Praise 1

"I have read every book in this series and loved them all...this one is no exception."
—*Soozers, Amazon reviewer*

"The writing is extremely good, and the plot and characters engaging. Closest author comparison probably Benedict Jacka and the Alex Verus series."
—*MB, Amazon reviewer*

"The books keep getting better and better."
—*Jim P. Ziller, Amazon reviewer*

"Have followed our expat mage from the beginning and this time around, it's a home run."
—*Amazon reviewer*

"I highly recommend the entire Alastair Stone Chronicles and this latest installment does not disappoint!"
—*Wendy S., Amazon reviewer*

Praise for *Core of Stone*

"Once again R.L. King has come up with another great story for Alastair Stone. I enjoyed this as thoroughly as all the others and look forward to more."
—*Tahlia Newland, Amazon reviewer*

"I love it when a writer starts out strong in her career and just gets stronger. I have loved The Alastair Stone Chronicles from the beginning, but this one just blew me away."
—*Shawna Reppert, award-winning author of* the *Ravensblood series*

"I have loved the series as a whole but have to say this is a favorite just for the character growth."
—*Amazon reviewer*

"The Alastair Stone Chronicles is one of the best series I have read in years…"
—*Judith A. Slover, Amazon reviewer*

Praise for *The Source*

"Perhaps the best addition yet to an already amazing series."
—*Greenlite350, Amazon reviewer*

"A continued thrill to the urban fantasy reader..."
—*Dominic, Amazon reviewer*

"I consumed the four pack in less than a week. This a great series and one of the best ones I have had the pleasure to read in a long time."
—*Skywalker, Amazon reviewer*

"If you like Harry Dresden and The Dresden files, or Nate Garrett in the Hellequin series than this series is for you."
—*Amazon reviewer*

Praise for *The Threshold*

"Once you enter the world of Alastair Stone, you won't want to leave."
—*Awesome Indies*

"Excellent story as are all the others in this series."
—*Tahlia Newland, Amazon reviewer*

"I LOVE THIS BOOK!"
—*Claryn M. Heath, Amazon reviewer*

Praise for *The Forgotten*

"Alastair Stone is like Harry Potter meets Harry Dresden with a bit of Indiana Jones!"
—*Randler, Amazon reviewer*

"I loved the first book in the series, but this book is even better! ... I didn't think I could be any more in love with the protagonist than I was in the first book ...My only hesitation in giving it five stars is that, if the next one is even better (as I suspect it may be) I won't have anywhere to go with the rating."
—*Shawna Reppert, award-winning author of* The Stolen Luck, Ravensblood, *and* Raven's Wing

"This is actually an original idea - such a rare thing these days. Well written too."
—*Tahlia Newland, Amazon reviewer*

"From the first paragraph I knew I was in the hands of a competent writer, and from the second paragraph I was hooked to read on...a novel deserving of the full 5 star rating."
—*Awesome Indies*

Praise for *Stone and a Hard Place*

"The magic is believable, the characters could be people you know, and the twists, turns and mysteries to be solved glue your eyes to the page. You will never forget these characters or their world."
—*Jacqueline Lichtenberg, Hugo-nominated author of the* Sime~Gen *series and* Star Trek Lives!

"Somewhat reminiscent of the Dresden Files but with its own distinct style."
—*John W. Ranken, Amazon reviewer*

"I am reminded of Jim Butcher here...Darker than most Urban Fantasy, not quite horror, but with a touch of Lovecraftian."
—*Wulfstan, Amazon Top 500 reviewer*

"Dramatic protagonist sucked me right in...I instantly wanted to spend more time with Alastair Stone...I definitely want to see more from this author!"
—*Shawna Reppert, award-winning author of* The Stolen Luck, Ravensblood, *and* Raven's Wing

"Fast-moving fun!...[t]he book is full of the things I like in a book, and they are presented in a clean, brisk style. This is a book well worth checking out.."
—*Jason M. Hardy, author of* Hell on Water, Drops of Corruption, *and* The Last Prophecies

"Stone is a completely believable protagonist, and, frankly, damned likeable. We all wish we had college profs as engaging as he is!"
—*Silas Sparkhammer, Amazon reviewer*

ALSO BY R. L. KING

THE ALASTAIR STONE CHRONICLES

Stone and a Hard Place
The Forgotten
The Threshold
The Source
Core of Stone
Blood and Stone
Shadows and Stone (novella)

SHADOWRUN

Shadowrun: Borrowed Time
Shadowrun: Wolf and Buffalo
Shadowrun: Veiled Extraction (coming in 2017)
(published by Catalyst Game Labs)

ALASTAIR STONE CHRONICLES: BOOK SEVEN

HEART OF STONE

R.L. KING

MAGESPACE
PRESS

To everyone who's read and enjoyed the series. I'm grateful to every one of you, and I hope I can continue to entertain you for many years to come.

ACKNOWLEDGMENTS

Second verse, same as the first: Thanks to my ever-understanding spouse Dan; to my ever-helpful editor John Helfers for pointing out all the places I could make the story better; to my Picky Beta Reader Mike Brodu (he didn't do as much this time, but he did help me work out a couple of knotty sections that needed massaging); and to everyone who's bought, read, and enjoyed the stories.

| CHAPTER ONE

MAGIC IS ONE OF THE most useful things in the world. It's great for getting you out of scrapes, and equally great for making it so you don't get *into* scrapes in the first place.

An abbreviated version of that thought flashed through Alastair Stone's mind as he caromed off the edge of the polished wooden bar and made a mostly vain effort to keep his feet under him.

Of course, for magic to do those things, you had to be sober enough to remember to use it, and that was where his current problem lay.

This is absurd. Stone scrambled backward to get the corner of the bar between himself and the three hundred pounds of bearded fury lumbering toward him. I *don't get into bar fights.* Jason *gets into bar fights.*

But Jason wasn't here. And to be fair, Stone didn't usually go to this kind of bar, either.

Get out of the house, he'd told himself.

Go drink somewhere besides your usual pub, he'd told himself. *It could be interesting. You could stand to meet some new people.*

In retrospect, the most infamous biker bar in Los Gatos had probably not been his best choice, despite the fact that one of his favorite local bands was playing there tonight.

Although to be fair, "biker bar" and "Los Gatos" were sort of like saying "strip club" and "Disneyland," or "cockfight" and "daycare center." The Highland Club's notorious reputation as an island of lawlessness notwithstanding, it still resided on the tony main street of a town usually populated by computer millionaires and Ferraris.

Stone might have been looking for a break from his usual Palo Alto pub, but he wasn't an idiot.

Actually, given current circumstances, the jury was still out on that one.

He scrambled backward again, trying to stay upright, but hampered both by his state of advanced inebriation and by his feet, which suddenly seemed to have grown three or four sizes and refused to cooperate with the rest of his body.

The biker, broad, glowering, and sporting a T-shirt reading *LOUD PIPES SAVE LIVES* and eyebrows resembling unbarbered caterpillars, swiped a mighty, beer-scented paw toward Stone as the surrounding crowd cheered him on. Stone somehow managed to dodge the blow, the only thing saving him being the fact that the biker was every bit as potted as he was.

"Hold still, ya fuckin' skinny geek!" the biker roared, attempting another awkward lunge. The crowd stepped back, content to watch and offer drunken advice, but unwilling to get involved directly. Up on the stage, the band played on as if this sort of thing happened every night.

Stone slipped around the corner and ducked behind a table. It was at that point that his alcohol-soaked synapses initiated sufficient connections to remind him that he was, in fact, one of the most formidable magical practitioners in the western United States. Cowering behind a table against a man who probably couldn't spell "magic" if you spotted him the first three letters was probably even more absurd than letting himself be dragged into this fight in the first place.

The good thing was that magic—at least the simple stuff required to deal with situations like this—came easily for him. When the biker shambled around the bar, his small piggy eyes cutting back and forth as he searched for Stone, he suddenly found that his legs were no longer performing as expected. One of his massive leather engineer boots slipped out from under him, yanked by an unseen force and pitching him backward with much comical flailing of tattoo-clad arms. The ensuing crash as all three hundred of his sweaty pounds impacted the bar's wooden surface shook the length of it, rattling the other patrons' beers like a hairy localized earthquake.

Stone took that opportunity to mutter a few words under his breath, summoning an invisibility spell around himself after a quick check to make sure no one was currently looking at him. He couldn't hold the spell for long, but the back door was close, and he had a few seconds while the biker was still trying to right himself.

He skittered across the floor, shoved the door open, and dragged himself to his feet against the alley wall, puffing as his jaw throbbed in rhythm with his pounding heartbeat.

Well. That *was fun.*

Some minutes later, slumped into the corner of a cab seat that smelled like pastrami and feet, he had time to examine the events of the evening in more detail. If he'd been smarter—and had fewer drinks—he'd probably have known better than to let his natural propensity for sarcasm get the better of him when the biker had ordered him to vacate "his spot."

Honestly, he was surprised the man had even understood the convoluted and anatomically impossible suggestion that Stone had offered regarding him, his motorcycle, and the "loud pipes" mentioned on his T-shirt. Ah, well. Live and learn.

Stone smiled, rubbing his jaw where the biker had connected with his first punch. He was going to regret all of this tomorrow when the buzz wore off and the long, slow hangover set in, but right now, his primary emotion was amusement.

That, and regret. He'd missed almost all of the band's set.

At least he didn't have to go to work early tomorrow.

| CHAPTER TWO

S TONE ALMOST CALLED IN SICK the next day. He'd awakened sprawled across his bed sideways, still in his clothes, his hair in crazed spikes and his mouth tasting like he'd wolfed some roadkill and washed it down with a gallon of industrial waste.

Magical scholarship, unfortunately, was stubbornly silent on the topic of dealing with raging hangovers. Pity—there was a fortune in it for anyone who could figure out how to brew up such a concoction, but alchemy had never been his strong suit. He settled for a cold shower, a change of clothes, and a large cup of weapons-grade black coffee he picked up at Peet's on the way to his Stanford office. By the time he got there, he was feeling at least passably alive.

His early-afternoon classes went better than he expected: for Stone, teaching was its own kind of drug, revitalizing him and driving off the last vestiges of the hangover. He prowled up and down the aisles of the tiered hall, regaling his Western Occult Symbology students with a lecture on the Salem Witch Trials that had them all on the edges of their seats. He had no false modesty about his abilities: he was good, and he knew it. Even with a stubborn headache and a bruised jaw that continued to throb after three Advil, he still managed to hold the interest of every student save one, a sleepy young man who looked like he'd indulged even more than Stone had last night. Stone left him alone: anything else would have been hypocrisy.

By later that afternoon, though, both the coffee and the Advil had worn off. He trudged back to his office, which was located about as far from the central core of the University as it could be while still being on campus, and told Laura, the administrative aide Occult Studies shared with a couple other small and obscure departments, that he wasn't feeling well and was blowing off his afternoon office hour.

She tilted her head. "What happened to your chin?"

"Bar fight with a three-hundred pound biker."

She nodded knowingly, no doubt thinking he'd slipped and smacked himself on the edge of the shower or something. "Okay, sure," she said. "Hope you feel better."

He thought about trying to get some work done when he got home. That lasted about as long as it took to drop onto the couch in the living room and start glancing through the research he'd left on the table from his last session. He didn't even remember falling asleep.

He dreamed of Lindsey.

He didn't do that often anymore. He had for a while, in the first few weeks after returning to the Bay Area from Ojai. Back then, the dreams had come several times a week. Now, four months later, they'd tapered off to a couple times a month.

They usually didn't come at night, either. The dreams most often accompanied unplanned naps like this one, the involuntary shutdowns when his body informed him that regardless of his other plans, it was clocking out for a while, thank you very much.

The ones that occurred all too often these days.

It was probably the aftereffects of the alcohol that did it. He always seemed to forget about the side effects—or just ignored them, because the temporary release was sometimes worth the consequences. The hangovers he was used to. The nightmares, not so much.

The blood wasn't the worst. Neither were the desperate screams, the confusion in her eyes, or the knife (in the dreams, it wasn't a genteel letter opener, but a wicked-looking, oversized steak knife with a gnarled wooden handle) sticking out from her chest at a crazy angle.

The worst was the knowledge, deep down in the back of Stone's mind, that her death had been his fault.

He hadn't killed her. His rational mind knew that. He hadn't plunged the blade into her chest. He hadn't held her down as she struggled and died. He hadn't even been present when it had happened.

He hadn't been charged with her murder, despite strong evidence pointing briefly toward his guilt. Even so, sometimes the dream included bits and pieces from his brief incarceration, magnified from a few hours in a small local cell to a full-blown prison experience—something he endured because he knew it was what he deserved.

No, he hadn't killed Lindsey Cole, former real-estate agent in a bucolic little resort town in southern California. But nonetheless, she was dead because of him. Because of what he was. And it looked like his subconscious had no intentions of letting him forget it any time soon.

The phone rang, startling him from his uneasy slumber. He jerked awake, his back protesting his awkward slumped position, half-on and half-off the overstuffed leather sofa. For a moment, his brain didn't register the sound, thinking it part of the dream, which was already fading.

Bugger it—let the machine get it. Stone sagged back, running a hand through his tangled hair. He didn't feel like talking to anyone right now. His heart still pounded as the blood and the screams and the guilt settled back down to rational levels, and his head felt like something was trying to beat its way out of it.

His gaze flicked to the clock as the phone rang again: eight thirty. That meant he'd been asleep for a couple of hours. On the coffee table in front of him, a disarray of items lay spread: three empty Guinness bottles from a couple of nights ago, a half-full carton of take-out chow mein he hadn't bothered to carry to the trash, a pair of open tomes showing complicated diagrams, and a notebook filled with scribblings that grew increasingly illegible as they progressed down the page. Stone didn't remember when he'd decided to give it up as a bad job and surrender to his fatigue, but he'd apparently stopped a thought in mid-sentence.

The phone rang again, and this time the machine picked it up. He heard the mutterings of his own voice on the message, a beep, and then another familiar one, this one female. "Dr. Stone? You there?"

Damn.

He blinked a couple times, sat up, and waved toward the other side of the room. The handset sailed toward him and slapped into his hand. "Yes, hello."

"Hey, Dr. Stone." Verity sounded surprised he'd picked up. "Didn't think you'd answer. We haven't heard from you in a while, so I thought I'd call and see how you're doing."

"Sorry." His voice sounded growly, which wasn't surprising. "Been busy lately. How are the lessons going?"

"Great!" Her enthusiasm came through clearly in her voice. "Things are still going great. Edna's fantastic. I'm learning so much from her. Remember when I told you she was teaching me some more advanced healing stuff?"

"I do." That had been a few weeks ago, the last time they'd spoken. The "advanced healing stuff" was part of the reason he'd arranged with Edna Soren to take Verity on for some "guest lecturing"—from the beginning of her training, his apprentice had shown a knack for the healing arts that Stone couldn't match. "I take it you're doing well?"

"Oh, yeah. She says I have a real talent for it. And..." She trailed off.

"And what?" He didn't miss the uncertainty in her tone.

"Well…" She paused. "I don't want you to take it wrong, but—I think my magic style is really meshing with Edna's. I can't wait to show you all the stuff I've learned."

Stone wished his head would stop pounding. "Why would I take it wrong? That's why I asked her to teach you—I thought it might be true. I'm glad things are going well for you."

"That's a relief. That's kinda why I didn't call, actually—I was afraid of how you'd react. I'll tell you one thing, though—it's *boring* down here, especially now that the holidays are over. When I'm not studying or helping out around Edna's place, there's not much else to do around here. Not without driving down to L.A., and I don't want to take Edna's truck that far. I miss the clubs, and San Francisco."

"Well, you'll be back eventually. You are planning on coming back, yes?"

"Oh, yeah," she assured him, though he thought she might have answered a little too fast. "Absolutely—as soon as Edna kicks me out."

"Well, good. Take your time. Learn everything you can—perhaps you can manage to get some of those healing techniques past my thick skull when you return. How's Jason, by the way?"

"Busy," she said. "I hardly ever see him, now that we're not living together. Fran's got him running like crazy, doing paperwork, studying the law, following cheating husbands—the whole bit."

Stone nodded. Fran Bartek, he knew from previous conversations with both Verity and her brother, was Jason's boss, a licensed private investigator he was apprenticing with as he accumulated enough hours to take the test for his own license. Stan Lopez, his late father's associate in the Ventura police department, had set up the gig. "Well, tell him I said hello when you see him."

"I'm surprised he hasn't called you." She paused, and when she spoke again, the pitch of her voice had changed, become more tentative. "Dr. Stone—?"

"Yes?"

"You're—okay, aren't you?"

He raised an eyebrow. "Why wouldn't I be?"

"Well—I know you kinda got used to having us hanging around, getting you out of your shell. And now that I'm not cooking for you anymore, have you gone back to getting takeout every night?"

Stone glanced at the half-empty carton of chow mein, then shoved it away with a sock-clad foot. "Of course not."

"Dr. Stone…"

"Verity, really—I'm fine." He forced cheer into his voice. "Everything's fine. In fact, as soon as I get off the phone, I'm planning to check out a new club I heard about." The lie came easily.

"Glad to hear it. We both miss you. You should come down here and see us sometime. Or maybe we can get up there one of these days."

"Absolutely, let's do that," he agreed. They'd talked about it before, a couple of times since Verity and Jason had decided to stay down there, but between Stone's own schedule and Jason's grueling work hours, it hadn't worked out yet. They hadn't even managed to get together over the holidays.

"Hey," she said, more slowly after a pause. "I know it's none of my business and I'm sure you'll tell me so, but are you—you know—seeing anybody?"

"You're right," he said. "That *is* none of your business." She started to say something, but he cut her off: "It's been lovely chatting, Verity. I'm glad you're still doing well with Edna. Must go, though—I have a few things I need to do before I head out."

"Okay," she said, obviously accepting that no more information about his personal life was forthcoming. "Take care of yourself, Doc. I mean it."

"I always do."

She didn't reply to that.

After she'd hung up, Stone remained slouched on the sofa. He sent the phone back to its spot with another flick of magic, then glanced at the remains of the chow mein. He noticed he didn't even bother to take it out of the carton lately, and contrasted it with the evening meals he used to have with Verity and Jason.

He flung himself off the couch, picked up the carton, and carried it out to the kitchen. The place was pristine, except for an untidy pile of newspapers and unread mail on the breakfast bar. He glanced down at the pile; a section of a two-day-old paper lay on top, folded open to an article about the new club he'd mentioned to Verity—the one he had no intention of visiting. He'd thought the place looked interesting when he'd first seen it, but the idea of dragging himself out among crowds of overhyped revelers—even to see a good band—didn't appeal to him lately. He'd slept for two hours, uneasy as it had been: that should give him the energy to spend the rest of the night working on the new ritual he'd been designing. And in any case, he doubted he'd be fit company for the rest of humanity tonight, given his current mood.

Still…

"Damn it, stop being pathetic," he snapped aloud. He snatched up the paper. Maybe he didn't feel like going out—but maybe he'd fallen into some unhealthy ruts over the past few months. He'd barely left the house in the last week except to go to work. If he forced himself to go out among people, and music, and life, his mood might change. Maybe he'd stop thinking about Lindsey and Verity and Jason—and maybe if he tired himself out, he might get a decent night's sleep so he'd stop passing out on his couch.

And if not, he could always come back home and work on his current research after.

| CHAPTER THREE

THE CLUB WAS CALLED THE NEXUS, and it was located in downtown San Jose, just off Market Street. It was a new place, opened only recently in a space where its predecessor hadn't managed to attract a sufficient clientele to keep the drinks flowing and the bands paid. That happened a lot in the area: the South Bay and Peninsula weren't known for their thriving club scene, with most people opting to head up to San Francisco for hotter bands and more action. Stone had done that himself on many occasions, but tonight he'd barely managed to summon the motivation to shower, shave, and exchange his faded jeans and old T-shirt for more upscale versions. That was about as far as he was willing to go to make an effort at dragging himself out of his current malaise.

By the time he arrived, the place was in full swing. He parked his big black BMW on the street a block or so away, and even from that distance he could hear the muffled sound of music. The mid-January air had a bite to it, a slight wind rustling the trees along the street; he thrust his hands into the pockets of his overcoat and strode off toward the club.

This is a mistake. It's pointless. I should just head home and get a start on that research.

Doggedly, he continued on. He still felt unsettled from the aftermath of last night's festivities and a lunch that wasn't agreeing with him, but it didn't matter. After the dream, he had no particular desire to find companionship, so he'd probably just mope in the shadows of some back table nursing a beer long enough to decide whether the band was any good. If they weren't, he'd be on his way back home in less than an hour.

If Verity were here, she'd be urging him to snap out of it. If Jason were here, he might commiserate and suggest going out to some bar where they could have a few beers and catch up on life.

But they aren't here, are they?

Even his usual Friday-night pub-crawling group would have been an improvement, but he'd even gotten spotty about turning up for that. Adding to that, this week one of them had a raging case of the flu, and another had to attend his daughter's school play. If Stone wanted to drag himself out of the house and do something, he was on his own.

Might as well make the best of it, now I'm here.

A few minutes and a brief wait in line later and he was inside, seated at a tiny table in a corner, where he could keep an eye on what was going on. The place was of medium size, and seemed to cater to a crowd mostly younger than him. Lots of neon, black light, trendy retro artwork, and quite a number of self-consciously hip twentysomethings trying to impress each other. Definitely not Stone's scene. He ordered a Guinness from a passing waitress and sat back to take stock of the place and decide if he planned to stay.

The music was good, at least, so that was something. The band, which he couldn't see through the crowd of people bobbing around on the dance floor, put out a passable imitation of classic punk rock. The dancers were mostly college students, but Stone spotted a few people older than he was at some of the tables and tapping their feet around the edges of the more vigorous dancers in the thick of things. Maybe it would be worth sticking around for a while after all. As long as nobody tried to convince him to dance, he could remain here in his corner for a while, and possibly see about chatting with some of the older punk-rocker types after he'd had a couple of beers. He contemplated his glass and focused on letting the driving beat of the music wash over him.

"Awesome band!"

Stone glanced up, surprised. Two attractive young women had pulled up chairs and sat down across from him while he'd been too busy staring into his glass to notice. About the same age as his students, they both wore slinky, tight-fitting minidresses and similar expressions that suggested a state of inebriation that had passed "mild" but had not yet reached "advanced." From the look of the drinks each of them held—oversized, colorful things with umbrellas, the minimum-quality, maximum-quantity concoctions marketed to college students—it might not be long.

Great. The last thing he was in the mood to do tonight was extricate himself from the tender mercies of a couple of drunken university students who should have figured out he was too old for them. He nodded politely, hoping they'd realize he was no fun and move on.

"Great music!" the first one agreed, a blonde who would have been stunning if her glazed gaze could settle on anything for more than a second or two, said. She extended a hand, several slender silver bangle bracelets tinkling on her tanned wrist. "C'mon! Dance with us!"

The other, dark-haired, dark-eyed and a little shorter than her friend, offered Stone a sideways smile. "You know you want to."

Stone glanced past them, hoping to spot more members of their party—like perhaps their male companions, if they had any—approaching, but no one seemed to be paying them any attention. The downside of choosing a table in a back corner of the club was that, the way the two women had situated their chairs, it would be difficult for him to make a graceful exit without shoving past one of them a lot closer and more forcefully than he wanted to.

"Sorry," he said with his best rueful grin, raising his voice to be heard over the band's pounding beat. "Not much of a dancer. I'm just here for the music."

The blonde grinned. "Oh, wow. Cool accent! Are you from Australia?"

Stone managed not to roll his eyes. It wasn't easy.

"Don't worry," she said without pausing to wait for an answer. "Dancing's a snap—just get out there and do whatever feels good. C'mon—you can't hear this music without getting up and moving."

"Aren't you two here with anyone?" Stone asked.

The dark-haired woman made a contemptuous sound, waving it off. "Yeah, but they're douchebags. Caught 'em hitting on the bartender."

Oh, this just kept getting better. Stone glanced around again, but still spotted no sign of anyone coming after his two new tablemates. He shrugged. "Sorry," he said again, indicating his glass. "I want to finish my drink. I'm sure you'll have no trouble finding someone else to dance with."

"No problem," the dark-haired woman said amiably. She settled back and took a pull from her own drink. "Okay if we sit with you for a while, then?"

"Maybe those pricks'll get a clue to fuck off if they see us with somebody else," the blonde added.

Stone doubted it, but he shrugged and acquiesced. He didn't plan to go anywhere until after he finished his Guinness anyway, though after that he'd already decided to head home. Whatever vibe he normally got from taking in a good band wasn't happening for him tonight. He wasn't sure why he'd thought it would.

"I'm Brianna," the dark-haired woman said. She nodded toward her friend. "This is Hannah."

"Pleasure," Stone said.

Neither of them seemed to notice that he hadn't returned the introduction. "We're at San Jose State. I'm a Bio major. Hannah's Kinesiology." She studied him for a moment. "What about you? You don't go to SJ State, do you?"

Clearly, finishing his drink in peace wasn't on the playlist for the foreseeable future. "Er…no. I teach, actually."

"Oh, yeah? Cool," Hannah said. "I've never seen you around campus. I'd have noticed, too," she added, with a glance that told him everything he wanted to know about the opportunities he might have if he had any interest in hooking up with women fifteen years his junior. "What do you teach?"

"Sort of—anthropology," he told her. It was his pat answer when asked about his field of study. Technically, it wasn't a lie: Occult Studies was part of the Cultural Anthropology department.

"Oh, yeah," Brianna said. "I took a class in that one time. I remember that guy—what was his name—like Dr. Leakey or something, right?"

"Different sort of anthropology," Stone said. "I—"

"Where the hell have you two been?" a voice, loud enough to easily carry over the music, interrupted.

Stone and both women looked up quickly. Two young men had come up behind Hannah and Brianna. Though they weren't dressed identically, they might as well have been: each had the beefy, handsome, square-jawed look that screamed "We play football and we always get what we want." Both glared, not just at them but at Stone. Like Hannah and Brianna, they both held drinks—oversized beers, already nearly empty.

"Fuck off, Troy," Hannah said over her shoulder.

"Huh?" the one who hadn't yet spoken said. "What's goin' on? Why'd you ditch us?"

Brianna snorted. "Don't play clueless. We saw you over there hitting on the bartender."

"We weren't *hitting* on her," Troy protested. He ran a hand through his brush-cut dark hair. "We were tryin' to get more drinks."

"Yeah, right," Hannah said. "Whatever." She turned pointedly away from him.

"Who's this guy?" The other football player asked, nodding toward Stone. His brow furrowed and he frowned. "He botherin' you two?"

"Actually," Stone said, "I was just leaving." He started to rise, hoping he could remove himself from the situation and let these four work out their differences on their own time. Although he had numerous options for doing just that should it become necessary, most of them involved magic and therefore were last resorts. If he could just get past Brianna, he could lose himself in the crowd and be outside before anyone decided to follow him.

"Siddown," Troy ordered. "Bri, he botherin' you?"

"Hell no," she said, with the sort of disdain attractive young women excelled at. "At least he's got some manners. And he doesn't ignore us while he goes off tryin' to score with somebody else."

"Wait, he's tryin' to score with you?" the other guy demanded, focusing his glare fully on Stone now. The remains of his beer sloshed in his glass as he waved it in Stone's direction. "Fuck, Hannah, look at him—he's gotta be like *thirty*. You some kinda perv, dude, checkin' out college chicks?" He directed this last at Stone.

Again, it took all of Stone's self-control not to roll his eyes at the absurdity of it all. It was why he tended to frequent smaller clubs—they attracted less of the horny-student demographic. He started to rise again, switching briefly to magical sight to get a read on the students' auras. Even before he did, he was acutely aware of the shift in the situation's emotional climate: in the past few seconds, Troy's and his buddy's ire had redirected from Brianna and Hannah to himself. Magical sight verified that not only was this true, but the two women were now regarding the two young men with less hostility. If he didn't play this just right, it could get ugly in a hurry. "Listen," he said, standing again. "I was about to leave anyway. Suppose I buy you all a round and we—"

Troy moved behind Brianna, blocking Stone's exit. "Maybe we oughta take it outside, asshole."

"Troy—" Brianna started.

"*There* you are," a new voice said.

A figure had appeared behind the main group. Stone took a quick look past Brianna—and stared.

| CHAPTER FOUR

THERE WAS REALLY NO dancing around the fact: she was beautiful. Not simply attractive. Not even simply pretty. The woman who stood, shoulders confidently squared, eyes glittering as she fixed her gaze on Stone, was the sort of drop-dead gorgeous you normally didn't see outside big-screen film productions and Paris runways. Everything about her—from her shimmering, shoulder-length chestnut brown hair to the direct look in her eyes to the way her snug-fitting but rather conservatively cut blue dress clung to her—looked out of place amid the pounding beat and sloshing hormones of this rather pedestrian club. Even the brief way she turned her head to take in the scene before returning her attention to him made Stone think of a panther on the hunt for a choice morsel.

"There you are," she said again. "Made some new friends, I see."

Troy and his buddy gaped at the woman, probably not even realizing their mouths hung open. Troy snatched a chair from a nearby table and plunked it down next to Brianna. "You wanna sit down?" he asked.

"What'cha drinkin', baby?" his buddy added. "Can we get you a refill?"

Brianna glared at both of them.

"Actually," the woman said, "I'd really just like to sit down here with my friend and have a drink. Would you all excuse us?" She smiled at the students, amusement and warmth in her cornflower-blue eyes. Their color nicely complemented the deep, jewel-like hue of her dress.

"Sure we will," Hannah said firmly. "Come on, you guys. Can't you see these two want to be alone?"

"But—" Troy's buddy began.

Brianna stood up and gripped his arm. "Come *on*," she said. "You can buy *us* drinks, and maybe we'll forgive you for macking on the bartender if you quit acting like assholes." She tossed a carefree smile back over her shoulder at Stone. "See ya, Mr. Anthropology."

"Cheers," Stone said, raising his glass to them. He kept the new woman in his peripheral vision, almost as if fearing if he let her out of his sight, she'd fade away into the darkness.

When the four students had disappeared into the crowd, he focused fully on the woman. "Thanks for the rescue," he said with an arched eyebrow. "You'll think me a fool for admitting it, though, but I'm afraid you must have mistaken me for someone else."

She chuckled. "No such luck. I've never seen you before in my life. You just looked like you could use a little help." Her voice was low, full of confidence and amusement.

"Well," he said, "avoiding pointless bar fights with drunken louts is almost always a good thing." He studied her for a moment, wondering if he should take a chance, and surprised to find himself feeling like a nervous schoolboy for the first time since he'd *been* a nervous schoolboy. Her kind of beauty didn't belong in a place like this—he wondered why every straight man and lesbian in the place wasn't staring at her—and more to the point, why she was standing here talking to *him*. Before he lost his nerve, he indicated the seat across from him. "The least I can do is buy you a drink."

"I just happen to be in need of one, so I'll take you up on that."

"Excellent." He waved the waitress over. She ordered a Cosmopolitan, and he got another Guinness. "I'm Alastair Stone, by the way," he said.

"Good to meet you, Alastair Stone. I'm Deirdre Lanier."

Stone's brain cycled through and rejected several responses, all of which would likely mark him as the worst sort of tongue-tied idiot. Finally, he settled on, "Do you always rescue strange men from potential violence?"

"*Are* you a strange man?" she asked with a little smile. She sat back in her chair, her posture confident and relaxed, clearly enjoying this.

He saw something else in her eyes too, though—something more primal, and something he was sure must be wishful thinking. "You don't know the half of it."

"Oh, you'd be surprised. I've known some fairly strange men. They're much more interesting than the so-called 'normal' variety. And anyway, I prefer to call them 'unusual.'" Their drinks arrived; she picked hers up and sipped it, leaning forward, watching him. "You definitely qualify. For one thing, I can tell you're a long way from home."

"I suppose I am...depending on how you define 'home.'"

She tilted her head. "From the accent...I'd say somewhere in southern England."

He raised an eyebrow. "Impressive. Most Americans can barely tell the difference between Cockney and BBC English. Except for the ones who think we're Australian," he added with a glance toward the direction where Brianna and her friends had departed.

"So...?" she prompted.

"Surrey. Little village there I can guarantee you've never heard of."

"You're probably right," she agreed. "I've been to London a few times, but always on business. I never ventured out of the city. I'd like to sometime—I hear it's beautiful."

"Indeed it is," he agreed. "And what about you? What brings you here?"

"Here as in this club?" She elegantly shrugged a bare shoulder. "I've been working too hard lately. I thought it might be fun to take a night off and get out for a while. Some friends suggested this place, so…"

"You're here with friends, then?" Stone asked. That explained it—if she wasn't here with a date, it made sense that she'd come with some girlfriends or coworkers.

"Nope." She smiled, obviously still entertained by his discomfiture, but the twinkle in her eyes was amused, not malicious. "All by myself. Does that surprise you? What about you? You must be here with someone."

"It does surprise me a bit," he admitted. "If you'll forgive me for saying so—I can't quite work out why a crowd of hopeful young men aren't following you around like a pack of lost puppies."

Deirdre laughed. "That's flattering. But I've never had much use for puppies. They're cute, but they need too much upkeep and they tend to make messes on the carpet."

"True enough," Stone agreed. "And no, I'm not here with anyone. In fact, I almost didn't come at all." Encouraged by the fact that her gaze hadn't left him since he'd started speaking, he leaned in closer across the table. "You know," he said, "this might be terribly presumptuous of me, but it's quite loud in here. Can't hear ourselves think. Also, the quality of the drinks isn't up to what I owe you for rescuing me from—well, who knows what that might have turned into?" He nodded toward the door. "I know a much nicer little place not far from here. What do you say?"

For a moment, she didn't answer. The moment seemed to stretch out interminably, even though he knew only a few seconds had passed. He waited, wondering if the thudding of his heart was visible. Why was he so *nervous*? He'd asked dozens of women out, and most of them had said yes. Why was Deirdre Lanier any different?

It was a stupid question, and he knew it. One look at her told him why. He was deluding himself: no way she'd say yes. She'd look at him with that appraising glance that said so much: *Seriously, why are you bothering? I'm so far out of your league that you can't even see me from where you are. Did you honestly think someone like me would be interested in someone like you? Where do you—*

"I say: I thought you'd never ask." There was that look in her eyes again: the one Stone had seen before, in other women, but couldn't believe he was seeing now, from her—and certainly not directed at him. "Do you have a car? I came in a cab."

He thought he might have stared at her for a moment too long, but she didn't seem to notice—or at least she was too polite to say anything about it. "I do," he said at last. And before she could reconsider and change her mind, he stood. "Shall we, then?"

| CHAPTER FIVE

STONE BARELY NOTICED THE WALK back to the BMW. As he opened the door for Deirdre and she slipped gracefully into the passenger seat, he took a moment to study her with magical sight. As dazzled as he was by her, he knew all too well that such beauty could come from many sources, not all of them natural: illusions, for one. Hell, he could whip up an amulet that would make him look like a movie star if he put his mind to it, so he didn't doubt that others could as well. It wasn't likely, of course, but it never hurt to be sure. He'd been fooled by illusions before, and in fact had been damned lucky not to be killed because he'd let his guard slip. These days, he took it as standard operating procedure to check out all potential romantic partners for hidden magical traps.

But no: a quick examination revealed no traces of magic on or near her, no supernatural subterfuge that he could identify. He did notice something else, though, something that once again raised his heart rate and stirred his body in anticipation: her aura, a strong, clear blue, pulsed with a vibrant, sensual red that could only mean one thing.

Careful, he told himself, getting in. *Don't get ahead of yourself.*

He took her to an elegant little bar tucked away in the back of the Fairmont Hotel. The bar, like the hotel itself, was one of the older ones in the area, more old-world charm than trendy neon and glitz.

When they were settled into a booth, Stone said, "I didn't even ask where you were from, or what you do that keeps you so busy."

"I haven't been in the area long," she said. "I've got a little place in Los Altos. I do most of my work out of my home, but I'm in the City two or three days a week. I'm a fashion designer."

"Ah." He indicated her dress with a nod. "Is that one of yours, then? It's lovely."

"It is one of mine, yes." She chuckled. "I like to take them for a 'test drive' now and then. Perk of the job."

"Again, this might be presumptuous of me, but you should model it as well as designing it. You look exquisite."

Her smile widened. "You're sweet. And what about you? Did I hear one of those girls call you 'Mr. Anthropology' before she left?"

The booth was semicircular; she sat quite close to him, so close that he could feel the warmth of her body next to him. "Cultural anthropology, actually," he said. "I teach at Stanford."

"Ah, so you're not far from where I am, then."

"Palo Alto, near downtown. Been there for a few years now." Stone forced himself to concentrate; his mental discipline, usually so adept at holding complicated magical patterns in his mind and resisting magical attacks, was proving much less helpful against the persistent thoughts currently threatening to overwhelm him. Her bare arm rested close to his, the faint, tantalizing scent of her light floral perfume rising each time she shifted position.

"Are you all right?" she asked. Once again her eyes glittered with amusement.

"Oh, quite all right." He ran a hand through his hair and took a sip of his drink. "Sorry—normally I'm not quite so…"

"You look like you think I'm going to eat you up." She laughed. "I promise I won't—unless you want me to, of course," she added, her voice dropping to a lower tone.

"That…could be quite nice, under the right circumstances," he murmured. He turned a little toward her, locking his eyes with hers. Hers were even bluer than he'd thought: lighter than his, brilliant and narrowed just a little, as if she were finding the entire scene to be great fun. Unlike him, she didn't seem nervous—but she didn't break his gaze, either.

"I'll be honest with you," she said, reaching out to cover his hand with hers. "I was looking for something—some*one* at that club tonight. That's why I went there."

"Oh?" Her hand was warm; he held his still to keep it from shaking. His voice sounded husky in his ears. He wondered if she noticed it too.

"Mm-hmm. Do you know what I was looking for?"

"Suppose you tell me."

She leaned in a little more. "A man I couldn't intimidate."

He raised an eyebrow. "So apparently you *can't* see my heart pounding like a jackhammer, then."

She laughed, squeezing his hand a little more. "But you invited me for a drink anyway. And you weren't a jerk about it. I like that."

"I honestly didn't think you'd say yes. But it never hurts to try."

"Exactly," she said. "Not a jerk, and not a puppy. That's rare—did you know that?"

He felt her leg press against his under the table.

She sipped her drink and tilted her head. "I was looking for something else, too."

"You were." Her leg was even warmer than her hand; he forced himself to hold still.

"I was. I told you I work a lot—I'm guessing you do too. I was out tonight looking for—a little fun. No strings, no obligations. But only with the right man." She leaned in even closer, until her face was only a few inches from his. "Are you the right man, Alastair Stone?"

He swallowed once, but when he spoke, his voice was soft, steady, and confident. "I...think I could be, yes."

She took another sip and smiled. "Then what are we still doing here?"

| CHAPTER SIX

S HE SAID LITTLE AS HE DROVE, except to give him occasional directions, but every time he glanced over at her, she was looking at him. He had a hard time reading her expression properly: a mix of amusement, anticipation, and the sort of hunger that he still couldn't quite believe someone who looked like her was aiming at him.

He'd checked her out more thoroughly with magical sight as they'd walked back to the car, but nothing dinged: nothing more than that pulsing, primal red around her brilliant blue aura that indicated better than any words could that she wasn't trying to deceive him about her intentions. Disguising one's aura was a seriously advanced magical technique, something even he had to work at. If she was hiding anything, she was doing a damned good job of it.

Or…maybe she *was* exactly what she seemed, and for some inexplicable reasons of her own, she wanted him.

Given that at this moment he wanted her more than anything else on Earth, he'd be a fool to argue with her.

She directed him into the gated underground garage of a genteel old three-story building that had been converted into upscale lofts, and didn't wait for him to open her door. Deftly exiting the car as soon as it came to a stop, she waited for him to come around and reached out to grip his arm. "Come on," she said. "Let's give the neighbors something to talk about."

They rode the elevator up without encountering any of the neighbors, however. When Deirdre opened her door, Stone got a brief impression in the dimness of soaring ceilings, elegant and minimalist furnishings, and a bold modern art print on the wall before she grasped his arm again. "We could have another drink," she said, her voice low and husky, her smile still playful. "You know...if you want to."

Even Stone's control had limits. "I...think not," he said in the same tone. He gripped her shoulders and pulled her into a firm embrace, inclining his head to cover her smiling, mocking lips with his own. A part of him was astonished at his boldness, especially given how he'd been feeling lately, but he ignored it. This wasn't the time to overthink things.

She responded instantly, her arms going around him, sliding his coat off his shoulders and letting it fall into a heap on the floor. She pressed into him, the full length of her body against his. Her hands worked their way under his thin black T-shirt, caressing his back, kneading his knotted muscles with proprietary insistence. "Mmm..." she murmured. "Yes..."

He kissed her again, cutting off anything else she might have intended to say. He explored her with his hands, stroking her back, her neck, burying his fingers in the luxuriance of her hair. Any thoughts, any doubts about why someone like her would want someone like him swept away as his body responded to hers, and hers to his; auras didn't lie. All he knew was that he wanted her, and as long as she was willing and enthusiastic, he would have her.

She didn't say anything, didn't break the kiss, but she seemed to be trying to steer them somewhere. He came up for air long enough to notice the shadowy form of a stairway, as elegant and minimalist as the rest of the place, off to one side of the open living area.

He got the hint, and somehow they managed to reach the top without breaking their embrace or toppling head over heels back down to the first floor.

They left a trail of clothes on their way across the room toward her bed. The only illumination came from the moonlight shining in through a skylight directly above it; as they stood for a moment next to it, Stone drank her in with his gaze. Only a few inches shorter than he was, her lithe, slender, body was athletically trim and perfectly proportioned. She studied him in return, her own gaze open, searching, with no hint of shyness or embarrassment.

"You're...beautiful..." Stone murmured. He didn't care if it sounded trite: it was true. It was more than true.

"And you talk too much," she said with a smile, pulling him to her in a crushing embrace.

After that, he didn't talk anymore. He kissed her again, letting go of anything that wasn't about her pleasure and his. He caressed her, the heat of her body and the insistence of her response spurring him on. She pulled his head down and kissed him even harder, her hands moving down to stroke his back, her fingernails digging into his skin. He arched as the pain and the pleasure joined together to form a sensation so exquisite that he didn't even have a name for it. His mind didn't have names for much of anything right now. He was beyond words, and he thought she was too.

He felt no resistance as he grew more insistent, and in fact her body, her hands, her low moans urged him on to something far more primitive, more forceful than he'd ever experienced in the past—they were more like a pair of lust-crazed animals than anything human. For a moment, just a moment, he switched to magical sight—her aura's brilliant red glow blazed so brightly that it nearly obscured every vestige of the strong, clear blue. The temptation to keep the sight going was strong, but even that simple magical expenditure required energy, and Deirdre's voracious appetite demanded every shred of energy he could muster if he meant to satisfy her. To do otherwise was unthinkable—to let her go was even more so.

He gave her his full attention, responding to her firm and urgent intensity with a heightened focus of his own. She moved in rhythm with him, their bodies in a perfect synchronization that he never wanted to end—except that if it didn't end soon, he feared the rising sensations would simply take him apart.

Her nails dug harder into his back, pulling him closer as if trying to merge his body with hers. Her hot, sweet breath sounded harsh in his ears.

And then it was over, in a moment of exquisite ecstasy that rose and kept rising until he didn't think it could rise anymore. He tried magical sight again—he couldn't help it—and their auras entwined, his purple-gold and her blue, both nearly obscured by a red so intense that he felt it more than he saw it. Deirdre's moan of pleasure rose with it until it became a soft little scream, and then she let him go and he fell back, spent, panting, his brain unable to form a coherent thought.

"Mmm…" Deirdre moved closer to him, draping her arm across his chest.

"Mmm…" he agreed.

They didn't talk more than that, but lay in companionable silence as their breathing returned to normal, until Deirdre shifted so she could look into his eyes. Hers glittered with mischief, and her hands began to move over him again.

"You're trying to kill me…" he murmured, eyebrow arching.

"But what a way to go."

He had no argument with that.

The second time proved every bit as good as the first: slower, more measured, less urgent, but no less intense. Deirdre seemed to know instinctively what he wanted, and how to communicate her desires to him with no words. He responded with enthusiasm, and once again her obvious pleasure was as much of a reward to him as his own.

She lay on her side, this time with both her arm and her leg draped over him, her head propped a bit on her other arm. Her sly smile was only just visible in the moonlight. "I think you're right," she said, tracing her finger over the quick rise and fall of his chest.

"About what?" His own arm was underneath her; his fingers played in her tousled hair.

"You are the right man."

"Good to know." Their auras had died down now, back almost to their normal hues, but the bright red of passion still flickered around the edges. He smiled back, lifting his head to kiss her and then letting it fall back on the pillow. His every muscle felt relaxed, his mind at peace and drifting, savoring the fading but still potent euphoria of what they'd just experienced.

She stroked his jawline, her touch feather-light. "Go to sleep," she said with a little laugh. "I know how you men are..."

But she sounded sleepy too; her head drooped to rest on his shoulder, snuggling into the crook of his neck, her flower-scented hair tickling his cheek. He drifted off to the sound of her soft breathing and the touch of her warm body against his.

| CHAPTER SEVEN

TONE AWOKE, REFRESHED, to sunlight streaming in through the skylight. He didn't open his eyes at first as the memories came back to him, convinced that the whole thing had been nothing but a particularly elaborate and pleasant dream—perhaps his subconscious mind's way of apologizing for all the unpleasant ones it had been sending him lately. He did remember a dream, vivid and sensual, but every time his mind tried to grasp it and re-play it, it danced tantalizingly away.

Finally, reluctantly, he opened his eyes. He was not, as he feared, lying in his own bed back in his townhouse, but stretched out and wound up in the disarrayed, scented sheets of a room that was, just for a moment, unfamiliar.

It hadn't been a dream.

He smiled, stretched languidly, and glanced over to the other side of the big bed.

It was empty.

Across the room, an open door suggested a bathroom. "Deir-dre?" he called.

No response.

He shivered against the early-morning chill and sat up. The sheet pulled at his back briefly before coming away; when he twist-ed to look, he saw small spots of dried blood that surprised him until he recalled her fingernails digging into his back and he smiled again.

No, definitely not a dream.

In his upright position, he spotted the folded piece of paper on her pillow, featuring a smiley face on the front. He unfolded it.

The note was short:

> Good morning, sleepyhead.
> Sorry to leave you, but I had to go up to the City this morning, and I didn't want to wake you. Please make sure the door locks behind you when you leave.
> I'd like to see you again. Call me next week if you feel the same.
> D.

Below it, she'd written a phone number.

Stone stared at it for several seconds, then refolded it. As he gathered up his clothes and took a quick shower (her master bath was spotless, minimalist, and sensual with a marble vanity, art-deco mirror, and simple Asian-inspired frosted glass shower door), his mind's eye kept returning to her: her sparkling eyes, her body, her smile, the willing, hungry warmth of her pressed against him. Already he wanted nothing more than to see her again.

Call me next week, the note said.

He wanted to call her tonight. Hell, he wanted to call her *now.* He stepped out of the shower, dried off and dressed quickly. *Stop it,* he told himself. He was acting like some kind of lovesick teenager. Sure, last night had been mind-blowing, but still.

He draped his coat over his arm and headed back out into the bedroom. He'd pushed the sheets down when he got up, and the small bloodstains from where she'd scratched him showed clearly against their dazzling whiteness. He contemplated them a moment: every mage learned from the days of his apprenticeship not to be careless with his own blood. Blood was a powerful thing, and anyone who had any could potentially cause another person—even a mage—a lot of trouble.

He thought about leaving it—he'd become intimately familiar with Deirdre's aura last night, and had found no hint of duplicity or malevolence in it—but, as the old saying went, there were old mages and there were careless mages, but rarely did the two qualities occur in the same person.

Stone sat down on the edge of the bed and used a simple spell to neutralize any trace of his aura that remained in the bloodstains. Not much lingered at this point even before he started, so it took him only a few seconds to complete the spell. When he finished he tucked her folded note away in his wallet and departed, making sure as she'd asked to lock the door behind him.

| CHAPTER EIGHT

MONDAY PASSED SLOWLY. Stone thought about calling Deirdre during one of his breaks, but forced himself to wait until the evening. He didn't care if she thought him too eager to see her again: after what they'd shared on Friday night, he couldn't imagine how she *wouldn't* think he'd want to see her again. The wait was more for his own purposes, to prove he could do it. Magic required discipline in all areas of one's life, not just those that affected the Art.

He managed to remain focused on his work through most of the day; when teaching, he entered a sort of flow state as he prowled the aisles and engaged his students with questions, observations, and demonstrations. A committee meeting took up most of his afternoon, and grading a set of essays claimed the rest. When he glanced at the clock, he saw it was already almost five.

He was gathering up his papers and getting ready to leave for the day when a knock on his office door startled him. He glanced up, annoyed. If some student had shown up outside normal office hours, he'd—

It wasn't a student. Stone didn't recognize the man who stood framed in the doorway: fiftyish, medium height, stocky, clad in simple buttoned workman's shirt, jeans, and sturdy boots. "Yes, may I help you?"

"You're Dr. Stone, right?" the man asked.

Normally, Stone would have replied with something like, "That's what it says on the door." However, one look at the visitor's face made it clear that he wasn't in the mood for such comments. "That's me," he said instead. "Please, come in, Mr.—"

"Wells. Ed Wells." Wells entered the office and perched on the edge of the guest chair Stone waved him toward. "I'm Tabitha Wells's father. She's one of your students."

"Ah. Yes, of course. She's in my Occult in America class this quarter." He narrowed his eyes. This was odd—university students' parents didn't usually come to see their professors about their children—especially not since the majority of Stanford students didn't have local families. In fact, Stone couldn't remember it happening even once since he'd begun teaching. Not even in America, where he'd found parents to be more directly involved—sometimes to the point of annoyance—in their offspring's educations. He waited for Wells to explain further.

The man's bearing suggested a mix of discomfort and resolve—as if he didn't want to be here, but perhaps felt that he had to. "I'm concerned about her," he said. "I thought you might be able to shed some light on something."

Stone frowned. He barely knew Tabitha Wells—he didn't make it a point to get to know his students beyond their work in his courses. He tried to picture her in his mind, but the only image he could come up with was one of an athletic, attractive young woman with long brown hair and a pixieish face. As far as he could remember, she'd never come to one of his office hours to seek personal help. Though she'd attended a few of his classes over the past few quarters, she was not an Occult Studies major. "I'll do what I can, Mr. Wells, but I have a lot of students. I don't know how much help I can be."

"Yeah," he said. "I get that." He paused, taking in the collection of odd items—books on the occult and supernatural, a stack of feathers, even a human skull—on the shelves behind Stone's desk.

"I found out recently that she's gotten involved in some stuff that concerns me, and I think you might have something to do with it."

This was getting even odder. "I've no idea what you're talking about, Mr. Wells."

"Have you ever heard of the Church of the Rising Dawn, Dr. Stone?" Wells leaned forward, meeting Stone's gaze now.

"No...can't say so. Should I have?"

"They're some kind of outfit down in San Jose, from what I understand. I don't know if you know it, but Tabby is a sociology major. She's only taking courses in your department because she's always been interested in that paranormal stuff."

"I'm aware of Ms. Wells's major," Stone said.

"I didn't even realize she was doing it until recently. She's here on a scholarship—no way I could afford to send her to Stanford if I had to pay for it."

Stone nodded. He glanced at the clock. "I'm terribly sorry, Mr. Wells, but I've got an appointment shortly, and I've got a fair walk to get to my car." He didn't add *so if you could get to your point, that would be lovely,* but it was implied in his tone. If he could deal with Wells's problem and get him out of here soon, he'd have time to get home and perhaps call Deirdre to see if she might want to have dinner with him.

"Yeah. Okay. I'll get right to it. Seems that Tabby has joined some kind of bullshit pagan 'church' down in San Jose, and she's been acting strange lately. Did you put her on to the place?"

"Of course not. I told you, I've never heard of it. What makes you think I've got anything to do with this?"

Wells sighed. "She doesn't talk to me much, but she does talk to her sister Taylor. She's seventeen, still living at home, but they talk a lot on the phone. Tabby's been telling Taylor about this church thing, and Taylor's worried that she might have joined some kind of cult."

"Have you asked Tabitha about this, Mr. Wells?" Stone forced himself to keep his voice even and respectful—after all, this *was* the father of one of his students. But sometimes the closed-mindedness of some people annoyed him to the point where he had a hard time keeping his opinions to himself. "Even if she *has* decided to join a pagan church, I can assure you, most of them aren't cults. No more than any other church is, at any rate." He gathered up some books and papers from his desk and began stuffing them into his leather briefcase. "And you still haven't explained why you expect I'd know anything about this."

"Because Tabby apparently has a pretty high opinion of you, Dr. Stone. Taylor thinks it might even be some kind of crush."

Stone froze in the act of closing his briefcase. "What?"

"You're saying you didn't know?"

"Of course I didn't know." Stone didn't try to keep the sharp tone from his voice. "How would I? She certainly didn't tell me, and I never noticed anything in her behavior." His mind flitted back over the quarter, trying to identify anything Tabby Wells might have done to indicate she was attracted to him, but he couldn't think of anything specific. She often sat up near the front of the class and paid particular attention to his lectures, but a lot of students did that. He'd dealt with the situation before: every young or reasonably attractive professor had stories about the occasional student crush. But if what Ed Wells said was true, Tabby had been more discreet about it than most.

Wells, however, didn't seem inclined to give up. His expression hardened, though he appeared more resolute than angry. "Be that as it may, Dr. Stone, I wonder if something you said might not have encouraged her to look into this…church…even if there wasn't anything…well…inappropriate going on between the two of you."

Stone stood. "Mr. Wells," he said tightly. "I'll thank you not to accuse me of inappropriate conduct with students. We take that sort of thing quite seriously around here."

Wells stood too. For a moment he looked like he would push it further, but then his shoulders sagged and he looked suddenly tired. "I'm sorry, Dr. Stone. That was rude of me, and I apologize.

I'm just worried about my daughter. She's never done anything like this before. I don't give a damn if she decides to go to some other church, or no church at all. But I do care if she gets herself involved in some cult. I just thought I'd see if you might be able to tell me anything before I talk to her, but I see that was a bad idea." He pushed his chair in. "Thanks for your time."

"I'm sorry I couldn't be of more help. But I think you should talk to your daughter, Mr. Wells, not me."

"Yeah. Maybe I'll do that." Wells turned and left without another word.

Stone watched him go in silence, then glanced at his watch. He was surprised to find his heart rate increasing as his mind once again turned to Deirdre.

| CHAPTER NINE

H E WAITED UNTIL HE WAS HOME to call, not wanting some other wayward student or disgruntled parent to make an unexpected appearance in his office mid-conversation. He pulled her note from his wallet and spread it on the table, though he didn't need to: he'd already memorized her number.

It rang several times before she answered, and then there she was. "Yes, hello?"

"I missed you these past couple of days," he said. "I hope your business in San Francisco went well."

She laughed. "So you *did* call me back. I'll be honest—I was about fifty-fifty that you wouldn't."

"After Friday night? I might be a fool, but I'm not an idiot. "

"You're the first, you know."

He leaned back. "The first what?"

"Would it surprise you to know I've done this before? But you're the first one I've given my number to."

A brief flash of something—it took him a moment to identify it as jealousy, since it was so uncharacteristic of him—gripped him, but it quickly faded. He covered it with a chuckle. "It wouldn't surprise me that you've done it before."

"Does it bother you?"

"Does it matter? I've only just met you. Your personal life is none of my concern, nor should it be."

"They don't even ask for it. I think I scare them off," she said, a note of approval in her tone. "But you don't need to worry, though—not only were you brave enough to call back, but Friday night…" she trailed off.

"Would it surprise *you* that you've been on my mind all weekend?" he asked.

"It was pretty amazing, wasn't it?"

"That barely begins to describe it." He paused, drew a deep breath, and took the plunge: "Deirdre…would you like to join me for dinner tonight? And perhaps…dessert, later?"

Her smile came through in her voice. "This is the time when I'm supposed to tell you I need to check my busy social calendar, then turn you down because you've waited too long to ask, isn't it?"

"You hardly seem the type who does what she's supposed to do," Stone said.

"Score another one for the man with the sexy accent." She laughed again. She had a lovely laugh, melodic and merry. "And I'd love to have dinner with you. Pick me up in an hour? You *do* remember where I live, don't you?"

"I think I could find it blindfolded."

"Well, don't do that. If you get pulled over, you'll miss dinner." She paused for a beat. "And I'd miss dessert. And that would be a shame."

He took her to a small, intimate Asian fusion place just off University. "I'm really the first, then, am I?" he asked teasingly when they were settled. "You don't tell that to all your conquests?"

"Now, don't go getting complacent on me," she said. "I like a man who can keep me on my toes. Most of them only have one thing on their minds."

He raised an eyebrow.

She laughed. "Well, it's not as if I don't have that on my mind too."

"I hadn't noticed."

"I'll have to try harder, then." She sipped her wine and regarded him over the top of the glass.

He hadn't misremembered, or miscalculated due to fatigue or too many drinks on Friday night: she was every bit as beautiful as he'd remembered. It was odd: for a woman who obviously enjoyed the effect she had on men, her style tended toward the conservative. Tonight, she wore a simple, elegant dress of deep blue under a long, sweeping coat; the dress fit her like a second skin, but had a certain old-world quality to it that Stone found charming. He wondered if it was another of her designs. In any case, as on Friday night he couldn't stop thinking about her, and when he wasn't looking at her, her image dominated his mind's eye.

Is this love at first sight? He rejected the thought. It was an absurd concept: love came as much from time and shared experiences as from physical attraction. Hell, he'd only ever been truly in love once before in his life, and that had been with someone he'd known for years.

His mind flitted briefly back to Lindsey Cole, which chilled him. He'd thought he might grow to love her too, given time, and look where it had gotten her. Was he a fool to risk it again, or was this some kind of bizarre trick of his mind to get him back in the game and show him that he wasn't a danger to any woman he was attracted to? To think that someone—and someone like Deirdre— whom he'd only met three days ago could—

He shifted to magical sight and wasn't surprised to see the red tinges coloring the edges of her aura again; at present they were dimmed, but the interest was clearly there. He wasn't deluding himself.

"What do you think about when you look at me like that?" she asked, head tilted.

Startled, he shifted back. "Like what?"

"I'm not sure. Like…you're reading my mind. You can't read my mind, can you?" she asked playfully.

"I wish I could," he said. "Then I'd know better how to make you happy."

"I think you did a pretty good job of figuring it out," she said, and laughed. "We'll see later how you are with…other types of dessert. I do love versatility."

"Perhaps you can show me some of your favorite recipes."

Her eyes sparkled. "Now *that* is a plan I can support." She took another sip of her wine and toyed with her fork. "So, tell me about cultural anthropology." She turned the words around, drawing them out, then added with a wicked grin, "Somehow, I've always thought of male college professors as either hopelessly nerdy, or old and stodgy."

"So, which one am I, then?" he asked.

"I think you break the mold. You're not old, and you're certainly not stodgy."

"And who says I'm not hopelessly nerdy?" he asked.

"You do." Her smile turned sly. "Or rather, you did, on Friday night. Don't tell me if I look in your closet, I'll find bow ties and jackets with leather elbow patches. If so, I might have to rethink my opinion of nerds."

"The only bow tie I own is the one that goes with my tuxedo," he said. "But seriously, I'd rather hear about you. I've never met a fashion designer before." He hoped she didn't notice his deliberate attempt to draw the conversation away from his occupation: given his track record in the past, he had no wish to drive Deirdre off with details about his true area of study. Especially if, despite her voracious appetite in the bedroom, she tended toward the conservative in other aspects of her life. Most mundane women, he'd found, had little patience for the odd occurrences that made up his everyday existence. Best if he gave her a bit more time to get to know him—*ideally a year or two,* he thought wryly—before he let her in on the specifics.

"There's not much to tell, really. I've only recently come to this area from Los Angeles, so I don't know too many people here yet."

"I'm surprised," he said. "As I said the other night, I'd expect you to have little trouble meeting people. In fact, I'd think you might have trouble *not* meeting people, whether you want to or not."

She laughed. "Puppies, you mean." She shrugged. "I know how to handle that kind of attention. It's one of those things most women learn young." She stroked his hand. "You men don't get the hint a lot of the time."

"Some of us do," he said. "Although sometimes we err too far the other way—seeing hints where none exist. It's troublesome, these days: some women prefer men to be bolder about their interest, but others find that annoying, or intimidating."

"You seemed to do all right," she said. She chuckled. "I'd imagine the accent helps, at least in America."

"It does," he said. "But I'm usually fairly good at picking up subtle cues, which has saved me from getting my face slapped more than once."

She leaned in a little closer. "I'm really glad you took a chance," she said softly. "And I'm glad you called back. You want to know a secret?"

"Of course."

"You won't believe me."

"Try me."

"I thought about you this weekend. A lot. I hoped you'd call. I told you you're the first one who called, but you're also the first one I ever actually worried might not."

He looked at her fondly. "That's very flattering. A bit perplexing, but flattering."

"Why do you say that?"

"Truly?"

She nodded.

He shrugged, and didn't meet her gaze. "I'm not a vain man—not much, anyway. I suppose I have my little vanities, like anyone does. I don't generally have too much trouble getting dates, when I want to. But…" he spread his hands. "I know this is going to sound like I'm fishing for compliments, but I'm not. I just don't see *why* I was the first. I mean—look at you. You're young. You're stunning. I mean it, Deirdre: you're the most beautiful woman I've ever met. That's not flattery, and it's not a lie. You could have any man you fancied. I suppose there's a small part of me that's trying to keep me from…fostering false hope."

"Hey," she said, and her tone was gentle.

He looked up.

"So you think I could have any man I fancied, but you can't get your mind around the fact that maybe I fancy you?"

"Well…I can certainly hope it's true."

"Don't sell yourself short, Alastair. I look for a lot of things in a man. Not just what he looks like—though you've got nothing to worry about there. But I've met a lot of pretty men, and every last one of them was boring."

He raised an eyebrow. "So you're saying I'm not pretty, then?" he asked with an impish smile.

She laughed. "You'll do," she said, looking him up and down. "Come on—let's go back to my place. When I get done with you, you won't have any doubt about how I feel about you."

| CHAPTER TEN

TABITHA WELLS SHOWED UP at Stone's office door the following afternoon. "Got a minute, Dr. Stone?" she asked.

Stone waved her in. He hadn't expected to see her—she'd been in class as usual, but he noticed she'd avoided his gaze and seemed overly interested in her notes during the lecture. He wondered if her father had talked to her—and if he'd mentioned her alleged "crush."

Tabby closed the door behind her, but didn't sit down. His mental assessment had been mostly correct: tall and dark-haired, she had a slim, athletic figure and the kind of fresh-scrubbed, healthy attractiveness that didn't need makeup. Stone hadn't noticed it before, but she superficially resembled Deirdre.

Right now, she looked troubled and a little annoyed, her dark eyes fixed on him. "I wanted to talk to you about my dad," she said. "I heard he came by to see you yesterday."

"He told you?"

"Actually, my sister did. I had no idea he was planning to come over here and bother you. I'm so embarrassed, and I wanted to apologize."

Stone shrugged. "You've nothing to apologize for, Ms. Wells. It's not as if you put him up to it."

She rolled her eyes. "I just…I can't believe he *did* it. I know he can be a little overprotective, but to come all the way over here just to talk to you about my personal business—" She glanced down at her bag, then back up at Stone. "You weren't planning to—you know—have a conversation with me about it, were you?"

"Of course not. What my students do on their own time is none of my concern."

She let her breath out. "Well, that's something, I guess. He thinks I've gotten involved in some kind of cult. I guess I didn't explain things to my sister very well, and she got it wrong when she told Dad about it. It's not a cult, you know," she added.

"I didn't think it was." Stone didn't miss the defensive edge to her tone. He wondered why she was telling him all this when a moment ago she'd seemed mortified that he knew anything about it in the first place.

"Well, it's not. It's a church. I found out about it a few weeks ago, and it sounded like something I'd enjoy, so I went to one of the services. I've always been interested in pagan traditions. I was raised a good little Catholic, but…" She trailed off as if suddenly realizing she was babbling. "Anyway," she said, picking up her bag, "I just wanted to let you know I'm sorry about Dad, and let you know I didn't have anything to do with him coming to talk to you."

"Think nothing of it, Ms. Wells," Stone said. He paused. "If you don't mind my asking—"

She'd been turning to leave, but she stopped and turned back at his words. "Hmm?"

"I'm familiar with most of the pagan and Wiccan groups in the area—it sort of goes with my subject. I've even attended a couple of services over the years. But I've never heard of this one of yours—what was it called again?"

She studied him a moment, as if trying to discern ulterior motives behind his words. Finally, she said, "It's called the Church of the Rising Dawn. It's in San Jose. I don't think it's been around long—maybe a year or two. It's a small church, and it's—different. Not Wiccan, not quite normal pagan, but the services are amazing. The high priest is this guy named Matthew Caldwell." She smiled, her gaze settling somewhere over Stone's shoulder. "If you didn't know better, you'd swear he was practicing real magic."

Stone raised an eyebrow. "You don't believe, then?"

"In magic?" She shrugged. "I'm not sure, really. But I think I could start to. This place—" She slung her bag over her shoulder. "I wish my dad would understand. I think he thinks they're doing human sacrifices in the nude under the moonlight or something. They're not doing any kind of sacrifices. It's all about love and belonging and accepting all kinds of people. They don't even ask for money." Her expression hardened. "So if Dad comes back and bugs you about it again, I'd really appreciate it if you'd tell him to talk to me instead of grilling my professors about my personal life."

"I doubt he'll come back," Stone said. "I think I impressed that sentiment on him the last time he was here." He began gathering papers and slipping them into his briefcase. "As I said, Ms. Wells— your personal life is no concern of mine, nor should it be."

Her gaze lingered on him for a beat or two too long, and then she nodded. "Good," she said at last. "Thanks, Dr. Stone."

"Ms. Wells?"

She turned back to face him. "Yeah?"

He paused a moment, unsure of how to say what he wanted to say without sounding either inappropriately paternal or patronizing. "I understand that you probably don't want my advice," he said at last, "so please don't be offended. This church is probably fine— most of them are, in my experience, even the ones that tend to unnerve the more...erm...conventionally-oriented. But I've run across a few that aren't what they seem."

She rolled her eyes. "I wouldn't expect to hear that from *you,* Dr. Stone." She indicated his office with a wave of her hand. "You're all about the unusual."

"I am," he agreed. "That's why I make it a point never to take anything at face value. All I'm saying is: keep your eyes open and your wits about you. If what they preach and what they practice line up—wonderful. But if they're teaching something and practicing something else, that's the time to consider what their true purpose might be."

"I'll keep that in mind," she said, her tone suggesting that she was sure she had the situation firmly in hand. "Thanks again. Gotta run—got class in a few."

Stone watched her go, then raised his hand and used magic to close the door behind her. She was right, of course: none of this was any of his business, and for him to get involved with a student's personal life was both potentially unethical and not something he'd normally even consider. Still, though, it wouldn't hurt to do a bit of simple digging. Tabby Wells wouldn't know, and if he found out the place was harmless, then she'd never have to.

He had a couple hours before his next class; he picked up his briefcase and headed out.

| CHAPTER ELEVEN

AS IT HAPPENED, Stefan Kolinsky still owed Stone at least one favor; he had consulted the black mage only a handful of times in a professional capacity since the whole Burning Man incident last year. It also happened that Kolinsky was free for lunch, so Stone let him recommend a restaurant.

Shortly thereafter, the two were settled in a patched rear booth of a dimly lit Middle Eastern café in northern Mountain View that looked like it was only one step ahead of the health inspectors. Kolinsky had never steered Stone wrong, however, and it quickly became obvious that the unsavory surroundings belied some truly impressive cuisine.

"So," the black mage said, swirling his glass of rosé with obvious appreciation, "what can I do for you?"

"Not much this time," Stone said. He'd taken Kolinsky's recommendation and ordered the lamb tagine; its sweet tang went well with the Moroccan red wine. Briefly, he caught himself wondering if he should bring Deirdre here, or if she would be put off by the lack of ambiance. "Have you heard of an organization called the Church of the Rising Dawn?"

Kolinsky paused to savor his latest sip before setting his glass down. "Of course."

Stone hadn't expected quite such a ready answer, and raised a questioning eyebrow.

"I assume that you're referring to the pseudo-pagan church in San Jose?"

"Yes."

"What about it?"

"I wanted to know what you knew about it. I've got a student who's begun attending, and her father's concerned. Thinks it's some sort of cult. It's none of my business, of course. This is more just—satisfying idle curiosity."

Kolinsky pondered that a moment. "It's been around for a couple of years. Near downtown, I think, though it's a bit hard to find if you don't know what you're looking for. The high priest is…" His gaze went unfocused for a few seconds. "…Matthew Caldwell, I believe his name is."

"That's what my student said. She also said that he made her believe he could do magic. I assume she was referring to the 'k' variety."

"Not surprised. He is a practitioner, after all."

Stone stared at him. "Is he?"

Kolinsky nodded, appearing not to notice Stone's reaction to his words.

"My team or yours?"

"He is a black mage. But I wouldn't be too concerned about him—he's quite harmless, as far as I'm aware. Rather more toward 'dark gray,' as you call it."

Stone let out a long, slow breath. "Stefan—I know some of you lot get what you need by purely voluntary means, but let's not take things too far. None of you are completely 'harmless.'"

"It depends upon your definition," Kolinsky said mildly. "Caldwell and I are similar in philosophy: we have those who choose to provide us with the energy we require to pursue our magical activities."

"Yes, but where's he getting the energy?" Stone persisted.

"That is none of my concern. Nor is it yours."

"You don't know, or you won't tell me?"

"I don't care," Kolinsky said. "But no, I wouldn't tell you if I did know, just as I've never shared the details of my own activities. Those sorts of transactions are purely private."

"So as long as someone isn't going around killing people to top off his tank, you're not bothered."

"Quite so." Kolinsky took a bite of his lamb and chewed thoughtfully. "Alastair, please take this as it is meant: as a suggestion from one professional associate to another. This isn't something you should investigate. As long as everyone involved is informed and capable of consent, it is no more the business of outsiders than is one's sexual history. And inquiries are likely to be received with the same negative response."

Stone rubbed his forehead. "So he's been at this for a couple of years, you say? I wonder why I haven't heard of him."

"He and his organization are somewhat secretive. Although this part of the country is unusually accepting of such activities, it's still not considered wise to advertise one's presence too widely."

"I suppose you're right about that." He focused on eating for a while, thinking about what Kolinsky had told him. Could Tabby Wells have gotten herself involved with a black mage? Did it even matter if she had? If this Matthew Caldwell was upfront about what he was doing, and offered something in exchange, who was he to interfere? Tabby was old enough to make her own decisions. "Anyway, thanks for the information. Don't know what I'll do with it yet—if anything—but at least it's satisfied my curiosity."

Kolinsky inclined his head and placed his utensils on his plate with care. "My pleasure."

Stone paid the check, and as the two of them prepared to go, he said suddenly, as if trying to get the words out before he changed his mind: "One more question, if I may."

Kolinsky's eyes glittered. "Of course. We grow ever closer to once again squaring up our balance sheet."

"Have you heard of a woman called Deirdre Lanier?" As soon as the words left his mouth, he regretted them. What kind of basis was that for a budding relationship: hitting up your friend the information broker for dirt on someone you were supposed to trust? Still, he didn't retract the question.

The black mage considered. "Not offhand. Should I have?"

"Doubtful. She's a woman I met recently. I've had—shall we say—a few unfortunate experiences in the past, and I'm trying to take this one a bit more slowly." He smiled as a vision of her face, her hair, her sparkling eyes flashed across his mind's eye.

Kolinsky gave him an odd look, but didn't comment. "I'm certainly not aware of any magical practitioners by that name in the area," he said. "I could investigate further, if you wish."

"No, that's quite all right." Stone waved him off. "Thanks, Stefan."

| CHAPTER TWELVE

S
TONE WAITED TWO DAYS before succumbing to his curiosity about Matthew Caldwell and the Church of the Rising Dawn. He thought about not doing it—and indeed he wouldn't have considered it if the church had simply been another in the ever-cycling series of new-age organizations that cropped up around the Bay Area. But Kolinsky's revelation that Matthew Caldwell was a black mage had put the whole situation in a different light.

As far as Stone was concerned, Tabitha Wells had every right to associate with anyone she liked—even a black mage. Hell, she even had the right to provide him with energy if she knew what she was getting into. It was the "if she knew what she was getting into" part he wanted to find out about.

Deirdre had left for San Francisco that morning, his day's classes were over at four, and the committee meeting he was supposed to attend at five was cancelled at the last minute. Faced with a free evening, he located the church's street on his map and drove down to San Jose. He figured he'd check the place out, possibly have a chat with Caldwell, grab a quick dinner, then head home and spend the rest of the evening grading essays and possibly getting back to his research.

A bronze plaque next to a closed set of double wooden doors read *Church of the Rising Dawn – All Are Welcome.* Stone noted that a casual passerby would be unlikely to notice the plaque, as the doors were set into an alcove well back from the street, behind a metal gate that was currently open. He paused a moment, inspecting the area with magical sight. He expected to find wards surrounding the entrance, and was surprised to see no sign of any magical activity. He took hold of the heavy handle and pulled, certain the door would be locked tight.

It swung open easily on silent, oiled hinges, revealing a vestibule lit by an old-fashioned, wrought-iron chandelier high overhead. Each of the three walls featured a closed door, and next to the door on the right side was a narrow table topped with a thick unlit candle in a holder and a small rack of buff-colored flyers. Stone couldn't read them from where he stood. Next to the rearmost door, a poster hung in an elaborate frame. A golden symbol that looked like a stylized eye with rays emanating upward from it dominated the poster; below it, written in golden script, a message read *Church of the Rising Dawn. Welcome Home.* The symbol reminded him, somewhat uncomfortably, of the triangle-and-rays symbol the Forgotten had used to indicate a good place. It occurred to him that he hadn't seen any new Forgotten graffiti in several months; he filed that thought away for examination at a later time.

Stone waited a moment longer, but it appeared that no one was coming out to reinforce the poster's welcome. He stepped in and closed the door behind him. Inside, the air smelled faintly of incense—sandalwood, perhaps. A soft, dark-red rug muffled his footsteps.

He tried each of the interior doors in turn: the left and right ones were locked, but the rearmost opened on a stairway leading upward. Like the vestibule, the stairway was covered in the same plush red carpeting.

"Hello?" he called, and started up the stairs.

No one had responded by the time he reached the top, which opened into an anteroom facing two ornate double doors carved with the same symbol he'd seen on the poster below. Small groupings of chairs and benches flanked the doors on either side, gathered around tiny tables decked with more unlit candles. Other than himself, nothing moved. He hesitated for only a moment, then crossed the room and pushed open one of the carved doors.

There were no lights inside, but he got the impression of a large, high-ceilinged space stretching out before him. He closed the door and turned to his left to search for a light switch along the wall. "Anyone here?" he called again. "Mr. Caldwell?"

A large hand clamped onto his upper right arm.

He stiffened and tried to spin, but before he could do so, another hand grabbed his left arm in the same fashion.

Several chandeliers blazed to life overhead.

| CHAPTER THIRTEEN

"WHAT THE HELL—?" Stone demanded. He struggled against his captors, trying to wrench free of their grips, but their fingers clamped tighter until his arms flared pain. Quick glances to his left and right revealed two big men, black-hooded and -robed; the only visible parts of them were their muscular forearms and the meaty hands holding him in place.

For a moment, he almost called a spell to fling them to either side, but so far, aside from their overzealous grips, they'd made no further threatening moves. Best to see what they wanted rather than reveal his magical abilities this early. He picked one at random and glared at him. "Let me go. There's no need for that. I'm not here to cause trouble."

"Are you quite sure about that?"

Stone stiffened as a man stepped out of the shadows on the other side of the room. Like the two others, he wore a black robe, though his was trimmed in embroidered gold symbols and his hood was pushed back to reveal his face. "I hadn't intended to," he said. "But if you don't call off your two goons, that might change."

The man considered. "Let him go, brothers," he said, nodding toward the big men. "That's no way to treat a guest."

The two hooded figures released their holds on Stone's arms and faded back a step to flank him on either side. Ignoring them, Stone focused his attention on the other man. "I'm surprised you get any recruits around here, if that's the sort of reception they can expect," he said. He made a show of shaking out his arms.

"Well, we don't normally get such…distinguished and formidable personages visiting our humble church," the man said.

"Matthew Caldwell, I presume?" Stone asked.

The man bowed. "At your service. And you, of course, are Dr. Alastair Stone. I've heard about you—it's a pleasure to finally make your acquaintance."

Stone frowned. Caldwell knew who he was—that might be a problem, or it might simply be a case of one magical practitioner hearing rumors of another. Black and white mages normally didn't interact often, but most of them were a secretive lot: it wasn't at all unusual for even those of the same persuasion to be unaware of each other's existence unless they had some reason to make contact. He inclined his head slightly, but didn't return the greeting.

Caldwell stepped forward. "Thank you," he said to the two hooded figures still hovering behind Stone. "Wait outside, please. I'm sure Dr. Stone means no harm."

"Sir—" one of the men began.

"You may go," Caldwell said again, more firmly. When the two had bowed and departed, he faced Stone again with a rueful smile. "They mean well, but sometimes they see threats where none exist." He paused. "You aren't a threat, are you, Dr. Stone?"

"That depends," Stone said. He paused to study Caldwell a moment: the man looked surprisingly unassuming for someone who was supposed to be the charismatic High Priest of an unorthodox church. A bit portly and pale, he had dark hair receding from a high forehead, heavy brows, and a prominent nose; dark eyes burning with intelligence and passion dominated his face.

"Please," Caldwell said, indicating for Stone to follow. "Come to my office and we'll talk." His voice was deep, with a pleasant melodic quality that no doubt served him well when leading his flock. "I admit to being curious about why you're here. If you'd like to attend one of our services, I can certainly arrange—"

"I want to talk to you about one of your members," Stone said. He followed Caldwell down a hallway and through another door.

Unlike the décor in the rest of the building, the High Priest's office looked more like it belonged to an overworked business executive than a mystical church leader. "Please, sit down," he said, indicating a leather guest chair. He settled himself behind his large wooden desk. "How I can be of service?"

"Tell me about Tabitha Wells," Stone said.

"Ah. Yes. Ms. Wells. Lovely young woman."

Stone narrowed his eyes. "I'm not interested in your opinion of her appearance, Caldwell. I suspect you know why I'm here."

"Actually, I don't," Caldwell said, unruffled. "Surely you don't expect me to reveal the secrets of our church to…outsiders."

"I don't give a damn what you get up to in your church," Stone said. "That's not my concern. But Ms. Wells is a student of mine, and she's informed me that she's started attending. That, also, is none of my concern."

Caldwell's brow wrinkled. "Then I'm not sure why—"

Stone leaned forward in his chair, gripping the arms and fixing Caldwell with a hard stare. "Are you using her to draw power during your rituals?"

"Yes."

Stone blinked. That hadn't been the answer he was expecting. He could easily be wrong about his suspicions, but even if he weren't, he'd assumed the man would lie about it.

"Does that surprise you, Dr. Stone?"

"It surprises me that you admit it. And it means we might have to revisit that question about whether or not I'm a threat."

Caldwell sighed, leaning back in his high-backed chair and spreading his arms in a conciliatory gesture. "Dr. Stone—as I said, I've heard of you. You have quite the reputation in our circles around this area, whether you know it or not. I know you try to maintain a low profile, but word gets around."

Stone wondered, as he sometimes did, whether other mages employed Stefan Kolinsky's information-brokering service. After all, Kolinsky didn't apologize for the fact that he was a business-man: if he was willing to provide Stone with information about Matthew Caldwell, it was entirely possible that he would likewise provide Caldwell and those like him with information about Stone, if they also agreed to his odd arrangements. "What does that mean?"

"It means," Caldwell said, "that I don't want you for an enemy. I heard about what happened at Burning Man a while back, and a bit about the unfortunate events in that little town down south a few months ago." He shrugged. "Despite our being on opposite sides of the practice, I suspect that your experience has made you far more adept at offensive magic than I'll ever be, or ever want to be." With an amused smile, he added, "In short, Dr. Stone, I'm a lover, not a fighter."

"If you don't want me as an enemy," Stone said tightly, "then leave Ms. Wells alone. I'm sure you have any number of other will-ing contributors. You don't need to add her to your stable."

"Ah, but I can't do that," Caldwell said. "The process is part of our rituals. She is fully aware of what she's doing, and I give you my word, she's completely willing."

"She knows you're a mage?" Stone asked, startled. That wasn't the sort of information one revealed to mundanes lightly, and Tab-by Wells hadn't mentioned anything about it, beyond her faith in Caldwell's alleged magical potential.

"Not *per se*. But she's aware that a certain—energy transfer takes place during the course of the ritual." Caldwell clearly caught something in Stone's expression, because he continued quickly: "I won't give you the details of our church and its practices, Dr. Stone. Not unless you join us, which you're certainly welcome to do. But I assure you, I have never harmed Ms. Wells nor any of the other members of my congregation, nor would I ever do so. Our relation-ships are built on trust, and mutually beneficial. I obtain the power

R. L. KING

I need to continue my work, and they in turn gain a family that loves and accepts them as they are, gives them a refuge from the troubles of the world, and provides for their spiritual, material, and physical needs."

"You're sleeping with her too, then, are you?" The whole thing was becoming clearer now. "And not just her, unless I miss my guess. This whole operation is nothing more than a front you've put up so you can shag young women and steal their power."

Caldwell leaned forward in his chair, putting his hands flat on his desk. For the first time, his smile faded and his expression grew serious. "Dr. Stone. First of all, what you're saying isn't true. There is far more to the Rising Dawn than mere pleasures of the flesh—and by that, I mean not only those of the more...carnal variety, but also good food and drink, stimulating discourse, and the appreciation of fine material things."

Stone sighed. "Save it, Caldwell. You're not the first of your kind I've encountered, and I doubt you'll be the last. This doesn't have to escalate. I'm certain that you have enough will-ing...congregation members to fulfill whatever desires your kinky little heart can manage to come up with. You don't need Ms. Wells."

"Of course I don't need her," Caldwell said, his features settling back into neutrality. "But that isn't the point."

Stone waited.

"The point, Dr. Stone, is that you can threaten me if you like. As I said, if it came to a magical battle, I'm sure you'd wipe up the floor with me—although you might find that we're a bit better de-fended here than you'd think. But what would it gain you? I thought you were a man of intellect, not one of force."

Stone had his doubts about Caldwell's assessment of his own abilities: that much power siphoned regularly from numerous con-tributors would render the man quite potent, even if he had no experience in magical combat. "I don't fancy seeing my students taken advantage of."

"Ah, but there's the disconnect. What makes you think I *am* taking advantage of her?" Before Stone could respond, he held up a hand. "Please—let me finish. Ms. Wells is an intelligent young woman. She's well past the age of consent. I haven't deceived her in any way regarding the nature of our rituals—nor have I deceived any of the other members of my inner circle."

"Inner circle," Stone said. "The ones you sleep with, or the ones you take power from?"

"Both," Caldwell said with undisguised frankness. "All of them know what to expect, and they're all willing participants. If you were to ask Ms. Wells, she would tell you the same thing." Again, he frowned. "In short, Dr. Stone, every person involved in our rituals is a legal adult, mentally capable, free of coercion, and fully able to make his or her own decisions about what he or she chooses to participate in. What right do you have to interfere with that?"

And there it was. Stone drew breath to respond, then let it out again without speaking.

Because damn it, the man was *right*.

He didn't want to admit it—hated to admit it, in fact. But the fact remained: assuming Caldwell was telling the truth, and that would be easy enough to discern with a quick and surreptitious look at Tabby Wells's aura, there wasn't a bloody thing Stone could—or should—do about it. She had every right to conduct her affairs in any way she saw fit, regardless of his approval. If she wanted to hand over a small and renewable portion of her life energy to this man in exchange for…whatever it was he claimed to give her, that was that. And if she chose to sleep with Caldwell—that was even less his business than their magical activities.

Caldwell favored him with a gentle smile that, to his credit, didn't appear condescending. "You see, don't you? I thought you would. You're a reasonable man."

Stone stood, expressionless. He kept his voice even. "Yes, Mr. Caldwell. I see. And you *are* right. This isn't my concern." He turned as if to go, but then paused and turned back. "But I'll tell you this, and I suggest you don't forget it: if it reaches me that Ms. Wells or any of your other…congregants have come to harm due to your activities, you will see me again."

"I wouldn't be at all surprised," Caldwell said, still showing no reaction. He rose and moved to open the door. "In fact, I'd expect it. Have a good evening, Dr. Stone. I hope you find your peace."

| CHAPTER FOURTEEN

TWO WEEKS PASSED. Stone heard nothing more from Tabitha Wells's father, nor anything directly from Tabby herself. She attended classes regularly, completed her assignments, and seemed normal in every way. The only indications Stone had that anything was unusual were that she relocated her usual seat closer to the middle of the hall, and she sometimes appeared tired early in the week. That could easily be explained by the normal weekend activities of a college student.

He'd taken the opportunity the day after he'd visited Matthew Caldwell to carefully examine Tabby's aura with magical sight while the class was busy watching a video presentation. What he saw was consistent with someone who'd had some of her power siphoned off by a black-magic practitioner, but other than that, it was clear, untroubled, and whole. Stone had seen enough such auras in his career to recognize someone who had contributed willingly. He decided not to ask her anything else about her new church, thinking that she—quite justifiably—might resent his intrusion into her personal life. Caldwell must not have said anything to her about Stone's visit either; no doubt she'd have given him an earful about it if he had.

He didn't have a lot of time to think about what was doing on with Tabby Wells, though—his mind, when not focused on his work, was most often occupied with Deirdre Lanier.

The two of them had spent every available evening together, whenever she didn't have to work late in San Francisco or he didn't have late classes or meetings. When they weren't together, Stone found himself missing her with an intensity that occasionally disturbed him.

He'd never felt this way about a woman before—even Imogen, all those years ago in England, hadn't affected him like Deirdre did. Every time he was with her, everything about her—her beauty, her wit, her sly sense of humor, her talents in the bedroom, the way she focused on him as if he were the most important thing in the world—contributed to a feeling of pleasure and satisfaction he used to wonder if he'd ever be capable of.

Still, his near-lifelong magical instincts didn't desert him: he continued to periodically check her aura to look for any kind of subterfuge, usually while she was drifting off to sleep next to him. He felt traitorous for doing it, as if he were betraying the obvious feelings she had for him. But he still did it, and he never found anything but affection, contentment, and a remarkably consistent passion.

Perhaps this was the real deal, and he'd allowed himself to become cynical for so long that he couldn't recognize it.

Stone didn't look forward to the department's upcoming shindig-slash-schmoozefest; ostensibly, it was a festive party for the faculty and their spouses or significant others to get together, drink too much, and take the edge off the middle of winter, but in reality it was an excuse to invite high-profile (read: loaded) benefactors and try to entice them to open their pocketbooks by plying them with small talk, free-flowing top-shelf liquor, and all manner of soft-sell sales pitches regarding the department's plans for the upcoming year.

Stone would have stayed home—he threatened to every time—but his department head always hinted none too subtly that doing so would be a politically unwise move. He knew why: they considered him a good draw. He was relatively young, attractive, looked good in a tux, and the rich ladies loved his accent. Despite his pathological dislike of small talk, he somehow managed each time to be witty and charming enough to convince the powers that be that he was responsible for some small extra measure of donations. He'd gotten it down to a science in the last couple of years: show up with his current girlfriend, turn on the charm for an hour, score a couple of primo drinks and chat up two or three old women, then take his leave before anyone figured out he was gone.

"So," he said one evening as he and Deirdre lounged in bed following their latest lovemaking session, "I've got to go to this party thing next Friday. Would you like to come with me?"

"You make it sound so appealing," she teased. She lay snuggled against him, her head on his chest.

"Well, to be honest it's normally a bit of a chore—it's a work thing. But if you'll accompany me, I think this one could be much more pleasant than usual."

He'd debated whether to ask her—of course he wanted her company, and certainly had no plans to ask anyone else, but bringing her to a University function essentially guaranteed that someone would mention his actual field of study within her earshot. He hadn't exactly lied to her about it, but he'd also made it a point not to bring up his work in anything but the most general way so as not to invite too many questions. The problem was, he couldn't show up at the party without a date (the one year he'd done that, he'd had to fend off the tipsy advances of a seventy-year-old widow who'd insisted her spirit guide had informed her he was her soulmate, and he should come back to her house to see her art collection). That meant Deirdre was elected.

Maybe she'd be busy that night, and he could play escort to Edwina Mortenson or something. That would be truly strange and probably unpleasant for both of them, but at least Edwina knew the score and would probably ditch him as soon as they arrived. And more importantly, he wouldn't have to reveal anything to Deirdre.

Ah, well. It had to happen eventually, if they remained together. He had to accept that her finding out might be the beginning of the end, the inevitable tipping point where every one of his previous girlfriends had twigged to the stranger corners of his life and begun the subtle disengagement that eventually led to their becoming his ex-girlfriends. Sometimes it was quick—one time it happened in a single night—and sometimes it took a few weeks, but so far his track record ran at a solid one hundred percent. He had no idea if Deirdre Lanier would be the one to break the streak, but he wasn't in a hurry to find out. Finally, it was the thought of showing up without her that made him bring it up at last.

"Might be fun," she agreed. "And if not..." She stroked his chest. "We can always sneak out and find something more fun to do, right?"

There was that, too. "I like the way you think."

| CHAPTER FIFTEEN

I N THE END, and after much debating back and forth with himself, he decided to head off the inevitable. "Listen," he said to her as they sat in the car parked along a side street a block down from the Rosicrucian Egyptian Museum in San Jose, where the party was being held. "There's something I want to tell you before we go in. You'll likely find out before the night's over, and I'd rather you heard it from me than from someone else."

"Oh?" She turned in her seat to face him.

She wore a short, slinky black dress that showed off the curves of her trim, athletic body to stunning advantage, and Stone was finding it difficult to concentrate. "I...haven't been quite truthful with you about my occupation."

Her eyebrow crept up. It was one of the many things he found irresistible about her: she was the first woman he'd ever met who could do the single-eyebrow raise. "Is that so? Wait, let me guess: you're really the janitor. Or you work in one of the dining halls as a lunch...er...laddie." She tilted her head, then reached out and playfully ruffled the front of his hair. "I can't picture you in a hairnet, but maybe that's why you have such trouble making it stay down."

"Either of those would be easier," he said. "Actually, I didn't lie: I just didn't tell you the whole truth. My department *is* part of Cultural Anthropology. But it's a bit more...specific than that."

"Specific."

He resisted the urge to tug at his tie. "My subject is only under that umbrella because they couldn't figure out where else to put us. I teach Occult Studies." He watched her closely for a reaction.

"Occult Studies." She considered that a moment. "So, things like the Salem Witch Trials, and ghostly visitations, and that kind of thing?"

"That and more, yes." He waited.

She smiled, and it lit up her face. "How fascinating! Why didn't you want to tell me that?"

He stared at her as he let himself relax, his nervousness ebbing away. Was that it? Just like that? Suddenly, he felt foolish for making a big deal of it. He'd been holding on to so much subconscious dread of how she'd react to the news that the relief hit him like a physical sensation. Of course she wouldn't be like the others—how could he ever have expected she would be? "You'd be surprised at how many people find it…off-putting."

"Oh, Alastair…" She reached out to straighten his tie, and let her finger trail down the stiff white front of his shirt. "I'm not most people. Haven't you figured that out by now?"

"Oh, yes…" he said, and his voice was husky. Suddenly the car's interior, comfortably warm before, was oppressively hot. "Suppose we just skip the party, then, shall we?"

She laughed. "No way. I want to spend the evening watching you trying to dodge rich ladies who want to have their way with you for donations."

"It's not nearly as amusing as you make it sound."

"I'll be the judge of that." With a smile and a final tweak of his tie, she added, "And then, after I've decided you've suffered enough for thinking I'd run away when I found out your real job…we'll go back to my place and find out what really goes bump in the night."

CHAPTER SIXTEEN

STONE HAD TO ADMIT IT: as venues for holding a meet-and-greet fundraiser for the Cultural Anthropology department went, the Rosicrucian Egyptian Museum in San Jose was one of their more inspired choices. The last couple of these he'd attended had been held at more conventional locations (the one last year was at the Mountain Winery in Saratoga) but this year, apparently, Occult Studies had had some input into the decision-making process.

The museum itself was only part of a complex that included an auditorium, a planetarium, a meditation labyrinth, and numerous winding paths that led past Egyptian sculpture and gardens. It wasn't generally open this late, but tonight all the lights along the paths were on, giving the place an otherworldly beauty.

"This is nice," Deirdre said as they followed the signs toward the museum. Other guests, clad in tuxedos, dinner jackets, and colorful cocktail dresses, lingered along the path; one older couple had paused to investigate the museum's life-sized outdoor game of Senet, an ancient Egyptian pastime. "Have you been here before?"

"A couple of times, yes." He didn't tell her about the library, tucked away in a building down a narrow path to their left and probably one of the few things not open for the party. It had surprised him when he'd first visited a few years back: it was one of the area's more impressive repositories of research material pertaining to the occult and the supernatural. Not only did it include numerous books and papers on the subject—some of them very old—that weren't duplicated in Stanford's libraries, but Stone had discovered that several genuinely magical tomes resided on its dusty shelves. After he'd chatted with the librarian (she was mundane, but remarkably knowledgeable on the subject) and determined himself that none of the magically active material posed any danger, he'd started sending some of his graduate students here to conduct various bits of research. "If you have any interest in ancient Egypt, you might find the exhibits interesting." He grinned. "And if you don't, they'll have plenty of good food and liquor. That's one thing I'll say for our department: they don't skimp on trying to impress the benefactors."

They rounded a corner toward the front of the museum. Beyond it, a walkway stretched out to the street, lined with an honor guard of more Egyptian-style statues. Several people milled around in front of the tall columns flanking the brass-clad front door, chatting, glasses in hand. Stone nodded greetings to them as he and Deirdre passed, noting with amusement how every one of the men's gazes followed her and barely seemed to notice him.

He was glad he wasn't the jealous type, or his anxiety level whenever he was with her would spend most of its time pegged to the maximum. This was a new experience for him—he'd dated his share of beautiful women over the years, but none as stunning as she was. He planned to make it a point to stay near her, not because he was worried she'd stray from him, but because some of these rich old donors could get a bit pushy with their attention. Two years ago he'd nearly had to pry one of them off his date when he'd cornered her in a side hallway with a drunken, long-winded story about how his wife didn't understand him.

Inside, dim light and soft music had transformed the museum into an inviting space for socializing. Two galleries opened out on either side of the large reception desk, and a short flight of stairs led up to the second floor. A few more guests mingled in couples and small groups.

"Welcome," the smiling woman behind the desk said. "The bar and buffet table are upstairs in the area between the galleries. Please enjoy yourself, and feel free to check out the exhibits."

"The bar," Stone said as they mounted the stairs. "I know this lot—that's where the action, so to speak, will be."

He was correct: as they reached the second floor, it quickly became clear that the majority of the guests were here. He estimated perhaps fifty people—mostly couples, mostly older—sipping drinks and drifting from one bit of Egyptian antiquity to the next. The low murmur of conversation or someone's amused laugh occasionally rose above the music, but so far things remained fairly civilized. Nobody had had time to get tipsy yet. It would come.

He'd just accompanied Deirdre to get a drink when he heard a voice from behind them: "Dr. Stone!"

"Here we go…" he murmured so only Deirdre could hear him.

Her eyes sparkled as she squeezed his arm in support.

Dr. Edwina Mortenson, head of the tiny Occult Studies department, stood there with a smiling woman who had to be at least seventy-five. "I'm so glad you made it," Mortenson said with a smile that didn't make it anywhere near her eyes. Around sixty, she wore a loose-fitting, caftan-like dress that swirled around her stocky frame, and had upgraded her usual abundance of bangle bracelets and mystical pendants to a single golden cuff with a gleaming blue gem on her right wrist and a sparkling golden pentacle necklace with a similar gem at its center. Her long, steel-gray hair was swept back into a soft bun, and her earrings were tiny claws clutching pearls.

She indicated her companion with a sweeping gesture. "This is Mrs. Feeney. She's recently moved into the area, and she's eager to find out more about our program. Mrs. Feeney, this is Dr. Alastair Stone. He's the newest member of our department, and quite the star when it comes to occult happenings. I'm sure he'll be delighted to give you some insight on your recent experiences."

"Oh!" Mrs. Feeney beamed. "I'm so pleased to meet you, Dr. Stone!" She clutched a half-full wineglass in one bony hand, but reached out the other to pluck his hand into her grip.

"And I you, Mrs. Feeney." He gave her hand a gentle squeeze, afraid he might break it otherwise. He nodded toward Deirdre. "This is Ms. Deirdre Lanier."

"Oh, a pleasure, a pleasure," Mrs. Feeney said, barely acknowledging Deirdre with a brief, vague nod before returning her attention to Stone.

"I'll leave you in Dr. Stone's capable hands, then," Mortenson said, with a sideways glance toward Stone.

He shot her a *thanks a lot* look as she edged away.

It took him nearly fifteen minutes before he could politely disentangle himself from the chatty old lady, who wanted to discuss the possibility that her late husband might be haunting his beloved golf bag. She also suspected he was trying to communicate with her by moving around the objects on his desk, which she hadn't touched since his death. Deirdre watched with amusement as Stone offered a few charming but noncommittal tips on ways she might determine this on her own, and gently declined her invitation to visit her at her home to check the situation out for himself. He only got away because he finally excused himself with the lie that he'd promised to meet someone else in another gallery and it wouldn't be polite to stand them up.

Deirdre chuckled as they headed off. "You weren't kidding, were you?"

"Did you think I was?" He rubbed the back of his neck and took a long drink. The event photographer passed them, pausing to snap a couple of shots before disappearing into the room Stone and Deirdre had just left.

"I thought you might be exaggerating," she said, eyes twinkling. She looped her arm through his. "I mean...*I* find your accent irresistible, but I had no idea you had such a fan club."

"Oh, hush," he said in mock annoyance, but he was smiling. Normally he found this sort of thing tiresome, but as was often the case lately, Deirdre's presence improved his mood significantly. He hadn't missed the fact that Mrs. Feeney had cast a few mildly vexed glances at Deirdre, as if she wished the younger woman would get the hint and find something else to do so the two of them could speak privately. "Come on—let's go top up our drinks."

"Who was that other woman? The one in the blue dress? She left before we could get introduced."

Stone sighed. "That was Dr. Edwina Mortenson. She's sort of the head of our little department, although with only three faculty members, we don't really need one."

"She doesn't like you, does she?"

"Not in the slightest." He grinned. "Not that I care—which is part of why she doesn't like me. Don't be fooled by that airy hippie demeanor—that woman can be a dragon lady of the first order when you get on her bad side."

Deirdre examined a collection of scarabs and other carvings in a glass case. "This sounds like a story. Why are you on her bad side?"

"Oh, it's not so bad anymore, really—we've come to a certain understanding over the years. Mostly, we stay out of each other's way unless absolutely necessary. She's good at her job and she likes all that administrative rubbish that bores me senseless, so I appreciate that. But she—" He considers his words. "—she *believes.*"

"Believes? In the occult, you mean?"

He nodded. "Tarot cards, psychometry, spirit visitations, vampires—the whole bit. She's convinced there's a secret world out there just beyond what normal humans can see."

"And you aren't?"

"I keep an open mind," he said, shrugging. "But mostly, I'm fascinated by the ways humans have integrated the unknown into their worldviews. Edwina's one of those serious types—she thinks I don't give the subject its proper respect." With another grin, he added, "Plus, she'll never admit it, but she's jealous because my student approval ratings are orders of magnitude higher than hers."

She moved in closer, her warm body pressing against his. "I'm not surprised," she murmured.

He swallowed. She was so close now that he could smell the fresh floral scent of her hair, and the faint hint of alcohol on her breath. He shifted to magical sight and wasn't at all surprised to see the familiar red glow hovering around her aura—and was sure it was around his as well. Once again, a nearly overpowering sense of desire swept over him. "Deirdre…"

"Hmmm?" She leaned over and planted a light kiss on his jawline.

He didn't trust himself to answer.

She rested her head on his shoulder. "I saw on the map as we came in that there's a scale-model Egyptian tomb around here somewhere. That sounds fascinating. Want to go look at it? It will be a nice break, and then you can get back to your admiring old ladies."

He should stay up here, with the rest of the crowd. That's what he was supposed to do—schmooze with the donors, charming the ladies and entertaining them and their husbands with anecdotes about the supernatural. But all the previous years, he'd barely stayed an hour before finding an excuse to make himself scarce. Tonight, with Deirdre at his side, he felt he could ride out the whole evening if he had to. If he took a little break now, what would be the harm? "Right, then," he said. "I'm all yours."

The "tomb" was down a flight of stairs off one of the galleries on the first floor. It consisted of a passageway that appeared to be carved out of rock, and opened out into a chamber lined on all four sides with hieroglyphs and Egyptian-style paintings of day-to-day life. Electric lights fashioned to look like wooden torches provided dim illumination, and a massive, closed sarcophagus on an elaborate bier served as a centerpiece. Currently, the chamber was empty.

"This is nice…" Deirdre said, examining some of the hieroglyphs. "Can you read any of these?"

"Sorry. Ancient Egypt isn't really my area of expertise." He remained close to her, looking over her shoulder. The scene depicted the goddess Isis and her beloved, Osiris. He nodded toward Osiris. "He didn't come to a good end, though—he ended up being cut into pieces, and Isis there had to go 'round gathering them up."

"That's true love," she said, gripping his hand more tightly. She glanced around as if verifying that they were still alone, then turned her attention back to him.

Warmth washed over Stone again. He wondered if she felt his hand trembling in hers—or if hers was doing the same thing. The wave of desire, even stronger than before, hit him so hard his knees weakened. He let go of her hand and gripped her shoulders with gentle intensity, leaning in closer to her. She leaned in to meet him halfway, her lips seeking his.

He pressed her back against the wall, eyes closed, mind and body on fire, as her arms snaked around him and one hand reached up to bury itself in his hair. Visions came unbidden to his mind: picking her up, laying her across the sarcophagus, and—

Someone cleared their throat behind them.

Stone jerked, startled, and stepped quickly back, whirling to see who had come in. The overwhelming sense of desire ebbed away as he spotted a familiar figure—a fiftyish man in a rumpled dinner jacket and baggy pants. "Hubbard. Er—how are you?"

Mackenzie Hubbard, the other member of the Occult Studies department faculty, stood with his wife in the entrance to the chamber. Hubbard eyed Stone with a sly expression, and his lips quirked into a smile under his large, salt-and-pepper mustache. "All right. Sorry to—interrupt." His gaze moved to Deirdre, and his eyes widened.

"Quite all right," Stone said briskly. "Deirdre, this is Dr. Mackenzie Hubbard. He's the third of our little band of miscreants up at the University. And his wife, Barbara. This is Deirdre Lanier."

"Pleased to meet you," Hubbard said. He wore an odd expression, intense and a bit stunned, and his gaze had not yet left Deirdre. "So, Stone here convinced you to come and rub elbows with the old and rich, did he?"

"Mac!" Barbara Hubbard said, shocked, hitting him lightly on the arm with her clutch bag. She was about Hubbard's age, plain but cheerful-looking. A bright glittery starburst pin added a touch of whimsy to her conservative gold cocktail dress. She smiled at Stone. "Don't mind him, Alastair. He didn't want to come tonight."

Stone knew that to be true—Hubbard hated these kinds of shindigs even more than he did, and made no secret of the fact that he'd much rather be home working on his writing. He'd been complaining about it just a couple days ago at the most recent department meeting.

"Well, I hope he's at least showing you a good time," Hubbard said, ignoring his wife's admonition.

"Oh, he certainly is. I'm pleased to meet you both as well," Deirdre said. Her eyes sparkled with amusement, and her arm slipped through Stone's.

Hubbard remained fixed on Deirdre. For a moment, all of them just stood there, at a loss for anything to say. Barbara glanced sideways at Deirdre and her expression clouded as she looked away.

"Well," Hubbard said abruptly, as if finally realizing he'd been staring. "We'll leave you two alone. Come on, Barb—I need another drink." He took his wife's arm and hustled her out the other side of the chamber, glancing back once over his shoulder.

As soon as they were gone, Deirdre burst out laughing. After a second, Stone grinned. "Well…what was awkward," he said.

She brushed a quick kiss across his lips. "I think it was funny." Stepping back, she took his hand. "We should go back upstairs, though, before anyone else catches us. I don't want to get you in trouble."

"It would be worth it," he said, but he let her lead him out toward the stairs. The wave of desire had passed now, leaving behind amused affection. Deirdre really was a good sport. "Did you see the way old Hubbard looked at you?"

Her arm slid around him. "Don't worry, love. You have nothing to worry about."

"Oh, I'm not worried. But I'll bet he'll be getting an earful from his wife when they get home. I thought his jaw was going to end up in his lap."

| CHAPTER SEVENTEEN

"**A**LASTAIR..."

"Hmm?" Stone rolled over on his side.

"I was thinking about the party tonight. I'm still fascinated by the fact that you teach the occult. I'll bet you've got some amazing stories to tell."

You don't know the half of it. "Oh, a few, here and there." They'd stayed at the museum for another hour after leaving the tomb. Stone had done his best to avoid both Mortenson and Hubbard, but had otherwise done his duty, chatting up several of the donors while making sure not to either drink too much or be distracted by Deirdre's decidedly distracting presence.

He thought he'd done all right, all things considered, but was nonetheless glad to be home. He'd shared his thoughts about the sarcophagus with Deirdre when they were in bed, and she'd been happy to add a few ideas of her own. Afterward, they lay next to each other as soft music played in the background.

"So...have you ever met a real ghost?"

He raised an eyebrow. "Deirdre, I teach it. That doesn't mean I go around looking for haunted houses built on top of mysterious Native American graveyards."

"So you don't believe in ghosts?"

He shrugged. "As I said before, I keep an open mind. Why, do you?"

"Oh, I don't know. I suppose not—not like you say Dr. Mortenson does. Though it would be fun if some of those kinds of things were real. My grandmother was quite a believer, though."

"Oh?"

She nodded, pulling up the covers and moving closer to him as if settling in to tell a good story. "I remember when I was a little girl, she used to tell me all about haunted houses, and witches, and things like that. My mother would get upset with her, thinking her stories would give me nightmares, but they never did."

"Interesting." He stroked her arm with two light fingers. "So she really believed, then, did she?"

"I think so. She had this old book...I still remember it, even though I haven't seen it for years. It was really old, and full of all these odd diagrams and words in some strange language that nobody in my family could read."

"Sounds intriguing." Stone stretched, with a lazy smile. It was another thing that often happened when people found out about his area of interest: inevitably, they'd trot out some old family heirloom and want to know if it was somehow supernaturally attuned. Mrs. Feeney and her husband's haunted golf bag was only the most recent in a long line of them.

She smacked him gently on the shoulder. "Oh, you're just humoring me, aren't you?"

"Er...yes?" He grinned. "I'm sorry, Deirdre. You'd understand if you knew how many people wanted me to tell them that Aunt Mabel's dusty old fox fur stole is possessed by the spirit of Sitting Bull or something."

"Well, if you don't even want to *look* at it..." Her pout was obviously affected.

"Oh, I'll be happy to look at it," he said. "I like musty old tomes. It might even be worth something. I could run it by a couple of colleagues in the History department if it doesn't end up being haunted. Because it won't be."

"I suppose not." She sighed, then feathered a kiss across his jawline. "But the stories were fun, though."

| CHAPTER EIGHTEEN

D EIRDRE SPENT THE NEXT FEW DAYS in Los Angeles, working on approving some designs that had come back from the production house, and Stone couldn't keep her off his mind. He almost missed a committee meeting following an office hour, because when no students showed up to consult with him, he soon drifted into thoughts of what he and Deirdre would do when she returned: restaurants she might like, clubs they could try, what they'd do when they returned home... by the time he glanced at the clock and startled himself from his reverie, he only had five minutes to make it halfway across campus. He had to run to get there, and showed up at the conference room breathless and disheveled.

"Sorry I'm late," he said, dropping into a chair. "Lost track of the time."

From across the table, Edwina Mortenson regarded him through narrowed eyes, but nodded, shuffled her papers in front of her, and continued what she'd been saying.

Stone leaned back, waiting for his heart rate to return to normal. He shouldn't be this winded from a quick run across campus. He routinely went for late-night runs and returned home less out of breath than he was now. It hadn't been recently, though. Not recently at all, now that he thought about it: he'd only gone running a handful of times since he'd parted company with Jason and Verity. He'd usually had an excuse why he'd do it later, and after he met

Deirdre...he had other more interesting things to do with his nights when she was around, and when she wasn't around, he'd been more concerned with trying to catch up on lost sleep.

Deirdre did keep him busy. Indeed she did. His mind spun off another pleasant fantasy...

"Something funny, Dr. Stone?"

He looked up, startled again, to find Mortenson eyeing him with suspicion. He realized he'd been smiling. "Er—no. Not really. Why?"

Mortenson shook her head and continued on. She had slides now, and was making some sort of presentation to the rest of the attendees about budgets and allocations. A couple other people gave Stone sidelong glances, but quickly returned their attention to Mortenson.

Stone tried to concentrate on her presentation as well, but Edwina Mortenson was not what one might call an electrifying speaker under the best of circumstances. Recitations of dry figures and charts didn't count as the best of circumstances. Before long, Stone caught himself nodding off again. His head fell forward slightly and he jerked it back up. Mortenson was watching him once more—and now so was Mackenzie Hubbard, the other Occult Studies professor. The former looked disapproving, the latter sly.

Stone managed to stay awake and mostly focused through the remainder of the presentation, wishing he'd had the foresight to bring a cup of coffee with him. When it was over, he got up quickly to leave while Mortenson was still gathering her papers—the last thing he wanted right now was to be drawn into a discussion with her. Perhaps if he hurried, he could get back to his office, collect his coat, and get the hell away from campus before she made it back. At least he *could* run if he had to; he'd never seen Mortenson move at faster than a determined waddle in all the years he'd known her.

"Hey, Stone, wait up!"

He let his breath out. He'd forgotten about Hubbard. He slowed to let the other professor catch up with him, but didn't say anything.

Hubbard fell into step next to him. "Heading back to the office?"

"I was, yes." Seeing no way to get out of the situation, Stone continued walking.

Almost as tall as Stone, Mackenzie Hubbard walked with a slight hunch and favored cardigan sweaters and baggy tweed slacks, which made him look even older. He didn't dislike Stone as much as Mortenson did, mostly because he couldn't rise sufficiently above his prevailing apathy to summon such a definitive emotion. Everybody knew he was just marking time in his position—his true passion lay in writing horror novels, an avocation he was certain would be rewarded any day now when the rest of the world finally made note of his genius. Last Stone had heard, he was shopping around his seventh manuscript and hadn't sold any of them yet.

"You all right?" Hubbard asked. "Not coming down with something, are you?"

"Why wouldn't I be all right?"

Hubbard shrugged and thrust his hands into his pockets. The mid-February air held a chill, and a light wind stirred up the dead leaves. "You don't look so good. I know those meetings are boring as hell, but I've never seen you nod off like that before."

Now that he wasn't running, Stone regretted forgetting to grab his overcoat from his office; his light T-shirt wasn't much protection against the cold. He picked up his pace a little. "I'm all right. Just haven't been sleeping too well lately."

Hubbard gave him a sidelong look, speeding up to match strides. "Ahh," he said with a knowing smile. "I get it. The girl at the party. What was her name again? Denise? Danielle?"

"Deirdre. And no, that's not it," Stone said, letting an edge of annoyance creep into his voice.

"Oh, sorry, I didn't realize you two had—"

"We haven't." *If it's any of your concern.* "She's down in Los Angeles this week on business."

"Got it," Hubbard said. He shook his head. "I have to hand it to you, Stone—I don't know how you did it. I know you don't have too much trouble with the ladies, but...*damn.*"

Stone couldn't decide whether to be annoyed or flattered, so he covered it with a chuckle. "I don't get it either, honestly. No idea what she sees in me, when she could have her pick. But I'm not arguing."

"Nice problem to have," Hubbard said. "Now you just need to keep up with her. Get some sleep, Stone. Women like that don't have patience for guys who can't keep 'em happy, if you know what I mean."

Stone raised an eyebrow. This conversation was going in an entirely odd direction, considering Hubbard's usual attitudes.

"Hey," the older man said, shrugging, "I'm just saying. I've been married a long time, so I'm out of the game. But I was your age once."

Definitely an odd direction. "Well...thank you for that. I appreciate the advice. But we're fine." He affected a shiver, which wasn't entirely feigned. "Listen—I'm freezing. Think I'll move a bit faster and try to warm up. Talk to you later, all right?"

Hubbard made a half-wave, half-salute. "Sure, no problem. Later."

When he got home, visions of a nice long sleep warring with fantasies of Deirdre, his message light was flashing. Two messages. He hit the button, then shucked off his overcoat and tossed it over a chair.

"Dr. Stone? You there?" Verity's voice came out of the speaker. A pause, and then: "Guess not. Ah, well. Just hadn't heard from you in a while, so I wanted to see how you were doing. Give me a call back when you get a chance, okay? Jason and I are both fine, and so's Edna. Later!"

Another beep, and it was Deirdre's voice: "Alastair, hi. I'm back in town. I've missed you, and I'd love it if you'd come over tonight. I've got something I want to show you." She laughed. "No, not that, silly. Well, okay—that too. But something else first. Come over at seven? I'll pick something up from Luigi's if you'll bring the wine. Bye!"

Stone glanced at his watch: it was already almost six. If he hurried, he'd have time to shower, change clothes, and get over there by seven. Already he felt more energized, thoughts of sleep driven away by the anticipation of seeing Deirdre again.

He was halfway to her place before he remembered that he hadn't called Verity back. Ah, well: he could do it later.

| CHAPTER NINETEEN

EIRDRE'S SMILE lit up her face when she opened the door. If he'd had any doubt about whether she was happy to see him, it quickly fled as she flung herself into his arms, drawing him into hard hug that morphed into a passionate kiss. He instantly responded, his own arms going around her slim figure. Every time he reunited with her after an absence, no matter how brief, he was reminded again how breathtakingly lovely she was. It was almost as if his mind's eye wasn't sufficiently developed to capture her true beauty accurately in his memory, but now, with her there in front of him—the sight of her, the subtle aroma of her perfume, the feel of her lips under his—he felt like he'd come home.

"I've missed you so much," she said after gently breaking the kiss and stepping back so he could come inside. "Did you miss me too?"

"Constantly," he said. He set the bag containing the wine he'd brought down on a nearby table and let her slide his coat off.

"I'd better stop with the coat," she said. "Or dinner will get cold."

"Who needs dinner?" he murmured.

She laughed. "Oh, come on, I'll bet you've been getting takeout all week while I was gone, haven't you?"

"You got takeout," he pointed out. He retrieved the wine, allowing her to lead him into the dining area. She'd already set the table with blood-red placemats, candles, and a vase containing assorted colorful flowers.

"Yes, but I won't be eating it alone over some student's essay about witch-burnings. And I'll put it on actual *plates*."

"You're too good to me," he said.

"Oh, you'll pay for it later," she called from the kitchen area. "But somehow, I doubt you'll mind the price very much…"

"You're making it quite difficult to concentrate on food, you know."

"Think of it as an exercise in willpower. And the sooner we finish up…"

"So what's this surprise you mentioned?" he asked when she returned a moment later carrying two fine-china plates of steaming veal piccata. He opened the wine and poured into two crystal glasses, then settled back in his chair.

"Oh, I'm afraid I've gotten your hopes up. It's nothing big."

"My hopes are up for later," he said. "The surprise is just a nice afterthought."

She smiled, eyes twinkling, and sat down across from him. "Remember that book of my grandmother's I told you about? My mother found it and sent it to me. It came today. It was waiting for me with the rest of the mail when I got home."

"Ah, yes. The haunted tome."

"Now, don't make fun of my Grandma," she said, but she was still smiling.

"I'm not making fun of your Grandma. I'm making fun of your book. But I'm sure I'll have a lovely time looking at it with you. As long as we don't look too long," he added with an arched eyebrow.

"That will be up to you, won't it?"

They chatted while they ate, mostly Deirdre telling Stone about her week in Los Angeles. When they finished, lingering over the wine, she got up, held up a finger, and hurried out of the room. She returned a few moments later carrying a cardboard box. Roughly eighteen inches by twelve by eight, it was covered in numerous layers of brown packing tape, as if it had been shipped or taped up for storage many times over many years.

"I'd forgotten how cool this was," she said. "I haven't seen it since I was a teenager. I think Mom was glad to be rid of it—she says it makes her nervous." She pushed Stone's empty plate out of the way and set the package down in front of him. "So, Dr. Occult Expert—give me your professional opinion. And remember to be kind, or Grandma's ghost might come back and haunt you."

Stone, amused, opened the box. He figured he could make a few noncommittal approving comments over it and that would satisfy her. At least it wasn't a moth-eaten fox-fur stole. No matter how lively they might be, fleas didn't count as a haunting.

Inside the threadbare cardboard carton rested another box, this one much more substantial: it looked like it was made of hard leather stretched over some stiffer frame, hinged in the back, with a locking clasp in the front. Each corner was reinforced with more leather. He lifted it free of the cardboard and set it on the table. "Have you got the—" he started.

She dangled a silver key on a chain in front of him.

He took it with a glance that was both amused and exasperated. Before he used it, he shifted to magical sight and examined the leatherbound box, confident that Deirdre wouldn't notice anything beyond a deep concentration.

The box appeared stubbornly mundane in all aspects, just as he'd expected.

He stole a quick look at Deirdre's aura as well: it was calm, with a hint of anticipation and excitement. The red tinges of another kind of anticipation were there too; as he watched, she walked around behind him and began kneading the knots out of his shoulders.

"If you're going to humor me," she said, "the least I can do is make you feel good while you do it."

He reached up to stroke her hand, then slipped the key into the lock. The sooner he got this over with, the sooner they could get to what was no doubt on both their minds. He opened the box.

And went still.

For a moment, he did nothing else, as different parts of his brain staged an interior struggle for control of his thoughts. It was nearly impossible not to notice Deirdre as she continued to massage his shoulders with strong, probing fingers.

But the book—

Inside the leather box, it sat nestled into a bed of crushed red velvet. It was almost as big as the box itself, bound in similar cracked, light brown leather. Two straps held it closed.

Without even thinking about it, he had shifted over to magical sight again when he opened the box. He'd expected to still see nothing—simply an old and impressive looking tome inside a similarly impressive looking container. Nothing about the box suggested otherwise.

What he hadn't expected was for the thing to light up his sight like a tiny sun. It nearly hurt his eyes to look at it. It nearly hurt his *brain* to look at it. He took a deep breath, finally succumbing and locking his eyes on it as he studied it.

He didn't even have to open the book to see it: Whatever else it was, it was without question one of the most magically potent items he'd encountered in his career.

And possibly one of the most malevolent.

| CHAPTER TWENTY

"**A**LASTAIR? ARE YOU ALL RIGHT?"

He almost didn't hear her.

"Alastair?" She stopped massaging.

"What? Oh. Sorry." He tore his gaze away from the tome and faced her.

"Are you all right? You went all pale, like you really did just see a ghost."

Summoning every bit of willpower at his disposal, he flashed a cheeky grin. "Fooled you, did I?"

She smacked his shoulder gently. "I have no idea why I keep you around. Actually I do—because you're great in bed." She pointed at the book. "But aside from that—okay, I get it. It's not haunted or anything. But take a look inside. It's pretty interesting, even if I can't understand a word of it."

Carefully, still forcing himself not to show any reaction, he turned back to the book. Without touching it, he examined it carefully for any traces of magical traps or misdirections. With the kind of power and black-magic vibes this thing was putting out, the possibility its original owner had put protections on it was strong, and the kinds of protections one put on a book like this were usually quite formidable—and quite deadly.

"What are you doing?" Deirdre asked. "Aren't you going to open it?"

He glanced at her again, this time sharpening his magical sight to pinpoint accuracy. He hated himself for doing it, but once again he was reminded that when it came to powerful magic, too much trust was a dangerous thing. But no, her aura remained as it had before: calm, a little excited, a little curious, and impatient to move on to the next stage of the evening. If she was hiding anything from him, she was damned good—probably so good that she wouldn't *have* to hide anything. "You say this belonged to your grandmother?" he asked.

She nodded. "Long as I can remember."

"And she opened it?"

"I told you she did." She frowned. "Why do you ask?"

He ignored the question. "Do you have any idea where she got it?"

"I think she said she found it in an old junk shop. You know," she said, "if I didn't know better, I'd swear you really *do* think it's got supernatural powers or something."

"No. But I think it might be more interesting than I thought, and I don't want to risk damaging it by opening it improperly."

"Do you think it's actually worth something? Not that I want to sell it, but…"

"I don't know," he said, still distracted. Satisfied that nothing was going to steal his soul, leap out and chop his hands off, or otherwise menace him if he opened it, he carefully unbuckled the two straps and pulled the cover open. He'd have liked to put up a ward around the table area, but that was far past what he could fool Deirdre into believing was mere professional curiosity. He'd just have to make this quick, and see if he could convince her to let him study it on his own later. If she agreed, he could take it home and examine it in the security of the heavily warded ritual space he'd set up in his attic.

What he did know was that it wasn't safe to let the kind of power this thing was radiating remain visible for long. Obviously the case was built to contain it, since he'd noticed nothing until he opened it. He glanced at Deirdre again: she'd sat down across from him and was watching him. He couldn't read her expression, but her aura clearly showed that she was tiring of the game and wanted to get on with the more one-on-one portion of the evening's activities. He did too—after not seeing her for a week, his body ached for her.

But this book...

Quickly, he flipped through several of the pages. Made of a heavy material that might have been thick parchment or possibly thin sheets of vellum, each one was packed to the margins with cramped notations, diagrams, and illustrations. He could tell right away that everything was handwritten, hand drawn, hand produced—he was sure that even the book itself had been lovingly crafted, probably by the same mage who had inscribed his spells and rituals on the pages within. Stone couldn't read it—he wasn't even sure yet what language it was written in—but bits of it looked maddeningly familiar. If he could get back home to his books, or even consult his more extensive library back in England, he was sure that, given time, he could decipher the strange inscriptions.

Deirdre's hand covered one of his, stroking the back of it with her finger. "If I'd known you'd be that interested, I'd have waited until *after* I got you into bed," she said. "Don't tell me I can't keep you more interested than an old book..." Her voice was low, throaty, sensuous.

Stone tore his attention from the pages again, but as soon as his gaze fell on her he was hit with a wave of desire so strong it nearly rocked him back in his chair. Why was he wasting time on studying the book *now,* when he had this beautiful, willing woman practically attacking him right there at the table?

Don't be a fool, he thought. *You'll probably never get another chance with a woman like Deirdre. Stop acting like a crusty old scholar and pay attention to your priorities.* His heart pounded, his body growing hot with anticipation. He covered her hand with his other one and smiled. "Not a chance," he said. "You know I want you, Deirdre…I've wanted you all week, ever since you left."

She smiled, running the tip of her tongue over her lips. "Don't worry," she said, indicating the book with a gesture of her chin. "You can look at it later, if it's so fascinating. Take it home with you if you want. Just…not now."

His arms went around her. "Not now…" he agreed, his voice as husky as hers. He maintained the presence of mind to return the book to its protective box and quickly close it, then pulled her down into his lap, his hands sliding under her thin blouse.

"Mmm, you *have* missed me," she murmured as she settled in, writhing against him.

"Did you have any doubt?"

"For a minute, I did," she said. "I thought I'd lost you to Grandma's haunted book."

"Leave Grandma out of this…" he said, pulling her in for a kiss. "I don't want her to haunt me for having impure thoughts about her granddaughter."

"She can mind her own business and go find her own boy toy." She ground herself more energetically into his lap.

"Is that all I am to you—a boy toy?" His teasing voice came out a bit strangled, through gritted teeth.

"Absolutely." She slid her hands up under his shirt and slipped it off. "Do you mind?"

"Not a bit."

As they made their way upstairs, though, Stone's mind alight with the possibilities of the evening, a small corner of it still churned over a different sort of possibilities..

| CHAPTER TWENTY-ONE

B Y THE TIME STONE left Deirdre's house the following morning, it was nearly eleven o'clock. He'd have to hurry to get home, change clothes and make it to campus in time for his twelve-thirty class, but he'd awakened at ten to the sight of her lying next to him on her side, her exquisite naked body uncovered by bedclothes. She'd been smiling.

"How long have you been watching me sleep?" he asked, rolling languidly over to take her into his arms.

"Long enough," she said. "You look different when you sleep. Did you know that?"

"Oh? How so?"

"More...innocent. Like you hide things from people when you're awake, and you let those masks down when you sleep."

"I hope I didn't give away any deep dark secrets," he said, and kissed her.

"Not yet, but I'll keep listening."

They shared a shower, and she sat on the edge of the bed afterward wearing a towel and watching him dress. "Do you seriously think that old book of Grandma's is interesting?" she asked.

"Fascinating."

"Well, I wasn't kidding. If you want to take it with you and read it at your leisure, you're welcome to. Two conditions, though."

He shoved his arms through his T-shirt sleeves and slipped it over his head. "Which are?"

"One: you have to tell me what you find out. You've got me fascinated now too."

"I will, assuming I can make any sense of it." Given the book's likely malefic origins, that promise probably wasn't one he could keep, but he'd cross that bridge after he'd made some headway. "What's the other one?"

She smiled and twitched at the towel, starting to let it drop. "I want priority. If I ever catch you neglecting me to stick your nose in a dusty old book, well...I'll have to punish you."

"Mmm," he murmured. "*That* has possibilities." With reluctance, he reached out and gently re-fastened her towel. "You've no idea how much I'd rather stay here and let you have your way with me. But if I don't leave now, I'll be late for class and have to endure more dirty looks from old Mortenson."

"You're no fun." She pouted, but she kept the towel where it was.

He promised to call her that evening, and left with the book under his arm, carefully locked into its protective case.

He actually considered calling in sick. The book mocked him as it sat on his passenger seat, and he wanted nothing more than to take it home, get it under magical protection so it didn't attract unwelcome attention, and spend the rest of the day poring through it.

As he got home and took it upstairs to his warded attic, he thought once again about Deirdre and her grandmother. Was she telling the truth about how the old woman had obtained the book? None of his surreptitious magical examinations of Deirdre had revealed even a scrap of potential magical talent, but he couldn't help wondering if the grandmother had been a practitioner.

He shook his head. While possible, it was unlikely. He couldn't tell for sure without much more thorough study, but you didn't find items like this outside the carefully guarded libraries of mages with the kind of power you didn't often see in the modern world.

Of course, you didn't often find them in junk shops, either.

Still, he thought, he'd encountered a similar situation personally, and recently, too. Maybe Suzanne Washburn's old tome, the one that now resided in Stone's own library back home in England, hadn't been of the power level this thing was putting out, but it was still old and dangerous, and it had ended up in a used bookstore when its owner had died and his heirs didn't know what they had. Mages might live longer than the general population on the whole, but they still died eventually. And sometimes they didn't have any more common sense than your average mundane.

He took one final look at the book to make sure it still wasn't emitting any magical energy, then locked it, case and all, in a safe inside a double-warded cabinet he kept in his lab for just such occasions. Anyone who could get past the wards on the house, the lab, and the cabinet was probably someone he didn't want to tangle with anyway. He slipped the key on its silver chain around his neck and stuffed it under his T-shirt. Where it rested against the skin of his chest, he almost thought he could feel a faint thrumming.

At least today was a short day. Assuming he didn't get too many students during his office hour this afternoon, he could be back home with a couple free hours to study the book before seeing Deirdre again that evening.

| CHAPTER TWENTY-TWO

T O STONE'S SURPRISE, Tabitha Wells showed up for his office hour. He hadn't heard much from her in several weeks; she attended class regularly, continued to sit in the middle of the lecture hall, and hadn't approached him again after the last time she'd come by. Right now, she hesitated in his doorway, as if unsure whether she wanted to come in.

"Ms. Wells," he called, waving her inside. "How are you?"

"Doing great," she said, a hint of defiance coloring her tone. She studied him for a moment as if searching for something, then shrugged and entered the office. She was dressed in her usual casual style, jeans and red hooded Stanford sweatshirt, with her hair pulled back into a loose ponytail.

"What can I do for you?" He glanced at his watch: it was a little after three-thirty. All day, his thoughts had been an uneasy mish-mash of fantasies about Deirdre and images of what he'd seen in his brief glances through the tome last night. It was a good thing he could deliver the material for his intro classes in his sleep, because he'd very nearly been doing so today.

"I wanted to talk to you about my midterm exam grade," she said.

"What about it?"

She sighed. "It wasn't as good as I hoped. Totally my fault, I know—I've been so busy lately, and I got a little behind on things.

Do you think I'll still have a chance to pull up my final grade before the quarter's over?"

He watched her as she spoke; she seemed preoccupied and possibly a bit tired, but otherwise looked like her usual self. Certainly no sign that Matthew Caldwell was draining debilitating amounts of energy from her during whatever rituals went on at the Church of the Rising Dawn. He pulled up her file on his computer terminal: her midterm grade was a solid B, which was indeed not consistent with her usual performance. "Well," he said. "You'd need to get As on the rest of your assignments and your final exam, but if you do that, you should be able to finish up with at least an A minus." He snapped off the terminal screen. "Do you think you can do that?"

She nodded. "Yeah. Thanks, Dr. Stone. I appreciate it." She got up to leave.

"Ms. Wells?"

She stopped, sighed. "You're going to ask me about the church again, aren't you?"

"Purely from a professional standpoint. You're still attending, then?"

"What do you mean, a professional standpoint?" Her eyes flashed with suspicion. "I thought we went through this before. I'm a big girl now."

"I know," he said, holding up a placating hand. "I'm not trying to dissuade you from anything. I was just curious—last time we talked, you mentioned that you almost believed the high priest—sorry, forgot his name—was doing real magic."

She smiled, as if remembering something. "Yeah. I did."

"Well…you've been attending for a while now. Do you still think so?"

Her smile changed, and her eyes narrowed. "More than ever, actually."

He nodded. "Well…given that magic is sort of my thing around here, I'd be interested in hearing more about some of the rituals they're doing that have impressed you so. If you wanted a bit of extra credit to help out that grade, you could write me a short paper on anything you're allowed to reveal without giving away church secrets."

She looked away. "I don't know…"

He shrugged. "It's completely up to you. Just making the offer, since you were concerned."

She considered. "I'll think about it. How long do I have to decide?"

"Drop it by any time before the final."

"Okay," she said. She looked at him again. "Hey, this is none of my business, but…"

He raised an eyebrow. "Yes?"

"Are you feeling okay?"

"Why do you ask?" Stone frowned, remembering that Mackenzie Hubbard had said the same thing to him yesterday.

"I don't know. You just seemed…out of it in class today. And you look tired. Maybe you should talk to Mr. Caldwell at the church. He's got some great herbal pick-me-ups."

I'll just bet he has. Given that he'd been examining *her* for signs of fatigue, though, he couldn't very well tell her to mind her own business. "I'm fine, Ms. Wells. I appreciate your concern, but there's nothing wrong with me that a few hours of sleep won't cure."

"Okay, sure. Well, anyway, thanks for the info about my grade. And I'll think about doing that essay." She waved, slung her backpack over her shoulder, and hurried away.

When Stone followed her a few minutes later, he stopped by the tiny department office on his way out to drop off some papers. Laura, the administrative aide, eyed him oddly, but said nothing except, "Thanks. I'll have those reports you wanted first thing tomorrow morning, if that's all right."

Stone nodded, his mind already on getting home to the book. "Fine, fine. I'm heading out now anyway. See you tomorrow."

"Take care of yourself, Dr. Stone."

Stone glanced at her in suspicion—why was everyone suddenly convinced he was ill or something?—but she had already opened the folder he'd handed her and was flipping through the papers. He shrugged and left.

| CHAPTER TWENTY-THREE

HE HALF EXPECTED THE TOME to be gone when he got home—that someone had broken into his townhouse and stolen it—but the cabinet and the ward around it both appeared undisturbed. It was a bit absurd to think otherwise, he realized: it wasn't as if anyone but Deirdre knew he had it, and unless she was a better actor than her aura suggested, she had no idea it was anything more than an interesting old book.

He flung his coat over a nearby chair and got right to it; he figured he had two hours or so before he could call Deirdre, and he wanted to make the most of them. Still, the task called for care and caution. He reached out with his magic and took hold of the strands of magical energy forming the ward around the cabinet, pushing them aside enough that he could open it, open the safe, and withdraw the leather case.

From there, he took it to a small table on the other side of the room. The table was stacked with books and papers; a small desk lamp perched on top of one of the stacks. Stone shifted several of them to the floor next to it, set the case down, and dropped into the chair.

His sanctum, the place where he did all of his magical experiments, was a large, open finished attic hidden behind a heavy steel door Jason had helped him install shortly after he'd rented the place. Aside from being physically formidable and featuring a hefty pushbutton lock, the door also included another security feature:

Stone had placed a spell on it to make it appear as a simple dead-end hallway. He'd put a lot of effort into that spell, and as a result he only had to refresh it a couple of times a year. The door simply wouldn't appear to any mundane who managed to break into the house, and even all but the most powerful mages would have a hard time penetrating the illusion. He'd placed a different kind of enchantment on the attic's only window: one that would divert curious glances in the same way he disguised his car to blend in with its surroundings. If anyone did manage to get a peek inside, they'd see nothing but a mostly bare floor with a few piles of dusty boxes.

All of that was in addition to the wards around the townhouse itself: those were designed only to repel magical efforts to attack or examine the place, and to deliver a nasty but nonlethal shock to anyone who tried to break into the house. He'd had a couple of years to work on the place's protections, and he was fairly sure that at this point they were as rock-solid as he could make them.

At least, no one had tried to break in yet.

He pulled the silver key from beneath his shirt and slipped it once more into the box's lock, then eased the box open. Instantly, waves of magical energy radiated outward, potent and pulsing. He could feel it even without switching to magical sight, washing over him, raising the little hairs on the back of his neck. Whatever else this thing was, it was *strong*, and it was not benevolent in its intent. In fact, even sitting in front of the pulsing energy made him feel uneasy, but he made himself ignore the feeling; he knew from experience how to notice the signs that the energy was causing him actual harm, and so far it was doing nothing more than giving him a slight headache. He slid on a pair of white cloth gloves and lifted the book from the case, putting the case aside on the floor.

Forcing himself to be patient—it wasn't as if Deirdre would demand the book back any time soon—he pulled a jeweler's loupe from a small collection of tools near the back of the desk and examined the cover. It was leather, as he'd suspected, unadorned except for the two straps with tarnished brass buckles that held the book closed. The leather itself was light brown, cracked and stained. A sudden insight rose in Stone's mind: it wasn't unheard of for the darkest of black-magic tomes to be covered in cured human skin, often flayed from one or more individuals who'd been sacrificed to provide ingredients or bits of power for the spells written within. A disturbing thought, but not one he could confirm or disprove at the moment.

He pulled the loupe from his eye and massaged the bridge of his nose. If this book *did* turn out to be as horrific as he feared it might, how could he give it back to Deirdre? Something like this in the hands of a mundane who couldn't protect it—he wondered how it could be that no one had tracked it and stolen it from her already. Perhaps she hadn't opened it; if it had rested, untouched, in a closet or a storage locker for all these years, perhaps anyone who might know of its existence was dead or had lost track of it long ago.

He was about to open the cover when the phone rang.

He glanced at his watch: after five already. He'd been here for nearly forty-five minutes, though he felt like he'd just sat down. He thought about not answering it, but perhaps it was Deirdre. He waved and brought the extension sailing into his hand. "Yes?"

"Alastair, it's me." It *was* Deirdre.

"I was just thinking about you. I thought we might go to that little sushi place that opened recently. What do you think? Pick you up at seven?"

There was a pause, and when she spoke again she sounded disappointed. "That's what I'm calling about. I got a call from my assistant. I need to head up to the City this evening to meet with some suppliers." She sighed. "I was looking forward to seeing you, too. Can we do it tomorrow?"

Stone glanced at the book, feeling irrationally guilty that while he wasn't quite *glad* for her call, the extra hours to study the tome couldn't have occurred at a better time. "Of course. I understand. Shall I come by later this evening?"

"I won't be in until really late," she said. "I promise—tomorrow we'll have dinner and…I've got a couple new types of dessert I'd like to try, if you're up for it."

"I'm always up for it," he said. "I live for dessert."

She laughed. "Oh, I know you are, and I know you do. Thanks for being understanding. This whole work thing should calm down soon. You're not worried I'm heading off to rendezvous with my secret lover?"

"Oh, terribly," he said. "But if this is what you're like when I'm sharing you with some other man, I'm not sure I could keep up with you if I had you all to myself."

"Yes, because you're *so* old and worn out," she teased. "Promise me you'll get some sleep so you'll be ready for me tomorrow. No all-nighters with Grandma's old book. My dessert recipes are fairly—complicated."

"I promise," he said. He fully intended to keep it, too.

"I'll see you tomorrow, then. Save room."

He hung up the phone and returned it to its spot, still feeling guilty. Even so, he decided as he returned his attention to the book, it wasn't as if they had to see each other every night. He thought briefly of her joking comment about going off to see a secret lover, and wondered if she'd said it to divert his suspicion away from her intent to do just that. But that way lay madness, and he knew it. He'd seen the way she looked at him. Why would she cheat on him when she could have any man she wanted? If she'd tired of him, she could simply tell him so and move on—and she hadn't done that. He'd never been the jealous type, and starting now would only lead to pain.

He sat down in front of the book again and opened the cover.

When he looked up, it was after eight. He stared in shock at his watch—he'd been at this for three hours and not even noticed the time passing.

His shoulders, neck, and upper back muscles twinged from being hunched for so long over the table, his legs felt stiff with disuse, and the mild headache he'd had from being around the thing for so long had grown into a full-blown throbbing pain. He hadn't gotten as far with the book's contents as he'd have liked, but after three hours of study, he'd come to a few preliminary conclusions.

Most importantly, he no longer had any doubts: he was now certain that he was dealing with an ancient and extremely potent— possibly artifact-level potent—magical grimoire. This was the kind of book that most mages, even at his power level and with his connections, never even got a glimpse of in their lifetimes. The few Stone knew of or had heard credible rumors about all resided in heavily warded, guarded, and hidden libraries belonging to some of the strongest and most reclusive individuals or magical societies on Earth. How this one had avoided discovery over all this time, he had no idea, but he was sure that any mage who got wind of it would be drawn to it like cats to catnip.

Worse, the thing wasn't only powerful, it was indeed full of the blackest of black magic. He still couldn't read the text—it looked maddeningly familiar, like something he'd seen a long time ago, though for now it continued to elude him—but the diagrams and the structure told him that it contained the instructions for numerous individual spells and rituals, all of which appeared to involve the sacrifice of one or more human beings. Dangerous stuff— particularly if it fell into the wrong hands. Stone knew there were black mages out there who wouldn't hesitate to take a few of these rituals for a spin if they had access to them. He wondered idly what Stefan Kolinsky would do with the book—in truth, he probably represented one of the safest places for it to reside, short of simply destroying it, but the chance always existed that his curiosity would get the better of him. Stone didn't plan to present him with the temptation.

Besides, while he had no intention of trying any of the spells (even looking at the diagrams made him uneasy), Stone's own curiosity dictated that he at least make an effort to study them before he decided what to do with the book.

The only thing he definitely did *not* intend to do with it was give it back to Deirdre. He wasn't sure how he'd manage that yet, but he had time to figure it out. He could stall for a while, at least, saying that he was on to something with his study. Maybe he could lie to her about the contents, make up a good story that would intrigue her, and then see if he could convince her to let him add the tome to his collection.

He closed the book, fastened it back together with the straps, and locked it into its protective case. Instantly, the intensity of his headache lessened. His stomach growled for attention, reminding him that he hadn't eaten since grabbing a cup of coffee and an energy bar at lunchtime today. He didn't have any food in the house beyond some canned soup, Guinness, and random condiments, so he'd have to go out and get something. He stood, stretching his arms upward, his back making satisfying little *pops,* and stared down at the thing. Suddenly, now that he knew what it was, his warded cabinet didn't seem so safe anymore. He checked the wards around the house: no one had tried to enter while he'd been occupied with his study.

You're being paranoid, he told himself. *No one even knows you have it.*

Still, though. With something like this, it was better to be safe than sorry. He knew where he could take it where it would be safe. It would take less than an hour, and he'd feel a lot better not leaving it in his townhouse.

He could even get something to eat in the process.

| CHAPTER TWENTY-FOUR

"Hello, Alastair. Bit late for you to be down here, isn't it?"

Marta Bellwood, proprietor of A Passage to India restaurant in Sunnyvale, smiled at Stone from behind the register. She was ringing up a takeout order for a man in a down jacket.

Stone waited for the customer to leave with his bag before replying, the spicy aromas wafting from the kitchen kicking his hunger up another level. "Got a taste for some chicken tikka. And a quick trip home." He had the book's case in a bag slung over his shoulder.

"Ah. Should I put something together for you?"

"Won't be gone long—half an hour or so, I expect. I'll get it when I come back."

"I'll have it ready for you."

"I appreciate it." Stone headed off down the hall past the kitchen. He glanced around to make sure no one was watching, then slipped through the illusion-hidden door leading down to the teleportation portal in the basement.

The portal looked as it always did, serene and beautiful with its shifting watercolor hues and amorphous rounded contours. Stone took a moment to calibrate it and stepped inside.

Ever since he, Jason, and Verity had thwarted the Evil's last desperate plans to establish a permanent portal back to their home dimension, magical travel had become much safer. Before the Evil's defeat, the Overworld, the strange, foggy dimension that mages used to travel between locations by way of carefully constructed teleportation portals, used to be crawling with larval Evil, always on the lookout for travelers unwise enough to attempt a journey while agitated, mentally fragile, or otherwise impaired. All but the most powerful mages had given up using the portals except for emergencies for just this reason, and most of them still hadn't started up again even though word had gotten around that travelers now rarely risked being ripped to pieces or driven insane if they weren't careful.

In less than five minutes, Stone emerged from the fog-shrouded tunnel into the darkness of the familiar crypt to which he'd pointed the portal. He summoned a light spell, took a moment to clear the calibration so no other travelers would end up here, and then climbed upward. A moment later he stood in the damp, chill darkness of his family's small private cemetery.

He moved quickly, tracing a familiar path up toward the drafty old manor house. It was nearly five a.m. here in England, so if he kept quiet he shouldn't wake Aubrey, the caretaker. He didn't want to talk to anyone now, but just to do what he came for and get back to California as quickly as he could.

Unlike his townhouse in Palo Alto, his home here, which had been in his family for countless generations, was uniquely suited for concealing and protecting an artifact of the grimoire's power level. Constructed on the confluence of three ley lines, it boasted some of the most potent wards in all of England, as well as numerous other permanent protections, detection spells, and misdirection magic put there not only by Stone himself, but by his long-dead family members. Further, the place he intended to take the tome for safe-keeping included even more protections specifically designed to conceal it and to kill anyone attempting to break in.

As Stone entered the house and headed for the hidden basement, he remembered Jason's objections when they'd been here two summers ago—were books worth killing people over?—and his own reply that some of these "books" were the magical equivalents of backyard nuclear weapons, and he had a responsibility to keep them from the wrong hands if he was going to have them. The grimoire definitely qualified.

It took him only a few more minutes to bypass the wards on the library and install the grimoire, still in its case, on one of the shelves high up near the two-story ceiling. "There," he said. "That should keep you safe." Whenever he wanted to continue his study, he'd just have to head back here to do it. Less convenient than keeping it at home, but at least this way he knew it would be there when he returned for it, and no one would be able to get their hands on it while it wasn't in his possession.

He didn't stay; his gnawing hunger refused his attempts to ignore it, and he wanted to get back home with enough time for at least a few hours' sleep. Fatigue clawed at him; he knew he'd been pushing himself harder than usual lately, between his nights with Deirdre, studying the grimoire, and work, but he was confident it wouldn't take him too much longer to sort out the grimoire and decide what to do with it. Until then, he could slip naps in when Deirdre was unavailable or he had some time after work.

Despite his exhaustion, he still wished Deirdre hadn't had to go to San Francisco for the night.

R. L. KING

| CHAPTER TWENTY-FIVE

B
Y THE TIME STONE EMERGED from the corridor and into A Passage to India's main dining room, it was nearly nine o'clock. Only two other customers remained: a young Indian couple seated at a tiny table near the front window. Marta looked up from wiping off another table. "Everything go all right?" If she noticed he was no longer carrying the shoulder bag, she didn't comment on it.

"Fine," he said. "I've been looking forward to that chicken."

"You're in luck, then—it's just about ready. Have a seat—unless you want it boxed up for takeaway."

"Think I'll stay this time. Barely had anything to eat all day, so I don't think I could bear smelling it all the way home." He settled himself into a booth under a large, colorful mural of Ganesh.

In a few moments, she brought out a steaming plate of chicken tikka masala and a pint of Guinness and set them down in front of him. "Haven't seen you in a while."

"Been busy," he said. "No time to head home."

"Have you heard from Jason and Verity lately?" Her tone was casual, but Stone didn't miss the undercurrents. Both of the Thayer siblings had spent considerable time working for Marta at the restaurant, Jason as assistant manager and Verity as assistant cook.

"Ah, that reminds me—I need to call Verity back." Already, the hot, spicy food was taking the edge off the last of Stone's dull headache. "They're doing fine, far as I know. We're all busy, so we don't talk that often." When Marta didn't answer right away, he looked up and was surprised to see her regarding him with an odd, searching look. "What?"

"You miss them quite a lot, don't you?" she asked gently.

He frowned. "Why do you ask?"

She nodded at the other side of the booth. When he waved her toward it, she sat down across from him. "Alastair…would you mind a bit of unsolicited opinion from an old friend?"

"Of course not."

"Please…I know you're a private person and don't like people fussing over you, but…you need to take care of yourself."

"What makes you think I'm not? I'm fine, Marta. Really." He took a long pull from the Guinness and did his best to look cheerful.

She pondered a moment, as if afraid to say more. "Well, you don't *look* fine," she said at last. "You look tired. I know this is none of my business, but…you aren't having any health problems, are you?"

There weren't many people who could ask him a question like that without getting a sharp and sarcastic reply. Unfortunately for him, Marta was one of them. "I'm *fine,*" he said again. "I'm not ill. Yes, I'm a bit tired. I've got several projects going right now, and it's a bit like trying to keep plates spinning. But everything's fine. More than fine, actually." As thoughts of Deirdre drifted into his mind, he smiled.

"Oh?" Marta's eyebrows crept upward. "Do tell."

"If you must know," he said, but his tone was fond, "I've met someone."

"Oh! Well, that's…wonderful." She smiled. "I'm glad to hear it."

He caught the skepticism in her tone and knew the reason for it—over the time she'd known him, he'd brought numerous women to the restaurant for dinner, and none of them had lasted past the six-month mark. "I know," he said softly. "But...this one might actually be the one, Marta."

He'd never said that before, and it startled him. *Was* Deirdre 'the one'? Was it too soon to tell? Did he even know her well enough yet to know?

"Well, then I'm delighted for you," Marta said, her long, angular face lighting up in a warm smile. "You deserve to be happy, Alastair. But tell her to let you have some rest, all right? She's going to wear you out." She dropped her voice to a near-whisper. "Is she...?"

He shook his head. "No, she's mundane. But that doesn't matter."

"No...of course it doesn't." Her voice grew wistful and her smile faded.

Stone reached out and gripped her hand in silent support. It had only been a couple of years since Marta's own mage partner, David Halloran, had been brutally murdered by the Evil.

She patted his hand. "It's all right. I'm all right now. It's just...hard sometimes, when mages come in to use the portal, and..."

"I know," he said. "I'm sorry."

"But I'm glad you've found someone. Please, bring her by sometime. I'll have Nikhil whip up something special for the two of you." She stood. "Anyway, must go—I have some more cleaning I need to do before closing. But if you talk to Jason and Verity, tell them we all miss them here."

"I will."

| CHAPTER TWENTY-SIX

AS STONE HEADED BACK HOME, he couldn't get his mind off what he'd said to Marta. It even, for the moment, drove away thoughts of the grimoire's contents. He drove up 101 almost on autopilot, thinking about his time with Deirdre.

He'd only known her for a bit more than a month, but already he felt more comfortable with her than any of the other women he'd had relationships with over the years. With one exception, of course, but that ship had sailed long ago and wasn't coming back in any time soon.

He wished he could see her tonight. After Marta's wonderful chicken he was no longer hungry and his headache had disappeared, but he couldn't shake the bone-deep weariness he always seemed to feel lately when he wasn't with her. It was as if he saved up all his energy to spend with Deirdre, and when they were apart he was forced to recharge—or, if he couldn't spare the time for recharging, to function in a less than optimal state. If he were wise, he'd go straight home, go to bed, and get several hours of uninterrupted sleep. His first class tomorrow wasn't until ten-thirty, so he could potentially sleep for ten or eleven hours.

He didn't go straight home, though. Instead, he exited the freeway and drove to Los Altos. She'd said she would be out late, so he had no reasonable expectation of finding her home, but something urged him to stop by and check anyway.

He pulled the BMW to a stop across the street from her building and looked up. The windows of her loft were dark, the shades drawn. The upscale neighborhood lay still and quiet under a clear, moonlit sky, and no other cars moved past him. After a moment, he got out of the car and crossed to the locked garage gate. She'd given him the code, but he didn't enter; instead, he just peered inside. Her space was empty, as he expected it to be.

It occurred to him as he walked back to the car that his actions might look suspicious: if Deirdre had been home, she might have been angry with him, thinking he didn't trust her. But it wasn't about trust. The thought that she might be with another man hadn't even entered his mind when he came over here. He wasn't sure exactly *what* the compulsion was to check on her, but it wasn't that.

He'd opened the grimoire inside her unprotected loft. Maybe he was just checking to make sure it hadn't attracted any of the wrong kind of attention. In any case, she wasn't there and his growing fatigue even blunted his body's normal responses to thoughts about her.

Time to go home.

Stone couldn't sleep.

He'd arrived home, checked the wards, checked his phone messages (nothing from Deirdre; Jason had called to see how he was doing, and he made a mental note to call him tomorrow) and then headed immediately upstairs. Too tired to do more than kick off his boots and slip out of his coat and jeans, he threw himself down on the bed, burrowing under the covers. With any luck, he'd pass out and not wake up until tomorrow morning.

He poked his head out what felt like a couple hours later, but when he looked at the glowing clock on his nightstand, he discovered it had only been twenty minutes. He spent the next half-hour tossing and turning, flinging himself around and trying to quiet his mind sufficiently that he could drop off to sleep, but that release stubbornly eluded him. His fatigued brain swam with disjointed images: Deirdre, Lindsey Cole, Jason, Verity, diagrams and bits of the odd handwritten script from the grimoire, the interior of the Church of the Rising Dawn, and still more images that flashed by too fast to identify. The overall effect was that every time he thought he might finally succumb to sleep, some other stray thought jerked him back to wakefulness.

Finally, he sat up and ran his hand through his hair in disgust. This was getting him nowhere. At this rate, he'd spend the whole night thrashing around in bed and be more tired in the morning than he was now. He wished he hadn't taken the grimoire to England; this would have been a good time to get in some more study. As it was, he had a few options: he could try taking a hot shower and see if that calmed him down; he could have a drink or a cup of tea; or he could go downstairs and try to read or put something mindless on the television and hope it bored him to sleep.

He got up and considered. His body felt sluggish, unresponsive, and more sitting around hardly seemed to be the answer. Maybe what he needed was a good run. Before Jason and Verity left, he went for long runs several times a week, usually right about this time of night. And he didn't do it only for exercise: it was the only reliable way he'd found to calm his racing mind.

He could certainly do with a bit of calming now.

CHAPTER TWENTY-SEVEN

OUTSIDE, THE FEBRUARY COLD sliced into him. Shivering, he locked the door behind him, did a few stretches in an attempt to get warmed up, and set off at a slow but steady pace. He'd have to take it a bit easy—he was out of shape following too many weeks of too much alcohol and not enough exercise, which was probably part of why he felt so wrecked—but just being outside and moving was already reviving him.

His T-shirt, lightweight jacket, and track pants barely afforded any protection against the chill of the air, but he knew from experience that he'd be fine once he got going.

One of his favorite places to run this time of night, when he didn't want to get in the car and drive up to campus, was along the Caltrain tracks that paralleled Alma Avenue. The trains came by less than once an hour this late, and the dirt path next to the tracks made for a more pleasant experience than constantly dodging traffic and waiting for lights. It was easy to get into a nice droning rhythm: just head in a straight line and keep going, letting his mind wander as it chewed over the events of the day. He never ran with headphones—not because he was afraid of anyone jumping him, but because he didn't like the distraction of music. Other than when he was asleep, the times he went running were some of the few when he could simply switch off and let his brain go wherever it wanted to. More than a few unconventional solutions to sticky problems had come to him in this way.

He'd been running along the tracks for about ten minutes when he spotted a pair of figures ahead of him.

He'd just crossed Palo Alto Avenue, where the tracks plunged through a small, wooded park. The figures lounged against a short, steel bridge that spanned a narrow creek—Stone had never looked at its name, but its bed was dry even this time of year. The only illumination came from the slender moon overhead and the lights at each end of the bridge.

Stone didn't slow down, though he kept a wary eye on the pair as he approached them. Probably a couple of homeless people getting ready to bunk for the night. There weren't a lot of them in Palo Alto, as the police tended to chivvy them along when they discovered them, but this area was remote enough that they sometimes took their chances under the bridge. Almost certainly harmless. They might try to stop him and ask him for a dollar or a joint, but most of the homeless he encountered along the tracks would take no for an answer if he had no money on him.

As he approached, Stone took them both in with a quick glance, and tensed. These two weren't homeless. He still wasn't worried—he'd never met a would-be mugger he couldn't deal with if he saw him coming—but he did step up his awareness, prepared to throw a spell if need be.

Under the pool of light at the edge of the bridge, the two bore a superficial resemblance to each other: both tall—taller than Stone, who was himself over six feet; both with the muscular, broad-shouldered, slim-waisted builds of serious athletes—football players, perhaps. One had short, neatly-cut hair and wore the pressed jeans, polo shirt, and expensive athletic shoes of one of Stanford's privileged elite, while the other was nearly shaven-headed, tattooed, in a leather jacket, ripped jeans, and combat boots. It was hard to tell how old they were in the dim light, but both looked about the right age to be students at the university.

"Hey," Polo Shirt said. He dangled the stub of a lit cigarette between two fingers; its tip glowed against the darkness.

"Evening," Stone said, stopping but continuing to keep a wary eye on them.

"How's it goin'?" Leather Jacket had his hands in his pockets and stood in a languid slouch.

They could be a threat, or they could just be a couple of buzzed frat boys out for a stroll. It was hard to tell, as both remained expressionless. Stone shifted to magical sight and relaxed a bit: their auras—Polo Shirt's gold and Leather Jacket's blue-green—were calm, unruffled, though both rippled around the edges with a red tinge that reminded Stone of his nights with Deirdre. Perhaps they were on their way home from visiting girlfriends or hooking up at a party, or perhaps they were a couple themselves. Regardless, he saw no threat. He shrugged. "Just out for a late run."

"That's cool," Polo Shirt said. "I like this time of night. Nice and quiet." He dropped his cigarette butt, stubbed it out with his shoe, and pulled a pack from his pocket. He withdrew another cigarette and held it out toward Stone. "You got a light, dude?"

"Sorry," Stone said. Despite the innocuous appearance of their auras, the little hairs on the back of his neck tingled. Something was odd about these two. He was probably wrong—his brain still hadn't sorted itself out—but best if he just moved along nonetheless. He nodded to them and started past them.

Polo Shirt grabbed his arm and pulled him up short. "Where's the book, Stone?"

Stone blinked, certain he'd misheard. He tried to wrench his arm free, but Polo Shirt's grip felt like it was made of steel. "What?"

"You heard me. Where's the fuckin' book?"

This was bad. How could they know about the grimoire? How did they know who he was? "What book?"

"One more chance to do this the easy way," Leather Jacket drawled. "We don't give a fuck either way—we kinda like the hard way. But you might not."

Polo Shirt's grip tightened again, digging into Stone's arm. "Where's the *book*?"

"You're both making a mistake," Stone said. Without giving them a chance to respond, he pointed his free hand at Polo Shirt and sent a potent concussion beam slamming into his broad chest. It should have tumbled him down over the bridge to land in the dry creek bed a few feet below.

Polo Shirt didn't budge.

His grip didn't weaken.

He smiled.

It looked creepy on his handsome, big-man-on-campus face. Then, with no change of expression, he released Stone's arm and buried his other fist in the mage's midsection.

Pain exploded. Stone staggered backward and would have fallen if Leather Jacket, moving far faster than he should have been able to, hadn't slipped around behind him, grabbing him around both arms and wrenching them backward.

"What the *hell*?" Stone bit out through clenched teeth. His body wanted to double over, but Leather Jacket held him upright. His heart pounded; that concussion beam should have sent Polo Shirt halfway across the parking lot, but he hadn't even moved.

"Surprise, motherfucker," Leather Jacket whispered in his ear. His breath was hot and sour-smelling.

Stone looked around wildly, hoping to see an approaching car along Palo Alto Avenue or any sign of other people in the area, but it appeared he and these two were alone. Puffing, he tried to pull up a shield around himself. If he could keep them from hitting him again, he could levitate out of their grasp and conceal his escape among the trees. He had none of this power objects with him in his running gear—he could deal easily with normal threats without them. But these weren't normal threats.

Polo Shirt hit him again: a one-two punch in the gut and the jaw. Leather Jacket held him still, then let him drop.

He fell to his hands and knees, the sharp rocks lining the tracks cutting into his palms, slashing through the thin fabric of his pants. Nausea rose and he fought it. Gritting his teeth, he struggled to his knees and pointed one hand at Polo Shirt and one at Leather Jacket. This was going to hurt, but he had to do something to get them out of his face. Snapping out a harsh word, he directed crackling lightning toward the two. It was a showy attack, but sometimes a display of power went further to intimidate threats than a more potent but less visually impressive assault. Without waiting to see if it hit, he flung himself sideways and tried to roll away.

The bright blue lightning danced around the two attackers like a hungry beast, but didn't even slow them down. Before Stone could get off another spell they were on him again.

"Bad idea," Leather Jacket said, jerking him back to his feet. Polo Shirt slammed another blow into his gut. Leather Jacket shoved him forward and he fell again, retching. One of them—he couldn't tell who—kicked him twice in the side, dropping him.

Damn it, focus!

But he couldn't focus. His mind on fire with pain, he struggled to form a spell—any spell. Anything to make them stop. Somebody kicked him again and he rolled into a ball, drawing his knees up and fighting get the nausea under control. He tasted blood and chicken tikka masala and Guinness.

One of them grabbed his hair and yanked his head up. Polo Shirt's grinning, frat-boy face appeared only inches away from his own. "Don't you get it yet, Stone? You're screwed. Tell us where it is or we'll kill you."

Stone glared at him, as well as he could with his vision swimming. He spat blood. Gathering every scrap of willpower he could summon, he pulled in energy. He shifted his gaze past him, fighting to focus on what was beyond. He didn't have long.

There—he spotted it: a fist-size rock. If he couldn't hit them directly, maybe he could hit them *in*directly. It was his only chance. Without thinking, without pausing, he snatched up the rock and flung it telekinetically toward the back of Polo Shirt's head.

Two things happened: The rock did what he intended and smacked into Polo Shirt, who yelped in pain and lurched forward.

Leather Jacket yanked Stone's head back and threw him hard to the ground. "Bad move."

In spite of everything, Stone grinned. "I'd say…" he got out between breaths, "it was…a good move…actually."

Polo Shirt, clearly not seriously injured by the rock, grabbed Stone by the front of his jacket and pulled him back up. "You're gonna pay for that, motherfucker."

After that, Stone couldn't construct a coherent narrative out of what happened next. It was just pain, and blood, and more retching as the two of them rained blows on him. After a time—it could have been a few minutes or a few hours, he wasn't sure—Polo Shirt pulled him up again by the ripped and ruined front of his T-shirt. "You're so pathetic, Stone. Your magic's useless on us, and that's all you got. You can't even fight like a real man, can you?" He let go and took a step back. "Go on. Try it. Hit me."

Stone swayed and would have fallen except for Leather Jacket behind him, who caught him.

"Go on!" Polo Shirt urged. "Hit me, you pussy! I won't even fight back." He pointed mockingly at his own chin. "Right here."

"Bugger off…" Stone whispered. He spat out more blood.

"Pathetic," Polo Shirt said again, his face twisting in disgust. "Where's the book? We can do this all night. Nobody's gonna come help you, and you're too useless to help yourself. Tell us where it is and maybe we'll let you live."

Stone glared.

Polo Shirt hit him again. "Where is it?" he screamed.

Leather Jacket grabbed his arm behind him and twisted it up, nearly wrenching it from its socket. "You're gonna give it up, man…do it before we fuck you up so bad nobody can help you."

Stone cried out at the pain. He hadn't wanted to give them the satisfaction, but he couldn't help it anymore. "I don't have it!" he moaned.

Polo Shirt was in his face again. "What do you mean, you don't have it?"

"I don't…" His voice shook. He hated himself for it, but he just wanted the pain to stop. Anything to make the pain stop.

Polo Shirt took a step back and visibly worked to get himself under control, then faced Stone again. "You still don't get it, do you, Stone? We *own* you. Nobody's comin' to help. We can do whatever we want with you, and there isn't a fuckin' thing you can do to stop us. Why don't you just tell us where it is and make it easy on yourself?"

"I…don't…have it," Stone whispered again.

Leather Jacket yanked his head up again, and wrenched his arm harder. "It's okay. We got time," he said.

Stone shrieked as his arm slipped out of its socket. He would have sagged if Leather Jacket didn't still have him.

"You're our *bitch*, Stone. What good's all that power now?" Polo Shirt grinned his unwholesome grin. He leaned in, his hot breath wafting over Stone's face. "We can have our *way* with you, man. How's that feel? We know all about you. We know what you can do. You're all about being in control, aren't you? You got all the answers. How's it feel now, knowin' you got nothin'?"

Stone tried to wrench himself free of Leather Jacket's grip, but even as he did it, he knew it was futile. He moaned again as his arm shot waves of agony through his body. Leather Jacket threw him down again, and he didn't get up.

"Just give us the fuckin' book. Tell us where it is. We'll even go get it." Polo Shirt crouched down next to him, hands resting casually on his knees, his bright white athletic shoes inches from Stone's head.

"…can't…" Stone said. His voice had nearly no volume now. He coughed; sharp rocks cut into his cheek, but the tiny pains barely registered next to all the rest. Hot tears of pain and shame pricked at his eyes.

"Why not?"

"…not…where I can get it…"

"You're lying," Polo Shirt said. He nodded to Leather Jacket, who took hold of Stone's injured arm again and wrenched it.

"I'm *not!*" Stone hated himself for the desperate, sobbing tone in his voice. "I *can't!*" He hated himself even more for knowing that if the grimoire had still been at his townhouse, he'd have handed it over. And even more still for wishing he hadn't moved it. Anything to make them stop.

"Fuck it," Leather Jacket said. "He's not gonna tell us anything."

"Hey, maybe that smokin' hot chick he's fucking knows where it is," Polo Shirt said. The leer looked even more horrific on his face than the smile had.

"She is *fine,*" Leather Jacket said. "I'd like to get me some of that."

"Oh, if we gotta find her, we will," Polo Shirt said. "We'll fuck her brains out. Let her see what real men feel like." He rolled Stone over and patted his cheek. "How about it, Stone? You tell us where the book is, or we teach your hot little fuckbuddy what it feels like to be with a real man…"

"Or two," Leather Jacket added.

"…instead of a skinny, pathetic little pussy like you?"

Stone didn't think he had anything else in him. He was wrong. At their words, a solid red wall of rage rose inside his brain, blotting out everything: pain, nausea, grayness, shame. Images of these two monsters touching Deirdre, hurting her, did what none of his own pain could have.

He wasn't going to use Trevor Harrison's magic again. Not until he had it under better control. His brief experiments following the incidents at Burning Man had helped him gauge it: how much he could get away with, and how it would affect him. But he was still feeling it out; normally the pain and the aftermath weren't worth the risk.

Right now, none of that mattered one damned bit.

With a sound that was half-growl, half-roar, he reached out, not within himself to the usual source of his magic, but outward, to the *other* source—the strange dimension brimming with power he could barely control even when he fought to keep the conduit closed so only the tiniest fraction of it could get through.

He pointed one hand at each of them and released it.

The energy ripped blazing holes in the night. Silvery-bright and impossibly potent, it traced visible patterns of agony along Stone's neural pathways. His body jerked as it fought to maintain control over the conduit in his weakened state.

The energy hit Polo Shirt and Leather Jacket full on in their chests.

For an instant Stone thought it wouldn't work. That it would contact them and dissipate like the lightning had, like the concussion beam had.

But no. Their screams—of pain, but also of surprise—rang out as both of them were blown back and disappeared, flailing, over the edge of the bridge.

The images of Deirdre had driven his rage, and his attack had been not to wound or subdue, but to kill. The energy should have torn them to pieces and left nothing behind. Maybe it had.

But maybe it hadn't.

Fortunately, those images also gave him a last reserve of strength he wouldn't have thought possible at this point. He didn't know if he'd stunned them, knocked them out, killed them, or if they were even now struggling back up the riverbank to come after him again. His only chance was to get the hell out of here.

Without looking back, he staggered off. His heart and head pounded, his arm burned, his legs barely functioned, but none of that was important at the moment. If he didn't get away, he was certain they would kill him.

Stone plunged into the trees with no idea where he was heading. He thought he heard them behind him, but couldn't be sure.

His only thoughts were those of a desperate animal—get away, find help, find a place to hide.

| CHAPTER TWENTY-EIGHT

ONSCIOUSNESS DID NOT RETURN EASILY, nor did it come all at once. Stone's body fought to keep him under the merciful grip of insensibility, but his mind, even after all that had occurred, refused to quiet. Even so, though he wasn't coherent enough to count them, he knew that there had been several abortive attempts to drag him to awareness before the latest one finally took hold. All he knew was pain.

Pain, and cold. It took him even more time to figure out that it was raining.

It was still dark. He lay…somewhere. He wasn't sure where. It wasn't the sharp rock-bed of the railroad tracks, but whatever was beneath him was uneven and yielding and wet. He was almost too cold to shiver.

He closed his eyes a moment and tried to focus his thoughts, then opened them. He didn't try to move his body. He couldn't even identify individual sources of pain.

Next to him, a high metal wall rose. He risked turning his head just a bit, blinking blood and water from his eyes, and identified it as the side of a dumpster. He turned the other way, and saw the other side rising up beyond a heaped pile of garbage.

He was in a dumpster.

A tiny memory came back: staggering, a desperate flight, the wild, absurd thought that maybe they could track him by scent. He didn't remember how he'd managed to climb into the dumpster, but he did remember thinking he'd used the smell of garbage to conceal himself once before. Maybe it might work again.

He shifted a little more. His arm exploded in pain, bringing back another memory: his attackers had dislocated it. Were they alive? Had he killed them, or had they searched for him, but given up when they couldn't find him—or perhaps when other people had shown up?

Either way, they'd nearly killed him. If it hadn't been for his last, desperate effort, one which would have doomed him if it hadn't worked, he couldn't have stopped them.

Nothing else he did could have stopped them. Shame and self-hatred rose, for a moment so intense that they even blotted out the physical pain.

For all the effect his magic had had on them, he might as well have been a small child shooting soap bubbles at a grizzly bear. So why had they—

Deirdre.

Gods, no…

He tried to struggle up, but couldn't do it. The garbage shifted beneath him. His arm lit him up again, and his ribs, his stomach, his head joined in. Aside from the bright agony of his dislocated shoulder, his limbs were so cold he could barely feel them. The sodden, tattered remains of his track pants and T-shirt did nothing to protect him against the sleety chill.

He had to get to Deirdre. How long had he been unconscious? Did Polo Shirt and Leather Jacket even know where she lived? Were they even now there, pinning her down as she struggled, their leering faces bent over her, their fetid breath in her face—

With his good arm, he tried to push himself upright, but his hand slipped on some piece of rain-slicked trash and he crashed backward again. A faint moan escaped him; he didn't have the energy for anything more.

"Somebody in there?"

Stone froze. The voice sounded nearby, frightened and alcohol-rough. After a moment, a faint metallic rattle joined it. "Help me..." he rasped.

"Who's that?" Whoever it was, they were closer now. Again, the metallic rattle.

"Help me...please..." He had no idea if he was managing enough volume to be heard. Rain beat down on him, spattering his face, getting in his eyes. He turned his head away. The smell of wet pavement mingled with the damp odor of garbage from the dumpster and the fainter, sour reek of vomit on the front of what remained of his T-shirt. Somewhere, he'd lost his jacket. He almost retched again.

"Whoa..." said the voice. "Dude...are you dead?"

Stone cracked open his eyes and looked up. A figure hovered there, peering over the top of the dumpster's wall, dressed in shapeless, colorless layers of ragged clothes. Under a floppy hat, squinty eyes glittered above a bulbous nose and a wild, curly beard.

"Please..." Stone whispered. "Help me..."

The man looked doubtful. He glanced around as if expecting someone else to be sneaking up on him. Then he stared down at Stone, studying him for several seconds before appearing to reach a decision. "Hang on, dude."

Stone's mind drifted; he didn't see what happened next until his arm once again exploded with pain as the man attempted to move him. He whimpered and tried to draw up into a ball, but that just made things worse.

"Dude...I gotta get you outta there and under this cover. It's rainin' all over ya. It's freezin'. Yer gonna get the nuhmonia, shiverin' like that."

Stone tried to focus on him. "Arm..." he moaned. "Dis...located." He didn't think the man would have any idea what to do about it.

"Whoa...bad news. Hang on...lemme see..."

"No…please…" He could barely get a breath, but he had to make himself heard. The last thing he needed was some old vagrant making things worse. He'd have to figure some way to pop it back in on his own. "Just…can you…call someone?"

"It's okay, dude. It's okay." And then the man was climbing into the dumpster, scrambling down next to him. He patted his other shoulder. "I can do this. Learned it in the Army. Gonna hurt like a motherfuck, though. Hold on." He shuffled through a bag he wore, and after a moment held up a stout dowel, eight inches long and an inch in diameter. "Bite down on this, man, okay? I ain't kiddin'—it's gonna hurt."

Stone glanced around, hoping that someone—anyone but Polo Shirt and Leather Jacket making a return—had spotted them, but wherever they'd taken him, it seemed otherwise deserted. He wondered what time it was. Resigned, he opened his mouth and allowed the man to insert the dowel, then clamped down on it. Then he nodded.

"You ready?"

He nodded again, and tried to brace himself.

It was over in a few seconds of unbearable pain. A scream rose in the back of Stone's throat as the bone popped back into the socket; he bit down on the dowel with such force that he thought he might break it, or his teeth.

He must have blacked out again; when awareness returned again, he lay on his back, staring up at the woven fibers of a blue plastic tarp. He couldn't see what the back of it attached to (presumably the side of the dumpster) but the front was tied to both ends of an ancient, rusting shopping cart full of plastic bags and other scraps. Beneath him was some kind of plastic ground cloth; it was damp, but the rain pattered on the tarp and didn't reach him. An old, ripped sleeping bag covered him.

"You back?" The bum sat next to him, huddled under the tarp as well.

Stone took stock for a moment before replying. His arm still hurt, but now it felt like the ache of a bad muscle pull instead of the agony of bone scraping against bone. He lifted it experimentally and the pain didn't increase. "Thank you…"

"No problem, dude."

"How…long?"

"Just a few minutes. Got ya outta there and all covered up, but man, you're in bad shape. You need a doc."

He was probably right. Stone had no way to know what kind of injuries the two had inflicted on him. The arm had been the worst of the pain, but nearly every other part of his body ached as well. And he was so cold…the sleeping bag helped, but the wind still sliced at him through his shredded clothes. He thought the man was probably right: injuries notwithstanding, he'd be lucky if he only came out of this with a bad cold instead of a case of pneumonia. The smart thing to do would be to call an ambulance, go to the emergency room, and get checked out.

If he did that, though, how long would they keep him? Who knew what might happen to Deirdre? Who knew what they'd already done to her? "What…time?" he whispered.

"Time? Uh…I dunno. Maybe like two-something? Ain't got a watch."

He remembered opening the floodgates to Harrison's power source. He'd hurt them; he knew that. How much, he didn't know, but he'd hurt them. But doing that still caused a temporary burnout of his ability to use his own magic. Had three hours been long enough for it to recharge? He shifted to magical sight to test it, and was rewarded to see a sickly yellow aura, riddled with black spots, flare up around the man. A wave of lightheadedness washed over him with even that minimal magical exertion. Doing what he planned to do was foolish in his condition. He didn't even know if he'd be *able* to do it.

It didn't matter, though: he had to try. He didn't have a choice. "Will you help me?" he rasped.

"Help you do what? I don't know no docs…"

"No…just stay with me for a little while. Don't…leave me alone here."

"I ain't goin' nowhere till this rain lets up, man. This is where I set up when it's wet."

Stone nodded. He had no wallet, no identification—he hadn't even brought his house key, since he could use magic to work the lock. "What should I call you?"

"Name's Pete."

"Pleasure to meet you, Pete. I'm…Al." He cringed inwardly at the name: it was what Jason called him and he hated it, but it was easier than trying to get 'Alastair' past a half-drunk homeless guy. "I think I'll be all right. Just need to…rest for a bit."

"You do what you gotta do, man. I'm gonna sit here and have a smoke." He dug a dirty pack from his pocket, carefully extracted half a cigarette, and flared a light.

Stone settled back and tried to get comfortable, which was essentially impossible. He made do with his best effort to relax as much as he could—almost as difficult, between the pain, low-grade nausea, the beginnings of a fever, and the cold.

Healing magic had never been easy for Stone, from his days as an apprentice. It was a topic he and Verity had spent many hours discussing and debating, supplemented by some enlightening conversations with Edna Soren, the irascible woman currently overseeing Verity's magical training.

To be truly good at healing, one had to have a strong innate sense of empathy, and a feel for subtle changes in the personal magical fields around the subject. Stone's form of magic was extremely potent—even more so because he'd trained under one of the premier mages in Europe—but, as Edna was fond of pointing out to him, it was all about control, about willpower, about commanding the forces of the Universe to do one's bidding. It made for formidable practitioners, and most of the top mages in the world subscribed to that school. However, in their areas of influence: subtle magic, the magic of harmony rather than force, the healing arts, and the exploration of the mind and the body, Edna's style of magic could accomplish feats that would be impossible for Stone's. He suspected that the reason mages of Edna's school didn't rank among the top talents wasn't that they didn't possess sufficient ability, but that such contests and comparisons were irrelevant to them.

Healing might not be Stone's forte, but it wasn't as if he had any other options. Verity and Edna were in Ojai. Madame Huan was out of the country, even if he could have contacted her at this hour. He hadn't had contact with the old Forgotten leader, Lamar, for over a year.

If it was going to happen, it was all him.

He took several deep breaths, punctuated by coughing fits that flared fire all over his body, closed his eyes, and focused his will on entering a state of meditation that would blunt the pain long enough for him to work on it. Too much time had passed since the injuries were inflicted to get anything close to a full healing, but he would do what he could.

No one disturbed him as he worked; Pete puffed away on his old cigarette butt, and rain kept pattering down onto the tarp. Finally, several minutes later, Stone let his breath out and allowed himself to relax as much as he could manage.

The magic was difficult: healing oneself was perversely harder than healing others, and the work had nearly depleted his already flagging stores of magical energy. He didn't realize he'd passed out again until he opened his eyes and found Pete crouching over him, peering down into this face with bloodshot, watery eyes. He jerked a little, startled.

"Sorry, man. Sorry. I was just checkin' on ya."

Stone nodded wearily. He took inventory again: the pain had definitely decreased. To his surprise, he'd discovered during the healing process that whatever else Polo Shirt and Leather Jacket were, they were good at what they did: inflicting maximum pain with minimal permanent damage.

That was why they hadn't killed him: they'd never meant to.

They'd been sending him a message.

"I need to go," he said.

Pete looked dubious. "Dude, you're wrecked. You look some better, but—"

He shook his head. "I need to go," he said again. He tried to sit up. Pain flared, but not nearly as bad as before. His head swam and for a moment he feared he'd be sick again, but he controlled the feeling with effort. "Is there...a phone around here?"

"Uh...yeah. Up the street, on the corner. But dude..."

Stone struggled to his feet. For a moment he didn't think he'd make it, but then Pete scrambled up and helped him. He ducked out from under the tarp. The rain had settled down to a drizzle by now, and the sun was just coming up.

"This is a bad idea," Pete said. "Yer gonna kill yerself."

Stone thought Pete might be right, but images of Deirdre at the mercies of Polo Shirt and Leather Jacket kept him going as little else could have.

He looked down at himself: he was a sorry sight. His light running pants were shredded, the knees bloodstained and torn. His T-shirt barely qualified as a shirt anymore, the front ripped out, the tattered remains stained and dirty. A network of scratches, bruises, and scrapes covered his chest and arms. He could only imagine what his face must look like. The only things about him that didn't look like they'd been through a war zone were his expensive running shoes, and even those were stained and water-soaked from his time in the dumpster. "Pete," he said, his voice still raspy and weak, "can you do one other thing for me? I promise—I'll find you and repay you for your kindness."

Pete tilted his head. "Yeah?"

"Do you have...something I could borrow to wear? An old coat...a sweater...anything like that?"

The homeless man looked away. Obviously he didn't want to part with any of his meager belongings to a guy he'd probably never see again. Finally, though, he nodded. "Yeah, lemme see. But you're not gonna fool anybody, man. Ain't nobody gonna pick you up lookin' like that."

Stone gripped the edge of the dumpster to remain upright, swaying, as Pete rummaged around in the bags hanging off his cart. In a moment, he returned and held up a gray sweatshirt. "This okay?"

In spite of feeling like he was about to pass out, Stone had to smile: the stained, ragged sweatshirt had *STANFORD* emblazoned across the chest. "Thank you. That'll do fine."

Pete helped him into it: it was too big and hung on him like a sack, but it covered up the worst of the damage. "Lemme show you where the phone is. It's a bit of a walk. I dunno if you can…"

"I'll make it."

In the end, Pete had to shuffle alongside Stone, holding him up to keep him from falling over. Fortunately the pay phone a block down still looked functional. "Thank you for everything," Stone said, holding on to it for support.

"No problem, dude. You take care o'yerself."

As the homeless man turned to leave, Stone called, "Pete?"

He stopped. "Yeah?"

"You don't…know any Forgotten, do you?" It was a long shot; most of the Forgotten had either faded into obscurity or left the area in the couple years following the Evil's defeat.

Pete looked confused. "I dunno what yer talkin' about, man."

"Don't…don't worry about it. Take care." He watched the old hobo as he shuffled off down the rain-slicked street.

| CHAPTER TWENTY-NINE

S TONE KNEW GETTING HOME would require all his magical re-
sources, so he tried to conserve them as much as possible
until he needed them. He called a cab, charging the call to his
home phone, and leaned hard against a phone pole to save energy
until it arrived. When he saw the green-and-white vehicle approaching, he pulled an illusion around himself, hiding the worst of
the damage under the image of an unassuming, generically-dressed
man. It took him a bit of effort to convince the cabbie that someone
had stolen his wallet so he'd have to pay when they reached their
destination, but finally he slumped into the back seat and the cab
rolled off into the sparse dawn traffic.

He couldn't close his eyes: if he passed out or fell asleep, the illusion would drop. Instead, he focused on the cabdriver in the
rearview mirror: his wooly black beard, utilitarian gray jacket,
cheerful bright orange turban. The man looked suspicious, his nose
wrinkling in distaste—Stone's illusion did nothing to hide how he
must smell—but Stone didn't care what the guy thought of him as
long as he got him home.

The drive took only a few minutes, as it was still only the leading edge of the morning commute and not many cars choked the
roads yet. The cab pulled up in front of Stone's townhouse. "We're
here," the cabbie said.

Stone swallowed hard. *You can do this. After all you've been
through tonight, you can do this.* He shoved open the door and got

out. "Come to the door," he rasped. "I don't want to walk back out here."

The cabbie looked suspicious, but did as instructed, following Stone as he staggered up the front walk to the door.

It was still locked. No one had busted it in. He didn't have the energy to check the wards, but at least the front part of the house looked undisturbed. That was a good sign. Stone's illusion nearly slipped when he diverted a bit of his focus to flip the door lock open, shielding the effort with his body. He fought down a wave of disgust: *you're just a bloody big deal, aren't you? Can't even open a damned door without falling on your face!*

He stumbled inside, nearly tripping over the threshold. "Be right back." For once, luck was with him: he'd left his wallet on the coffee table in the living room, not upstairs in his bedroom. He dug out some bills (enough that the tip would more than equal the fare) and, holding on to various bits of furniture and walls, got back to the door still on his feet. "There," he said, pressing the bills into the man's hand. "Thanks." He closed the door in his face and let the illusion go.

All he wanted to do was drop, right where he was. Just pass out right there on the foyer floor. Every part of his body hurt. He was shivering like a Chihuahua in a snowstorm. His clothes were still wet from the rain and stiff with dried blood. But he'd made it home. If he could just lie down for a few minutes, then...

Deirdre.

Her image flashed in his mind again, followed by the leering faces of Polo Shirt and Leather Jacket.

He might be home, but they were still out there somewhere.

He slipped down to a seated position against the front door. Now that he wasn't holding the illusion anymore, he could spare the power to summon the phone to him. His hands shook so hard he misdialed three times before gripping his wrist with his other hand to steady it. He punched in her number, stuck the receiver between his head and his shoulder, and waited while it rang.

One ring. Two. Three.

Where was she? Why wasn't she answering?

Four. Five. Six. "Answer…please…answer…" he whispered.

Was she asleep? What time had she gotten in last night? Had she decided to stay in San Francisco?

Would one of *them* answer?

The machine picked it up. Deirdre didn't have an outgoing message, just a beep. Stone gathered his thoughts for a moment, and when he spoke, his voice was weak, shaking, and gravelly. "Deirdre…it's me. It's Alastair. Please…if you're there, pick up." He waited a moment, but no one did. "Not home…Deirdre…I'm sorry about this, but…you might be in grave danger. Please call me the instant you get home. I'm at my place. Please. This is extremely important. Call me."

He let his hand drop to his side, his exhausted mind already spinning dire scenarios of what might have befallen her at the hands of the two men. He knew, somewhere in the back of his mind, that he would have to start putting effort into figuring out who—and what—those two were. No mundane could be nearly immune to magic. Mages could resist it, but their methods would be obvious: shields, protective bubbles, and other defensive spells. Why would a magic-immune creature want a book of black magic spells?

Yes, he'd have to think about that—but not now.

He raised the phone again, called the department office at Stanford, and left a message that he was ill and wouldn't be in to-day. From where he was still seated with his back against the front door, the stairway looked very high, and very steep. If he tried to climb it, he'd probably fall over backward and break his neck. It would be so much easier to just stay here…

He gritted his teeth and hauled himself back to his feet. The familiar muzzy grayness in his head informed him that he might have another few minutes, at best, before he passed out. *Hello, spir-*

it? This is flesh. I don't give bugger-all what you've got planned: we're out of here in 3...2...1...

In the end, he crawled up the stairs. It wasn't pretty, and it sure as hell wasn't dignified, but he made it to the top in one piece, more or less. He reached his bedroom, kicked free of his shoes, shucked off the damp, bloody, smelly remains of his clothes, and used the last of his strength to fall onto the bed and drag the covers over him. He was gone before they settled back down.

| CHAPTER THIRTY

THE RINGING PHONE jerked him awake. He scrambled to roll over and grab it—if the machine got it, he'd have to go downstairs to find out who it was. He fumbled the receiver and glanced at the clock on the nightstand. Nine-twenty. He'd been out for about three hours. "Yes, h-hello?"

"Alastair?"

The relief that washed over him almost made him pass out again. "Deirdre. It's you...thank gods..."

"Alastair?" she said again. Her voice sounded puzzled and worried. "What's going on?"

"Are you all right?" He shoved himself up to the top end of the bed and propped himself on two pillows, still under the covers.

"Are *you* all right? I just got in—I got your message—you sounded terrible. You said something about danger—?"

"Is anyone there with you? Did you check?" He knew he sounded disjointed—crazy, even.

"With me?"

"Was your place secure? Anything disturbed?" *Other than me, that is.*

"Uh—no. Nothing disturbed. Everything's fine. Will you please tell me what's going on?"

"I will...I'm coming over there." He had no idea how he planned to do that, since right now getting out of bed seemed like more effort than he could manage.

"You are not coming over here," she said firmly. "You sound awful. Are you sick? I'll come over there and you can tell me what this is about."

"No." He said it quickly. There was no way in hell he wanted her to see him looking like this. "No. I'm...I'm fine. Just...a bit under the weather. But I need to tell you this."

"I'm coming over," she said, in a voice that allowed no argument. "I'll be there in half an hour, and you can tell me." She hung up.

Stone slumped back into the pillows, dropping the phone.

Half an hour.

That was how long he had to make himself presentable before she got here.

From the way he felt, that was a tall order. He suspected that once he saw what he looked like, "tall" might turn into "no bloody *way*" in a hurry.

He flung the covers off and sat up, closing his eyes when the world tilted off in a crazy spin. Nothing hurt any worse than anything else: everything was at an equal-opportunity level of pain, but at least it seemed like the minimal healing he'd done and the three-hour stupor had taken the edge off the worst of it. Possibly a handful of ibuprofen would sort out the rest enough that he could function. Some of the dizziness was probably from hunger, given that he hadn't eaten since A Passage to India and that hadn't stayed down.

When the dizziness seemed to abate a bit, he got up and half-padded, half-staggered into the bathroom. He gripped the edge of the sink and stared at himself in the mirror.

He let his breath out slowly when he saw what he had to work with.

"No bloody way" was looking a lot more likely.

His dark hair had dried while he slept, sticking out at every conceivable angle. His eyes, bloodshot and exhausted, peered out at him from pitch-black hollows. His cheeks were sunken, his jaw shadowed with dark stubble, his face bruised and traced with scratches. His mouth was crusted with dried blood and he didn't want to think about what else.

Yes, quite the charmer, he was. This was the face that had somehow managed to attract a woman who looked like Deirdre Lanier.

His gaze shifted downward. Like his face, his chest, sides, and arms were a riot of cuts, colorful bruises, and scrapes, all covered in a layer of grime. His lower body fared a bit better since the track pants had afforded more protection, but his knees were shredded from the rocks on the track-bed, and his legs sported their share of bruises as well.

One thing was certain: he was going to have to burn his bedsheets.

Still holding on to the sink for balance, he turned on the shower, then rinsed his mouth about five times and brushed his teeth while he waited for the water to heat up. That simple act went a long way toward making him feel human again.

He'd have liked to stay in the shower for at least an hour. The hot, high-pressure blast sliced at his scraped skin and pounded his bruised muscles, but it was a different, more cleansing kind of pain. It had seemed for a while that he'd never be warm again, but it didn't take long for the water to loosen him up and take some of the stiffness and most of the chill from his battered body. It didn't do anything about the heaviness in his head, though. He was definitely coming down with something, but with luck it would take a day or two to develop.

By the time he got out and glanced at the clock, he only had ten minutes before Deirdre would arrive. Damn. He'd have to get dressed: while normally he had no problem with her seeing him in a towel, or less, the towel wouldn't do much to hide all his injuries. He wiped fog from the bathroom mirror and peered at his face: the cuts and bruises were still there, but some of the hollowness had left his eyes.

R. L. KING

He decided against shaving, since his hands still weren't steady and he didn't want to add any new cuts to his existing supply. He threw back four ibuprofen tablets, then dug a long-sleeved black thermal shirt and jeans from his closet and pulled them on, taking much longer than normal. Finally, he stared at himself in the full-length bedroom mirror. His efforts wouldn't fool her, but maybe he could redirect her attention and convince her that he'd fallen off his bike or something.

He didn't have a bike, but she didn't know that.

The doorbell rang.

He pulled in a deep breath through his teeth and left the bedroom.

| CHAPTER THIRTY-ONE

HE MADE IT DOWNSTAIRS without falling, with the help of a death grip on the railing and taking the steps one at a time like an old man instead of his usual headlong descent. The bell rang again. He opened the door.

She stood there on his porch, looking as radiantly beautiful and perfectly put together as she always did. Dressed in gray slacks, a thin white silk blouse, lavender infinity scarf, and a long, dark gray coat, she looked like she'd just stepped off the pages of a fashion magazine.

Just looking at her made Stone feel better. Knowing she was safe made him feel better still. He smiled faintly, hoping she didn't notice how hard he was gripping the doorjamb. "Good morning."

She stared at him. "My God…What…happened to you?"

So much for getting anything past her. "Nothing to worry about. Really. Come in." He stood aside to let her pass, and closed and locked the door behind her.

She narrowed her eyes and frowned. "You're not fooling anyone, you know. Out with it."

"Come on…let's go sit down." He waved her ahead of him toward the living room.

Thankfully, she did as indicated. He followed her in and dropped down onto the couch, unable to conceal a wince. Before she could say anything, he said, "I need to talk to you."

"That's what you said. Something about me being in danger. But first I want to know what's wrong with you."

"Nothing. Nothing serious. Think I'm getting a cold or something."

"Colds don't give you scratches, or bruises. You look like somebody hit you in the face." She sat at the other end of the couch, but moved closer to him.

"Deirdre. Please. This is important." He swallowed, and gathered his energy. This wouldn't be easy. "Are you sure no one broke into your place? No glitches in your security system? Anything?"

"No, nothing," she said. "I got home early this morning, and everything was fine." Again, she frowned. "Why do you expect that there would be problems? What do you know?"

Instead of answering, he did something he didn't want to do: he shifted to magical sight and watched her aura carefully as he asked her a question of his own: "Deirdre, what do you know about that book?"

"Book?" For a moment, she looked perplexed, and then her eyes widened. "Grandma's book? The one you have?"

He nodded. "Are you sure you've told me everything you know about it?"

"What kind of question is that?"

Her aura didn't change. As Stone had told others before, though, the aura wasn't a lie detector. Some people were good at concealing duplicity so well that it didn't even show in their auras. She was either an adept liar or she had no idea what he was talking about. "An important one," he said. "Please, Deirdre. It's critical that if you know anything more about it, you tell me."

She shook her head. "I don't know anything else about it. I told you, my grandma used to show it to me when I was a little girl. My mom had it in storage, and she sent it to me when I asked. I brought it straight to you. You saw—I hadn't even opened the package."

He let his breath out. He swiped a hand across his forehead; it felt hot. "Okay. Okay."

She reached out and took his hand. "Alastair. Tell me what's going on."

"I—" He held her gaze for a few seconds, then looked down into his lap, at their two hands together. "I was out running last night. Late."

"Yes...?"

He almost couldn't get it out. He didn't want to. This was just the sort of thing—albeit usually some less violent version of it—that brought on the beginning of the end of his relationships. The ache in his chest had nothing to do with injury, and everything to do with fear. But regardless of what might happen, he had to tell her. The two attackers had seemed as vulnerable to physical damage as anyone else—which meant if she were warned, she might be able to protect herself from them if they came after her.

She squeezed his hand. "And...?"

"And...I got jumped. They wanted to know where the book was."

"What?" Her aura flared alarm. "How can that be?" She leaned in, looking at him more closely. "What did they do to you?"

"I got away from them," he said. "But not before they worked me over a bit." He gently gripped her upper arms. "But that's why I need to know if there's anything you haven't told me about that book."

She was still staring at him, wide-eyed. "That's...horrible," she said. "They beat you up to get my book? You should have just *given* it to them!" Tears sprang to her eyes. "My God, it's just a crazy old book. I have no idea why they wanted it, or even knew you had it, but it's not worth getting hurt over."

"It's all right," he said. "You're sure you didn't mention it to anyone else? One of your coworkers? Or perhaps your mother told someone she was sending it to you?"

"Of course I'm sure…Well…I'm sure *I* didn't tell anyone." She swiped at her hair with a perfectly manicured hand. "This is awful. I'd never have even shown it to you if I'd thought something like this would happen. Please—just give it back to me. I'll…I'll destroy it."

He patted her hand. "That won't help. They know it exists now. I've got it hidden somewhere very safe, where they'll never find it. And I have to admit, this has gotten me more curious than ever to find out what it's all about. I'd like to keep it a bit longer, if you don't mind."

"You…said I was in danger too. You're saying they know about me?"

He nodded. "They do. I feared when I got away from them, they might try to find you. I tried to call, but you didn't answer your phone."

"The meeting went late, so I spent the night at my place up in the City," she said. She stared at nothing for a moment, as if taking in the enormity of it all. Then she scooted over and tried to pull him close to her. "What do we do?" she asked. "We—" She stopped when he winced at her touch, and pulled back. Her eyes narrowed again. "You're holding something back, aren't you?"

"No. I—"

Gently, she reached out and pulled up the bottom of his shirt, and gasped at what she saw. "Dear God…" she breathed. "What did they do to you?"

He bowed his head and didn't answer. He didn't resist as she gently pulled the shirt up the rest of the way and slipped it off, and once again stared in shock. "It's all right…" he said, but his voice held no volume. "Deirdre, it's all right."

"It's *not* all right. You should be in the hospital. At least have a doctor look you over. Come on—I'll take you—"

"No." More firmly, this time. "Really. I'll be all right. It's not as bad as it looks." *Should have seen it last night.*

"This is what they did to you before you got away from them? How many of them did you say there were?"

"Two."

"Did you call the police? Can you describe them?"

He shook his head. "Didn't get a good look—all I saw was that they were big. A lot bigger than I am. And there's no point in calling the police."

"Why not? Maybe they can catch them. When did this happen? How long ago?"

Her frown cut him. Already she was unraveling his lies, and suddenly he was too exhausted to continue them. "I barely got away from them," he mumbled, sinking back into the couch cushions.

"What? What do you mean?"

"It was luck…that was all." He didn't look at her; couldn't look at her. "They…I couldn't stop them. I couldn't fight them, Deirdre. I got lucky—did something they didn't expect long enough so I could run away like a coward. I couldn't do a damned thing to stop them. I was bloody *useless*." He hated the way he sounded, hated what he was saying. He hadn't wanted to tell her any of this, so why was it all coming out now?

He truly expected her to get up and leave, or at least to regard him with the kind of disdainful disappointment she no doubt felt for him now that she'd seen his true colors. Behind the mask, behind all the charm and the sarcasm, this was all he was. And now she knew it.

He didn't expect her to take one of his hands in both of hers. "Come on," she said gently. "I know you feel rotten right now, but none of that. This is all my fault for giving you the stupid thing in the first place. Come on. Let me help you."

"Deirdre—"

"Shh." She stood and stepped back. "Lie down. That's an order."

In spite of himself, he had to smile. "Forceful…I like that…"

"Good, because I'm about to take your pants off."

He swallowed. "Much as I'd enjoy that, I don't think…"

"I just want to get a look at you, silly. Stretch out."

He did as he was told, and she carefully removed his jeans. When she got them off, she spent several silent seconds taking a long look at him. "My God," was all she said.

"Listen," he said, "it's not important. None of this is serious—it will heal. What's important is that they know about you, and I don't want them to hurt you."

She sat down carefully on the edge of the couch. "They won't hurt me. I'll be careful. I'm always careful. I don't go places alone at night."

Stone sighed. "It might not be enough. You didn't see them, Deirdre." He closed his eyes, his perverse mind serving up more visions of what the two hulking men would do to her if they cornered her somewhere.

"I have a gun," she said matter-of-factly. "I know how to use it, too, and I've got a permit to carry it. I'll keep it with me whenever I go anywhere. Will that make you feel better?" She perched on the edge of the couch and gently stroked his chest.

He shivered. Suddenly he felt very exposed—and very warm—lying there on the couch in only his shorts. Despite the fact that his body ached, his head pounded, and he was sure he was getting a fever, her touch and her closeness affected him as they always did. "Deirdre—"

"Shh," she whispered. She moved her hand up to stroke his jawline, and smiled as her eyes glittered. "I like the stubble. The look works for you."

He covered her hand with his own. "Deirdre, please. I—" He shook his head. How could he tell her how he felt? He'd thought she would get up and leave, and yet here she still was.

"Shh," she said again. She looked him up and down once more, and her smile widened. "I'm not so good for you right now, am I?"

"You're always good for me. I want you…" he said, his voice husky. He hadn't realized it, hadn't even thought about it, until she was sitting there, so tantalizingly close to him. But now, despite all his aches and pains and exhaustion, it was all he could think of. "I want you so much right now…but…I don't think…"

"Don't worry," she said. "I want you too. You know I do. But I'm not going anywhere. Let's get you healed up, and then I'll give you a workout. I promise. But for now, let's make sure you have what you need."

"I need to figure out why those men want that book," he said. He used a little surreptitious magic to pick up the old throw he had at the foot of the couch and pull it up to cover his lower half. "If I know that, I might be able to figure out who they are."

"There's time for that," she said. "When you're feeling better. Now, what else can I help you with?"

In the end, she cleaned up some of the scratches and cuts he hadn't done a very good job on, got him a bowl of soup and a Guinness, and went upstairs to retrieve a spare comforter from his linen closet.

"Are you sure you don't want me to stay?" she asked as she arranged it around him. She was back on the edge of the couch again. "I can call in and tell them something came up…"

"No," he said, stroking her hand. "I'll be fine. Seriously—I'd rather you see me a bit more at my best, when I can be more…entertaining."

"I'll hold you to that," she said. "Okay. But you have to promise to call me if you need anything."

"I promise." Of course, he had no intention of letting her play nursemaid, but she didn't have to know that. "And *you* must promise to be careful. Stay with other people, and keep your security system on. And please call me now and then to let me know you're all right, or if you see anything suspicious. Anything at all. I expect I'll be dead to the world for a few hours today, but leave a message. If I don't hear from you, I'll come over to investigate."

"I will." She kissed him. "I'll see you soon."

The door closed behind her. He settled back, already feeling like some important part of him had left with her, leaving an empty spot. He tried to concentrate: he had so many things he needed to think about now, such as who his attackers were, why they seemed to be nearly immune to magic, and why they were after Deirdre's black magic grimoire. Such as why Deirdre's grandmother was in possession of a tome of such power in the first place. Had she been a mage? Was there some connection between her and the attackers, or someone who knew them? Was there some specific bit of content in the book that they were looking for, or did they want the whole thing? Had they been sent by someone else to retrieve it? If so, by whom?

He drifted off with these questions still spinning uneasily in his mind.

"Help me...Please...Oh, God, help me!"

At first he couldn't see her face. He ran toward her, but no matter how fast he ran, he didn't get any closer. He yelled her name, but it was lost on the whipping wind. Around her, hulking figures circled: looming, muscular, naked things, too big to be human. They stalked her as she stood in the center of the circle, their faces leering, their hairy, grasping hands reaching for her...

And then he was no longer on that dream-treadmill, unable to get any closer. Running as hard as he could, he reached the edge of the circle. He grabbed one of them and tried to pull him backward, out of the leering ring, but the thing turned to him with a mocking grin on its slope-browed face and slapped him backward with no more effort than it would take to bat away an annoying fly. He fell hard, skidding to a stop. Inside the circle, her screams rose. He still couldn't see her face.

He scrambled back up, throwing himself at them again, battering his fists against their broad backs, trying to break through their ranks. They only laughed at him, shoving him this way and that. They had thick necks and tree-trunk legs and massive bulging biceps, and they stood shoulder to shoulder, reaching for the terrified figure inside the circle who darted this way and that, desperate for escape. Her screams kept pace with her rising panic, as one or another of them caught her and pulled her in.

"No!" he yelled. Every now and then he'd get a glimpse of her face, wide-eyed and horrified. Sometimes it was Deirdre's face. Sometimes it was Lindsey's. He redoubled his efforts to get past them, flinging himself down and trying to dive between their legs, or to slip between a pair of them as they surged forward, but each time they rebuffed his increasingly desperate attempts with no effort of their own.

They never spoke, only laughed and grunted and leered. They hardly appeared to even notice him except to mock his ineffectual attempts. Another one lunged, big body coming down on top of the screaming figure. For a moment, he saw her face—she was Deirdre now, and she was looking, not at the hulking male creature on top of her, but at him—*and her expression was accusing...and disappointed.*

And then she turned away from him.

She closed her eyes for just a moment, and then the rest of them moved in and she screamed.

He snapped awake, his heart pounding, his hands gripping the comforter so tightly that he'd ripped little holes in it. Rage rose, then faded with the shreds of the dream. He sank back down and let the out the breath he'd been holding in a rush.

He must be out of it—usually his dreams weren't that obvious.

In fact, that one had been so literal it was very nearly insulting.

Except for the fact that it had done an uncomfortably good job at encapsulating how he was feeling right about now. Maybe his subconscious had figured out that his brain wasn't running at full capacity at the moment, so it had better serve up the message in easily digestible form so he didn't miss anything.

He sat up, shivering, and pulled the comforter around him. He didn't have time for this. If he had any hope of figuring out who the men who'd attacked him were, and making damned sure they didn't come after Deirdre, he'd have to answer the question of why they wanted the grimoire.

He gritted his teeth, picked up his clothes from where Deirdre had left them on the coffee table, and began pulling them back on.

CHAPTER THIRTY-TWO

H E REACHED A PASSAGE TO INDIA in the middle of the lunch rush. The spicy aromas of the various Indian dishes, which normally made him hungry, now made his stomach squirm uncomfortably. He swallowed hard and plunged forward through the dining room.

Marta looked up as he swept past, and her eyes widened. "Alastair?"

"Not now, please, Marta. I'm in a hurry." What he didn't say was that he was afraid if he stopped, he wouldn't start again.

"But—"

"Please," he said again. Without stopping, he continued past her and headed down the hallway toward the portal door. Marta followed him, but only as far as the door itself.

He paused a moment in front of the portal. He shouldn't be doing this. Every ache in his body, the shivers despite his heavy overcoat, the gray exhaustion weighing him down, told him it was a bad idea. But every time he was tempted to stop, to turn around and head back home to the comfort and solace of his warm bed and his wards, new images of Deirdre and Polo Shirt and Leather Jacket spurred him on.

The grimoire was his only lead, and he knew he was close to cracking it. If he waited, who knew what might happen? And if it happened because he chose to coddle himself, he'd never be able to look in a mirror again.

❖

It was a little after eight p.m. in Surrey, already dark as he emerged from the crypt near his house. At least it wasn't raining tonight. He moved as fast as he could (which wasn't very fast); once again, he'd prefer not to run into Aubrey because it would mean a lot of long explanations he had neither the time nor the energy for.

He almost made it. He would have, except that he tripped on the steps leading up to the front door and dropped to his knees with a grunt of pain. As he dragged himself back to his feet, he heard the *snik-klunk* of a rifle behind him.

"Stop right there," said a cold voice. "Who are you, and what are you doing here?"

Stone sighed. "Aubrey. It's me."

"Sir?" The voice went from implacable to astonished. Footsteps on gravel, and then the old man was next to him, crouching and setting a lantern down next to him. "Oh, I'm sorry, sir. I didn't know you were coming, or I'd—"

"I didn't tell you I was coming," Stone said. He got back up and turned a little away from the lantern, hoping if he stayed out of the light, Aubrey might not notice his current state. "I just need to take care of a couple of quick things. No need to trouble yourself."

"It's no trouble. It's good to see you. Let me get you some—" His eyes widened. "Dear God, sir! What's happened to you?"

"Long story," he said, waving him off. "I don't have time for this right now. I'll be down in the magical library. We'll have to chat some other time—this is rather urgent."

"But—"

He already had the front door open and was heading inside. "Sorry, Aubrey. I know I'm being rude, but I feel rather ghastly right now and I know my energy won't last too long. I need to get this done right now. I promise you—I'll be fine."

He knew Aubrey wanted to protest. After all, the man had known him since he was born, and had seen most of his dodges and excuses. "Listen—if you want to help, could you put together a plate of something for me? Just leave it on the table at the end of the hall by the cellar entrance, and I'll get it when I have a break." He stopped, turning back with an encouraging smile. "And then go back to whatever you were doing. Please, don't let me interrupt you. I was trying to get in without you seeing me, but—" He spread his hands.

Aubrey regarded him for a long moment, then sighed and nodded. "Yes, sir."

He spent two hours in his magical library. The grimoire was there, right where he'd left it, undisturbed. That didn't surprise him. Only one person had ever managed to breach the library's wards, and he'd retuned them since then to be both more sensitive and more deadly. He'd liked to have spent longer, but wisdom eventually prevailed: if he left now, he'd still have the energy to get back through the portal and drive home. If he waited too much longer, he couldn't count on that.

Aubrey, good old Aubrey, had left him a covered plate including a large sandwich, a shiny red apple, and a glass of iced tea, counting on the frigid temperature of the unheated wing to keep it cold. He paused to devour it, taking the fact that he was ravenously hungry as a good sign. He carried the plate to the kitchen when he was done; Aubrey was nowhere to be seen. After scrawling a note (*"Thanks, Aubrey. See you soon—maybe during the spring break. I'll call you. A."*), he left it on the counter and headed out.

When he got back to A Passage to India and emerged from the portal room, he sneaked out the back door to avoid Marta. He wasn't proud of it, but he didn't want to talk to anyone else. He waited until he was on the road before allowing his mind go back over the discoveries he'd made about the grimoire to keep him engaged on the drive home.

He hadn't cracked it yet, but he was closer. He thought if he could manage to make it back there for a few more hours, he'd get it. The thing definitely contained a series of spells and rituals. It was written in an ancient ciphered language used thousands of years ago by mages who wanted to keep their research secret from those who would persecute or exploit them: clergy, the aristocracy, or powerful merchants who would steal their work and sell it to other mages. He hadn't gotten any specifics yet, but the spells and rituals all seemed to be related to the pursuit of power, immortality, and youth. As far as Stone knew no modern mage had access to such spells—he'd certainly never heard of any such thing—but magic in the old days had been both more potent and more widely practiced than it was today. While he doubted any of these spells would work properly, and he certainly didn't intend to test them since they all required human sacrifices of varying horrific degrees, neither could he rule out their validity.

This time when he got home, he checked the wards, and was relieved to find no disturbance. He was even more relieved to find two phone messages from Deirdre, both informing him that she was still fine and asking him to call her when he woke up to let he know how he was doing. He noticed the one from Jason was still there too; he'd have to call him back, but not today.

He sat down on the couch with the phone, intending to return Deirdre's call. As soon as he got off his feet, though, exhaustion overwhelmed him. He knew if he called her she would want to come over—a thought that at any other time would fill him with anticipation. But if she did come over and saw him like this, she'd insist on taking care of him, and he didn't want that.

He also knew that, given her usual effect on him, he'd be tempted toward more pleasurable activities. Much as he hated to admit it, though, he wasn't sure his body wouldn't betray him—which he also didn't want. *I'll call her tomorrow,* he thought, swinging his legs around so he was lying on the couch. *First thing.*

Before he got past that thought, he was asleep.

| CHAPTER THIRTY-THREE

THE NEXT DAY he went back to work. Probably not one of his wisest ideas, but after a full night's sleep (he found two more messages from Deirdre in the morning, but he'd slept so deeply he hadn't even heard the phone ringing), a hot shower, and a small handful of ibuprofen, he felt human enough to give the day a try. He still didn't shave: Deirdre had said she liked the look, and besides, the stubble covered up some of the bruises on his jaw.

He only had a couple of classes; he decided if he felt well enough after those and his office hour, he'd head back to England and see if he could make more headway on the grimoire translation. Before he left, he called Deirdre and left his own message, apologizing for missing her last night and asking her to call him at his office if she wanted to see him tonight.

He made it through the two classes and lunch, and thought he did a reasonably good job of hiding most of the injuries and stiffness. Some of the students gave him odd looks, but no one was brave enough to approach him. He stayed out of Mortenson and Hubbard's way, and by the time he slumped into his chair in his office at 3:00, he was feeling like he might be able to pull this off. He was about to try calling Deirdre when a figure appeared in his doorway. He looked up to see Tabby Wells waiting.

"Ms. Wells," he said.

"Hi, Dr. Stone. Can I come in?"

"Of course." He waved her toward a chair.

She sat down and pulled her backpack into her lap. "I decided to do that extra-credit assignment," she said. She removed a three-ring binder and extracted a thin sheaf of printed sheets, stapled together. "I can't tell you everything—exactly the way the rituals go is kind of a secret—but I hope it's enough to get my grade up." She pushed it across the desk at him.

"Thank you," he said. He picked it up and skimmed the first page, then slid it off to the side of his desk. "I'll take a look and let you know in a day or two."

"Thanks, I appreciate it." She paused a moment, as if unsure of what she wanted to say next. "Uh—Dr. Stone?"

"Yes?"

"I saw that you were out yesterday. Dr. Mortenson took over your class, and she said you were sick."

He frowned. "Nothing to worry about, Ms. Wells." Why was she asking him about that?

"Yeah," she said. "But…well…don't be offended, but you haven't been looking too well for a while now. Tired, you know?" She rummaged in her backpack and pulled out a small brown bottle, about the same size as one that would hold cough syrup. It had no label, and a wax-wrapped cap held its contents in. "I don't know if you're interested, but I thought you might be able to use this."

His frown deepened. Now she was offering him some kind of medication? "Ms. Wells, I don't know what that is, but it's probably not wise for you to—"

"I got it from Matthew," she said, meeting his gaze. "Remember that herbal pick-me-up I was telling you about before? I told him how tired you were looking, and asked him to give me some for you. I use it sometimes myself when I need to pull all-nighters—we all do. It's amazing—like one of those energy drinks, but better."

"Ms. Wells—" He looked at it, then at her.

"There's nothing illegal in it," she said quickly. "It's not drugs. Come on—I'm not stupid enough to give drugs to one of my *professors*. You don't have to try it if you don't want to. I just thought it might help you out. If you decide to use it, just use a capful at a time. And not too often." She zipped up her pack and got up. "Anyway, I hope the paper was what you were looking for. Thanks, Dr. Stone."

And then she was gone, leaving Stone sitting at his desk staring at the bottle and the stapled papers she'd left behind. He glanced up to make sure no one else was coming to see him, then picked the bottle up. It was about three-quarters full of some syrupy liquid— maybe ten doses, if each was a capful.

So this came from Caldwell, did it?

I wonder...

He shifted to magical sight, and was rewarded by the sight of a faint glow around the bottle. Magic, then. Interesting. Was Caldwell an alchemist? That kind of magic was rare—the only other mage Stone knew who practiced it at all was Madame Huan, who specialized in subtle concoctions like concentration enhancers. But what was this one's true purpose?

He dug the telephone book from his bottom drawer and riffled through it, sure he'd find nothing, but no, there it was: a tiny listing in the business white pages for the Church of the Rising Dawn in San Jose. He punched in the number, and after having to deal with two different underlings, got Matthew Caldwell himself on the line. "Caldwell. Alastair Stone."

"Dr. Stone. What a pleasure. What can I do for you?"

"I want to know about your little...gift."

"Ah, yes. The elixir. Ms. Wells mentioned that you'd been looking under the weather lately, and she thought you might find it useful. I was happy to give her a bottle for you."

"You're an alchemist."

"I dabble at it a bit," he admitted. "The elixir's quite harmless, I assure you. I use it myself, to help me stay awake when I have...projects."

"And you're giving this to your—congregants. Mundanes. To help them stay awake."

"Yes, of course." There was a pause. "I thought we covered this ground during your last visit, Dr. Stone. I'm not doing anything wrong—not by mundane laws, and certainly not by magical guidelines. My little concoction doesn't contain anything illegal or addictive."

"What *does* it contain, then?" Stone asked. He held up the bottle again, swirling it.

"Proprietary recipe. But I'm sure if you give it a moment's thought, you'll have no trouble figuring out the primary ingredient."

Stone narrowed his eyes. Could Caldwell be saying what he thought he was saying? "You're…infusing the elixir with the energy you take from your donors." So *that* was where all that extra energy was going. It made a strange sort of sense.

"I'll neither confirm nor deny that. But in any case, you have my word, Dr. Stone: it's quite safe, as long as you don't abuse it."

Stone stared at the little bottle in disgust. Even though using energy drawn from others as an ingredient in an alchemical mixture wasn't technically the same as drawing off that energy to power one's own magical efforts, he still found the concept distasteful on principle. He sighed. "I'm still keeping tabs on you, Caldwell. Remember what I said about Ms. Wells."

"Ms. Wells is fine and happy, as I'm sure you know. She's been attending your classes, has she not?"

"She has."

"And she doesn't look distressed in any way?"

"No more than any other student," he said reluctantly.

"Well, then. It sounds like I have nothing to worry about. Have a good day, Dr. Stone. The elixir is a gift—use it or not as you wish. I won't be offended."

After he hung up the phone, Stone leaned back in his chair and let his breath out. He shoved Tabby's paper into his briefcase and swept the elixir bottle into his top drawer, closing it with rather more force than necessary. He pulled on his coat and headed out.

He got as far as the door before he paused. After a moment, he whirled back around, yanked the drawer open, and dropped the bottle into his pocket. Then he left the office.

| CHAPTER THIRTY-FOUR

"**Y**OU LOOK BETTER TONIGHT," Deirdre said.

She sat across from him at a trendy little French place in Menlo Park. The dancing candle flame in the middle of the table caught the sparkle in her blue eyes.

"Told you it wasn't as bad as it looked," he said. He had a hard time keeping his eyes off her, but forced himself to scan the restaurant every few minutes, still convinced that Polo Shirt and Leather Jacket lurked nearby and planned to jump them as soon as his vigilance faltered. "You haven't seen any sign of anyone suspicious, have you?"

When he'd picked Deirdre up at her place, he'd paused to glance around with magical sight, but saw no lingering traces of potential trouble. He wished he could put a ward around her building, but wards took a lot of time and energy, and he doubted the people in the area would ignore him walking around the place for several hours, muttering to himself and tracing symbols in the air.

She shook her head. "Not that I'm aware of." She patted her bag on the chair next to her. "If they try to bother me, though, I'm prepared."

Stone wondered privately if she truly were: he had little experience with guns himself, but Jason had told him once that shooting a human being, even one who was trying to hurt you, wasn't as easy as they made it look in the movies. "I'm surprised they haven't come after you. Very relieved, but surprised. Obviously they know about you, and think you might know where to find the book."

She shrugged. "I'm not going to worry too much about it unless I see them. Maybe they gave up." She reached across the table and took his hand. "Are you sure you won't just give it back to me and let me get rid of it? It still upsets me that someone I care about got hurt over something so stupid."

"No, not yet. I'm getting somewhere with it. And it's not stupid—it's quite old, and probably very valuable. That's likely why they want it—they're working for some rich collector who wants to stay anonymous."

"If that's true, then why did they attack you? Why not just make an offer for it? It's not like the thing means anything to me, really. I'd probably have just sold it to them."

"Who knows? It just disturbs me to think they still might try to get it from you by force."

"You said you're getting somewhere with it. What does that mean? Are you telling me you can read that gibberish?"

"Yes—or rather, I'm getting close. It's an ancient language, and not one that's widely known."

"Interesting…" she said. She took a sip of her wine. "Can you tell what the point of the book is yet? Is it a storybook? Some kind of religious thing?"

"Not…exactly." He paused a moment, thinking about how much he wanted to tell her. He supposed it wouldn't hurt to tell her a bit of the truth, given that she'd never believe him anyway. "I think it's a kind of…spell book. A lot of people in those days fancied themselves wizards, and a lot of other people believed them."

"Wizards? You mean like Merlin or Gandalf or something?"

"Sort of, yes. Quite a lot of monarchs and aristocrats had their court magicians and diviners—you know, reading cow entrails and casting horoscopes and putting curses on people they didn't like."

"And this tells how to do things like that?" She tilted her head. "How strange."

"Strange and rather fascinating," he said. "That sort of thing is right up my alley—thug attacks notwithstanding, of course."

"Well, don't forget, you promised to tell me about what you found. And now I'm even more curious."

"I'll let you know when I get far enough to tell you something interesting. I've been spending a fair bit of my free time on it. When you're not available, of course. I haven't forgotten the other promise as well."

She nodded. "You really *do* look a lot better," she said, eyeing him across the table. "What's your secret?"

"I told you it looked a lot worse than it was. I just needed good night's sleep. Sorry I didn't answer your calls last night."

"I figured you were probably asleep. So..." she said with a sly grin. "Are you feeling up to some...dessert?"

"You *are* insatiable, aren't you?" he asked, chuckling.

"Are you complaining?"

"What kind of fool do you think I am?"

Her grin grew wider. "I'll go easy on you. At first. Need to build your strength back up again. I notice you kept the stubble, by the way."

"You said you liked it."

"Oh, yes. Very sexy. In fact, I kind of want to throw you over this table and ravish you right now."

"I think they have a surcharge for that."

"Worth every penny."

"No doubt. But in any case, I think I owe *you* a good ravishing."

She looked delighted. "Then consider me officially collecting."

CHAPTER THIRTY-FIVE

O N THE DRIVE to Deirdre's place, Stone let his mind drift back over the afternoon, and took stock of his current condition. He'd driven down to Sunnyvale after work and managed to slip past Marta while she was busy with customers. Aubrey was nowhere to be found, which left him two undisturbed hours to continue his studies before he'd have to return. The sleep last night had helped, but he still felt like he was getting a fever, his body ached, and as he sat at his old table surrounded by reference books and papers, he began to doubt he'd be able to concentrate sufficiently to get anywhere.

Almost without thought, he slipped his hand in his pocket and pulled out the bottle of elixir. He held it up and stared at it again, watching the thick liquid move back and forth against the brown glass.

Doing what he contemplated would be foolish.

He knew very little about Matthew Caldwell, and trusted him less.

The man was using energy he'd drawn from mundane donors to infuse an alchemical mixture. Black magic, no two ways about it. Just because it wouldn't affect Stone the same way as if he used black magic himself, it didn't mean it was a good idea to take chances.

Still, Kolinsky had said the man was harmless. And Kolinsky had never been anything but upfront with him.

Maybe Caldwell—or more likely, Tabitha Wells, who had no idea what she was doing—really *was* just trying to help him. To bring one of her favorite professors something to make him feel better when he was obviously tired and in pain. She'd said she used the stuff herself, and he'd seen nothing in her appearance or her aura to indicate it had harmed her in any way.

The fact was, he needed to finish translating the grimoire, and he had to do it fast. He knew of no way to trace who was trying to get hold of it—who had almost certainly hired Polo Shirt and Leather Jacket to retrieve it—without knowing what secrets it held.

If that meant taking a mild risk in order to keep Deirdre safe, he was willing.

He broke the wax seal on the bottle and unscrewed the cap.

The aroma that wafted upward was strange, but not unpleasant: sweet, with overtones of a sharper tang. He poured a capful; outside the brown bottle, the liquid was a deep purple hue.

He set the bottle and the cap down on the table and looked at both with magical sight. The faint glow he'd spotted in his office was stronger now, especially around the capful. Definitely potent magical stuff.

In the end, it was thoughts of Deirdre that made up his mind. He'd try it once and see how it went. Caldwell and Tabby Wells were probably overselling the stuff anyway, but if it took his headache and some of the pain away so he could concentrate, it would be worth it. He picked up the cap and swallowed the mixture.

It went down sharp and cold, with a bite that burned all the way down. Almost instantly, his mind seemed to sharpen, the fever-fog that had been settled over it for the last couple days burning off like early-morning haze. Likewise, the low-grade exhaustion gave way to a crisp clarity of thought, a level of focus he'd almost forgotten he was capable of. The pain didn't go away, but it was as if it didn't matter anymore. He didn't have to think about it—he had more important things to think about, and now he could get to them without the failings of his body getting in his way.

He wondered how long it worked, and decided since he didn't know, he'd better get to it. He spread out his notes and reference books, opened the grimoire to the page where he'd left off last time, and began to read.

By the time he returned to A Passage to India a couple hours later and once again sneaked out the back door, he'd made more progress on his translations than he had in any of his past sessions. He'd added almost five new pages to the sheaf of handwritten notes he'd left on the table. Even if he didn't use any more of Caldwell's concoction, that kind of headway wasn't something he would turn down.

Now, nearly five hours later as he pulled up to Deirdre's gate and punched in the code, the feeling of energy and vitality had barely faded. The jury was still out on what he'd feel like when the elixir finally wore off, but if he was lucky, he could keep it going long enough for a pleasant evening with Deirdre and then sleep off the aftereffects and be back to normal (or at least his current, somewhat diminished version of "normal") in the morning.

"What are you thinking about?" Deirdre asked as she got out of the car. "You're smiling."

"You," he said.

"Dessert?"

"That too."

"Something else?"

He slipped his arm around her as they entered the elevator, feeling the warmth of her against him. "Thinking about what a lucky man I am."

She leaned her head against his shoulder. "I'm the lucky one. But I still feel guilty: I got you hurt."

"Doesn't matter," he said. "I'd do it again, a thousand times, for the chance to be with you."

She leaned in a little closer, only pausing to pull out her key to open her door. "Come on," she said. "Let's go upstairs and see about that dessert."

"No arguments here."

He followed her upstairs; she didn't turn the light on, and by now he was familiar enough with her place that he didn't need it. When she reached the top, she paused a moment.

"What?" Stone asked.

"I'm…not sure. Something feels…off."

| CHAPTER THIRTY-SIX

STONE TENSED, shifting immediately to magical sight. "Turn on the light."

She did so. Her bedroom looked as it always did: elegant, understated, perfectly put together.

Stone swept his gaze around, but saw nothing out of place. "What is it?" he asked, already crossing to the bathroom to check for intruders hiding there.

She sighed. "I don't know. Probably nothing. I'm probably just jumping at shadows. Come on back out. I'm sorry."

No one hid in the bathroom, nor in Deirdre's walk-in closet. When Stone emerged, she was staring at her low, mirrored dresser, which had a small collection of personal items arrayed on its surface. "Something wrong?" he asked.

"I can't be sure." She pulled open a couple of drawers, looked inside, and shook her head. "It feels like someone's been here. Like they've...moved things. But only a little bit. And I can't even be sure I'm not just seeing things that aren't there."

Stone froze. Had Polo Shirt and Leather Jacket been in Deirdre's loft, carefully sifting through her things? Hunting the grimoire? "You did have the security system on, right?"

"I always turn it on, especially after...what happened. You saw me turn it off when we came in."

"Let's take a look around downstairs. You're right—you might be imagining things. But better safe than sorry."

She followed him down, and he watched her as she moved around the living room, the kitchen, and the tiny dining area. When she finished, she shook her head. "Still can't be sure. I feel like things are just a little bit...off. But not enough that I can be sure."

Damn. Again, Stone tried to figure out a way he could ward her loft without arousing suspicion, but once again he couldn't. "Come on," he said. "We'll go to my place tonight. Tomorrow we'll sort it out."

"Do you really think those men were in here?" She shivered a little and moved closer to him.

"No way to know. But it disturbs me that, if they were, they managed to get in without setting off your security system."

She nodded. "I don't want to call the police with no proof."

"No," he said with a sigh. "And if they were careful enough to leave next to no trace, they'll certainly have worn gloves."

Stone checked the parking garage with care when they left, looking for any sign of hidden auras as they headed back to his car. He did the same thing when they arrived at his townhouse, pausing in front for a moment to examine the wards. He found no sign of tampering. "What are you doing?" Deirdre asked.

"Nothing. Just...thinking." He waved her ahead of him and hurried inside.

For the first time since the night they'd met, Stone found it difficult to focus on Deirdre during their lovemaking. The effects of Caldwell's elixir were finally beginning to wear off, but he was sure that wasn't the problem.

As he held her in his arms and felt her warmth pressed against him, he couldn't stop thinking about Polo Shirt and Leather Jacket. *Had* they been in her apartment, sifting with care through her things, searching for the grimoire? He had previously assuaged his fear by thinking that if they had any idea what the tome was, if they or their mysterious employer had any idea who *he* was, they couldn't possibly think that he would leave something so magically potent in the care of a mundane with no way to protect it.

But if that weren't true—if they were somehow still convinced that she might have it, or worse, that they could use her to get to him, then that brought up a whole new series of problems. Could he protect her? Even if he could, could he do it without revealing to her what he was?

"Hey..." Her soft voice broke into his thoughts.

He gave her a faint smile. "I'm sorry. I'm not giving you my proper attention, am I?"

She tilted her head. Her face was only a few inches from his, her eyes troubled in the dim light of the bedroom. She draped her arm over his chest and snuggled her head into the crook of his arm. "You're still thinking about tonight, aren't you?"

"I can't help it," he said. "The thought that those two might have been in your home—" He gently stroked the soft, silky skin of her back.

"But we don't know they were," she pointed out. "I might just be jumping at shadows after what happened to you. Please...don't worry about it. It's a secure building. If the neighbors see anything wrong, they'll call the police."

He nodded. He wasn't convinced, but he tried not to let her see it.

"Do you want to just go to sleep tonight?" she asked. Her tone was still gentle, understanding. "I know you've been tired lately—maybe you weren't quite ready for—"

"I love you, Deirdre."

Stone tensed, startled. That had just popped out. He hadn't intended to say it, but yet...there it was.

She pulled back a little, propping herself up on her arm and looking into his eyes. For a moment, he couldn't read her expression, and feared he had made a terrible mistake.

Then she smiled. It was a tiny thing, tentative and faint, but her eyes glittered in the dimness. "Alastair…"

"I do." His voice came out a little husky. "I love you. When I'm not with you, I'm thinking about you. When I *am* with you, there's nothing else in the world. And the thought of anyone hurting you—"

She kissed him. It wasn't a sensuous kiss this time, but long and slow. Her arms went around him. "Nobody's going to hurt me," she said when she pulled back at last. "I know they won't. I know you would never let that happen."

For a moment, just a moment, he thought about telling her. Everything. What he was, what the grimoire was, and why it was so important that he finish his translations so he could figure out who might be after it.

Not yet. It's not the time yet.

He pulled her to him in a tight embrace. "No," he said, and there was a hard resolve to his voice. "I won't let that happen. I promise you, Deirdre. I won't."

Caldwell's elixir was definitely wearing off now, the fog beginning to settle over his head again.

"Shh…" Deirdre whispered, brushing his hair off his forehead. "You sleep now. You'll feel better in the morning. I pushed you too hard, and I'm sorry."

"Mmm…" he murmured, but his mind was already wandering as the exhaustion of the day caught up with him.

Just as he drifted off, some back corner of his mind pointed out that she hadn't said she loved him as well.

CHAPTER THIRTY-SEVEN

NEITHER OF THEM MENTIONED the conversation the next morning. Stone was half-convinced that the whole thing had been a dream borne of his fatigue, but didn't want to ask Deirdre about it in case he was correct. He hadn't quite decided whether that would be a good thing or a bad thing.

Deirdre had to fly down to Los Angeles for the weekend to finish up some work and meet with clients ("Unfortunately," she told him with regret, "when there are upcoming shows, I don't get weekends off"), so Stone took the opportunity to spend more time in England with the grimoire.

His bruises faded, slowly, over the next couple of days, and with them some of the pain from the attack. The exhaustion and constant feeling that he was developing a low-grade fever, however, didn't. He managed to avoid the temptation to use any more of Caldwell's elixir on Saturday, but by Sunday afternoon he was so tired that he was afraid he'd simply drop off to sleep over his research notes if he didn't do something.

Just one more, he told himself. *I'm so close to cracking this thing.* With the clarity of mind and the jolt of energy from the concoction, he was able to add another ten pages to his notes.

By now, he'd determined that the grimoire contained a lot of reference material, mostly long descriptions of how to create or procure the various components required to perform the spells and rituals it included, followed by an annotated, cross-referenced, and heavily illustrated collection of techniques. By the end of Sunday, he had good translations of six out of the nine major ones, all of which represented the sort of hardcore black magic that you didn't see often in the modern world.

Stone, though unusual among white mages with his keen interest in understanding black-magic processes even though he had no interest in actually practicing them, found these to be more distasteful by far than almost anything he'd ever seen before. Most modern black-magic rituals did require blood, other bodily fluids, or magical energy, but almost without exception these were either given voluntarily or taken from a living contributor without killing the person. The grimoire's rituals, on the other hand, required human sacrifices—most of them a single person, but a couple detailed the ritual murders of no less than five. A couple of them specified children. The night following his translation of that one, Stone's increasingly frequent nightmares featured not only Deirdre, but a vivid and horrific depiction of several screaming children stretched out on an altar, falling one by one under the ritual knife of a shadowy, robed figure—a figure that, when he looked into a mirror conveniently hanging nearby, he realized was himself.

How the hell had something like this turned up in a shop? Even a "mage dies and his heirs don't know what to do with his stuff" situation, which occurred far more often than one might think, seemed farfetched in this case. He'd examined Deirdre for signs of magical talent while she slept and found none, but with each successful translation, his suspicions grew that there might be more to her grandmother than met the eye. He'd have to ask Deirdre about that some time—but the hard thing was working out a way to do that without making her think he was insane. "So, my love, was your gran a diabolical and frighteningly powerful practitioner of the black arts, perchance?" didn't seem like the best way to endear himself to a woman he was desperately attracted to.

All of these thoughts spun and roiled in his mind as he returned to California through the portal after studying in England until nearly one a.m. They preoccupied him so fully that he didn't realize he'd traced a familiar path out through A Passage to India's dining room instead of ducking out the back door as he'd done the last few times until he heard Marta's voice calling to him. "Alastair?"

Bugger.

It had been nearly 1:00 in England, but he'd lost track of the time difference: it was only five p.m. in California. The restaurant was not only open, but the early wave of the usual Sunday-evening dinner crowd already occupied many of the tables.

He glanced up, fixing a rather manic smile on his face. "Marta! How are you? Sorry—in a bit of a rush, but we should chat soon."

She eyed him critically, and he didn't miss the suspicion and worry on her long, rather horsey face. "Please—I'd like to talk to you. It'll only take a couple of minutes."

He sighed. While he *could* reiterate that he was in a hurry and couldn't spare the time, Marta was an old and dear friend, and he hated to see her looking at him like that. "All right," he said. "Come on, though—not out here."

She took him back to the break room, which was currently empty. "Would you like something? You look like you could use a cup of coffee."

He almost declined, but his latest dose of Caldwell's elixir was fading, and the muzzy-headed feeling of fatigue loomed. "Thanks."

She got him one and waved him toward a chair.

"Can't. I told you—I need to get going." He took a long sip of the coffee; the hot, strong liquid felt and tasted wonderful.

"All right, then. I'll get right to it." She regarded him in silence for a moment, then said, "I'm worried about you, Alastair."

"Why? I told you, I've just been busy."

"You look terrible," she said. "I'm sorry to put it so bluntly, but if I can't tell you the truth, then what kind of friend would I be?" When he didn't reply, she continued, "You're pale—"

"I'm always pale. So are you. We're English. It's what we do."

Her brow crinkled and she frowned. "Don't deflect, Alastair. I've known you too long for that, and it won't work."

Again, he didn't answer.

"You're pale," she repeated. "You've got cuts and bruises where I can see, and I can only imagine where else that I can't. You've lost weight. Every time I see you, you look like you're about to pass out any second." She moved closer and put a hand on his shoulder. "If there's something wrong, please…let me help. Let *someone* help, at least. You mentioned you've met someone—are you two still—?"

"We're still together," he said. "We're fine."

"How can you be fine when she lets you go 'round looking like you're—" she trailed off, her face clearly showing that she thought she'd taken it too far.

"Like I'm what?"

She shook her head. "Will you answer a couple of questions for me, Alastair? Will you give me honest answers, knowing I'm a friend and I care about you?"

"I might. Depends on the questions."

She fixed her gaze on his. "Are you ill? Have you got some sort of—something that needs to be treated?"

"No," he said, too quickly. He took her hands gently and smiled. "Marta. I haven't got anything dire. I promise. No cancer. Nothing horrible like that. I might have a bit of a fever, I'm not sure. But that's it. And I'm not addicted to anything, if that was your next question."

She held his gaze for a few more seconds, as if trying to read his face and determine if he was telling her the truth. Finally, she nodded. "Okay, then. I notice you've been using the portal a lot more than usual lately. Are you involved in something that's harming you?"

"No," he said again. He sighed. "Marta, honestly—I know you're a dear friend and I don't want to tell you that what I'm up to isn't your concern, but—well—it isn't. You know I do a lot of research. I'm on to some interesting bits right now, which means that between work, my—personal life—and the research, I don't have as much time to sleep as I should. That's part of why I'm doing my research in England—I can get eight hours in and then still have some daylight left when I come back here. It's sort of like poor man's time travel."

"You know it doesn't work like that, right? You know it's going to catch up with you—it looks like it already has, actually."

Stone nodded. "I know that. And I accept it. It's a short-term thing. I should be done with the research fairly soon, and I've got the Spring holiday week coming up, so I'll have plenty of time to catch up on lost sleep then." He smiled. "I need to go home, Marta. I'm tired, and I'm planning to head to bed straight away when I get there. Don't *worry*, all right?"

"I'll try not to," she said with a sigh. "You don't make it easy, though, do you?"

| CHAPTER THIRTY-EIGHT

MONDAY KEPT STONE BUSY: between teaching classes, attending committee meetings, and fielding questions from students concerned about their upcoming final projects and exams, he didn't have a chance to sit down until nearly four that afternoon. The day was gray and blustery; cold rain had begun falling in earnest about an hour ago. He trudged the quarter-mile back to his office with his long black wool overcoat buttoned up, a scarf draped around his neck, and his industrial-strength umbrella deployed against the windblown droplets. It was times like this he was glad he'd brought one over from England: he'd found American umbrellas, at least in California, to be laughably inadequate for anything but the mildest rainfall—which Californians didn't bother using umbrellas in anyway.

When he entered his office, shaking water drops off his coat and unwinding his scarf, he found Deirdre seated in his guest chair. She flashed him a radiant smile.

"Hi. I hope you don't mind me waiting for you in here." She wore a thin green sweater and a gray skirt over high-heeled black boots; the way she sat, leaned back with her legs crossed, gave her the elegant look of a woman from another time.

"You've just made my day," he said, bending down to kiss her. He hadn't seen her since Saturday morning, and up until now, she'd never come to his office. He tossed the coat and scarf over his chair. "Nothing's wrong, is it?"

"No, no, not at all. I was just in the area, so I figured I'd stop by and see if I could catch you instead of calling." She picked up her black leather bag and held it on her lap. "I've got something I hoped I could interest you in, actually."

"Indeed you do," he said, raising an eyebrow. Instead of sitting behind his desk, he took the other guest chair and faced her.

She laughed. "Not that, silly. I *know* I can interest you in that." She slipped her hand into her bag and withdrew an envelope. "A friend at work had tickets to the symphony in San Jose tonight, but she can't make it, so she gave them to me. Would you like to go? It's at eight. I know it's short notice, but…"

"I'd love to go," he said. He glanced at his watch. "If I head home soon, I can change and pick you up at six. We can go somewhere for dinner beforehand. You choose."

"Are you sure you're not too tired? I hope you got some sleep this weekend."

"I did," he said. He felt reasonably good today—as he'd told Marta, he'd gone straight home the previous night and fallen into bed. Though a couple times today he'd been tempted to take just one more dose of Caldwell's elixir, he'd resisted the temptation. Both Caldwell and Tabby had said not to overdo it, and if he did take any more, he wanted to save it for the last push to finish up the translations. "Have you been home since you got back?"

"I stopped by this morning," she said. "No sign of anything wrong. I think I must have just been seeing things on Friday night."

"Probably," he agreed, though he wasn't so sure. "Good to hear, anyway."

She stood, "I should be going—I need to do a couple of things before I go home. See you at six?"

He got up too, and held her coat for her. "Six it is." He pulled her close to him and kissed her. She responded with eager hunger, leaning into him and giving as good as she got. Once again, he was overwhelmed with longing for her—the feeling that he wanted nothing more than to take her right here in his office, across his desk. From the way her strong, grasping fingers dug into the back of his shirt, he was sure she felt the same way.

A sound outside the door startled him, and it was only then that he remembered he hadn't closed it. He almost jerked back, guilty as a schoolboy caught necking in a dark corner, but instead he simply stepped backward and glanced at the doorway, just in time to spot the retreating back of a female student walking quickly back down the hall. Even from behind, he recognized the backpack.

Tabitha Wells.

"Ms. Wells?" he called.

She took another step, then came to an abrupt stop and turned back around. "I'm—sorry, Dr. Stone. I didn't mean to…interrupt you."

"No—it's fine. Please come back. Did you need something?"

"I should go," Deirdre said.

"Just a moment—I'll take care of this." He stepped outside the office.

Tabby hesitated in the hallway. "Really—I can come back later." Her gaze darted past Stone to the open door to his office, and clouded for a moment.

"No need. What can I do for you?"

She paused. "Nothing, really. I…uh…was just wondering if you'd gotten a chance to take a look at my extra-credit paper."

Damn. He hadn't even thought about the paper—in fact, he'd forgotten he'd put it in his briefcase. "I have not. I apologize—been a bit…busy. I'll look at it and let you know by the end of this week. Fair enough?"

"Sure," she said. She glanced sideways again, then hitched up her backpack on her shoulder. "Thanks, Dr. Stone. Sorry for…uh…"

"Not a problem. Have a good evening, Ms. Wells."

She looked like she was about to say "You too," but didn't. Instead, she nodded, turned on her heels, and hurried off.

When Stone turned back around, Deirdre was lounging in the doorway, watching her go. "Who was that?" She had an odd, impassive expression.

"One of my Occult in America students. I owe her a grade on an extra-credit assignment I gave her a few days ago."

She nodded. "She's got a thing for you. Did you know that?"

He looked at her, startled. "What?"

She shrugged, and smiled. "Men are funny—you either see things that aren't there, or you miss the blindingly obvious. Oh, yes, she's got it bad for you."

He considered, remembering the visit from Tabitha's father a few weeks ago. "Someone else told me that too. I suppose you're right—I don't see it. And I assure you, even if it's true, it's certainly not mutual. You can't possibly be concerned about that, can you?"

She laughed and shook her head. "No, don't worry. I'm a bit more secure than that."

"Well, good. Because I'd be the biggest idiot in the world if I even *looked* at anyone else while I've got you."

She laughed again. "You can look. Just don't touch." She kissed him again, quick but passionate, then tapped a playful finger on his nose. "See you at six."

| CHAPTER THIRTY-NINE

STONE'S MUSICAL TASTES ran more toward rock concerts than classical symphonies, but he'd have cheerfully attended anything from a country-music festival to a polka extravaganza if Deirdre had asked him to.

"Have I told you lately that you're beautiful?" he asked when he spotted her waiting for him in the lobby. She wore a short, form-fitting black dress in her usual style that combined old-world class with modern-day sensuality, stiletto heels that made her stand almost as tall as Stone, and a glittering necklace that, if it wasn't made of genuine diamonds, was the best imitation Stone had ever seen. She held her long, sweeping coat over one arm along with a small clutch bag.

She smiled. The rain still fell hard outside, and he'd dropped her off before heading off to park the car. "Did you have to park far away?"

"Couple of blocks," he said, shaking out his umbrella. He'd learned shortly after he'd moved to California that it didn't rain that often here, and when it did, the vast majority of the motorists forgot how to drive. Tonight was no different, which meant that by the time they arrived, all the nearby parking lots were already full. He'd finally found space in a small lot on a tiny side street.

She looked rueful. "Sorry about that. I forgot about what the rain would do to traffic."

"No trouble," he said, and kissed her quickly. "Come on—let's check our coats and find our seats."

For the next hour and a half, Stone mostly split his time between sidelong glances at Deirdre and letting his mind chew over the grimoire translations. It wasn't that he didn't enjoy the music: the concert featured the works of several of the more energetic Russian composers, and the pounding beat of some of the pieces affected him the same way many of his favorite rock pieces did. But between the warm closeness of Deirdre's leg against his and of their arms resting next to each other on the armrest, and the fact that his brain refused to let him completely forget a problem when he was in the middle of it, he missed large portions of the program.

At the intermission, when everyone filed out to the lobby to stretch their legs and refresh themselves at the bar, she took his hand and squeezed it. "You've been looking like you're off in another world," she said teasingly. "Not a classical fan?"

"Oh, I am," he said. "You're just—distracting."

"Distracting." She moved a little closer to him, and took a sip of her drink.

"Very…distracting. That dress is…" He tugged at his tie. "…Distracting," he finished.

She chuckled. "Then it's doing its job."

"It is. Admirably. But I have to admit, I've also been thinking about your book."

"Really?"

He nodded. "I'm getting close. I made a lot of headway this weekend. I've got almost all of it translated now. Just a few more bits and I'll be done."

"That's wonderful," she said, brightening. "I can't wait to hear about it. Can you tell me anything now?"

"Not just yet. Soon. Once I've got it all sorted out." He paused; it was almost time to return to their seats. "Deirdre…"

"Yes?"

"Would you consider selling it to me?"

She looked surprised. "The book?"

He nodded. "As I mentioned before, it's just the sort of thing I find fascinating, and it would make quite an addition to my library. I hope you'll consider it. I'll offer you a fair price, of course."

She took his hands, then leaned closer to him and gently kissed his forehead. "Alastair...you've spoiled my surprise. I was planning to give it to you."

He stared at her. "You...were?"

"Of course I was. I saw the look in your eyes when I showed it to you. And then when you got hurt because of it...if you want it, it's yours. On one condition," she added.

"Name it."

"You have to promise me that you'll tell me what's in it. Even if it's something horrible. I'm dying of curiosity. Will you do that?"

He considered. He could lie to her—she'd never know the difference. That was what he'd intended to do all along. But—

"All right," he said. "I promise. I'll tell you. I warn you, though: it is fairly horrible."

"It's all right," she said. "I used to love horror stories when I was a kid. Come on, though—we'd better go back before they close the doors."

For the second half of the concert, Stone had even more trouble concentrating on the music. Now, in addition to Deirdre's tantalizing closeness, the translations, and his growing fatigue, he had his astonishment that Deirdre had decided to simply give him the grimoire. He'd never expected that. She'd never shown any indication that she was motivated by money, and seemed to be sufficiently well-off that she didn't have to worry about it, but he'd been indulging in a bit of wishful thinking when he'd told her he'd make her a fair offer for the book. Even if he cashed in all his investments and raided his various bank accounts both here and in England, he wouldn't come close to gathering what the book was worth. Admittedly, the market for such a thing was vanishingly small, and finding a buyer willing to pay that kind of money would be difficult, but if she did, such an item could easily fetch an exorbitant sum.

Part of him—the part that loved her, the part that wanted to be honest with her—insisted that he reveal the whole story about its worth before allowing her to give it to him. But this thing wasn't just some work of art, some first-edition bit of literature that belonged in a museum. When you got right down to it, the grimoire, in the wrong hands, was a powerful weapon. Stone had an obligation to keep that weapon out of those wrong hands—hands such as those of whoever was pulling Polo Shirt's and Leather Jacket's strings—even if he had to deceive Deirdre to do so.

He hadn't reached any definitive conclusions by the time the hall rang with the thundering final chords of the last piece, followed by loud and enthusiastic applause from the audience. Deirdre squeezed Stone's hand as around them, people began to rise from their seats. "That was wonderful."

"It was," he agreed, even though he'd barely heard half of it.

They joined the exiting crowd and let it sweep them out to the lobby. Stone retrieved their coats and his umbrella and settled Deirdre's coat over her shoulders. Outside, the rain still fell, cold and steady. "Wait here," he told her. "Stay warm. I'll go get the car—watch for me just out front."

He set off at a brisk pace, wishing he could have gotten away with wearing his Doc Martens with his suit. His thin leather dress shoes sloshed through the frequent puddles dotting the sidewalks, and already his feet were soaked. Once more, he let the chattering crowds carry him along, but it wasn't too long before people began to break off, in pairs or small groups, and head toward their cars parked in the nearer lots. By the time he'd reached the end of the first long block, he was walking alone. Cars still drove by, though, their headlights making crazy multicolored patterns in the oily puddles on the streets. Stone remained vigilant, as always, but wasn't terribly concerned.

It wasn't far now, though: just another half-block up this street, then a left and another block or so to the lot. He increased his pace again, not wanting to keep Deirdre waiting any longer than he had to.

This street was narrower, choked on both side with parked cars. The intermittent streetlights cast eerie yellow glows over the cars and the street, which was lined with small blue-collar business-es like auto-repair shops and plumbing contractors. All of them were closed at this time of night.

The lot was just ahead now. Stone slowed his pace a bit, feeling suddenly exposed. He switched to magical sight, doing a quick sweep for auras, but the only one he saw was the tiny glow of some small animal—a cat or a large rat, maybe—darting across the street.

Don't be stupid, he thought. *They're not here. And you can handle anyone else.*

As he approached the lot, which was on the same side of the street he was, he noticed two things right away: the first was that it was nearly empty now. It was far enough away from the symphony venue that most likely whatever event the people in the other cars here had attended had finished up well prior to the concert.

The second was that most of the lights were out.

Perhaps he was mistaken—he couldn't remember how well lit the lot had been before, because when he'd arrived, other cars had been driving in and out, illuminating the area with their headlights. Now, only a lone streetlamp on the far side of the lot provided any light. In it, Stone could pick out only a half-dozen cars, including his own BMW, scattered throughout the open space.

He glanced around again, doing another scan for auras. When he still saw none, he called up a shield around him and headed to-ward his car. A bit of shame gripped him—admitting fear wasn't something he did easily—but in a moment, he'd be back inside his car. He could go pick up Deirdre and soon he'd forget about the whole thing.

"Smarter this time, I see," said a drawling, familiar voice from behind one of the cars closest to the BMW.

| CHAPTER FORTY

"**Y**OU THINK THAT PUSSY BUBBLE of yours can stop us?" came a second voice from behind the BMW itself.

Stone froze as the two of them rose up: Polo Shirt, now wearing a down jacket, jeans, and a backward-facing baseball cap, and Leather Jacket, dressed similarly as before except for the addition of a black knit stocking cap, swaggered around the cars and faced him, maybe twenty feet away. Both were smiling, their teeth flashing white and predatory in the dim light.

"You won't find me such an easy target this time," Stone said, but his heart pounded and doubt nudged at a small corner of his mind: *could* they get past his shield? They seemed immune to normal magic, but did that mean magical shields would be useless as barriers against them? He lowered his umbrella but held on to it; if they came after him and the shield didn't stop them, it was substantial and might be useful as a weapon.

"We'll see about that," Polo Shirt said. He lounged against the side of the BMW and crossed his arms over his chest. "We got time to wait."

"You can't hold that thing forever. Magic takes energy, and you ain't got much of that right now." Leather Jacket let out a nasty laugh. "How you feelin', Stone? Still fucked up? That's a nice suit, but it ain't hidin' anything. You walkin' like an old man."

Stone examined his options. They were right: he couldn't keep the shield up indefinitely. Maybe five or ten minutes straight, assuming they didn't do anything to stress it, like attacking him. Both of them stood between him and the BMW, so there was no way he could make a break for the car.

He could try throwing something at them, but he saw nothing to throw, except cars—and those were a bit out of his power range at present—or his umbrella, if it came down to that. He might be able to skewer one of them—but then what about the other one?

He could levitate himself away, but he wasn't certain that in his current shape he could keep the shield up at the same time, and in any case, levitation wasn't flight. As fast as they moved, he might not be able to get far enough away from them before they could grab him.

The only other option he saw was to try using Harrison's magic again. It had hurt them, sure, but clearly it hadn't taken them out. And when you added the fact that he hadn't worked out yet how to control it without collapsing and burning out his magic for an indefinite period, that seemed a poor choice as well.

"So," Polo Shirt said. "Let's talk while we wait for your bubble to pop. Where's the book?"

"Somewhere you'll never find it," Stone said.

"That's too bad," Leather Jacket said. He, too, leaned against the BMW, hands in the pockets of his jacket. "We were hoping our little…demonstration convinced you we're not fuckin' around."

"Hate to have to do it again," Polo Shirt said. "'Cause if we do…well…you never know what we might do to you next time. We were bein' careful before. Maximum pain, but no real damage. We're good at that. We wanted you to be able to lead us to the book."

"Won't be careful this time, though," Leather Jacket said with a leer. "You'll *really* be our bitch this time." He made a suggestive motion with his hips.

Stone forced the memories of the beating away—or tried to. He rolled his eyes. "Seriously? That's what you've got?"

Polo Shirt shrugged. "Hey, it's not our thing, but we do what we gotta do, you know? We'd much rather plow that hot chick of yours. Where is she, by the way? She waitin' for you? Maybe we should go find her."

"Why?" Stone asked. "The book isn't at her place. You know that—you've already checked, haven't you?"

The two of them looked at each other for a moment, and Stone caught an odd look passing between them. Was it confusion? "Yeah, we checked," Polo Shirt said quickly. "Didn't expect to find it, though—you'd have to be pretty fuckin' stupid to let somebody with no magic keep hold of it."

"You'd want to study the fuck out of it," Leather Jacket said. "Just like our boss. Fuckin' mages are all alike."

"Who is your boss?" Stone asked. He had to think of a way out of this situation fast, but if they were in the mood to talk instead of coming after him, maybe he could get some questions answered.

Polo Shirt snorted and didn't reply. Instead, he pushed himself off the BMW and moved closer to Stone, casually circling the barrier around him. He poked a finger out, but stopped short of touching it. "Hmm...can we get through it or not? You don't know, do you?" Quick as a striking snake, he lashed out with a fist and punched it, right at the level of Stone's face.

Stone flinched backward as the barrier flared bright under the thug's hand, but it didn't break.

Polo Shirt grinned. "There's your answer. Yeah, your little pussy shield will stop us...but not for long. Look—it's already a little weaker." He resumed pacing around it. "So...how many licks does it take to get to the soft, squishy center?" He punched the shield again, this time from behind. "What'cha gonna do, Stone? C'mon— dazzle us with your brilliance."

Stone did nothing, beyond concentrating on keeping the barrier going. The temptation to plunge the pointy end of his umbrella into Polo Shirt's throat clawed at him, but he resisted it. The umbrella represented his only weapon at the moment. He swept his gaze around the lot, hoping he'd missed something else he could use, but aside from the parked cars, everything else was firmly attached to the ground.

He had to do something soon—the shield weakened with every one of Polo Shirt's blows, and every minute he had to focus on keeping it powered. Even with the help of the focus items he had with him, it wouldn't last too much longer. And Deirdre was still waiting for him. What would she do if he didn't show up soon? Would she come looking for him?

Polo Shirt came back around in front of him, stopping to face him down. Leather Jacket pushed himself off the car and ambled over too. Rain still fell hard, soaking them both, but they didn't seem to notice or care. "Last chance, Stone…" Leather Jacket said.

Stone smiled.

His sudden idea was crazy. It might not work. Even if it did, he'd have to pull it off perfectly, with a level of precision he might not even be capable of right now. But being out of options does wonders for focusing the clarity of one's mind.

He should have thought of it before, but he supposed he'd been a bit off his game during their last encounter.

Magic didn't work on them—at least any he could easily use didn't. They'd proven that.

But what if he didn't target *them,* but something attached to them?

He pulled power to him, gathering it from within himself and from the remaining shreds contained within his focus items.

"You gonna try to zap us again?" Polo Shirt's teeth bared in a mocking grin. "You saw how well that worked for you last time—"

Leather Jacket cracked his knuckles.

And then, suddenly, both of them lifted off the ground and flew in two different directions, yanked by their shoes and flung through the air, each one landing hard about twenty feet away with two loud crashes and individual variations on "what the *fuck?*"

Stone ran. He dropped the shield and took off toward the car, ignoring every pain his protesting body tried to hit him with, ignoring everything but the BMW's door in front of him. As he ran, he jammed his hand into his pocket and hit the unlock button on the keyfob.

He almost made it. He would have made it if he hadn't hit a puddle and his foot, clad in a slick-soled dress shoe instead of his usual boot, slid momentarily out from under him.

He didn't fall—he barely faltered. But it was enough. In the second it took him to right himself and yank the car door open, they were on him.

They still moved fast—faster than normal humans, agile as hunting cats taking down prey. They both slammed into him at the same time, throwing him face-first into the closed back door of the car, holding him there with his cheek pressed against the window. He struggled, trying to duplicate the spell to fling them off again, but he couldn't do it.

"Nice try, Stone," Polo Shirt said, casually shutting the BMW's driver door. "I'm impressed. You almost got us that time."

"Almost," Leather Jacket repeated. He continued pressing Stone into the side of the car with one beefy arm, while his other hand gripped his hair and wrenched his head up. "And now, we're gonna have some *fun* with you."

"Alastair!"

Stone's blood froze at the voice.

No...no...dear gods, no...

| CHAPTER FORTY-ONE

"LASTAIR! IS THAT YOU? What's going on?"

He wrenched his head around, nearly ripping it free of Leather Jacket's grip, and his knees sagged.

Deirdre stood at the entrance to the parking lot, her long coat whipping around her in the wind. She'd gotten hold of an umbrella from somewhere. "Deirdre! No! Run!" he tried to yell, but it came out as a strangled croak as Leather Jacket got a handful of his hair again and jammed his cheek back into the window.

He couldn't let them go after her. As long as they were focused on him, maybe she'd have a chance to get away. Was she already running? He couldn't tell. All he could see was the front of the car, and Leather Jacket's broad upper body blocking the rest of his view. He closed his eyes and concentrated with everything he had, trying to summon one last bit of energy to at least keep their attention.

And then Leather Jacket let go of his hair, and his arm. He shoved him toward Polo Shirt, who caught him and threw him to the ground next to the car. "Looks like it's your lucky day, Stone," he growled, reaching up to swipe rain off his face. Together, he and Leather Jacket turned and took off into the night. Stone roared and flung a concussion beam at them, more out of frustration than anything, but they kept running without seeming to even notice. They disappeared into the darkness on the far side of the parking lot.

"Alastair!" Footsteps hurried across the parking lot toward him.

Stone dragged himself back to his feet, leaning against the car, puffing, his heart pounding hard in his chest. "Deirdre..." he whispered.

"Are you all right?" She came up next to him, holding her umbrella over them both.

He nodded. "I...yes. Fine." That wasn't quite true, but beyond relatively minor aches where they'd slammed him into the car and grabbed him by the hair, he hadn't sustained any new injuries. "Bit soaked, but fine." He looked at her, seeing her for the first time. "Why did you come after me?"

"I got worried," she said. "Everybody else was gone, and I didn't see any sign of your car."

He collected his umbrella from where he'd dropped it, and went around the other side of the car to open the door for her. "You got all the way here that fast on those?" he asked, pointing at her stiletto heels.

"It's a skill," she said with a shrug. Her expression immediately clouded when she got in, though, as she seemed to put two and two together. "Were those—the same guys who attacked you before?"

He nodded, but didn't reply. He started up the car and drove out of the parking lot, scanning the area illuminated by the headlights in case Polo Shirt and Leather Jacket changed their minds and decided to come back for seconds. Slowly, his heart rate returned to normal, and his mind stopped conjuring images of what might have happened if the two men had decided to chase after Deirdre instead of remaining with him.

They drove in silence for several minutes. Stone, driving by rote, got back to the freeway and headed north. Traffic this time of night was sparse, especially with the rain. He moved over to the fast lane and nudged the car up to what was probably an unsafe speed.

If Deirdre noticed, she didn't comment. She continued to sit quietly in the passenger seat until they'd driven several more miles. "What are you thinking about?" she asked at last.

He shrugged. "A lot of things. None of them particularly pleasant."

"We should call the police," she said. "They got away again. This is twice they've attacked you, and they're still out there somewhere. What if they won't stop coming after you?"

"Well…" he said softly, "that's the thing, isn't it? Why did they run away at all?"

"I…don't understand."

"They had me. They didn't catch me by surprise that time, but I was still no match for them. But then you showed up, and they just…took off." He turned to her. "Why do you suppose that is?"

She frowned. "I don't know. Maybe they thought I'd run away and call someone?"

"There weren't any phones nearby. They probably knew that."

"Maybe they thought I had a cellular. Or…could they have been afraid I'd seen them? That I might be able to describe them to the police?"

"I saw them," Stone pointed out. "Unless they planned to kill me, I could have described them."

Her hand crept across the console and rested on his leg. "This is so horrible," she said. "And all because of that stupid book."

He nodded, still facing forward, his gaze fixed on the rain-slick road. He didn't say anything for a long time, and when he did, reluctance tinged his voice. "Deirdre…" he said at last.

"Yes?"

"I think you'd best tell me the rest of what you know about that book. Don't you think so?"

She was silent for a long time. Then she nodded. "I…think so," she said at last. She didn't look at him either.

| CHAPTER FORTY-TWO

HE DIDN'T SPEAK AGAIN until he'd taken her back to his townhouse. He checked the wards, then headed inside. Without asking, he went to the kitchen and put a teapot on. He took off his coat, suit jacket, and tie and tossed them over one of the breakfast-bar chairs, then stood watching the teapot until it whistled. Then he put together two cups and carried them out to the living room.

Deirdre followed him, and sat down in the spot he indicated on the couch. He sat next to her and offered her a cup of tea. When she took it, he leaned back and regarded her with no expression.

She took a sip of her tea. "I'm sorry," she said. Her eyes glittered. "Before I say anything else, I want you to know that. I never thought anyone would get hurt, least of all you."

He said nothing.

She put the teacup down on the coffee table, then leaned forward and took his hand. "I'll tell you the truth, but when I do, I think you'll see why I didn't before. I didn't think you'd ever believe me."

"Try me," he said. "You might be surprised."

She swallowed. "What would you say if I told you that I think the book is magic? Really magic, I mean."

He raised an eyebrow. "Magic?"

"See, you don't believe me." She sighed. "That's why I showed it to you in the first place—when I found out you taught the occult,

I thought if I could get you curious, maybe you'd...I don't know...figure it out. Or know somebody who could."

"Figure it out," he said, still in the same even, measured tone. Under his calm surface, his emotions smashed into each other in a storm of confusion. Part of him questioned everything she'd told him since they'd met—but even with doubts nagging him, he still couldn't take his eyes off her. "Did it really belong to your gran, then?"

She nodded. "But she didn't find it in a junk shop. I think..." She took a deep breath. "I think she was some kind of witch." She squeezed his hand. "Please, Alastair—don't look at me like that. You told me one time, back at the party at the museum, that you were afraid to tell me what you did because you thought if I found out, I'd get freaked out and leave you. Now I'm scared of the same thing."

"You're afraid I'll leave you because you think your grandmother was a witch?" He sighed, suddenly exhausted as the evening's adrenaline at last began to wear off. He pulled her into his arms. "Deirdre...the other night...I was so tired, but think I told you I loved you. Did I do that, or was it a dream?"

"It wasn't a dream," she whispered. She snuggled into him, resting her head on his shoulder and drawing her legs up. "And...I love you too, Alastair. I was afraid to say it the other night because of...this."

"Because you were afraid of what I'd think of you?"

He felt her nod; he couldn't see her face.

He remained silent for a long time, thinking over what she'd said, and trying to decide how he felt about it. "How long have you been deceiving me?" he asked at last, softly.

Her head rolled back and forth; then she tightened her hold on him and raised her head to meet his gaze. "I haven't deceived you about anything important," she said. "It's killing me that you might think I have. You're the best thing that's ever happened to me. I don't want to lose that." She sighed. "Just...forget the book. Keep it,

R. L. KING

burn it, do whatever you want with it. I don't care. But please…please don't hate me over it."

He looked into the blue depths of her eyes. For once, looking at her didn't stir his body with overwhelming desire, but with something deeper. He brushed her hair off her forehead. "How can you think I could ever hate you, Deirdre?"

Her grip tightened again.

"In fact…" he said, choosing his words with care, "I might even be able to help you a bit more than you hoped."

She raised her head again. "How so?"

He held up a hand. "Wait a moment. First, you need to answer some questions. They might sound strange, but I need you to answer them properly. No more deceptions."

"No more deceptions," she agreed. She pulled back a little and sat up, though she didn't move far from him and kept hold of his hand.

"What made you think your gran was a witch?"

She shrugged. "I'm not sure. The book was part of it. But every now and then, when I was a little girl, I'd see her do things when she didn't think I was looking. Like bringing things to her from across the room. Floating above her chair. I thought I was dreaming."

"Did you ever ask her about it?"

"No. I was scared to—or else I thought she'd laugh at me."

"Did your mum ever make you think she was too?"

Deirdre shook her head, frowning as if she thought it an odd question. "No…Mom was always the practical type. Didn't like fairy tales or fantasy at all. I told you—the book gave her the creeps. Even when Grandma got sick and came to live with her, she wouldn't let it in the house. That's how it ended up in storage."

Stone nodded, thinking. "But your gran never did anything that made you uncomfortable?"

"No. She was just a sweet old lady, as far as I ever knew. Strong, but sweet. She was always good to me." She tilted her head. "Why all the questions about Grandma?"

"We'll get there," he said. "So you thought to ask me about this when you found out what I teach?"

"Yes. When I found out you were an honest-to-goodness scholar of that kind of thing, it reminded me of the old book. I hadn't thought about it in years, but it all came back to me that night. I wasn't quite honest about what I told you about that—she didn't want me to look at it. But I was so curious that she ended up showing it to me to keep me from trying to sneak peeks at it. She told me I shouldn't look at it on my own."

Stone nodded. "I was going to ask you about that as well." He retrieved his teacup from the table, took a sip, and leaned back. "So what was it you were hoping I'd find?"

"I'm not really sure," she said. "Maybe I wanted to find out once and for all if I was right about Grandma being a witch, and if she was, what kind of spells she was casting."

"So you believe in witches?"

"I don't know," she said again. "I know what I saw, and I don't think I was dreaming. When I was a kid, I used to wonder if there were other witches—if there were lots of them, you know, just living among us like regular people."

Stone chuckled. "So you didn't just show me the book because you thought it would appeal to me—you really do want to know what's in it."

"I do," she said. "Like I said, I want to know—if Grandma really was a witch…" She paused. "You said what you found in the book was horrible."

He nodded. "Yes."

"But it's not really magic, right? Kids are like that—they'll believe anything they see. They don't question it, they just roll with it. But there had to be an explanation."

He didn't answer.

She gripped his hand. "Right?"

"There's always an explanation," he agreed. "It's just that sometimes it's a bit harder to believe." Abruptly, he twisted around, facing her head-on. "Tell me about those two men."

"Tell you?" she asked, startled. "I don't know anything about them."

He sharpened his gaze. "Are you sure?"

"I'm sure," she insisted.

"So you don't know why they want it. Your gran didn't have any enemies that you know of? Or anyone who might have been interested in the grimoire?"

"Why would it matter? Grandma died ten years ago. Even if there was, why would they wait that long to try to find it?" She frowned, tilting her head. "What did you just call it? A...grim-something?"

Stone took a deep breath. As was always the case when he made the decision he was about to make, he felt as if he were preparing to step through a one-way door. No turning back.

He let out his breath, slowly. "A grimoire," he said. "A magical tome."

She stared at him. "You're saying...that this thing really *is* magic?"

"Yes."

"And..." She spoke slowly, each word coming out with measured care. "How...do you know this?"

"I think you've already worked that out, haven't you?" He took her hand, his voice soft and even. His heart rate increased; he was surprised she couldn't hear the beats thudding in the silence that hung in the air between them.

She swallowed, her gaze fixed on his. She didn't pull her hand back. "You're...like Grandma, aren't you?"

He inclined his head.

"You're a...what do they call a male witch? A wizard?"

He smiled faintly. "Depends on the tradition. Sometimes male practitioners are called witches too. My tradition prefers 'mage.'"

"Mage." She tried that out. "So...you...don't just teach about the supernatural, and magic. You actually *do* magic. And nobody knows?"

"A few do. It's not something I spread around," he said. "For obvious reasons."

"But yet you told me..."

"I love you," he said. "If we're to stay together, I'd have to tell you eventually. And I can't tell you what I need you to know about the grimoire without telling you how I know."

She remained silent for almost a full minute, sitting there next to him, still holding his hand. He didn't try to hurry her along: that sort of information took time to process.

Finally, she drew back, leaning into the sofa's soft cushions. She picked up a pillow and put it in her lap, toying with it. "What do I need to know about it?" she asked.

"It's powerful," he said. "And it's quite evil."

"Evil?" Her eyes widened, glittering in the dim light.

"Malevolent. I told you I've almost got it translated—it contains a series of extremely horrific black-magic rituals and techniques."

She took a breath. "So...my grandma wasn't just a witch? She was doing black magic?" She turned to him, fear flashing across her face. "You...don't do black magic, do you?"

"No. No, of course not."

She nodded, taking that in. "What kind of rituals?"

"Deirdre—" He paused. How do you tell someone that their loving grandmother might have moonlighted as a practitioner of the blackest of the black arts? Hardly the sort of thing that endeared you to someone you've just professed your love for.

She shifted over, leaning against him again. "Please," she whispered. "I have to know."

He put his arm around her and pulled her in close. She came readily as she always did, her own arm going around him as well. He could feel the tenseness in her slim body, and wished he didn't have to answer her question. "The kind that require…sacrifices."

"Sacrifices?" She tensed even more. "You mean, like…goats or something?"

He could tell from her tone of voice that she was grasping at straws, even though she already knew what he was going to say. "No."

"People?" she whispered. "Human…sacrifices?"

He didn't answer.

"Oh, my God…" She shifted her weight, looking up at him with wide, fearful eyes. "My grandma did human sacrifices?"

"We don't know that," he said. "She might have been like me— a scholar. Someone whose interest was purely academic." He stroked her hair. "Believe me—the sorts who practice that kind of magic are easy to identify. You'd have noticed something." He didn't want to go into the whole lecture about black vs. white magic and how neither was inherently good or evil, but this was different. "They're quite rare, that type. Which brings us back to my original question: did your gran have any enemies?"

"You didn't tell me how they'd know, even if she did." She still looked shell-shocked by the information he'd given her.

"You said the grimoire was in storage until your mum sent it to you, yes?"

She nodded. "Like I said, Mom wouldn't let it in the house. She didn't even want to go find it and send it to me."

"That could explain it, then. It's stored in a protective case— the case itself is a potent magical artifact. Magical items, especially powerful ones, put out…energy. Other mages can pick up on that energy—sometimes from a great distance, if they're looking for it."

"So you're saying when you opened it, it let out this energy?"

"Yes. It's possible that if someone knew your gran had the book, and wanted it, they've got magical detectors set to pick it up if it should surface."

"Even after all this time?"

"For an item this powerful, it wouldn't surprise me."

She mulled that over a moment. "So...how can you study it without letting out more of the energy? Is that how those guys found you?"

"Bit hard to explain without going into more detail than you probably want to hear right now. Let's just say I've got...magical protections in place, sort of like the same thing the case does. That, and I've taken it somewhere that's nearly impossible to find. I can study it there without risking anyone locating it."

"Wow..." she whispered. "This is unreal. I...can't even get my mind around all of this. It's like some kind of bad dream."

"Don't worry," he said. "It's a lot to take in. All you need to know right now is that it's safe, and you're safe."

She tilted her head up and looked at him, her expression fearful. "But what about you? Whoever those guys are, they know you have it, and they want it. They won't give up, will they?"

"I doubt it. But once I finish the translations—which should be very soon—I'll see if I can figure out who might be looking for it. Someone hired them—they're just muscle. There's someone powerful behind them."

"How do you know that?"

"Because they're immune to normal magic, which means they're not human, exactly."

"Immune to magic?" She paused a moment, then gripped his arm. "That's how they got you, isn't it?"

He nodded, but he didn't look at her. "I'm fairly formidable magically, but rubbish at physical fighting. As you probably saw. I had to take a dangerous chance to get away from them."

She must have picked up something in his voice, because she gave him a gentle smile and slipped her hand inside his shirt. "You're plenty physical enough for me, you know…"

"Deirdre—"

"Come on," she said, snuggling closer to him. "I'll be honest—this whole business has me freaked out, and scared, and confused. And I don't want that right now. Time enough to deal with it tomorrow. For now…" Her smile changed, growing more languid and sensual. "For now, you know what I want?"

"I…can guess," he said, mirroring her smile. She was so beautiful…and she was right. The grimoire could wait. Right now, he wanted her more than anything else. "I couldn't stop looking at you in that dress tonight…"

"Think you can carry me upstairs?" she asked with an impish grin. "Then you can look at me *out* of it. And maybe show me a different kind of magic."

"That's the best offer I've had all night," he said.

| CHAPTER FORTY-THREE

O NCE AGAIN, classes, committee meetings, and answering students' questions about their final projects filled most of Stone's next day. Tabby Wells showed up to her Occult in America class, but sat with her nose firmly buried in her notebook throughout the hour, scribbling furiously. Stone glanced at her a couple of times as he stalked up and down the aisles during his lecture, but she avoided meeting his eyes. When the class ended, she hurried out the door. He still hadn't had a chance to look at her paper, so he didn't try calling her back.

All day, his thoughts raced between his night with Deirdre, the story she'd told him about the grimoire and her grandmother, and the two magic-immune thugs who'd now taken their second shot at him. Between all of that and concentrating on things like teaching and not nodding off during another boring meeting, by the end of the day he was back to being exhausted. Most of the physical injuries from the first beating had faded by now, but their cumulative effects on his body had not, and last night's abortive attack had left him with some newly stiff muscles.

On any other day, he'd have simply headed home, picked up some take-out on the way, and called Deirdre to invite her to spend a quiet night with him. Now, though, the urgency to finish the grimoire translations nagged at him until it became almost a physical compulsion. He'd worked out the language now—if he could just get one more decently long session in, he thought he could complete deciphering the last of the book's rituals. And once he'd done that, he could get to work trying to figure out who might be after it. He wished he could ask Stefan Kolinsky about it—odds were good that the black mage could give him some good leads on powerful practitioners dark enough that they might be interested in getting their hands on it at any cost—but a quick stop by Kolinsky's shop at lunch time revealed a note on his door, hidden behind wards, stating that he was out of town until the weekend. Stone wasn't sure whether to be disappointed or relieved: as potentially helpful as Kolinsky could be in situations like this, revealing the grimoire's existence to him wasn't necessarily a wise thing to do.

He didn't completely duck Marta's notice at the restaurant, but when he arrived he found her in the middle of a transaction, so he was able to slip past her without letting her engage him in conversation. With the aid of another dose of Caldwell's elixir (good thing he was almost done with the translations—he only had a few more doses left, and he didn't think after the scene in his office with Tabby Wells she'd be inclined to bringing him any more) he finished up his notes in a little less than three hours.

He leaned back, swiping a hand through his hair, and contemplated the stack of notes he'd collected over his last few sessions. Almost fifty pages, describing a series of gruesome rituals ranging from a recipe for (alleged) immortality to a means for siphoning off the life force from a collection of sacrificial victims—not to provide a temporary magical power boost, as some of the darker black mages sometimes did, but to add years to one's physical lifespan. Each spell, ritual, or technique included a carefully annotated (and quite grisly) list of components and ingredients required to perform it. Looking at the notes didn't make Stone feel quite as uneasy as looking at the actual grimoire did, but close. This was the kind of magic no one should be performing, ever.

This wasn't the only black magic book he had in his collection, not by far. In fact, he had an entire shelf of his library, high up near the ceiling and protected by additional wards, devoted to such tomes. A few of them even contained techniques he could see the justification for performing—since black magic was nothing more than drawing power from other living sources: usually either human energy, blood, or other bodily fluids—some of the uses to which it could be put were not inherently harmful. Stone had performed one of them himself a few years ago, using a bit of Jason Thayer's blood and a bit of his own to summon a demonlike creature to track Verity when he couldn't find her any other way. He'd participated in another last year with Kolinsky. But in both those cases, the components had been given freely, and the end results had been, if not positive exactly, certainly not what most reasonable people would call "evil."

This grimoire was different. This thing was, not to put too fine a point on it, an abomination—something even Stone's legendary curiosity and thirst for knowledge couldn't justify keeping around once he'd finished his study of it.

What he should do was destroy the foul thing right now.

He didn't think it would be difficult. Magical tomes, for all their enchantments to keep them fresh and usable even after hundreds of years, generally didn't include protections from things like burning. Most mages assumed that when they created such an item, it would remain in their libraries, safe and away from any potential harm.

All it would take would be a simple fire spell. He'd keep his word to Deirdre and tell her what it had contained—mostly—and tell her that it was simply too evil to be allowed to exist. Now that she knew about magic—and about him—she'd certainly see the reasons behind it.

Except…

He stared at it for a long time as it sat there on the table, closed now and looking as innocuous any of the other hundreds of books in his library. He glanced at his watch: a little after four a.m. If he returned now, it would be shortly after eight p.m. in California.

Later than he'd intended, but at least the work was done now. He could call Deirdre and perhaps they could have a late dinner.

He stood, packed the grimoire away in its protective case, and levitated upward until he reached the empty spot on the shelf where he'd been storing it. It wasn't in any danger here. No one could find it or steal it.

Technically, Deirdre hadn't given it to him yet. She'd said she was going to, but she hadn't done it. Thus, he owed it to her to tell her what he wanted to do before he did it.

He'd tell her tonight. He'd give her a full report on what he'd found, and then explain to her that the grimoire must be destroyed, and why. After she agreed, he'd return tomorrow and do it, keeping only enough intact that, if Polo Shirt and Leather Jacket came after him again, he could show them that it was pointless—that no matter what they did to him, the book was lost.

Of course, there was still the matter of figuring out who was after it in the first place, and what connection, if any, they had with Deirdre's grandmother.

CHAPTER FORTY-FOUR

STONE CALLED DEIRDRE as soon as he got home. He hadn't quite managed to get out of A Passage to India without Marta spotting him; he saw her standing at the other end of the hallway leading to the back door when he sneaked out. It hurt to duck her again—her expression of sadness and disappointment tore at him—but he still didn't have time for a long discussion. He promised himself he'd come back and apologize to her properly once this whole grimoire thing was sorted out.

Deirdre answered right away. "Hi," she said. "I was starting to wonder if you'd call tonight."

"I'm sorry I'm so late," he said. "But I've been busy, and I've got some news. All right if I come over?"

"Always," she said. "I hope it's good news."

"It's productive news, in any case. I'll see you soon."

"So," she said when she met him at the door with a passionate kiss and a Guinness. "What's your news?" She was dressed casually but with her usual flair, in loose-fitting pants and a scoop-neck lavender T-shirt.

He waited until they were both seated on her sofa, her head on his shoulder. "I've finished the translations," he said.

"That's great!" Then she frowned. "It...*is* great, right?"

"Well..." He paused. "Yes and no."

"Is it really about evil magic with human sacrifices? All of it?"

He nodded. "Every last bit. I wasn't having you on about it being horrible."

"Tell me about them," she said. She shifted around until she was lying stretched out with her head in his lap and her bare feet propped up on the pillows at the other end.

"You really want to hear?"

"I do," she said. "I guess it's not really about feeling connected with Grandma anymore…I hope you're right about her just being a scholar and not actually doing awful things like that. But after all the time you've spent, I want to hear about it. Just tell me what the spells are. I don't need all the gory details or anything."

He paused a moment to organize his thoughts and decide how best to tell her. "There are nine of them altogether. Most of them are fairly complex rituals. It's got lists of what's needed for performing them—most rituals require a collection of components."

"Like eye of newt and tongue of bat?" Her eyes twinkled for a moment, but then she shuddered. "I'm sorry. I'm still getting my mind around the fact that this stuff is real."

"It's quite real, and quite dangerous. Whoever created this grimoire seemed to be obsessed with eternal youth, power, and immortality. All the spells and rituals are concerned with aspects of those."

"Immortality?" she asked, frowning. "That's possible with magic?"

He shrugged. "It's one of those holy-grail things, really. I've certainly never heard of anyone actually working it out. Magical practitioners tend to live quite a bit longer than non-magical people, but that's not always true. And magic to make you immortal? That's…" He shook his head. "As I said, I've never heard of it, and I'm fairly knowledgeable about what's been done."

"So the spells won't work?"

"Who knows? Some of that old magic is far more potent than anything around today. But I doubt it." He shifted a little and pushed her hair gently off her forehead. "In any case, it doesn't matter. Those rituals will never be performed. That's what I wanted to talk to you about."

"About what?" she asked.

"You said last night that you were planning to give me the grimoire. Is that still true?"

"Of course it is."

He took a deep breath. "Then I plan to destroy it."

She stiffened a little, startled. "Destroy it? I thought you said you had it somewhere safe."

"I do," he said. "But that's not enough. This thing has no redeeming features—it doesn't even have proper scholarly value for most mages. It's a weapon, more than anything. If it somehow got into the wrong hands, someone who might be tempted to try some of the rituals, it could be disastrous."

She sighed. "You're right, of course. I guess I need to stop remembering it as 'Grandma's old mysterious book.'" She rolled her head over, looking up at him. "Alastair…"

"Yes?" Her eyes were so beautiful, deep and blue and expressive, so bottomless he could almost lose himself in them. He shifted position again.

"Before you destroy it…I'd like to see it again. One last time. Even with…what it is…it was still part of my childhood. I know what!" she said, brightening. "Let me see it one more time, and then we'll destroy it together." She paused. "Can it be burned with normal fire? We don't have to…I don't know…take it to Mordor and drop it in a volcano or anything, right?"

"Nothing so ambitious," he said, chuckling. "Normal burning should do the trick."

"Good," she said. "Because you're way too tall for a hobbit." She sat up with a wicked grin, gracefully swung her legs around, and snuggled herself in next to him. "Can we do it tonight? Burning an evil magical tome at midnight and then making love afterward seems kind of romantic."

He shook his head. "I can't get it tonight. And anyway...Deirdre...I'm not sure it's really a good idea to do it."

"Why not?" She draped her arm around him and slipped her hand up under his shirt.

"Well..." He let his head drop back against the cushions, stretching languidly as her gentle fingers stroked his chest. She made it so hard to think about anything but her, sometimes—how lovely she was, how she made him feel, how the day's tension seemed to drain away whenever he was with her. "Well..." he said again, "we'd have to take it out of the protective case to do it. Someone might notice."

"Mmm..." she said contemplatively. "So you don't have it around here? Not hidden away somewhere at your place?"

"No."

"Hmm..." she said again. Her hand got more insistent. She stretched her neck up and planted a series of little kisses along his stubbled jawline. "Well," she said after a moment, "I'm sure you can keep it safe long enough for us to burn it, can't you?"

He thought about it, which wasn't easy. "I...I suppose I could," he said. "It wouldn't have to be out for long."

"I knew you could do it..." she said with a smile.

"I can..." he said. "I'll get it tomorrow."

"Perfect." She got on top of him, flowing more than moving until she straddled his lap, and kissed him. "Come on. Let's go upstairs and practice for tomorrow night."

| CHAPTER FORTY-FIVE

S TONE BARELY REMEMBERED the next day. He felt as if he were navigating it in a haze, but attributed the feeling to his ongoing exhaustion since he managed to get through teaching his classes without any of his students or colleagues mentioning anything odd. The only exception was the knowing look he got from Hubbard during his afternoon meeting—he almost didn't recognize it for what it was until he remembered the conversation they'd had about him and Deirdre a couple of weeks ago.

Nobody showed up for his office hour, which was unusual—the closer they got to the end of the quarter when final projects would be due and final exams given, the more students tended to drop by to ask questions or advice. He spent the time catching up with grading some quizzes, but when forty minutes had passed without any visitors, he thought about packing it in a little early and heading out. He'd promised Deirdre to bring the grimoire over to her place that evening so they could burn it together.

His mind drifted to Matthew Caldwell's elixir again; he went as far as opening his briefcase where he kept the bottle before changing his mind. He could get through tonight without assistance, and after the grimoire was destroyed, he could go back to having a normal life with Deirdre. In fact, it had even occurred to him last night that perhaps it might actually be a good idea to burn the grimoire in a non-warded area—if Polo Shirt and Leather Jacket's mysterious employer had indeed put out magical feelers to track it, those same feelers might sense its destruction. That didn't guarantee he and Deirdre would be safe from further attacks, but it did increase the odds. He might never know who the mage behind it all was, but he could live with that. He didn't like it, but he could live with it. Especially if it put an end to all of this.

He was just about to close the flap on his briefcase when he spotted Tabby Well's extra-credit paper poking out. Damn, he'd forgotten about it again. It was already Wednesday, and he told her he'd have it back to her by the end of the week. He glanced at the clock: four forty-five p.m. Surely he could skim it in fifteen minutes. He'd already determined that he'd give her a couple of points for it unless it was terrible; if she actually gave him any interesting information about the Church of the Rising Dawn and its practices, he might even add an extra point. He pulled it out and began to read.

The first page was the typical PR stuff about the church: how she'd found it when she was at a low point and looking for some spirituality in her life, how she felt immediately at ease when she entered the building, how Caldwell had made her feel important from the beginning, and how much the mysticism, the symbology, and the actual practice of the rituals calmed her and brought her a feeling of deep well-being.

Stone skimmed that part and turned to the next page, where she described some of the rituals at a high level, apologizing for not going into more detail. She mentioned how when she participated in the ritual with Caldwell and her fellow worshippers, she came away feeling cleansed, as if the accumulated emotional baggage gained over the course of living life was drained away, leaving only peace behind. It wasn't difficult for Stone, reading between the lines, to figure out that most of the "rituals" seemed to involve a lot of sex, both one-on-one with Caldwell and with groups, but Tabby was so vague about it that he wasn't sure he'd reach that conclusion if he hadn't already expected it. He sighed, flipping pages. All in all, nothing new and nothing specific, so she'd get the two points he'd been planning to give her, but not the extra one.

He skimmed the rest, then flipped to the final page and read her last paragraph, which was addressed directly to him:

Dr. Stone, I hope this is what you were looking for. I know you've met Matthew—he told me so. I know you're probably wondering how he could make me feel the way he does. I guess it's just something I can't explain. When I'm with him, I feel like everything's going to be all right, like the world's a better place and maybe I can be part of that. He's kind, and wise, and patient, and generous…and I know looks don't matter that much, but it doesn't hurt that he's gorgeous, too! (I know, you're my professor and you don't need to hear that—sorry!) I just want you to know that I'm happy, and that my life is much better since I've joined the Church. I hope you'll come to a service some time. I think you'd enjoy it.

Stone sighed; he hadn't expected the paper to take a sharp turn from "mildly interesting write-up of church rituals" to "Harlequin romance." He flipped the paper back to its first page, wrote on the top: "*2 points. Does indeed sound like an interesting experience,*" and put it back in his briefcase so he could return it to her tomorrow. As he left, he thought idly (and, he had to admit, not entirely kindly) that Matthew Caldwell must be very good in bed indeed to make someone like Tabby Wells consider him "gorgeous."

| CHAPTER FORTY-SIX

H E DREADED HAVING TO FACE MARTA again, but she'd stepped out when he arrived at A Passage to India so he didn't have to. This time he made the trip quickly: once through the portal, he hurried up to the house and retrieved the grimoire, making sure it was sealed securely in its protective case. He was back through and on his way back to Deirdre's place in less than twenty minutes.

She greeted him as she always did, with a sensual kiss. When she saw the case, she smiled. "I know you must think I'm horrible for wanting to see that awful thing again, but you have to remember—it was a big mystery for me when I was little."

"It's fine," he said. "Where do you want to do it? I'm not sure about your fireplace—it might put out unpleasant fumes. I've never burned something this powerful before."

"It will be fine," she said. "The chimney's in good shape, so all the fumes will go up and out." Her arms slipped around him. "Come on, though. Let's eat first. I picked up something from that little Thai place you liked last week."

Seated at the table with the grimoire next to him, Stone discovered he wasn't hungry. He picked at the food, but his mind refused to quiet.

"Are you all right?" Deirdre asked.

He nodded. "Just still not convinced this is a good idea. I should have done it inside my wards."

She got up and came over to massage his shoulders. "Come on," she said, and kissed the top of his head. "Let's get it over with. Then it will be done and you can stop worrying about it."

"Yes, all right." She was right about that part, anyway: he'd be a lot more settled when the vile thing was destroyed once and for all. He got heavily to his feet and carried the case over to the fireplace. She'd already started a cheery blaze going before he'd arrived. He crouched down in front of it.

She knelt next to him. "Just let me have a quick look, all right? Then we'll toss it in together."

He pulled the key on its chain from beneath his shirt and slipped it into the lock. *This is a bad idea...*

Deirdre smiled and put her hand over his. He glanced at her, and had to return the smile. He pulled open the case and removed the grimoire. As it always did, it seemed to resonate with unwholesome energy. He shivered.

"Cold?" she asked.

"No. Just...hurry up. Let's be done with this. Having it out of the case without wards around it makes me nervous."

She wrapped her arms around him. "Thank you so much for bringing it back. I know it's silly, but..." She pulled him close, gently turning his face so she could kiss him.

Stone started to protest, but her lips, her hands were so insistent...he could let himself relax for just a moment.

The sound of rain pattering on Deirdre's skylight woke him the next morning.

"Hi," she said. "I was about to wake you. I wasn't sure what time your first class was today."

He rolled over and did a long stretch, smiling. "Not for a bit," he said. "I've got plenty of time."

"Feeling better today?" She propped herself up on her arm and faced him, returning his smile.

"I am, yes." He let his thoughts drift for a moment, back over the previous evening. The burning of the grimoire had been anti-climactic—he'd half-expected it to scream, or begin emitting toxic fumes the fireplace flue couldn't cope with, or start firing off protective magic in all directions, but it had done none of these: it simply caught fire like any normal book would have done. They'd sat there next to each other, his arm around her, wineglasses in hand, and watched the blaze, watched the smoke—it might have been a bit oilier than typical wood smoke, but was otherwise unremarkable—curling and wafting up and out. The whole process had taken about half an hour, and Stone could feel some of his own tension borne aloft along with it. Afterward, they'd finished their wine, gone upstairs, and celebrated the tome's destruction.

"You certainly seemed like you were, last night," she said, leaning over to kiss him. "Very...energetic."

"I love you, Deirdre," he said softly.

"And I love you," she said. "But I'd better let you get up and get to work." She kissed him again, running her hands up and down his back, then pulled back and smiled. "You have some errands to run today, right?"

He nodded. "I...do."

Her smile widened, and her eyes sparkled. "Great. I'll see you tonight, then."

CHAPTER FORTY-SEVEN

Oak View, California

JASON THAYER ALMOST DIDN'T PICK UP the ringing phone until he heard the voice on the machine. He'd just trudged into the house, slammed the door behind him, and tossed his jacket mostly over the couch. His mind was on nothing but getting the hell off his feet for a while when he heard the beep and then a British-accented voice he recognized—but an unexpected one—speaking his name.

"Jason? Are you there? It's Marta Bellwood."

Jason bounded over and snatched up the phone. "Hey, Marta," he said, breathless. "How's it goin'?" He grabbed a beer from the fridge, then carried the phone over and slumped down on the big overstuffed sofa, shoving aside yesterday's newspaper. After a moment he switched on the TV and began cycling idly through the channels with the sound turned off.

"It's going well," she said. "How have you been? How's the job?"

"Busy. Really busy. Fran's got me running like crazy. Just got back from an exciting afternoon of researching public records, and tonight I get to follow a woman to find out if she's cheating on her husband."

"We miss you at the restaurant," she said. "But I'm glad things are working out for you." Her voice had an odd, tentative edge, unlike her usual confident tones.

Jason frowned at the phone. What a strange call: Marta had never called him since he moved down here—he'd called her once, a week after settling in to his room in Stan Lopez's house, just to tell her he and Verity were fine. She'd sent him a Christmas card (he hadn't sent one back; he hoped "bachelor guy" was a sufficient excuse) and had kept meaning to check in with her, but he'd always either been too busy or forgotten about it. Hell, he was lucky if he saw his own sister more than once a week these days. "Uh…Marta…not that I'm not glad to hear from you, but is something up?"

"It might be," she said after a pause.

Uh oh.

It didn't take superhuman intuition to figure out what she must be referring to, at least in general terms. Now that he and Verity were down here, they and Marta had only one person in common who still lived in the Bay Area. "Something's going on with Al, isn't it?"

Another pause, longer than the first. "Jason, I'm not sure I should be saying anything. It's absolutely none of my business, and he's going to be furious with me if he finds out."

Jason sighed. "What is it?" He'd last spoken with Stone shortly after he called Marta, but once again chalked up the subsequent infrequency to both of them being busy. Verity had told him she'd talked to him sometime in January, and he'd sounded fine then. Both he and Verity had called and left messages more recently, but they'd gone unanswered.

"I think there might be something wrong with him."

"What kind of something? You know he gets into those moods sometimes, but he always gets over it."

"I know that. And I wouldn't be calling if it were just that. He's been coming in to the restaurant frequently to use the portal—

several times a week, in fact, and he's been avoiding me when he does it."

"You don't know where he's going?" Jason frowned, flicked off the TV, and sat up a little straighter.

"No idea. He says he's going home, but I've no way to know if that's the truth. Jason—" There was a long silence. "—I don't know what he's gotten himself into, but the one time I was able to get a close look at him, he looked ghastly. I think he might be ill, to be honest. And I'd swear that someone's hurt him. He had bruises, and he walked like his whole body was in pain."

What the hell? "Are you sure about this?"

"Believe me, it's impossible to miss. And when I managed to corner him and asked him about it, he told me he was fine, and just needed to get some sleep."

Jason scrubbed at his face with his hand. "Do you know anything else about what might be going on? Anything at all?"

"I wish I did. He won't tell me anything. Oh—there are a couple of other things, but I've no idea if they're relevant. The first time he came to use the portal, he had something with him in a bag. I didn't see what it was, and when he came back, he didn't have it with him anymore. And…he says he's met someone."

"Met someone? You mean like a new girlfriend?"

"That's what it sounds like. He didn't tell me anything specific about her, but his whole face lit up when he mentioned her. He seems quite taken with her, whoever she is."

Jason let his breath out in a long, slow exhalation. "Uh…wow," he said at last. "Sounds like I should give him a call. Maybe I can get something out of him."

"Jason…" Again, she sounded tentative. "I think it's gone beyond that. I can promise you, if you call, he'll just tell you he's fine and brush you off. Is there…any way you could come up here, even for a couple of days? Even better if you can bring Verity. Perhaps she can…take a look at him and see something the rest of us can't."

"Uh…yeah." Jason took a long pull from his beer and got up. "Yeah, okay. I'll talk to V, and we'll see what we can do. Thanks for letting me know, Marta. This sounds weird, even for Al. I'll see if we can get up there this weekend."

"Thank you, Jason." For the first time, Marta's voice held relief, as if she were glad to be sharing this burden with someone else.

| CHAPTER FORTY-EIGHT

J ASON WASN'T DUE TO CHECK IN at the office until later that evening to get his marching orders from Fran Bartek about the surveillance job, so he got in his car and drove out to Matilija Hot Springs, just outside Ojai. One nice thing about living down here was that everything was a hell of a lot closer together than in the Bay Area: less than twenty minutes later his old Ford was jouncing its way up the rutted dirt road leading to Edna Soren's rough-hewn home.

He found Verity around the back, cutting some brush with an electric trimmer. "Hey!" he called. Then, louder: "V!"

She jumped a little, shut off the trimmer, and turned. When she spotted Jason, she grinned. "Hey! Didn't expect to see you!"

Jason was still getting used to her new look: since she spent a lot more time outside down here than she had up north, it wasn't practical for her to wear her leather goth gear, so she'd swapped to a more simple style consisting mostly of jeans and hoodies, along with the Doc Martens Stone had bought her back when they'd first met and she'd needed a wardrobe. She hadn't changed entirely, though: she still kept her dark hair in its familiar short, spiky style.

"Working hard on the magic, I see," he said, returning the grin.

"Oh, stuff it," she said fondly. "C'mon. I'll put this away and we can go inside. I'm just about done anyway." When he fell into step next to her, she said, "Besides, you should have been here last night. Edna and I healed a deer that got hit by a car up the road."

"So, what, you're going for your Doctor of Magical Veterinary Medicine degree now?"

She rolled her eyes, shaking her head in exasperation. "We can't exactly go to the hospital and ask them to let us work healing techniques on real patients, can we?"

"True," he admitted. "Where's Edna, by the way?"

"She went into town to get some stuff. Should be back soon." She looked him up and down. "So, find any lost cats lately?"

"Three last week," he said. "And one that was cheating on his insurance company."

"Excellent!" She led him inside and waved him toward the living room. "Take a load off—you look tired. Back in a sec with something to drink."

Edna Soren's house had the rustic, wooden-beamed feel of an oversized log cabin. Jason sank onto a brown leather sofa, noting that nothing had changed since he'd been here last a few months ago: still the same colorful Native American rugs and artwork, still the same heavy, comfortable wooden furniture, and still the same spectacular view of the forest out the big picture window.

"Here we go," Verity said, coming back in with two tall glasses of iced tea. She gave Jason one and dropped into a chair across from him. "So what's up?"

No point in being evasive. "Marta called. She thinks something's going on with Al."

Her eyes narrowed, and she frowned. "Something's going on? What does that mean?"

He told her what Marta had said.

She stared at him. "Wow," she said at last. "I know he gets weird sometimes, but this sounds a lot worse than that. Especially the stuff about somebody hurting him."

"She wants me—well, us—to go up there and check it out. Without telling him we're coming."

"Oh, he'll *love* that," she said. "You know he'll tell us to go get stuffed, right?"

He nodded. "Yeah, I know. But still...this is some pretty weird shit. Between looking sick, somebody beating him up, a new girl-friend, and all those mysterious trips through the portal—sure as hell looks like *something's* up." He leaned back and sighed loudly. "I'm gonna talk to Fran and see if I can get a few days off. You want to come too? Maybe we can corner Al and get him to tell us what's going on. And if he won't tell us, maybe you can do that aura thing and figure something out."

"Yeah," she said. "Yeah, I'd better come too. Let's wait till Edna gets back and I'll tell her."

"Tell me what?" came a voice from the kitchen. A moment later, Edna Soren stood in the doorway. "Oh, hello, Jason. Haven't seen you in a while." She was dressed in her usual style of loose-fitting shirt and faded jeans, with her long, steel-gray hair tied back in a loose ponytail.

"I need to go with Jason for a couple days," Verity said. "Maybe a little longer. A friend called, and something might be going on up there we need to deal with. It's about Dr. Stone."

Edna frowned. "What about him? He's a big boy—he can take care of himself, can't he?"

"We think he might be in trouble," Jason said. "And he's avoiding our friend, so she's not sure what's happening."

"That sounds like him, all right," Edna said with a snort. "Self-sufficient to the end, even if it ends up killing him." She sighed and shrugged. "Go if you must. It might give you a chance to test out some of your new techniques in a real-world situation, if he's got-ten himself into trouble again. Besides, I've been meaning to visit some friends down in L.A."

She turned to head back to the kitchen, then stopped and faced them again. "Be careful," she said. "I know he's a good friend, and I hope you can help him if he needs it, but if he's gotten in over his head again, don't let him drag you in with him. Remember what I taught you."

| CHAPTER FORTY-NINE

A FTER VERITY PACKED A BAG and tossed it in Jason's trunk, they drove back to Ventura to tell his boss he was taking some time off.

Fran Bartek's office was nothing impressive. Located on the second floor of a threadbare old building just off Main Street, it consisted of a tiny beige waiting room with a coffee machine, water cooler, and two ancient and mismatched couches, and a single office. A faded landscape print hung askew on the longest wall. Bartek hadn't intended to take on a student—she'd done it as a favor to Stan Lopez, an old friend of hers and of Jason's late father.

"This is…nice," Verity said, looking around.

"Yeah, isn't it? I don't even have my own office—just a desk in the supply room. Fran says I shouldn't be spending much time here anyway." Louder, he called, "Hey, Fran—you here? I need to talk to you."

The door to the office opened, revealing a woman standing in the doorway. "You get those records?"

"Yeah." He handed over a file. "Fran, this is my sister Verity. V, my boss."

Bartek nodded to her. "Yeah, hi." Then, to Jason: "You ready for tonight?"

If Jason had any visions of a classic femme-fatale type when he learned he'd be studying under a female PI, they'd been put to rest the moment he met her. In her late forties and looking every bit of it, Bartek was five-three in stocking feet, built like a fireplug, and had a face like a grumpy pug. She kept her bottle-blonde hair cut short and didn't wear makeup; Jason had thought at first she was a butch lesbian, and was surprised to find out she and her husband had been happily married for over twenty years.

"Yeah, I need to talk to you about that," he said. "I gotta take a few days off."

Her eyes narrowed. "What? Now?"

"Yeah. Something came up and I need to deal with it."

She frowned. "Thayer, you can't just go takin' off whenever you feel like it. We got stuff to do."

"Look," he said. "You know I wouldn't do it if it wasn't important. I haven't taken a day off since I started working for you. I might even be back on Monday. But I gotta do this."

Bartek turned and tossed the folder onto the desk in her office. "What if I say no?"

Jason took a deep breath and let it out slowly. When he spoke, it was in a careful, controlled way. "Then I guess that's the way it's gotta be." When she started to say something, he held up a hand to cut her off. "A good friend needs my help, Fran. A guy I owe my life to, more than once. So if you make me choose between this job and helping out my friend…well, I think maybe you know how that's gonna end up."

Bartek regarded him for a moment, her small, shrewd eyes revealing nothing. Finally, she shrugged. "Okay. Go. I'll do the Roth case tonight. Just get back here as soon as you can—I've gotten used to havin' somebody around to do the grunt work."

"Thanks, Fran. I'll try to be back by Monday if I can."

"I'll be sure and save all the paperwork, 'cuz I know how much you *love* it."

"So, she always that much of a bitch?" Verity asked once they were on the road heading north.

R. L. KING

Jason grinned. "Bitch? That was her bein' nice. If she was a bitch, she'd have told me I was fired. She's okay—you just have to get used to her. Kinda like Edna."

"Edna's not gonna boot me out of her house if I come back a day late."

"Fran won't fire me. I do good work and she knows it. But let's try to wrap this up quick if we can."

"Maybe it'll be nothing," Verity said. "Maybe Marta's just over-reacting."

Jason snorted. "This is Al, V. What are the odds he's gone off looking for something man wasn't mean to know, and now he's in over his head?"

"Pretty good," she said, staring out the window at the ocean rolling by. "I just hope we can help. Anything that's over his head will be over ours by even more."

"Maybe not," Jason said. "Marta says he's got a new girlfriend. Maybe it's related to that."

"What, you think his girlfriend is beating him up?" Verity rolled her eyes. "Not unless he's dating She-Hulk or something."

Jason shrugged. "Maybe she's got a nasty ex. Who knows? Not much point speculating about it till we get there and get a look at him."

"If he'll even talk to us," Verity said. "Marta said he wouldn't talk to her."

"We can be a lot more persuasive than Marta."

| CHAPTER FIFTY

STONE DIDN'T REALIZE he'd forgotten about a mid-afternoon department meeting until he returned to his office and Edwina Mortenson appeared in his doorway, her carefully painted brows furrowed in disapproval.

"Oh, bugger," he said softly. "We had a thing this afternoon, didn't we?"

"We did," she said, frowning—she didn't approve of profanity, even British profanity. She held up a couple pieces of legal paper, marked with her precise, purple-inked notes. "Just a few things you need to be aware of. Nothing terribly important."

Stone took the papers. "Thanks." How could he have forgotten about the meeting? It was a one-off end-of-the-quarter thing, not one of their usual weekly get-togethers to discuss the regular topics, but even so, he'd gotten the memo on Monday and put it on his calendar. He ran a hand through his hair. "Sorry, Edwina. Had a few errands to run after lunch, and I guess I lost track of time."

"Quite all right," she said, even though both of them knew she didn't mean it. She paused in the doorway for a moment, then stepped into his office. "Do you have a moment, Alastair?"

"Er—of course." This was odd—Edwina Mortenson usually tried to avoid him as much as possible. She always maintained an aura of propriety and professional courtesy around him, but he couldn't remember the last time she'd actually done more than pop her head into his doorway to deliver a memo or return a book she'd borrowed.

She came in and closed the door behind her (odder still), then settled her ample frame into one of his guest chairs. As usual, she wore a flowing, bold-print top over an ankle-length skirt; today, she'd accessorized it with a scarf tied around her long gray-and-black streaked hair, and several silver bangle bracelets that rattled against each other as she sat down.

"What can I do for you?" Stone asked.

"I wanted to know if there was anything you'd like to—discuss," she said.

Stone tilted his head. She sounded uncomfortable, as if she were saying something she felt she had to. Officially, she was the head of their little three-person department, mostly by virtue of the fact that she'd been there the longest, but in everyday practice that meant next to nothing except that she had to attend an extra meeting every week. Occult Studies was such a small department that most of the administrative tasks it required got rolled up into the Cultural Anthropology department as a whole. "Discuss?" he asked, then shrugged. "Don't think so. Why?"

She paused, obviously organizing her thoughts. That was another down side to being the department head: she had to remain professional, even when talking to people she didn't particularly like, or about subjects she didn't particularly want to talk about. Under any other circumstances, Stone would have been amused watching her squirm; now he just wanted her to say whatever she'd come to say and get out so he could finish the last few things he wanted to do before he headed home.

Finally, she said, "You've been—acting a bit uncharacteristic over the last few weeks. If there's anything you're…having trouble with…you're aware that the University has…options you can seek out if you need help, right?"

Stone stared at her. "Are you suggesting you think I need some sort of counseling?"

"I'm not suggesting anything," she said, her expression tightening. "I'm merely saying that if anything's going on that might be causing you...stress... either here or outside work, I hope you'll make use of the options you have available to you."

He sighed. "Edwina...I appreciate your concern, misplaced though it might be. I'm fine. As I keep telling everyone, I haven't been sleeping too well lately—been working on a project that's been taking up most of my free time."

Mortenson's sculpted eyebrows lifted.

Stone didn't miss the implication. "I've been doing some translations of an old book I got hold of," he said coldly. "Fascinating stuff. I lose track of time when I'm working on it. But I'm finished now. So you can stop worrying that I've become a drug addict or something."

Mortenson started a little at his last words. "I—"

So that was it. He'd hit a nerve. "That's what you thought, isn't it?"

"I don't know what to think," she said, puffing up in her chair. "You're late to meetings or forget them outright, or nearly fall asleep in the middle of them. You look like you haven't slept in days. You can't blame me for wondering what's going on." She subsided back into her usual settled posture. "Is it so odd that I might be concerned about your well-being?"

"Well, you needn't be. And I won't be late to any more meetings. I don't need counseling, and you're welcome to insist I take a drug test if you're worried I've become a junkie." He leaned forward, hands on the desk. "Is that acceptable, then?"

She stood. "That won't be necessary," she said stiffly. Before she opened the door, she turned back. "Have a good weekend." Then she slipped out and closed the door behind her.

Stone sat there a moment, watching the closed door. Suddenly, he had no desire to spend another hour there grading final projects. Next week was Dead Week—he'd have plenty of time to do them then. And besides, if he left now, he could take care of a couple more errands before heading home.

Deirdre would be happy to see how much he'd gotten done already.

CHAPTER FIFTY-ONE

"**Y**OU KNOW THIS ISN'T GONNA make him want to talk to us, right?" Verity asked. "He's not even *functional* this early in the morning on a weekend."

She and Jason sat in Jason's car, parked in front of Stone's Palo Alto townhouse. They'd arrived in the Bay Area the night before, but by the time they found a motel room and got settled in, they decided it would be better to wait until the following morning before going to see Stone. It had been Jason's suggestion to show up at eight a.m. ("If we get there later, he might be out already. This way we know he's home and he can't ditch us.")

"Yeah, well, maybe if he's half asleep he'll let something slip before he kicks us out."

"Okay," she said. "Just warning you. Let's go."

Jason took the place in as they walked up toward the front door. It didn't look any different than he remembered: a small, freestanding two-story townhouse with a steeply pitched roof, a single car garage—currently closed—and a no-nonsense front yard with a tiny lawn and a row of hedges separating it from the sidewalk. The heavy drapes on the front sitting room window were shut tight. In contrast to the house, some of the neighborhood was already awake: during the time he and Verity had sat in the car, they'd seen several joggers go by, including a couple pushing a baby in a stroller and a young woman clutching the leash of a large, exuberant dog.

They stood on the front step for a moment. "Let's do this," Jason said, reaching out and decisively knocking three times on the heavy wooden door.

They waited for nearly a minute without any sign of an answer.

"You think he's not here?" Verity asked.

In response, Jason knocked again: four sharp raps that time.

Again, nearly a minute passed in silence.

Verity sighed. "Come on," she said. "Let's—"

The door opened, and a familiar voice said, "Yes, what—" and stopped.

For a moment, neither Jason nor Verity said anything. Verity found her voice first. "Uh...hi, Dr. Stone."

Jason took the mage in in a brief glance, the additional observational skills Fran Bartek had been teaching him automatically filing away information to sift through later. His immediate assessment, however, was clear:

Marta was right.

Alastair Stone stood in the doorway, his expression closed and unreadable. Clad in nothing but faded jeans, he looked pale and somehow twitchy, shifting from foot to foot. His hair was in its usual disarray, his face shadowed by at least a three-day growth of stubble, and his bright blue eyes sunken into hollows. Most worrisome of all, the fading vestiges of several bruises stood out on his chest and sides. "Jason. Verity. What a...surprise." His voice sounded rough.

Jason recovered quickly. "Hey, Al. We—uh—were in the area, so we thought we'd drop by and say hi." One thing that surprised him: he detected no hint of alcohol. He know from past experience that when Stone got into his black periods he often drank too much, but this time it didn't seem to be the case.

"At eight in the morning?" Stone leaned on the doorframe, making no move to invite them in. "Without calling first?"

"We wanted to see how you were doing," Verity said.

"You don't answer your phone," Jason said. "We've both tried calling, left a bunch of messages—you never call back."

"So you thought you'd nip up here and check up on me, did you?" His voice was still inflectionless—not quite cold, but certainly not in any way inviting further inquiry.

"Like we told you, we were in the area," Verity said.

Stone shook his head. "Don't. You of all people should know you can't lie to me that easily, Verity."

"Okay," Jason said, louder. "Yeah. We came up here to check up on you. See how you were doing."

"I'm fine," he said. He took a step back. "I appreciate your concern, but it's early. If you'll excuse me—"

"Al, wait a minute!" Jason stepped forward. He didn't quite put his foot over the threshold so he'd block the door if Stone tried to close it, but he was close enough he could probably move before Stone did. "Look at you, man. What's going on?"

"Please tell us, Dr. Stone," Verity said. "Maybe we can help—"

Stone's expression hardened. "As I said—I'm fine. And even if I weren't, it's not really any of your concern, is it? Now, if you'll excuse me—I've got a guest. I'm not having this conversation right now." He took another step back and started to close the door.

Jason put his hand on it. "If you're not gonna have it now, you're gonna have it later, Al. You might be able to blow Marta off, but it won't work on us. We've seen a lot more of your bullshit than she has. Give us your word you'll talk to us today, and we'll go now."

"Or what?" Stone asked softly. His eyes narrowed. He looked pointedly at Jason's hand on the door, and then met his gaze again. "Or what, Jason?"

Verity sighed loudly. "Stop it, both of you." She moved up next to Jason. "Dr. Stone, please. Talk to us. Let's have lunch or something. If you really are fine, we'll just have a nice lunch and catch up on each other's news. Okay?"

Stone didn't move, except his gaze shifted between her and Jason, finally settling back on her. "Tell your brother to get his hand off my door."

Verity touched Jason's shoulder. "Come on, Jason. Do it." And to Stone: "Will you promise? Meet us for lunch?"

Stone didn't answer for a few seconds. His jaw twitched, his expression remaining chilled and distant, and then he sighed. "Fine," he said. "Fine. I'll meet you at—there's a little place on University called Otto's. I'll meet you there at noon, and we'll have our chat. All right?"

Jason pulled his hand back. "Okay. All right. Noon."

"Brilliant," Stone said. "Until then." And he closed the door in their faces.

"Who was that?" Deirdre asked as Stone came back into the bedroom.

He slipped out of his jeans and slid back into bed. "Just some old friends who were in the area."

He lay back and stared up at the ceiling, his heart thudding hard. Why was he so angry? They were his friends—and he had to admit, he'd been far more lax than he should have been about returning their calls. They had every right to be concerned about him. But still, to come all the way up here—he suspected Marta was behind it. He'd have to talk to her about that. "I promised I'd have lunch with them today."

"Ah. That works out, actually—I need to go up to the City for a few hours." She moved in closer, snuggling her head into its usual position on his shoulder. "Friends from where?"

"Used to be here—they moved down to southern California a few months ago to continue their studies."

"Mmm," she said. She turned her head a little and looked into his eyes with a lazy smile. "How are the errands going, by the way? Will you have time to get some of them done today?"

He stroked her hair and returned the smile. "Very well. Got quite a lot sorted yesterday, and I should be able to do a bit more today. Not everything, though. I think I can finish up on Monday." Already he could feel his tension draining away, his heartbeat returning to its normal steady rate.

"That's wonderful," she said. "Really great. I'll see you tonight, right?"

"Absolutely," he said.

She kissed him, long and deep, and then unwound herself from the covers and got up.

"You don't have a few minutes to spare?" he murmured, rolling over to face her. She paused there by the bed, naked and lovely, every line and curve of her body perfect like some kind of living statue.

"I need to get going, and it sounds like you do too," she said. "Stay in bed, love. I'll make it up to you tonight. I promise."

He watched her go until she disappeared into the bathroom, then drifted off to sleep again, still smiling, as the shower started up.

CHAPTER FIFTY-TWO

JASON AND VERITY ADJOURNED to a coffee shop near their former apartment in Mountain View. They didn't say much until they sat across from each other at a back booth, with steaming cups of coffee in front of them.

"Holy shit," Jason said. "I thought Marta was overreacting, but it's worse than she said it was. What the hell's wrong with him?"

"I don't know," Verity said. "I took a look at his aura while you were talking to him—there's definitely something going on, but I can't tell what it is. He's really good at concealing stuff."

"I'm surprised he came to the door looking like that—he must have been pretty out of it to let us see those bruises."

"Yeah. And you know if we ask him, there's no way he'll tell us where they came from."

"Even if he does, he won't tell us the truth."

Verity paused for a sip of her coffee, looking troubled. "Do you have any ideas about what we can do?"

"We can't exactly kidnap him and stage an intervention," Jason said. "You might be better at magic than you were when you left, but I'm guessing you still can't take him."

She shook her head. "Not a chance—and even if I could, what would we do with him? I'm hoping maybe he'll give us some clues at lunch today."

"If he even shows up."

She narrowed her eyes at him. "You're gonna have to keep your temper under control, though. You two are like a couple of bulls running into each other—you get pissed and he gets nasty. That won't help any of us."

He sighed and took a long drink. "Yeah. I know. Just keep your eyes open—your regular ones and your magic ones. We're gonna need all the intel we can get."

Otto's turned out to be an upscale little sandwich and pasta joint a few doors down from the Stanford Theater. Jason and Verity got there early, which was a good thing because they had to park some distance away and the place was starting to fill up. They found a table in the back, ordered drinks, and settled back to wait.

At ten after noon, they began to get nervous. Jason glanced at his watch, then up at the door. "He's not usually late. You think he's gonna blow us off?"

"Maybe he had trouble parking," Verity pointed out. "We did, remember, and we got here before the lunch rush." By now, the restaurant was packed, with several more people loitering around outside waiting for a table. The waitress had been by twice attempting to take their orders; finally, to placate her and make her stop shooting them nasty looks, they both ordered small salads.

By twenty after, their salads had arrived and they were doing their best to eat them slowly while taking turns scanning the huddle of people out front. Jason was about to suggest that they'd been stood up when Verity said, "There he is!"

The Alastair Stone who came sweeping through the crowd, scanning the tables for familiar faces, looked so different from the pale, twitchy version they'd seen this morning that it was hard to believe he was the same man. He was back in his usual style: black T-shirt with the logo of some London pub, jeans, long black overcoat, and Doc Martens. His hair was as neat as it ever got, his eyes bright and no longer sunken into dark pits. The only thing out of place with Jason and Verity's usual image of him was that he still hadn't shaved. He spotted them, smiled, waved, and deftly slipped through the crowd until he reached their table. "Jason. Verity. Sorry I'm late—had to park three blocks away."

"Hey, Al," Jason said. "No problem. Sit down."

Stone took off his overcoat and tossed it over one of the two empty chairs and sat down in the other. "It's good to see you two. Sorry about this morning—you should know by now that I barely qualify as human before ten a.m."

The waitress came over again and left a menu with Stone; he paused to examine it. "Excuse me," he said. "Starving."

Jason took that opportunity to study him, and a quick glance at Verity told him she was doing the same: she had that fuzzed-out look he was so used to in Stone, the one that meant she was checking things out with magical sight. She caught his eye and shrugged.

After a moment, Stone tossed the menu down. "So," he said. "You've seriously come all the way up here to check on me because I got busy and didn't return your phone messages?" His tone was light.

"It wasn't just that," Verity said. "We haven't exactly been great about keeping in touch, either."

"How's Edna?" he asked. "I'm surprised she didn't come up here with you."

"She's fine. Good. She's gone down to visit some friends in L.A."

The waitress returned again; this time, all three of them gave her proper orders and she left looking mollified.

Stone nodded. "Good, good. I'm glad to hear your studies are going well."

"What have you been up to, Al?" Jason asked, trying for the same lightness of tone that Stone was affecting.

"Oh, this and that. Working, mostly. Next week's Dead Week, and then finals after, so I've been grading projects and sorting out exams." He'd been glancing back and forth between the two of them and the rest of the room as he spoke, but now his gaze locked on Jason. "This is Marta's doing, isn't it?"

"Huh?"

"Don't be coy about it. I told you, you can't lie to me. *You* might be able to," he said, switching over to Verity, then back to Jason. "But not you. So, she did, then?"

"Yeah," Jason said. "She did."

"She's worried about you," Verity said. "She said you kept avoiding her, and that you looked like there was something wrong with you."

"Where'd you get the bruises, Al?" Jason asked.

Stone waved him off. "Those are nothing. They're almost gone now."

"That's not what I asked."

"And you might note that I didn't answer." His tone was still light, but his eyes went still. "Unless you can give me a good reason why it's any of your concern, I won't be."

"It's our concern because we're your friends," Verity said. "We care about what happens to you. If somebody's hurting you—"

"It's nothing," Stone said again. "It's over. And in any case it's nothing you could do anything about. I hardly need rescuing. Let's change the subject, shall we?"

Jason started to protest, but Verity gave him a quick head-shake and he subsided. Instead, he took a slow deep breath and said, "I hear you've met someone."

Stone frowned. "Marta's a regular little fountain of information these days, isn't she?" He leaned back in his chair, the frown morphing into a smile that lit up his face. "But yes, she's got that bit right."

"Who is she? Can we meet her?" Verity asked.

"She's away right now—up in San Francisco for the day, doing some work."

"Well, tell us about her," she said, matching his smile. "Come on, Doc—we want to hear. What's she like? What's her name?"

R. L. KING

Stone shrugged. "Not that much to tell, really. Her name is Deirdre, and I met her at a club back in January. She's a fashion designer. She's amazing, and she's beautiful. Can't believe she even gave me a second look, honestly, but for whatever reason she seems to fancy me."

"That's awesome," Verity said. "I'm so happy for you. Do you have a picture of her?"

"I don't," he said. "But then, I've never been much of a 'carry photos around in my wallet' sort of person."

"We'd love to meet her," Jason said. "Will she be around tonight after work? Maybe we can all have dinner together."

Stone considered. He almost looked like he would decline, but then he said, "Sure, why not? I'll see if she's interested—can't imagine why she wouldn't be—and get back to you. How long are you here?"

"Not sure yet," Verity said.

"Not sure how long it'll take to get me sorted?" Stone asked, arching an eyebrow. "If that's so, then there's no point in staying long. As you can see, I'm quite sorted."

Jason and Verity exchanged glances, but neither responded to that. Instead, Verity stood. "I'm gonna run to the ladies' before the food gets here," she said. "Be right back."

Stone looked at Jason expectantly when she'd disappeared into the crowd. "So—?"

"So, what?" Jason asked, confused.

"I thought perhaps Verity left to give us some privacy so you could ask me something." He didn't look disturbed by the idea.

He shook his head. "Nah. She's too curious for that." He paused a moment, trying to decide how to proceed. Finally, he said, "So, you met Deirdre at a club?"

"Little place down in San Jose. I wasn't even going to go, but I'm glad I did." He smiled again. "She really is quite incredible."

Stone's smile was infectious; Jason grinned. "I've never heard you talk about anybody like this before, Al. I really am happy for you."

"I've never known anyone like her before. You'll see what I mean when you meet her." He leaned forward a little. "I've not told anyone else this, so keep it to yourself, but...I've been thinking I might ask her to marry me."

Jason stared at him. "Seriously? Uh...wow. She must really be something, if she's made that kind of impression that fast."

"You're surprised. You're more than surprised." The waitress arrived with their meals, so he leaned back in his chair and waited for her to finish before continuing. "I'd expect you to be—I know this is hardly normal behavior for me. And I know it seems sudden. But—as I said, you'll see when you meet her."

"Does she know about—" He waggled his fingers.

"She does," he said. "I told her recently."

"And she's okay with it?"

He nodded. "I was concerned, of course. But that's part of the reason I've been thinking about proposing. She's seen the worst of me, and she's still here."

Jason wasn't sure what he meant by *the worst of me,* but he didn't think it only meant magic. "Al, you gotta know we're just concerned about you. First you don't ever call, and then we see you looking like somebody beat you up—what are we supposed to think? What would you do if it was reversed?"

Stone nodded. "I understand. I do. And I do apologize for my behavior this morning. I was tired, and I'm afraid I misplaced my manners. But even so—I don't need a minder. I don't come down there to Ventura every time you forget to return my call or get yourself into a bar fight. Give me the same courtesy."

"You got in a bar fight?"

"Not recently."

Verity came back and sat down. "What'd I miss?"

"Al was just about to tell me about a bar fight he was in," Jason said.

She stared at Stone. "Seriously?"

"Not really," Stone said with a sigh. "It was a misunderstanding. And it was months ago."

Verity looked like she was going to say something, but changed her mind. She focused on her pasta and remained silent.

They kept the conversation light for the rest of the meal, with Jason telling Stone about his private investigator training and Verity bringing him up to date with her magical progress. Stone peppered Verity with questions about what she was learning from Edna, and she answered them with enthusiasm.

"Sounds like you won't be back any time soon, then," Stone said.

"Is that okay?" she asked. "You know I'm coming back—I know there are still a lot of things I need to learn from you—but I sometimes can't believe how well this healing thing is working out for me. It's like…it just makes *sense,* you know? Not just physical healing, either. I'm actually thinking I might like to go into some kind of counseling as a mundane job, once I finish my apprenticeship."

"It's not a problem," Stone said. "I'd be rubbish as a mentor if I didn't give you opportunities to discover where your strengths are, and to pursue them. If this is your passion, then you absolutely should put your effort into it. Edna will know when you're ready to come back. "

She gave him a faint smile. "Thanks."

"And if you're still serious by then about wanting to study counseling, I might be able to help you find a program. Possibly even at Stanford. No promises, but I'll do my best."

Her smile widened. "That'd be great."

"Who knows?" he continued. "Perhaps when you return, there'll be a few things you can teach *me.* You've been at this for nearly two years now—that's half the standard apprenticeship period, give or take a few months."

"You mean you'll actually listen to me?" she asked with a grin. "*That'll* be a first."

"We'll see," he said. "I could stand to get my mind around healing magic, at least better than I can do now."

"It's a plan," Verity said.

They finished lunch. Stone insisted on picking up the check, and the three of them reconvened on the sidewalk outside the restaurant. "So we'll see you tonight?" Jason asked.

"If Deirdre's willing," he said. "Leave me the number at your motel, and I'll call you with the details." He regarded the two of them for a moment. "It's good to see you. I'll try to be better about keeping in touch in the future."

"So will we," Verity said.

She and Jason watched him as he headed off down the street toward where he'd parked. "So," Jason said, "Did you really go to the bathroom?"

"Yeah. But not the whole time. I wanted to get a look at his aura when he didn't think I was around. I thought maybe if he thought I was gone, he might not hide it as carefully."

"Were you right?"

"Yeah. Hiding your aura's hard. As soon as I left, he let it slip a little."

He started walking, and she fell into step next to him. "And?" he asked.

"There's definitely *something* going on with him," she said. "I can't figure out what it is, though. I've never seen anything like it before."

He frowned. "What kind of something?"

"I don't *know,*" she said, spreading her hands. "It's like there's some little extra bit around his aura. It's really hard to see, but definitely there. I wouldn't even have noticed it if I hadn't been studying that stuff with Edna just a couple weeks ago."

"But you have no idea what it means? Could it be from whatever hurt him?"

"Maybe, but I doubt it. Physical injury's easy to spot. If you made me guess, I'd say this is more related to his mind than his body."

"He seems fairly crazy about this Deirdre. Maybe it's that. You've never seen him in love before."

She sighed and shook her head. "Could be, but I'm pretty sure that's not what love looks like."

"Well, see if you can get another look tonight if we end up going to dinner with them. Maybe when they're together he'll let something slip again."

"I don't like it," she said, looking down. "It seems dishonest to spy on him like that."

"We're not spying. We're helping. You know Al. He never has *simple* problems. It takes more than simple plans to deal with 'em."

CHAPTER FIFTY-THREE

STONE DIDN'T GET HOME until after five o'clock, and when he arrived, a message from Deirdre waited for him. He called her back right away.

"Hi," she said. "Back in town. How did your lunch go?"

"Very well," he said. "Better than I expected, actually."

"Glad to hear it. Want to come over? You can tell me all about it."

"I'd love to, but probably later on. How would you feel about having dinner with my friends tonight? I told them about you, of course, and they're quite excited to meet you."

She paused a moment. "Sure. I'd love to meet them."

"Brilliant. I'll set up a reservation—somewhere not too fancy, since I doubt they brought clothes for it."

"Sounds good," she said, her smile coming through in her voice. "Did you get a chance to get to any of those errands today?"

"I did. As I said, I should be done by Monday."

"Wonderful. That's great."

"Shall I pick you up at seven, then? This should be fun. I think you'll like my friends, and I'm sure they'll like you."

She chuckled. "I hope so."

Jason and Verity pulled into the parking lot of the restaurant Stone had told them about. "I gotta admit," Jason said, "I didn't think he'd go through with it. I half expected to get a call saying he forgot they'd already made other plans or something."

Verity nodded. "I kinda did too, and I feel bad about it. Maybe there really *isn't* anything really wrong with him anymore."

"Yeah, but like I said, keep your eyes open."

They checked in with the hostess, who informed them that the rest of their party hadn't arrived yet and invited them to wait in the bar. "You don't think he's gonna stand us up, do you?" Verity asked after they'd settled themselves at one of the tiny, tall tables and ordered drinks.

"Who knows? He—Ah, no, there he is." He pointed. And then he stared.

"Jason?"

Jason shook his head as if clearing something from it. "Uh…sorry. But holy shit—Al wasn't kidding!"

"About what?"

He glanced sideways at her, then back at the woman who strode into the bar, her arm linked through Stone's. Everything about her was gorgeous, from her face to her slim, lithe body to the lines of her impeccable outfit. "Deirdre. *Look* at her."

"I am looking." She shrugged. "She's hot, yeah. But I wouldn't call her falling-off-your-chair hot. Close your mouth, Jason. Don't drool on Dr. Stone's girlfriend."

Jason shot her another sideways glance when he caught an odd tightness to her tone. Her expression was uncharacteristically flat. "V?"

Verity didn't get to reply, because at that point Stone and Deirdre reached their table. "Jason. Verity." Stone's sharp features lit up with his smile. "Hope we didn't keep you waiting long."

"No, we just got here a few minutes ago," Jason said.

"Good, good." He nodded toward Deirdre, slipping his arm around her waist. "I'd like to introduce you to Deirdre Lanier. Deirdre, these are my friends, Jason Thayer and his sister Verity."

"Great to meet you," Jason said. Close up, she was even more beautiful than she'd looked from across the room.

She smiled at him. "Likewise."

Verity got up too. "Nice to meet you," she said. "I think our table's ready."

"Perfect. Let's go, then." Stone turned and, along with Deirdre, headed back toward the hostess's station.

Jason hung back a little, watching them—mostly Deirdre—go. To Verity, he said, "What was that about?"

"What?" she asked, starting after Stone.

"You. You're acting weird."

She shrugged. "*You're* the one acting weird. Dr. Stone's gonna be pissed at you if you keep staring at her like that."

"Like what?"

"Like you want to do her right here in the restaurant," she said under her breath, flashing him a look of exasperation. "Keep it in your pants, big brother."

He glared at her. "Stuff it, V. She's gorgeous, yeah. But I'm not—"

"Trust me. You are. And you better quit it, because he *will* notice."

Before he could sputter a reply, she sped up to catch up with Stone and Deirdre as they followed the hostess to their table. He took a couple of deep breaths and hurried after them.

The restaurant was crowded, but the layout did a good job of providing each table with at least an illusion of privacy. They reached theirs and settled into their seats. Jason studied Stone and Deirdre surreptitiously over his menu, watching as they exchanged quick glances as if sharing some private amusement. He had a hard time dragging his gaze down to decide what he wanted—Deirdre's stunning beauty was difficult to look away from. Even though she wasn't his usual type—he preferred blonde surfer girls to sophisticated brunettes—she had the effortless ability to draw the eye.

Verity kicked him gently under the table, and he returned his attention to his menu.

"So," his sister was saying, "Tell us how you met at this club."

Stone chuckled. "Deirdre rescued me from a potentially touchy situation," he said. "I'd somehow managed to anger a couple of drunken young men who thought I was trying to seduce their dates."

"Were you?" Jason asked with a grin.

"I'm not even going to answer that."

Deirdre smiled, her eyes twinkling in the dim light of the table's candle. "He just looked like he could use a little help. And he looked like someone I might want to meet." She redirected her smile at Stone and gripped his hand on the table.

"And she's managed to put up with me since then," Stone said. "I'm baffled, but I've learned not to ask too many questions."

They placed their orders and made small talk as they waited for their meals to arrive. Jason noticed that neither Stone nor Deirdre brought up the subject of magic, so he didn't either. Instead, they chatted about the Stone's job and Deirdre's experiences as a designer, and Stone asked Jason and Verity about what was keeping them busy in southern California.

Jason kept up with the small talk and answered when he was addressed, but for the most part he split his attention between casting surreptitious glances at Deirdre—a couple of times she caught him and flashed him a dazzling, amused smile—and watching Verity. As the meal went on, he forced himself to do less of the former and more of the latter.

Verity was acting, for lack of a better word, odd. She said little, responding to direct questions but volunteering little information of her own. Jason caught her doing the same as he was—sneaking glances at Deirdre—but she, unlike him, didn't look as if she liked what she saw. Her face remained set in a neutral expression; however, Jason's long familiarity with her allowed him to spot the telltale tightness in her jaw and narrowing of her eyes that let him know she was disturbed about something.

Once, halfway through the meal, he nudged her with his knee and looked at her questioningly. She shook her head a single time without returning his gaze.

They finished their meals, and the efficient waiter removed their plates and took their after-dinner orders. As they waited for their drinks to arrive, Deirdre stood. "Excuse me," she said. She squeezed Stone's shoulder and leaned down to kiss him. "Be right back."

After a moment, Verity said, "Yeah, that's a good idea. Think I'll do the same thing." She got up and headed off in the same direction Deirdre had.

Jason leaned back in his chair and smiled lazily at Stone. "Al, I gotta hand it to you. She is one beautiful lady."

Stone nodded. "She is indeed."

"So—when are you thinking about proposing? Soon?"

"I thought I might see about asking her to take a little trip with me during the spring break week. Perhaps a cruise, somewhere warm."

"Nice," Jason said. "I can see why you want to. I have to admit, I was a little skeptical—knowing somebody for two months and already asking her to marry you? That's not like you at all. But yeah...I get it. All that and she's okay with the magic, too? You want to hang on to her."

"As long as she'll have me," Stone said.

Verity pushed open the door to the ladies' room to find Deirdre standing in front of the mirror, touching up her makeup. For the moment, the area appeared to be otherwise deserted.

Deirdre glanced sideways and then turned a little, fixing Verity with a cool, appraising gaze. She said nothing, though.

Verity positioned herself at the next sink over from Deirdre's. "You're not fooling me, you know," she said.

"I beg your pardon?" In the mirror, Deirdre's elegant eyebrows lifted. Her lips twitched in a tiny, amused smile.

"I said, you're not fooling me. I don't know what's going on between you and Dr. Stone, but I'm going to figure it out."

Deirdre tilted her head. "Are you all right?"

"What happened to him?" she asked.

"What?"

"You know what." Verity narrowed her eyes. "You've seen him. You've seen the bruises, and how tired he looks."

"Tired? I think he looks great tonight," Deirdre said.

Verity turned on the water and washed her hands to keep from clenching her fists. "You know that's not what I mean. We saw him this morning. We saw the bruises. If you're that close to him, you should know where they came from."

"I do," she said. "But if he didn't tell you, why would I?"

"Because we're his friends. Because we want to help him. And we want to make sure you're not—doing something to him."

Deirdre shook her head, looking astonished. "Listen," she said. "I don't know what you're trying to imply, but I'd never do anything to hurt Alastair. He's the best thing that's ever happened to me." She tilted her head again, and her blue eyes narrowed. "Wait a minute," she said. "Are you jealous?"

Verity stiffened. "Why would I be jealous? We're friends. There's nothing between us. There never has been."

"But you wish there was, don't you?" She smiled. "I understand. He's too hard on himself sometimes—can't quite get it through that women find him attractive. No harm in that. I think it's kind of adorable, actually."

"It's not gonna work," Verity said. "So you might as well give it up. Here's the bottom line: Dr. Stone's a good friend. I want him to be happy. So if you're right—if you really are good for him, then you and I will get along great. Same with you and Jason."

"I think Jason and I are getting along just fine already," she said with a chuckle.

Verity glared at her. For a moment, she shifted to magical sight. Deirdre's aura was brilliant blue, unruffled and serene. Nothing about it indicated any agitation or duplicity, which seemed odd to Verity. She let her breath out and switched back. "Look," she said. "Let me try this again. If it ends up that there's nothing wrong and I screwed up, then I'll be the first one to apologize. I *want* there to be nothing wrong, because I've never seen him look at anybody like he looks at you. If that's real, you're good for him and that's a good thing. But if you end up hurting him…"

"I'm not going to hurt him," Deirdre said again. "I have no idea where you're getting this. But seriously—I'm glad he has such good friends who look out for him like that."

"He does," Verity said, grabbing a wad of paper towels from the dispenser and drying her hands with more force than she needed to. "Just because we're not around right now doesn't mean we won't be keeping in touch."

"I hope you do," she said. She put her lipstick back in her small bag and smiled. "He could use more friends like you." She swept past Verity on the way to the door, and closed it behind her.

Verity paused, gripping the edge of the counter and staring into the mirror at her troubled reflection. Suddenly, she felt guilty, and foolish. What had Deirdre done to invite such a reaction from her? Stone was clearly smitten with her, and she with him. Hell, she'd even been reasonably civil dealing with Verity's sudden tirade. Her aura looked fine.

So why couldn't she shake the nagging feeling that there was something off about Deirdre?

She sighed, tossed the paper towels in the trash, and left the restroom.

| CHAPTER FIFTY-FOUR

"**Y**OU'RE QUIET," Jason said on the drive back to their motel.

"Just thinking." Verity pressed her cheek against the car's cool window and stared out at the buildings rolling by.

"About Al?"

"Him, yeah. And Deirdre."

"What about her? Did you check her out when you went back to the bathroom with her?"

"Yeah. And I might have done something stupid."

Jason turned his head to look at her for a second, then focused back on the heavy El Camino Real traffic. "Stupid?"

"Yeah." She pushed herself off the window. "Speaking of stupid, what was going on with *you?*"

"Me? What are you talking about? I think things went great."

"Yeah, except for you practically drooling all over Deirdre all night."

"I wasn't drooling," he protested. "C'mon, V. She's *gorgeous.* I'm a straight guy. I noticed. It's not like I'm trying to lure her away from Al or anything."

"I doubt you could," she said. "Those two seemed like they were stuck together with glue. But it was embarrassing, the way you kept staring at her."

"She didn't seem to mind," he said. "Neither did Al. I didn't see him glaring at me or anything, did you?"

"That's only because he's not the jealous type," she said. She sighed. "But come on, Jason—she's pretty, yeah. But you act like she's some kind of...supermodel or something."

Jason's eyes widened. "Hell, V, you need to get your eyes checked. She looks like she *is* some kind of supermodel." He glanced at her again. "I mean, c'mon. You like girls. You mean to tell me she didn't hit all your buttons?"

"Yeah. I meant to tell you that. Like I said, she's pretty. I wouldn't kick her out of bed. But..." She spread her hands. "I didn't see what you two were so amped up about. Ah, well. Doesn't matter, I guess. Different strokes."

"So what's this stupid thing you did?"

She looked down at her hands. "I sort of...confronted her."

"About what?"

"About her and Dr. Stone. I dunno, Jason—there's just something about her that rubs me the wrong way, and I can't put my finger on what it is. She accused me of being jealous."

"Jealous?" He frowned and snatched another glance. "What, of her and Al?"

"Yeah. She wouldn't believe me when I told her there wasn't anything between us, and never has been."

"There...isn't, is there?"

"What the hell's that supposed to mean?"

Jason shrugged. "I guess I never thought to ask. Maybe because you've mostly gone out with women. He's a little old for you, but not like that's ever stopped a lot of people."

She sighed. "No, Jason. There's nothing between me and Dr. Stone, except a whole lot of magic lessons. I don't know where she got that. But anyway—I just felt bad after she left. She handled it pretty well, and she said he makes her happy and she wants to make him happy."

"Did you look at her aura?"

"Yeah. That's part of why I felt stupid. It looked fine. No weirdness or agitation—not even that strange thing I thought I spotted in Dr. Stone's earlier today. It's just...a nice clear blue."

"Does that mean anything? The color?"

"The specific color doesn't, usually. Everybody's is different. It's changes that you need to notice: spots, or odd patches. That's how you can sometimes tell if somebody's lying, or hiding something, or sick. But hers didn't have any of that."

"You said it's really hard to hide, right?"

"Yeah. If you're a mage, it's hard. If you're not, it's pretty much impossible, since most mundanes don't even know they *have* auras, let alone how to hide stuff about them."

Jason pondered that for a while, then shook his head. "So you saw something about her that makes you nervous, but it's not her aura. Maybe you're just being overprotective after what we saw this morning."

"Maybe," she admitted. "I also want to know how Dr. Stone went from being a wreck this morning to looking fine today and tonight. You saw him—that wasn't just his usual early-morning grouchiness."

"Yeah, I wondered about that too." He was quiet for a long time again, and when he spoke again, his tone was a bit more tentative. "I wonder..."

"What?"

"Do you think it would be rotten of me if I called Fran and asked her to do a little digging?"

"On Deirdre, you mean?"

"Yeah. It's probably nothing, but...can you keep a secret? Al will kill me if he finds out I told you."

"I'm pretty good about not letting the world know I can shoot lightning bolts out of my hands," she said wryly. "I think I can handle this."

He pulled into the parking lot at the motel and shut off the car, but didn't get out. "At lunchtime today, when you were in the bathroom, Al told me he's thinking about proposing to her."

She twisted around in her seat and stared at him. "Really? But he's only known her like two months."

"Yeah. You see what I'm trying to get at."

She thought about it and shrugged. "It happens, though."

"Not to Al. He thinks things through a lot more before making a big decision like that."

"Well…" she said. "No, I don't think it would be rotten. I think it might be a good idea. But you'd better make damn sure he never finds out about it—or she doesn't."

| CHAPTER FIFTY-FIVE

"So," STONE SAID. "What did you think of Jason and Verity?"

Deirdre leaned back in her seat, stretching her legs out in front of her. "I like them. Jason needs to learn to be more subtle about his staring, though."

Stone chuckled. "He's never been subtle about that sort of thing."

"Not jealous, are you?" she asked, stroking his hand on the steering wheel.

He shook his head. "I don't think you'll run off with Jason. Besides, I'm not the jealous type, remember?" He gave her a quirky smile. "Do you *want* me to be jealous?"

"Oh, no," she said. She leaned over until her head rested on his shoulder. "I like that about you—you're secure. And you should be."

"Hey, I still can't quite work out what you see in me," he said with a grin. "But whatever it is, I think I still have it, so I figure I'm safe."

"Absolutely," she said. "I don't think Verity liked me very much, though."

Stone frowned. "I noticed that too. Perhaps she just wasn't feeling well or something."

"You two never…?"

"Oh, no. No. She mostly fancies women anyway, and besides that, I'm nearly old enough to be her father."

She took that in, nodding. "You never told me how you met them," she said. "I don't think I remember you mentioning them before today."

Stone realized with guilt that she was right. That was odd—during all the time they'd spent together, was it really possible that he'd never said anything about two of his best friends? "I've only known them a couple of years," he said. "But we've been through a lot together."

"Oh?"

"I didn't mention that Verity's my apprentice, did I?"

She shook her head, rolling it back and forth on his shoulder. "Mmm, no. I think I'd have remembered that. So mages have apprentices?"

"It's an old-fashioned system, but it works. It's how we train new mages."

"Interesting. You didn't mention she was a mage, either, actually. Is Jason one too?"

"No, he's m—er—non-magical. The talent usually passes along gender lines. That's why I asked if your mum showed any sign of it, when you said your gran did."

"I see," she said. "And I guess I'm not either, or I'd have noticed something by now."

"Not necessarily," he said. "There are quite a lot of latent talents out there who never find out about it. But no, you're not."

"How do you know?"

"I checked."

She turned to look at him. "You checked? How did you do that? When?"

"A while back, actually. Shortly after we met. I've had a couple of instances of rather bad luck with women who turned out to be mages, so I've gotten in the habit of checking when I start a relationship. I checked again after you told me about your gran."

She was silent for a while. "Well," she said, "I guess I can't lose what I never knew I didn't have." Another pause. "How can she be your apprentice if she doesn't live here? Doesn't an apprentice have to be where you can teach her?"

"She's taking a break—sort of a year abroad, with 'abroad' being southern California. There's another mage down there whose style is more in line with hers, so I arranged to have them study together. That's why Jason's down there as well, working on his private investigator's license."

"Must be rough, having your friends leave like that." She tilted her head up to kiss his jawline, and smiled. "I'm glad I came along to keep you company."

"So am I," he said. "Very glad. So—my place or yours tonight?"

"Yours. I'd like to see what you picked up today." Her smile became seductive. "And anyway, your place is closer. I want you all to myself, because I have to work tomorrow. Hope you weren't planning on getting much sleep."

He kissed her. "Sleep is for people who haven't anything better to do."

| CHAPTER FIFTY-SIX

A FTER DEIRDRE LEFT FOR SAN FRANCISCO on Sunday morning, Stone set off for East Palo Alto to see if Kolinsky was back in his shop. He, Jason, and Verity hadn't made any definitive plans for the day—he'd forgotten to ask them when they planned to head back down south—and he didn't see any particular need to call them yet. Despite the fact that they'd had a pleasant time yesterday catching up with each other's activities, the fact remained that even when Jason and Verity were still living in the Bay Area, the three of them rarely chose to "hang out" when they had no purpose to do so.

That, and his latest dose of Caldwell's elixir from yesterday had worn off, so if he wanted to see them again, he'd have to either take another one of the few that remained, or let them see him looking tired again, and probably set them off on another round of intrusive questions.

The sign no longer adorned the hidden door to Kolinsky's shop, so Stone slipped through the wards and entered. He passed through the threadbare front section and found the black mage in his usual spot in the back room, using a large magnifying glass to examine what looked like a vellum scroll.

"Alastair," Kolinsky said without turning or changing position. "An unexpected surprise. I wasn't aware that you were awake at this hour on a Sunday morning."

"Morning, Stefan. Good trip?"

Kolinsky put the magnifying glass down and swung his chair around. His gaze lingered for the barest beat too long on Stone, but he said nothing about the younger mage's altered appearance. "Quite productive, yes," he said. He indicated the scroll. "I picked this up, as well as several other fascinating pieces, from an auction in Amsterdam. Please, sit down," he added, waving him toward a chair.

Stone did so, glancing as he did at the scroll. All he saw were line after line of text written in some runic language, along with a couple of diagrams he couldn't make out.

Kolinsky rolled up the scroll and settled it back into a satin-lined wooden box, which he closed and pushed off to the corner of his desk. "What can I do for you? I cannot imagine you've come here at this hour simply for a social visit."

Stone couldn't remember the last time he'd ever come to Kolinsky's for a social visit. He raised an eyebrow. "I've still got one more favor on our balance sheet, and I want to claim it."

"Indeed." He leaned back in his chair and steepled his fingers. "How may I be of service?"

"What do you know about a magical grimoire—quite old, quite malevolent—that might have resurfaced recently?"

Kolinsky's expression went still, and he leaned forward nearly imperceptibly. "Why do you ask?"

"I'm specifically interested in whether you've heard anything from that vast web of feelers you keep active, regarding anyone who might be either missing it or searching for it."

"And I repeat—why do you ask?"

Stone shook his head. "That's not how it works, Stefan. I'm calling in a favor to see if you have information that might help me. If you want me to give *you* information in return, then that alters our arrangement."

"You have this grimoire." Kolinsky's voice was even, soft, and his gaze locked on Stone. "Somehow, you've come into possession of it."

"Who's looking for it, Stefan?"

Kolinsky leaned back. He looked past Stone rather than at him. This lasted for nearly a minute, during which Stone said nothing. Finally, he shifted his gaze back. "I have heard only rumors."

"Tell me."

"I will tell you what I know—but first I will tell you this, at no cost: If you do possess this grimoire, I hope that you have a secure location in which to store it. It is not a safe thing to have in one's possession. Further, I cannot fathom *why* you might have it. It is hardly the type of artifact you might find interesting. I warn you, Alastair, even your well-known curiosity would be better served by leaving this one alone."

"I appreciate your concern," he said. "Now tell me: who's looking for it?"

"The rumor," Kolinsky said, turning back to his desk, "Is that a man named Elias Richter recently returned from an extended absence to discover it missing from the place where it was stored. He is said to be seeking it. I do not know if he has any leads as to its current location."

"What do you know about this Elias Richter? I've never heard of him."

"He is quite old, and quite reclusive. I know little about him, except that he is rumored to be an extremely powerful practitioner."

"And a black mage. Blackest of the black, yes?"

Kolinsky inclined his head. "From what little I have heard of this grimoire, it contains the sort of techniques that even I would find distasteful—except as the subject of research, of course."

"So you said he discovered it missing. Does he know who took it?"

"I do not know. All I have heard is that it was stolen from him, and he seeks to retrieve it."

Stone frowned. "And all this happened…recently?"

"Relatively so, yes. Sometime in the last six months." He narrowed his eyes. "Alastair, it is almost worth it to me to tip our balance sheet yet again in your favor to find out whether you do have the grimoire, and if so, how you came to obtain it."

Stone sighed, his mind whirling. If what Kolinsky said was true, then how did that reconcile with what Deirdre had told him? If the grimoire had been in storage for more than a decade, then how could it have been stolen from a powerful black mage only a few months ago? "I'll tell you something I promise you'll find useful, Stefan," he said at last. "And you won't have to owe me a favor later, because I'm claiming it immediately."

Kolinsky tilted his head and made a subtle 'go on' gesture.

"I want you to give me your word that you won't mention any of this to anyone else," he said. "As far as you're concerned, I never came in here today. We never talked about any of this. Can you do that?"

"I can," Kolinsky said. "Assuming the information you give me is worthy of such a promise."

Stone paused again, then came to a decision. "I had the grimoire," he said.

Kolinsky's eyebrows rose. "Had?"

"Yes. I destroyed it."

That got a measurable reaction from the black mage. He leaned forward in his chair, gripping the arms. "You what?"

"I destroyed it," Stone said. "It's gone. Burned."

Kolinsky took a long deep breath. His grip quivered on the chair arms. "Why…did you do such a thing? If rumors can be believed, it was of immeasurable power, and immensely valuable merely for its artifact status."

"It was also immeasurably evil," Stone said. "You know as well as I do that as long as it exists, some black mage out there will be tempted to try out some of the rituals. And every last one of them is vile. No one should ever be performing them."

"You…are familiar with the rituals, then?"

Stone gave him a look. "Seriously, Stefan—have you ever known me to get hold of any sort of magical item without studying it thoroughly?"

Kolinsky nodded in concession. "True. Perhaps we can discuss them at some point. Purely for the sake of research, of course."

"Of course. Right now, though, I need to know if you know anything else about Richter. You haven't heard anything about him being in this area, have you?"

"Not at present," Kolinsky said. "But I am not certain I would hear such a thing, given his secretive nature. And if you have indeed destroyed the grimoire, then you know as well as I do that the chances are good that he is aware of its destruction."

"I hope so."

"Then it simply becomes a matter of whether he considers seeking out the destroyer to be worth his time. For your sake, I hope he does not."

"You and me both," Stone said. "Not really up for dealing with world-class black mages at present." He stood. "Thank you for the information, Stefan. As for the grimoire—yes, I took notes, and I might be convinced to discuss them with you. But not today."

Kolinsky leaned back in his chair. "I am nothing if not patient."

| CHAPTER FIFTY-SEVEN

"THANKS, FRAN." Jason hung up the phone and lay back on his bed. "Well, it's done. I hope it wasn't a big mistake."

"Me too," Verity said. "But he's not gonna find out. How could he? And besides, it'll probably come back fine. Even if he *does* find out eventually, they'll already be married and then you can just tell him you were concerned about him."

"Yeah, you and I both know how well that'll work out. Let's just hope he doesn't find out, okay?"

It was late Sunday morning, but as Jason had expected, he'd found Fran Bartek in the office when he called. She hadn't been happy about what Jason asked her to do ("I got enough work around here already, especially with my main flunky out runnin' around instead of doin' his job,"), but she'd agreed to do some digging and see if she could find out anything about Deirdre.

"She won't be able to get much until tomorrow, though," Jason said, sitting back up. "Lots of places aren't open on Sundays."

"I guess we'll have to stay until then," she said. "You want to call Dr. Stone and see if he wants to get together today?"

"Maybe a little later. How about we go down to Sunnyvale and have lunch at A Passage to India? We should see Marta while we're up here—and we kinda need to warn her that Al's on the warpath about what she did."

They arrived at the restaurant in the middle of the lunch rush, to find most of the tables filled with well-dressed families. "Forgot about the post-church crowd," Verity said. "Maybe we should come back later."

"Jason! Verity!"

"Or not," Jason said, as they spotted Marta, her bony face lit up in a smile, shoving her way through the crowd toward them. He grinned. "Hi, Marta. How are you?"

"It's so good to see you!" she said, gathering first Verity, then Jason into brisk hugs. Then, more quietly, "I'm so glad you made it."

"You're busy," Jason said. "We'll have lunch and then we can talk when things settle down. Unless you need some help."

"Of course not. You're guests!" She pointed at an empty table near the back. "Sit right down, and I'll tell Nikhil you're here. Lunch is on the house, of course. Try the chicken biryani—it's exceptionally good today."

They thanked her and sat down at the indicated table. "I'd forgotten how busy this place could get," Verity said. "I think I blanked out what it was like cooking for rushes like this."

"Yeah, no kidding," Jason said. He looked around. "*I'd* forgotten how *normal* it could be. I mean, look at all these people. Just regular people, going to church, hanging out with their families, doing normal stuff. It's hard to reconcile with the extradimensional portal in the basement, you know?"

Verity chuckled. "Never thought about it that way."

Despite the crowds, Marta made sure they got their meals quickly. By the time they'd finished, most of the other groups had gone, leaving the place about a quarter full. Marta finished ringing up a take-out order and came over to their table, brushing a stray strand of hair off her forehead. She looked tired, but pleased. "That's another Sunday crowd sorted," she said. "It amuses me sometimes how this place doesn't need to earn a penny to stay open, but somehow it's become quite popular."

"Well, the food's good," Jason said. "And so's the location." He waved at one of the empty chairs. "Sit down, if you have time."

She fell into the chair with a grateful sigh. "So…have you seen Alastair yet? When did you get in?"

"We got here Friday night," Verity said. "Saw quite a bit of him yesterday, actually."

"And…how was he?"

Verity paused before answering. "Weird," she finally said. She told Marta about the meeting on Saturday morning, followed by their lunch and then dinner with him and Deirdre.

Marta nodded. "Saturday morning sounds about like I've seen him the past few weeks. Odd that he was fine later that same afternoon."

"That's why I said weird," Verity said. "By the way, he got it out of us that you told us about him, so be aware if you see him again—he wasn't too happy about it."

Marta waved it off. "I can deal with him," she said. "That's not a problem. If it gets him the help he needs, it's worth it." Without seeming aware she was doing it, she straightened the napkin dispenser and the condiments on the table. "Tell me about his new lady friend. I haven't met her yet."

"She's beautiful," Jason said, smiling. "Absolutely gorgeous."

"Jason's got a crush," Verity said. "But yeah, Dr. Stone's pretty crazy about her, and she seems to be about him too."

"Good to hear," Marta said. "I think he could use someone like that in his life. Please don't tell him I told you this, but I think he's taking your being gone a lot harder than he wants to admit." She paused. "Did he say what his mysterious project was?"

"We didn't ask him about that," Jason said. "Didn't want to set him off again. We'll ask him if we see him again tonight."

"How long are you staying?"

"Not sure yet," Verity said. "At least until Monday. We—" She dropped her voice, looking over Marta's shoulder. "That's an unusual-looking guy."

Jason and Marta both turned to look. A man had just emerged from the hallway leading back toward the restrooms. Of medium height, he was slim, looked to be in his sixties, and wore an immaculate suit. He carried a fine leather satchel in his right hand. His dark eyes glittered, scanning the room from beneath heavy silver brows. When he noticed the three of them watching him, he inclined his head politely, then continued forward and exited the restaurant.

"I don't remember seeing him in here when we were eating," Jason said. "He'd be hard to miss."

"I don't think he was here," Marta said slowly.

Verity stared at her. "You think he's a mage using the portal?"

"Quite probably. We get a lot of them, and they're usually fairly easy to spot. You remember how it is. Never seen that one before, though. Maybe he's new to the area, or just passing through on his way somewhere else." She shrugged. "Anyway, I'd be interested to hear about Alastair's project if you can get it out of him, but I'll understand if you'd prefer not to tell me."

"Yeah," Jason said, turning back around. "He probably won't tell us anyway."

"Hey, I've got an idea," Verity said. "Let's call him up and see if he wants an old-fashioned home-cooked dinner at his place tonight. He might let something slip if he's on his home turf and feels comfortable."

"I think that's a wonderful idea," Marta said. "I wish you the best of luck—and please let me know how it went."

"If we can even get him to agree to it," Verity said. "Deirdre's probably already got plans for him."

| CHAPTER FIFTY-EIGHT

DEIRDRE DIDN'T HAVE PLANS for Stone, as it turned out. When Jason called him after they left A Passage to India and returned to their motel room, he even sounded enthusiastic about the idea of getting together for a home-cooked dinner. "Yes, that would be quite nice. Deirdre's out of town all day—she's working up in San Francisco again and won't be back until tomorrow, so I'm on my own tonight."

"Great," Jason said. "V says we'll go shopping and come by your place around six."

Stone tried to spend the rest of Sunday afternoon catching up on sleep. He wanted to avoid the temptation to take another dose of Caldwell's elixir to convince Jason and Verity he wasn't as tired as he was, but his mind refused to quiet.

He hadn't said anything to Deirdre when she'd called to tell him that she'd be remaining in San Francisco that night. "Sorry," she said ruefully. "Another late meeting, and a dinner thing I have to go to with some clients after. You can come up later and come along if you like—believe me, I'd love to have you—but I don't know when the meeting's over and you'd probably just be bored."

"Quite all right," he said. "I need to get on with grading some projects anyway, and catching up with some work around here. I'll see you tomorrow."

"Great," she said. "Oh—that reminds me. I've got a surprise for you tomorrow night. You don't have plans, do you?"

"Not that I'm aware of. What kind of surprise?"

She laughed. "It wouldn't be a surprise if I told you, would it? But you'll love it. I've been working on it for a while. So try not to work late, all right?"

"I'm all yours, love."

After that, he lay down on the sofa in the living room and tried to sleep, but his conversation with Kolinsky that morning kept coming back to him. If the grimoire had been stolen from this Elias Richter sometime in the last six months, then how had Deirdre's mother had it in storage since her grandmother died?

The most obvious explanation was that Deirdre had lied to him about where she'd gotten it. But if that were true, then that brought up several questions he couldn't answer.

The first one was: why? What would she possibly have to gain from convincing him that the grimoire had languished in a storage locker for many years?

For that matter, if she'd somehow come into possession of such a powerful artifact and actually knew what it was, then why would she have allowed him to destroy it? Had she *wanted* him to destroy it? Perhaps she'd gotten hold of it for the sole purpose of taking it to someone who could do so? But that didn't make sense either: the grimoire had burned readily in a normal mundane fireplace. She could have done it herself. Perhaps she didn't know that, though. Since she wasn't magically talented, she could have feared some sort of backlash.

The final, and probably most compelling, question was: how had she obtained the grimoire in the first place? He had examined her thoroughly both shortly after he'd met her and after she'd revealed her awareness of the magical world. In both cases, his examinations had come up negative. Further, the second time, he had done the examination while she slept, carefully studying her aura for any anomalies or indicators that she might possess magic talent. Concealing one's aura was an advanced technique even when the practitioner was awake; it was, as far as Stone knew, impossible to do it while sleeping. While identifying someone as a mage required a fairly in-depth study at close range (mages couldn't pick each other out of a crowd merely by switching to magical sight and scanning auras), she couldn't have hidden it from such a careful examination.

So Deirdre wasn't a mage. If she was telling the truth, her grandmother might have been. But Kolinsky had said Elias Richter was an old and powerful practitioner, which meant that if he owned such a thing as the grimoire, he'd have kept it safely locked away, concealed behind both magical and mundane security measures. And probably quite nasty ones, given Kolinsky's assessment of his status as a truly black mage. Stone couldn't imagine how she would even know such a person, let alone have any chance of stealing a powerful item from him. Did Polo Shirt and Leather Jacket work for him? Had he sent them to locate the grimoire? They had mentioned that they worked for a mage, but Stone had no way to know if it was the same one or if another black mage had somehow found out it had been stolen. Had they given up their search because their employer had felt the book's destruction?

He sighed, rolling over on his side. He'd have to discuss it with Deirdre when she returned. Possibly she had a perfectly reasonable explanation for the whole thing. After all, she hadn't originally told him about her knowledge of the grimoire because she'd feared he'd react badly to it. Perhaps there was some other bit of information about it that she hadn't felt comfortable enough to confide in him. Now that the grimoire had been destroyed, she might be more willing to talk about it. He made a mental note to ask her tomorrow, following whatever surprise she planned to share with him.

After she'd explained it and they had no more secrets from each other, he would set about arranging some sort of special getaway for just the two of them. And see to finding a ring.

He drifted off, smiling, as those more pleasant thoughts took the place of his previous ones.

| CHAPTER FIFTY-NINE

"HAVE YOU EVEN *used* your kitchen since we left?" Verity stood in the middle of the room in question, her astonishment clearly visible on her face.

"I have," Stone said from his position leaning in the doorway.

"For what? Heating up leftover Chinese food?" She began going through the bags on the counter, pulling out various items and arranging them.

"Well...that too," he said. "I do make coffee and tea fairly often. And sandwiches occasionally."

She sighed, amused. "Some things never change. Well, at least I know where everything is, since you haven't touched any of it."

"You seriously need to learn how to cook, Al," Jason said. He sat at the breakfast bar, paging through a two-day-old newspaper. "Even I've learned a few things from Stan."

"Yeah, Jason can make *pancakes* now," Verity said, in the tone of a proud mother discussing her two-year-old child's latest accomplishment.

"Hey, not just pancakes. I did a pretty damn tasty grilled-cheese sandwich a couple weeks ago," Jason protested.

"So," Stone said before they got going, "What exactly is it you're making here?"

"I wanted to keep it quick and simple," Verity said. "But still home cooking. So I'm making herb chicken along with a salad and vegetables."

"Excellent," Stone said. "I do appreciate it."

"I take it Deirdre doesn't cook much either?" Jason asked.

Stone shook his head. "No, she's busy more than I am, what with running around dealing with clients and suppliers and what-not. The only difference is, fashion designers get treated to a lot of high-end free meals. University professors generally don't."

"Well, you should have at least a couple days' worth of lefto-vers with this," Verity said. "I'm making a lot more than we can eat tonight." She grinned. "That way I'll know you're eating right for at least a day or two."

"What would I ever do without you two to look out for me?" Stone asked. If his tone had contained any more good-natured sar-casm, it would have been visible to the naked eye.

"Well, I know Marta feeds you occasionally when you go down there," she said. "So there's that. By the way, I was curious about something. You don't have to answer if you don't want to, so promise not to jump down my throat, okay?"

Jason leaned forward a little and looked over the top of the newspaper. He didn't miss the careful casualness in his sister's tone.

"You can ask," Stone said. "No guarantees I'll answer, though."

"Well," Verity said, focusing on pulling pans from the cabinets and getting water started boiling, "when Marta told us you weren't looking so good, she mentioned that you'd been using the portal a lot, and that she saw you go through with something in a bag that you didn't bring back."

"Yes, that's so," Stone said with care. His slouched posture against the doorframe got a little less slouched.

Verity shrugged. "Well, as your apprentice, I'm supposed to be curious, right? Did you get hold of some interesting magical doo-dad and take it back to your place in England for safekeeping?"

There was a long pause. Jason glanced over the top of the newspaper again, watching Stone. The mage wasn't looking at Veri-ty; instead, he appeared to be working through something in his mind.

Finally, Stone nodded. "Yes," he said. "I did."

"What was it, if you don't mind saying?"

Stone paused again. After a moment, he began pacing around the dining area. He stopped with his back to them and stared out the dining-room window. "It was a grimoire," he said. "And it's been troubling me recently."

"What's a grimoire?" Jason asked.

"It's a book," Verity said. "A magical book."

"More specifically," Stone added, "it's a magical book containing spells, invocations, rituals, that sort of thing."

"Kind of like that one Suzanne Washburn had down in Ojai?" Jason asked, turning his chair around.

"Very much like it in some ways, yes." Stone spun back around and returned to his spot in the doorframe. "I took it home because it's quite powerful, and it was putting out significant magical energy. I wanted to get it behind proper wards so I could study it in peace."

Verity dumped pasta into a large pot and turned up the heat. "I don't get it," she said. "You do that a lot. What was different about this one?"

"Marta said you used the portal a lot in the last couple weeks," Jason added. "Was there some reason you had to study this thing in a hurry? Was there something you needed in it?"

"No, nothing I needed. It didn't contain the sorts of spells I'd ever want anything to do with. In fact, its contents were so completely vile that once I finished my studies, I destroyed it."

Jason frowned. "Why? If you didn't intend to do any of the spells, why not just keep it in your library? You didn't think it would tempt you, did you?"

"Not at all. The spells required human sacrifices. Nasty stuff. While I'll admit to the occasional temptation to try out a few of the milder black-magic techniques, something like that would never tempt me." He sighed and pushed off the doorframe. "No, I destroyed it because I didn't want anyone else to have the chance to get their hands on it. But that's not what's troubling me."

"What is?" Verity asked. She put a lid on the big pot, got out a cutting board, and began chopping up vegetables.

"Where it came from in the first place. Or where I *thought* it came from." He began pacing again. "As you may or may not know, when I meet someone I don't tend to advertise my specific area of study right away. So I didn't tell Deirdre what I taught until we'd been together for a month or so. Once she found out, not only did she find it fascinating, but she offered to show me something that belonged to her late grandmother—something she'd had in storage for the last ten years or so."

"The book?" Verity said, stopping in mid-chop. "*Deirdre* gave you that thing?"

"You did check to make sure she's not a mage, right?" Jason asked.

"I did. And she's not. She's one hundred percent mundane. She led me to believe that her gran might have been, though." He took a deep breath, and once again appeared to be considering something. "You asked what happened to me before—what caused the bruises. Someone was after that book—someone powerful. I don't know who it is, but they apparently sent a couple of associates out to try convincing me to tell them where it was."

Jason narrowed his eyes. This was making less and less sense. "Wait a sec. What kind of associates? Mages? You don't get bruises from magic battles, do you?"

"You can," Verity said. "If you get tossed around a lot."

"But…you're not exactly a slouch in the magic-battle department, right?"

"It wasn't a magic battle," Stone said. He didn't meet either of their gazes. "It was physical."

"How can that be?" Verity asked. "You don't *get* into physical fights, do you?"

"I didn't have a choice," Stone said. "These two were immune to magic. By the time I realized it, they'd made sure I couldn't get away from them."

Jason gaped at him, wide-eyed, and noticed that Verity was doing the same. "Immune to magic? So they just—beat you up?"

Stone nodded. "They were good—no permanent damage, and I was able to use my minimal healing abilities on the worst of it, after I woke up a few hours later in a dumpster."

"Holy *shit,* Al," Jason said.

"You didn't tell them where the book was, though, right?" Verity asked. "They didn't break into your house and try to steal it?"

"I think they broke into Deirdre's place," he said, still not looking at them. "But by then, I'd moved the grimoire to England. I couldn't have given it to them if I'd wanted to."

"So they just left you there? Have they tried again?"

"Once. I'm still not quite sure what ran them off that time. Deirdre and I were out at the symphony. I went to get the car and they tried to attack me again. They ran when Deirdre turned up."

"That's weird," Verity said.

"It is," Stone agreed. "Especially since they spent a fair bit of effort trying to intimidate me by cataloguing all the horrible things they planned to do to her if they got hold of her." He paused, his gaze focused somewhere far away. "That's something else that disturbs me—even more so, now."

"What's that?" Verity asked. She started up chopping the vegetables again, scraping each type off into a different bowl with the edge of the knife.

"The fact that they didn't attack Deirdre."

"Are you sure they knew it was her?" Jason asked.

"Not positive, no. She wasn't close by, and as far as I know they've never met her. Who else would I be out with, though?" He paused, thinking. "In light of what I found out today, I think I need to talk to her some more about this situation."

"What did you find out?" Verity set the bowls aside and began slicing a baguette.

"I have an associate—we share information sometimes. Jason, you remember him—I called you to his home a year or so ago, shortly before Burning Man."

"Oh, yeah. Your fellow cat and partner in magical stupidity." Jason tossed the paper back down on the breakfast bar.

Stone ignored that. "Now that the grimoire's been destroyed, I felt it safe to ask him if he'd heard of anyone looking for it. He told me about a powerful black mage it had apparently been stolen from some time in the last six months."

"Wait," Verity said, frowning as she stopped cutting bread. "You said it's been in storage for like ten years. How can—"

"You begin to see the problem," Stone said. He looked troubled.

"So you think Deirdre lied to you?" Jason asked.

"If she did, she probably had a good reason," Stone said. "Just as she had a good reason for not telling me initially that she thought the grimoire was truly magical instead of some sort of curiosity."

"Al…" Jason said, speaking slowly and with care. "Are you…" He sighed. "Are you sure about Deirdre? Are you sure she's what she claims to be?"

"What else would she be?" Stone asked. "She's not a mage—I'm certain of that. I doubt she stole the grimoire, since it would be nearly impossible for a mundane to steal something like that from a mage—especially one as powerful as Richter. And if she did, then why would she allow me to destroy it? Aside from claiming a bit of childhood nostalgia and wanting to see it once before I did it, she had no objection to my destroying it. In fact, we did it together. She helped me. That's hardly the action of someone with malevolent intent."

"Yeah…" Jason let his breath out. He glanced at Verity. "Any thoughts, V?"

She shook her head. "I looked at her aura in the bathroom after I confronted her—all I saw was normal, non-weird, and mundane. Even if she stole it, wouldn't she want to sell it? Or figure out how to use it somehow? Not destroy it."

Stone sighed. "I'm meeting her tomorrow night for dinner. I think we'll be needing to work a few things out. I don't doubt she's got a reasonable explanation for what's happened, but I need to hear what it is."

CHAPTER SIXTY

S TONE WENT TO WORK early on Monday. Since it was the first day of Dead Week, he didn't plan on doing much instruction; when he showed up for his Occult in America class at ten a.m., most of the students had the stressed, shell-shocked expressions that told him they'd been spending the entire weekend cramming and would probably do the same for the remainder of the week. A quick swap to magical sight revealed a veritable lightshow of agitated auras, overlaid with a heavy coating of fatigue. And this was only Monday.

Oddly, Tabitha Wells wasn't in attendance. Stone wondered if she'd decided to blow off the class in favor of more study, or if her activities at the Church of the Rising Dawn had finally tired her out sufficiently that she was unable to keep up the pace. He hoped it was the former, and expected she'd show up for her final the following week.

He headed back to his office at lunchtime; he had a free period afterward, and planned to use the time to continue grading final projects. When he settled into his seat, he noticed the red light was on his phone, indicating that he had voicemail. Hoping it wasn't anything he had to deal with urgently, he hit the button to play the messages.

The first two were the usual: one from Edwina Mortenson reminding him of the time change for the department meeting on Wednesday, and the other from the dealership where he'd bought the BMW informing him that it was due for service soon. The voice on the third message, however, made him stiffen and sit up straight in his chair.

It was Stefan Kolinsky.

Kolinsky never used the phone. He hated phones. If he deigned to do so, whatever he wanted must be urgent indeed. Stone leaned forward, gripping the edge of the desk with one hand and waving his other to close and lock the office door.

"Alastair. I must speak with you, preferably today if you can spare the time. I have information that you will find of utmost interest. Please come to my shop at your earliest convenience." The line went dead.

"Brilliant," Stone muttered, standing. He didn't have time for this today, but that didn't matter. If Stefan was using the phone, he had no choice but to find out what he wanted. He grabbed his coat and swept out of the office, pausing only to inform Laura the admin aide that he'd be back soon.

"What's going on, Stefan?" Stone asked as he strode into Kolinsky's back room. "I'm assuming it's important since you actually managed to unearth your phone and call me."

"Sit down," Kolinsky said, as unruffled as if he had done nothing of the sort.

"I don't have a lot of time today," Stone said, letting a little impatience creep into his voice. "I've got a pile of papers to grade, and—"

"I have obtained some information about Elias Richter," Kolinsky said. "I thought you might find it useful."

"What kind of information?" Stone leaned forward. Was Richter on the move after all, even though the grimoire was destroyed?

Kolinsky leaned back and laced his fingers. "You know my methods, Alastair. What have you to offer in exchange?"

Stone let his breath out in a rush. The black mage could be maddening sometimes, with his balance sheets and tallies. "I don't know—what do you want? I can't do your wards for you—they still look like they'll last another several months."

Kolinsky nodded. "I am aware of that. And frankly, this information is too valuable for mere ward maintenance."

"What, then? I see you've got something in mind, so out with it, please. I need to get back to work."

Kolinsky let the silence hang in the air for a beat. "You told me at your last visit—the one which did not, of course, occur—that you studied the grimoire and took extensive notes before destroying it."

"Yes…" Stone thought he knew where Kolinsky was heading.

"I would like access to those notes," he said.

Stone propelled himself out of the chair. "I'm sorry, Stefan. Out of the question."

"Why?" Kolinsky asked with a raised eyebrow.

"I wouldn't give *anyone* access to those," Stone said. "Especially someone who might be curious enough to try some of the techniques."

"You are speaking of human sacrifices."

"Yes. Of course I am. That's what that thing was about. A whole book full of rituals that require killing people to perform. You can hardly blame me for not wanting that sort of information to get out."

Kolinsky considered that. "You are saying that you think me capable of performing magic that requires killing another person?"

"Absolutely," Stone said. "Come on, Stefan. We've known each other for years. We're associates. We share information. But I know you: you do what you do, and you don't give a damn about who might get hurt in the process. I overlook that most of the time because I value the service you provide. But I'll be buggered if I'll give you access to that kind of power."

Kolinsky did not appear to take offense at Stone's words, nor did he deny them. "Make me a counteroffer, then. If I cannot convince you that my interest is merely scholarly—which I assure you it is in this case—then perhaps we can still do business with a...subset of what I seek."

Stone fixed a hard gaze on Kolinsky. "Tell me more about what you've got," he said. "What do you know about Richter?"

"I know how to find him," Kolinsky said.

"Why do I care how to find him? As long as he's not in the area, I—" Stone stopped. He stared. "He's in the area, isn't he?"

Kolinsky didn't answer.

"Damn, damn, damn." Stone clenched his fists and began pacing around the room. If Kolinsky was correct and Richter had come to the Bay Area, that probably meant he was looking for him, and perhaps for Deirdre as well. He'd been so sure that revenge would be too much trouble if the grimoire was gone, but he'd been wrong before. Some mages—especially black mages—were just that vindictive. He sighed. "All right, then, what about this: I'll let you look at my notes, but only with me in the room. You won't make any notes of your own, and you'll give me your word that you'll neither try to re-create any of the rituals, share them with anyone else, nor even let anyone else know they ever existed. And once again, this meeting never took place. That's the best I'll do." He stopped pacing and faced Kolinsky, waiting.

The black mage paused. He closed his eyes, leaned back in his chair, and clasped his hands in his lap. After a few seconds, he opened his eyes and nodded. "I accept your terms."

Stone hadn't expected him to accept without making another counteroffer. He blinked. "Uh—all right, then. I'll bring them by later this week. You know you can trust me. Tell me this urgent news about Richter."

"He is indeed in the area. He has put out word, discreetly through an intermediary, that he has traced the grimoire to this area and he seeks information about where it might be found. He offers a substantial reward for any such information."

Stone narrowed his eyes. "That's odd," he said. "He's obviously not going to find it. How is it that he doesn't know it's been destroyed?"

"I have no idea," Kolinsky said. "I can only pass along what I have been given."

"So where is he?" Stone asked. "How is someone meant to get hold of him if they have information for him?"

"I have only a telephone number," Kolinsky said. "As you might expect, he is reluctant to provide more specific information." He pulled a piece of paper from one of the numerous cubbyholes in his antique roll-top desk, selected an exquisite fountain pen from a stand holding several, and wrote down a number in his heavy, precise hand. He handed the paper to Stone.

Stone stared at it. The area code was 650, meaning it was somewhere not too far from Palo Alto. It wasn't much to go on, but perhaps Jason might have some ideas on how to trace it further. He thought he remembered hearing somewhere that telephone numbers could be traced to their location. "Thank you, Stefan," he said. "As I said, I'll bring the notes by later this week. I'll bring some projects to grade and you can look them over to your heart's content."

"I will look forward to it. And I wish you luck. A bit of unsolicited advice, if I may."

Stone had been about to head back out, but he stopped and turned back. "Yes?"

"Be careful, should you elect to pit yourself against Elias Richter. He is a powerful practitioner, and one of the oldest currently alive. He will not be easy to defeat."

"Thank you, Stefan. I hope I won't have to. If he doesn't bother me, I won't bother him." He held up the phone number. "I consider this to be defensive ammunition."

| CHAPTER SIXTY-ONE

B Y THE TIME STONE GOT BACK to his building, he had about half an hour left in his free period. Laura looked up from her desk as he went by. "Oh, Dr. Stone?"

He stopped. "Yes?"

"There's someone waiting in your office. I told him I wasn't sure when you'd be back, but he insisted on waiting for you. I hope you don't mind that I let him in."

"No, that's fine. Thank you, Laura." Stone continued down the hall toward his office. He expected that the unknown visitor was probably Jason, stopping by to let him know he and Verity were heading home, and maybe to invite him to lunch beforehand. He regretted that he'd have to decline, since he had another class soon, but he could at least give Jason the phone number and ask him to look into it.

The visitor stood as soon as Stone opened the door, and whirled around to face him. "Stone," he said. "Where have you been? I need to talk to you."

It wasn't Jason. It was Matthew Caldwell.

Stone almost hadn't recognized him out of his black hooded robe: currently, he wore slacks and a button-down shirt under a gray sweater, and looked more like a middle-aged professor than the high priest of a pseudo-pagan magical sex church. His face was flushed, his hands moving with a jerkiness that belied his normal grace, his eyes alight with concern.

Stone stared at him. "What are you doing here, Caldwell? Is something wrong?"

"Have you seen Tabitha Wells?"

"What? Why are you asking me that?"

"Was she in your class today?"

Stone shook his head. "No. But it's Dead Week—I thought she'd skipped class to get in more study time. That happens often." He got a good look at Caldwell's face. "What are you so concerned about?"

His eyes narrowed. "Are you *sure* you don't know where she is?"

"Why the hell would I know where she is?" Stone demanded. He glanced at his watch. "Listen, Caldwell, I've got a class I need to prepare for—"

"She didn't come to the service last night," Caldwell said. "She's never missed one since she joined."

"I told you, she's probably studying—"

"No. I checked with her roommates. She left to go running yesterday afternoon, and she never came home. They don't know where she is either."

"I still don't understand why you're asking me," Stone said. "The last time I saw her was last week, when she came to class. If you're concerned, perhaps you should call the police."

"They won't do anything until she's been missing for longer than this," Caldwell said. He paced the tiny office, then his shoulders slumped and he sighed. "I'd best get back to the church, then," he said. "I was hoping you might be able to give me some insight. I'm quite concerned about her—she's very reliable, and never misses appointments without letting me know. It's completely unlike her to simply vanish like this." He faced Stone with an intense, probing gaze. "She didn't seem upset about anything that you noticed, did she? Not doing well in her classes, anything like that?"

Stone shrugged. "I've no idea how she's doing in any of her other classes. She's doing fine in mine—in fact, she turned in an extra-credit paper that I need to return to her." He paused. "There was one thing, but it was a week ago, and she's been back to class since then."

"What was it?"

"She walked in on my girlfriend kissing me in my office last Monday, and seemed a bit flustered. As I said, though, she came back to her next class and seemed fine." He paused. "Are you planning to do a ritual to find her?"

Caldwell sighed. "I might be. I don't want to intrude on her privacy, if she was trying to get away for some reason. But—" He spread his hands and sighed. "I don't know. I'll decide when I get back."

A thought occurred to Stone—one that he wasn't proud of, but with his recent focus on misinformation, it was where his mind was. "Mr. Caldwell," he said evenly, "It occurs to me that you could potentially be quite aware of what's happened to Ms. Wells—and that this whole visit here could merely be a smokescreen, a way to establish an alibi if you end up needing one."

Anger flared in Caldwell's eyes, but drained quickly away as he slumped again. "Yes, I can see how it might look like that. You think perhaps one of our rituals went awry, don't you? That she was injured or killed and I'm trying to cover it up."

"Stranger things have happened," Stone said in the same flat, even tone.

Caldwell sighed. "I don't know how I can convince you that you're wrong, so I won't try. I need to go back to San Jose and decide whether I should use magic to find her. If you hear anything from her, please let me know."

He turned to leave, then stopped and turned back. His face looked ten years older, haunted and pallid. "I'm very fond of Tabitha, Dr. Stone. I want you to know that. She is of me as well, hard as you might find that to believe. I know you don't trust me, but I promise you, I'd never do anything to hurt her. Good day." He slipped out and closed the door behind him.

Stone stared at the closed door, is mind sifting through possibilities. Caldwell *could* be lying, or Tabitha Wells really could be missing. And if she *were* missing, any number of reasons could exist for her absence, many of which had nothing to do with foul play. Perhaps she'd just had enough of Caldwell and his ways, and not been brave enough to tell him about it to his face. Or it was possible the stress of the quarter was getting to her and she felt the need to get away for a while. Stone had seen his share of students snap under academic pressure, both at Stanford and at the university back in England where he'd begun his teaching career.

He thought for a moment about giving Ed Wells a call—hell, Tabby's father lived close enough, it was conceivable that she had taken off to spend some time at home—but decided against it: the situation wasn't any of his concern, and wouldn't be unless someone official chose to question him about it. He'd meddled enough in Tabby's personal business by visiting Caldwell's church in the first place—he doubted she'd be pleased if she turned up from wherever she'd gone and found out her professor had gotten her father involved.

He made a mental note to check back tomorrow; if she still hadn't reappeared, he'd go see Caldwell, find out more about what he knew, and offer his assistance if necessary.

For now, he had a class to get to.

| CHAPTER SIXTY-TWO

B Y THE TIME HE FINISHED with classes, a brief afternoon meeting, and dealing with the parade of students who wanted "just a couple of minutes" of his time, Stone didn't get away from campus until after five, and didn't get home until almost six. He came in through the kitchen from the garage, tossed the mail on the pile, and headed out to the living room.

Deirdre was sitting on the sofa. She smiled at him. "Hi."

He stopped, startled: he hadn't remembered giving her a key, but he supposed he must have done it at some point. No matter— he certainly didn't mind that she was here. "Well, hello. This is a nice surprise," he said, tossing his briefcase on the side table. "I was about to take care of a couple of things and then call you."

"Hope you don't mind that I let myself in. I tried to call, but you didn't answer."

"Work was insane today," he said. He dropped down next to her, leaning in to kiss her. "How was your dinner last night?"

"Oh, boring as usual," she said. "I missed you the whole time. How was your home-cooked evening with your friends?"

"Quite nice," he said. "It's really been good to see them again."

"Have they gone back home, or are they still visiting?"

"I think they went home today. I know they've got jobs and whatnot, and we said our goodbyes last night. I've got some nice leftovers from dinner, if you're interested—but wait. You said you had a surprise for me, didn't you?"

"I do. I'm so excited about it. Like I said, I've been working on it for a while now. And I just know you're going to love it." She turned to face him, her blue eyes twinkling with amusement.

"Can't wait to see it. And I'd like to chat with you about something after," he said.

"Oh, really? What?"

"It can wait," he said. "Show me your surprise."

"I can't show it to you here," she said. "We need to go to where it is." She stroked his jawline.

"And where is it?"

"Well, that's part of the surprise, silly. Remember all those errands you've been doing this week? You did finish the last of them today, didn't you?"

He nodded. "I've got the rest in my car. That last bit was hard to find, since I couldn't go to my usual suppliers. I had to improvise."

She kissed him. "I'm sure you did fine, love," she said.

"I hope so," he said, and smiled. Sometimes it amazed him that, even after all the time they had spent together in the last couple of months, he never failed to get lost in the deep, fathomless loveliness of her eyes.

"And now, you get to see what I wanted you to pick up all those things for," she said. "Come on—my surprise doesn't include dinner, so let's have some of those nice leftovers you were talking about. And then we can go. You drive, and I'll tell you where we're headed. We'll finish up tonight, and then afterward…oh, I want to make love with you all night."

"That sounds wonderful," Stone murmured.

"Oh, it will be." She kissed him again, her lips hot and hungry and sensual. "You just wait and see."

Verity lounged on the lumpy motel bed, reading a fantasy novel she'd picked up at a nearby drugstore. "How long are we gonna wait?" she asked Jason. "Maybe Fran hasn't got anything. Wouldn't she have called back by now if she did?"

Jason shrugged. "Yeah, probably. But at this point, we might as well wait and go back tomorrow." He glanced at his watch. "Getting close to six. If we left now, we wouldn't get home until after midnight. You want to get some dinner? Maybe we can catch a movie or something."

"Might as well." She tossed the book on the bed and sat up. "We—"

The phone rang.

Jason grabbed it. "Hello?" He paused. "Oh. Hey, Fran. Hang on, let me put you on the speaker so V can hear too." He hit a button on the phone.

Fran's gravelly voice came out of the tinny speaker: "…know I got other things t'do besides track down info for you for free, Thayer. Had to deal with the payin' customers first."

"That's fine," Jason said. "Thanks, Fran. We appreciate anything you got. So, did you get anything?"

"You sure you got the name right? Deirdre Lanier, right?" She spelled it out.

"I'm not sure how it's spelled, but that sounds right. Why?"

"And you said she's some kinda fashion designer, and lives in the Bay Area? Five-ten, Caucasian, brown, blue, super hot, about your age?"

Jason glanced at Verity, who shrugged. "Yeah, that's our best guess. We didn't exactly sneak a peek at her driver's license or anything. That's kinda the point of this—we're tryin' to do it discreetly."

Fran's sigh came through even out of the crappy motel-phone speaker. "I got nothin', Thayer."

"What do you mean?" He exchanged another glance with Verity. "You mean you didn't find anything about her?"

"I mean, she don't seem to exist. I found nobody by that name anywhere in the Bay Area for the last three years. There's a few

Laniers and a whole shitload of Deirdres, obviously, but never to-gether. Couldn't find any records of her renting a house, no Social Security number, no driver's license, no tax records, nothin'. I even called a couple o' friends of friends in the fashion industry, and they checked with contacts up there. Nobody's ever heard of her. If she's as hot as you say, *somebody* would have remembered her. Even gay dudes notice women like that."

Jason stared at the phone. "So…she's either using an assumed name, she's hiding from something, or both."

"Dunno. Could be any number of things. She might be tryin' to get away from an ex, or some kinda stalker. Women sometimes change their names and move far away to do that. But if you can't give me any more to go by—like where she maybe came from in the first place—I can't get too much more without a whole lot more digging than I'm gonna do for free. I just don't have time, Thayer. You know how swamped we are. Which reminds me—when you comin' back?"

"Soon," he said. "Next day or two, I hope." He let out a loud sigh. "Thanks, Fran. I owe you one for this."

"Oh—one more thing, in case you care: I didn't find her on any wanted lists, and nobody with that description's escaped from a prison or a funny farm, at least around here or the Bay Area."

"That's…uh…good to know. Thanks, Fran."

He hung up the phone slowly, slumped down onto his bed, and faced Verity. "Well…fuck. I don't even know what to make of any of that."

"Except it sounds like she's not who she claims to be," Verity said.

"Yeah."

"And much as he's gonna hate us for digging in his business, Dr. Stone really ought to know about it."

"Yeah," Jason said again, heavily. "C'mon. Let's go over there and see if he's home."

| CHAPTER SIXTY-THREE

S TONE GATHERED UP the plates and carried them to the kitchen. "See?" he called. "I told you Verity is quite an amazing cook."

"She is," Deirdre agreed. She lounged in the doorway like a satisfied cat. "Come on...leave the dishes, though. We'll do them when we get back."

He smiled, coming over to pull her into an embrace. He gently kissed along the edge of her ear. "Are you sure you won't give me any hints about your surprise?"

"Oh, no. That would spoil everything. We—"

The doorbell rang.

"Just a minute," Stone said, irritated. "It's probably the Jehovah's Witnesses or something, trying to save my soul. I'll get rid of them."

He hurried down the hall and opened the door.

Jason and Verity stood on the front step. Both of them looked tense, unable to stand still. "Oh, thank God," Verity said. "You're here."

Stone stared at them, puzzled. "What are you two doing here? I thought you went back home today."

Jason dropped his voice so it barely carried to Stone. "Listen, Al. We've got something important we need to tell you. Can we come in?"

"This isn't a good time—" Stone said. He glanced back over his shoulder. Deirdre lounged at the other end of the hall, watching him. She smiled.

"It's really important," Verity insisted, trying to look past Stone. "Is Deirdre here?"

Stone frowned. "Yes, she's here. We were just about to leave—"

"Look," Jason said. His gaze shifted from Stone to some point over his shoulder as if looking for something, then back to Stone. "It's about Deirdre. You can hate us later, but we have to tell you this."

"Tell me what?"

"Alastair?" Deirdre called. "Are you coming? We're going to be late if we don't leave soon."

"There's something up about Deirdre," Jason said. "Something weird. Like, there's no record of her anywhere. As far as any official records around here are concerned, nobody by the name of Deirdre Lanier exists."

Stone stiffened. "You checked up on Deirdre? Why in the hell would you--?"

Jason shoved into the house before Stone could stop him, and Verity followed behind him. "Look, Al," he said, louder now. "Like I said, you can hate us later. But something fishy's going on here. Maybe you don't see it because you're too close to it, but it is."

Verity closed the door behind her.

Stone glared at them. "You two have overstepped yourselves," he said, his voice tight with anger. "I suggest you get the hell out of here before I escort you out. You won't like how I do it."

Jason ignored him and moved past him. Deirdre still stood in the same place at the end of the hall, leaning in the doorway with her arms crossed over her chest. "What's going on with you?" he asked her. "Why don't you show up in any public records? Why are you faking your identity? What are you hiding?"

She smiled. "Oh, Jason…it's so great the way you're trying to protect Alastair. You're a good friend, you really are. Smart, too.

You're the first one who's figured it out. But I really do have a good explanation. If you'll calm down, I'll tell you. All right?"

Jason stopped. For a moment, he stood without moving, a few feet away from Deirdre. "Yeah…" he said slowly. "Yeah, okay. I'm sure you do."

"Of course she does," Stone said. What was Jason talking about? Deirdre was using an assumed name? That was the first time he'd heard anything about that. But of course she must have a good explanation for it. "Come on," he said. "Let's go sit down, and you can explain it, Deirdre."

"Have you people all gone *crazy?*" Verity yelled. She looked back and forth between Jason, Stone, and Deirdre. "Jason, what the hell are you talking about?"

"Come on, V, let's just listen to her. We kinda screwed up coming over here guns blazing like this. Let's just let her talk."

"Yes," Stone said. "Come on."

Verity stood for a moment, her gaze shifting away. "Jason," she said, "Listen to me. You've got that same weird thing on your aura that Dr. Stone had. Remember I told you about it before? She's *doing* something to you. Both of you! Can't you see it?" She took a step forward toward Deirdre, eyes alight with anger. "Whatever it is, you'd better fucking knock it off *right now.*"

Deirdre glanced at Verity, then turned her attention to Stone and Jason. "Alastair…Jason…I think there's something wrong with Verity. I don't understand why she hates me so much, but she's scaring me. Jason, maybe you should take her home. I'll explain everything to Alastair, and he can tell you tomorrow."

Jason nodded. "Yeah, maybe you're right. She's been acting weird lately—I think she's just tired." He turned. "C'mon V, she's right. Deirdre and Al can work it out. It's really not our business anyway."

Verity, eyes wide, took a step backward. "Jason, damn it, snap *out* of it! I'm telling you, she's doing something to you! To your mind!"

"Delusional," Deirdre said, shaking her head sadly. "Too much stress."

"Like *hell!*" Verity backpedaled a couple more steps, then pointed both hands at Deirdre. Magical energy crackled around them for a moment, and then she released it.

It arced down the narrow hall, past Jason, and hit Deirdre in the center of her chest.

"*No!*" Stone yelled. He lunged forward past Jason and flung a concussion beam at Verity.

It happened so fast she didn't have time to get a shield up. The beam hit her in the side, driving her backward. She made a little yelp that was as much surprise as pain, crashed into the wall, and slid down to the floor in a heap.

Jason went stiff. "Fuck!" he yelled, his face reddening with rage. He whirled around and, moving fast and without warning, lashed out with his fist at Stone.

Stone had no chance to react. His vision filled with Jason's rage-wreathed face. Jason's fist came in too fast for him to do anything, except to begin raising his hands to ward off the blow. He didn't get them high enough in time.

Jason's fist slammed into his jaw.

Stars sprang up in his vision.

The blackness rose and took him before he hit the floor. The last thing he saw before he passed out was Deirdre, standing at the end of the hall, unharmed.

| CHAPTER SIXTY-FOUR

STONE BLINKED. Urging his leaden arms to action, he brought his hands up to scrub at his face.

Pain flared. He jerked his hand away from his jaw.

With frustrating slowness, the fog lifted from his brain. He lay on the floor, pushed against the wall in the hallway of his townhouse. What was he doing here? What had happened?

It came back, all at once. He sat up fast, then slouched back against the wall when the dizziness hit.

The house was quiet. An instinct, a sort of deep-down affinity over his years living in the place, told him he was alone.

Deirdre was gone.

Jason and Verity were gone.

Dear gods—had he really hit Verity with a concussion beam? His heart thudded in his chest, and his breath came faster as a chill fell over him. He replayed the scene: his enraged strike, her yelp of pain and surprise, the way she reeled back and slammed into the wall.

The way she'd fallen.

Had he hurt her badly?

Had he killed her?

And what about Deirdre? Verity had hit her too.

Why were they all gone?

Why had they left him here, sprawled against the wall like some toy everyone had tired of playing with?

He rubbed his jaw again, wincing. Jason hadn't held anything back when he'd hit him. It might be cracked.

I have to get going. I have to find them. The compulsion to leap up and go after them, even though he had no idea where they'd gone, was so strong he could barely resist it, but he did so nonetheless. He leaned his weight back against the wall, took a few deep, centering breaths, and tried his best to concentrate sufficiently to manage a healing spell.

Verity should be doing this. She's better at it than I am.

You attacked Verity. You might have killed her.

He drove the thought down, seeking calm, tranquility, peace where none existed.

A few more deep breaths.

Relax. *Relax…*

He felt the warmth growing, and closed his eyes, directing it where it was needed. It settled around his jaw, enveloping the injury in a cocoon of soothing, golden healing energy. This was easier, even for him, than healing what Polo Shirt and Leather Jacket had done to him—single injuries were always less complicated to heal than multiples.

When he finished, he let himself stay there for just a few seconds, relishing the absence of pain. He probed his jaw with two fingers; nothing flared. A bit of the dizziness still remained, but he ignored it. He didn't have time to rest.

He dragged himself up. "Deirdre?" he called. "Jason? Verity?" He knew it was futile, that they were all gone, but he did it anyway. "Is anyone here?"

Silence.

He glanced at his watch: a little after six thirty.

Where *was* everyone?

He strode out to the kitchen, snatched up the phone, and called Deirdre's place. It rang several times, and then the beep sounded. He hung up without leaving a message.

Next, he dug the number of Jason's and Verity's motel room from the pile of papers on the breakfast bar and called that. Once again, it rang several times before redirecting to the motel's front desk. He hung up again.

Where were they? Had he hurt Verity badly enough that Jason had to take her to the hospital? That didn't make sense, though: Jason wouldn't have taken her away on his own if she was injured. And if he'd called an ambulance to the house, they wouldn't have left Stone unconscious in the hallway. If Verity had hurt Deirdre, they wouldn't have left her, either.

Except Verity hadn't hurt her. He'd seen his apprentice's magical blast hit her in the center of her chest, but she hadn't been harmed.

Had she?

Had Verity's spell missed?

As he stood there in the kitchen, his gaze fell on the door leading to the garage. He remembered telling Deirdre that he'd left something in the trunk, but he couldn't remember what it was. That was odd. It had seemed very important to him earlier today— something she'd wanted him to be sure to get. If Verity had somehow missed her with the spell, might she have gone out there to retrieve it before she left?

Stone took another look around the kitchen, then opened the door and switched on the light. The black BMW sat undisturbed in the narrow, single-car garage.

He reached into his pocket and hit the button to open the trunk.

Inside was a small duffel bag made of green canvas. Stone didn't recognize it; it certainly wasn't something he'd brought with him. He bent, unzipped it, and peered inside, but it was too dark to see the contents. Heart still beating hard, he picked up the bag and took it back into the kitchen, where he dumped it onto the breakfast bar.

Several items tumbled out. He stared at them, blinking in confusion.

Rolling around on top of his pile of old mail and discarded newspapers were several vials containing what looked like blood, along with a small collection of gnarled, desiccated objects that might have come from animals, two large, black-feathered birds' wings with dried blood on the points where they would attach, and a sealed jar with what appeared to be a miniature preserved organ of some sort floating in it.

Stone gripped the edge of the counter, shaking. What had he done today? He didn't remember collecting any of these items, but he did remember stopping to do something on the way home from work. Perhaps someone had left the duffel bag and the items in his trunk, or he'd stopped somewhere and allowed them to put it there. He squeezed his eyes shut, trying to force his brain to bring back the memories that eluded him. At first, all he got was that Deirdre had asked him to run errands. He'd done the same thing over the weekend. She'd wanted him to pick something up.

Then, as suddenly as if someone had just placed it there for him to find, another memory returned. This one hit him so hard he swayed on his feet, and would have fallen if he hadn't been maintaining a death grip on the breakfast bar.

No.

This can't be happening.

She can't be involved in this.

He stared at the items again.

The items that were some of the components in one of the grimoire's rituals.

Weakness and nausea slammed into him like a cresting wave, his hands going white where they gripped the counter. He swallowed several times, forcing down the nausea. *No...*

The doorbell rang.

He stiffened.

Who could that be? Had Jason and Verity returned? Had Deirdre? Hastily, he gathered up the items on the counter and tossed them back in the bag, which he zipped up.

The bell rang again. More urgently this time.

He dropped the bag behind the kitchen counter and hurried down the hall. He opened the door.

Deirdre stood there, her hand in mid-reach toward the doorbell.

Stone stared at her in shock. Every time he had ever seen her, even first thing in the morning when she'd just woke up, she always looked utterly put together, with every line of her clothes perfect, her face smooth and lovely.

She didn't look that way now. Her eyes were wide, her expression terrified, her clothes in disarray. "Deirdre? What's happened?"

"Alastair," she said, with breathless urgency. She grasped his arm. "You have to help me. Everything's gone wrong!"

| CHAPTER SIXTY-FIVE

MOVEMENT, THE SENSATION OF starting and stopping, brought Verity back to wakefulness. She cracked open her eyes, and her first sight was the familiar tattered tan headliner of Jason's car. She was belted into a seat, which had been pushed all the way back until it was almost reclining. Twisting, she saw her brother in the driver's seat, both hands gripping the steering wheel, looking straight ahead. "...Jason?"

Jason glanced over at the passenger seat, then went back to watching the traffic without acknowledging that his sister had spoken.

"Jason?" she said again, louder. "What's...going on?" She fumbled at the side of the seat with her right hand until she found the control to return the seat to its upright position. Her left arm throbbed, and blazed pain when she tried to move it.

"Don't worry," he said. "Everything's gonna be fine."

She shifted again. "Ow. Where the hell are we?" Memories came back: her anger at Deirdre, hitting her with a spell. Stone's enraged roar. The concussion beam slamming her into a wall. Jason's wild lunge. Why weren't they back at Stone's place? "Jason, why are we driving? Where's Dr. Stone?"

"Back at his place, I guess. I don't know. I don't give a damn."

She grabbed his arm, hard, ignoring the pain in her own. "Jason! Damn it, what's going on with you? We have to get back there!"

"We're not going back. He hurt you, V."

"I know—but he didn't mean to. I hit Deirdre with a spell. I had to stop her from doing whatever she was doing."

"She wasn't doing anything. Why'd you hit her?"

"Where are we?" She looked around, trying to figure out where the car was headed. The freeway was packed with commuter traffic, creeping along at about twenty miles per hour. Taillights flared bright red as the whole line of traffic periodically ground to a halt. "Are we in *San Jose?*"

"I guess. I've just been driving."

"Jason!" She squeezed his arm again, and shook it. "Pull *off* the freeway. *Now.* We gotta get this straightened out. We need to get back to Dr. Stone before Deirdre does something to him."

"She's not gonna do anything to him, V. I don't know why you keep thinking that."

Verity let out a loud sigh. Every time Jason got near Deirdre, his common sense went out the window, and he forgot every bit of his distrust of her. "*Listen* to me," she said, loudly. "Don't your remember? We were going over there to tell Dr. Stone about how Deirdre doesn't exist. Remember? You had Fran check? After we said something about it, that's when everything got fucked up." She shook him again. "Damn it, *remember!*"

It almost seemed for a moment as if he was beginning to. His grip on the wheel loosened, and his eyes shifted to her and back to the road. Uncertainty flitted across his face.

"Pull this car off the freeway *now,* Jason, or I swear, I'll knock you out right here." She raised her right hand, flaring energy around it in a passable imitation of Stone's favorite magical intimidation gesture.

Jason glanced over at her again. "Fine," he said. "Fine. But we're not going back there."

"Just pull off. Go park somewhere. I'm gonna heal my arm."

She waited long enough to make sure Jason was making headway toward moving the car in the direction of an exit, then closed her eyes and concentrated on generating healing energy, pulling it from the Earth's aura just as Edna had taught her. She still amazed herself sometimes at how much easier it was to do it this way—to work with the energy that surrounded the Earth in harmony with her own body, to set right what had been disrupted, to restore the proper pattern to the body's integrity. It still wasn't *easy*—Edna had told her that magic worth doing was almost never easy—but healing this way made so much more sense than the way Stone had tried to teach her. In less than five minutes, the cracked bone in her upper arm had been restored to wholeness, and the pain that remained was only a vestige of its former self.

She opened her eyes, half afraid to find out that Jason had continued driving south on the freeway, but he'd pulled off at an exit and was now cruising down a crowded street she didn't recognize, past a procession of strip malls and fast-food restaurants. "Pull off," she said. "Just pick a parking lot somewhere."

He did as he was told, still looking like he was half in a daze. He didn't even ask her about whether her healing efforts had worked. He guided the Ford into a parking space in the back corner of a McDonald's lot, switched off the ignition, and waited, still staring straight ahead.

"Talk to me," she said. "Come on. I'm fine now. See?" She waved her arm in emphasis. "All good. We need to go back and find out what's going on."

He shook his head. "I don't think so."

"Jason. Didn't you hear me before? There's something up with your aura. Deirdre did something to you. I don't know what, but it's the same as she did to Dr. Stone. We—"

She stopped, because he didn't appear to be listening to her. He stared out through the windshield, fixated on a rusting *Customer Parking Only* sign on the wall in front of them.

She let her frustration out in a loud sigh, then shifted to magical sight and focused on Jason. His vivid blue aura blazed as brightly as ever, but just like before she noticed a faint red overlay.

As she'd learned from both Stone and Edna, red in an aura (at least in one that wasn't red to start with) was usually associated with strong emotion—most commonly either anger or sexual desire. Since Jason didn't seem angry—in fact, he appeared surprisingly complacent, especially given what had occurred back at Stone's place—she suspected that whatever Deirdre had done to him focused on the sexual end of things. That could explain why both Jason and Stone considered Deirdre abnormally beautiful, when Verity herself saw only an attractive woman.

If they were going to get anywhere fast, she'd have to do something about this herself. She couldn't afford to wait for it to wear off—*if* it even wore off. If Deirdre had Stone under some kind of compulsion, it had clearly been going on for quite some time—possibly since shortly after they met.

"Argh," she said under her breath. Aura manipulation was tricky stuff. She'd only begun to study it with Edna, who made it a point to reiterate before every session that any kind of magic that messed with the mind or the aura directly was both more difficult and potentially more dangerous than magic that healed the body. If a physical healing spell went wrong, the worst that might happen is it didn't work, or possibly a bone would knit wrong or something. If mental healing magic went wrong, it could have devastating effects on the patient's mind.

Carefully, slowly, she reached out with her magical senses to touch Jason's aura. She felt its familiar strong, steady pulse: whatever Deirdre had done, it wasn't inherently harmful. Jason was still there—she'd just added something extra.

That would make things easier.

"Jason…" she murmured, keeping her voice low and soothing. "I'm going to try something. Don't freak out if it feels a little weird, okay? I promise it won't hurt."

Jason shrugged. "Sure, go ahead."

She leaned in a little closer, narrowing her eyes. She took several deep breaths to center herself, then reached out toward Jason's aura. She wasn't sure what would happen when she touched it—how the red part would react—so she forced herself to go slow even though her mind was screaming to hurry.

Jason shifted in his seat when she contacted his aura, but the red part didn't react. Verity let her breath out. Passive, then. That meant it would probably wear off on its own given time, especially since it hadn't had much time to take root. With Stone, she thought it would be much harder. She wasn't even sure she'd be capable of helping him—she might need to call Edna. But for now, she moved her perceptions around Jason, poking with gentle care at the red overlay, gauging its boundaries. When she thought she had them, she mentally took hold of part of it and gave it a small tug.

It came away readily, and in the place where it broke free of Jason's blue aura, it dimmed and faded like smoke. Once again, Jason shifted in his seat, though he continued to stare at the battered sign as if it were written in hieroglyphs and his life depended on deciphering them.

Still moving slowly—*can't be impatient now*—Verity peeled up one edge of the empty space between the two bits of red and tugged again, a little harder this time. The same thing happened, with more of the red going hazy and drifting away. It took her several minutes to finish; she probably could have gone faster, but she didn't want to take the chance. Once all of the red was gone, she focused on building a barrier that, with luck, would make it more difficult for Deirdre to get through to Jason again if she tried. She had no idea how well it would work, but it couldn't hurt. When she finished, she slumped back into her seat, drawing her shoulder blades together against the cramping from sitting still too long. "Jason?"

He blinked a couple times as if awakening from sleep. "V?" He looked around, confused. "Where are we?"

"Somewhere in San Jose," she said. "Are you okay? Is it gone?"

"San Jose?" He spun around to look out the back window. "What the hell—we were at Al's place. He hit you. Deirdre—"

"Yeah. And we gotta get back. C'mon. I'll explain everything on the way."

Jason didn't ask questions. He turned on the car, backed out, and headed back for the freeway.

CHAPTER SIXTY-SIX

STONE NARROWED HIS EYES at Deirdre. "What's going on? Where are Jason and Verity?"

She took several deep breaths, her shoulders rising and falling rapidly. "I'll tell you," she said, voice shaking. "I'll tell you everything. But you have to help me!"

"Help you do what?" He stepped aside and let her in. "Deirdre—something's happening, and I want to know what it is. Why do I have components for one of those grimoire rituals in the trunk of my car?"

"I—I don't even know where to start," she said. "There isn't time to talk for too long. You're going to hate me—you might even want to kill me, Alastair, when you hear what I have to say. But you can't—not yet. Not if you want to stop something horrible and save your friend."

Stone went cold. "My friend?" He gripped her arms. "Jason? Verity? Where the hell are they? Have you done something to them?"

"No!" She shook free of him and took a couple steps back, still looking scared and frazzled. "No. I sent them away so they wouldn't get involved." Tears sprang to her eyes. "Nobody was supposed to die, Alastair! I promise you! You're still going to hate me, but please remember that!"

"Deirdre…" Stone fought to keep his breathing under control, to remain calm. "What did you do? If you're not talking about Jason or Verity, then who—"

"Your student," she said. "The woman. The one who caught us kissing in your office."

"Tabby Wells?"

"I don't know her name. But if she was the one—"

He surged forward, gripping her arm so hard she winced. "Deirdre, *what did you do?* Is Tabby dead? Did you kill her?"

"No!" She didn't try to wrench free of his grip this time. "No…I never meant for her to die. I give you my word on that."

"Then *what?*"

"He took her! I went back to where she was, and she was gone. And—" She met his gaze with big, haunted eyes. "So…was the grimoire."

Stone froze. "The…grimoire?" he asked. "What do you mean? We destroyed that, Deirdre. We threw it in the fire. We watched it burn!"

She shook her head. "No. We didn't. That's what I made you think. Once you'd told me you did all the translations and under-stood the rituals, I…" She looked down, her shoulders hunching.

Stone yanked her forward by her arm. With his other hand, he grabbed her chin and forced her head back up. "Have you been mucking with my mind?" he asked, his voice deadly calm. He shook her. *"Have you?"*

"Yes! *Yes!*" She tried to pull back, but his grip was too strong. "You're hurting me, Alastair. Please let me go. I won't run."

He didn't let go. He shook her again. "Are you doing it now?"

"No!"

"How do I know that?"

She gaped at him in astonishment. "Can't you tell?"

He glared. "How can I tell?"

"Don't I—don't I look different to you now?"

He stared at her. Her hair was windblown, her eyes reddened, her face blotchy and tearstained—but aside from that, she looked like the same beautiful Deirdre he'd known since the night he'd met her in January. He flung her hard onto the couch. "If I catch you messing with my mind, I will kill you."

"I know. I know. I deserve it!" She sat up, but made no attempt to rise. "But you have to help me first. You have to stop this!"

"Stop what?" He replayed what she'd said. "Who's 'he'? Who's got the grimoire? Who's got Tabby?"

"Elias Richter. He's—"

That froze him again. "Richter? The black mage?"

"You know who he is?"

"Yes. I knew he was searching for the grimoire, but I didn't pursue it because I thought we'd destroyed it." He took some more deep breaths, trying to get himself back under control. "What's your connection with him?"

"I stole it from him," she said.

"Impossible." He whirled and began pacing, burying both hands in his hair as if trying to squeeze the answers from his own head. "You're lying. You're not a mage." He faced her again. "What *are* you?"

She looked down at her lap. "There isn't really a name for what I am," she said. "There aren't many of us left anymore."

"So you're not human?"

She shook her head. "Not…completely. We—I—can influence men. Make them see me as more beautiful than I am. And…"

"And…?" Everything began to make sense to him now, though his mind screamed against accepting the truth. All this time, she'd been using him, manipulating him…insinuating herself into his mind to make him do what she wanted. And he'd *let* her. Hell, he hadn't even noticed she was doing it! He clenched his fists and felt the magical power rising within him. He wanted to scream. He wanted to run from the room.

He wanted to kill her.

Instead, he asked in the same tone of deadly calm, "And what?"

She still didn't look up. "Once they fall in love with us...once we...make love..." She swallowed. "Once we have access to their blood...then we..."

Stone went still, remembering their first night, how her fingernails had sunk into his back, leaving bloody scratches. "You can control them," he said. The rage rose again. "Is that what you've been doing? Controlling me? All this time?"

"No!" Her head came up, and her eyes were wide. "Only enough to make you see me as beautiful. I didn't...I didn't start until the night we destroyed the grimoire. I had to make you think it was gone, so I could...set up the rest of..."

"The rest of what?"

"The rest of my plan," she said, looking at her lap again.

"Your plan."

She nodded.

"Your plan to do what?"

"To..." She paused. "To keep from dying," she said. "To stay young and beautiful." She sighed. "And to punish Elias."

"Punish him? Why? What did he do?"

She blinked away tears again. "We don't have time for all this right now, Alastair. If he's got Tabby, he'll use her for the ritual. He wants to be immortal."

"When did he take her?" Stone asked, pacing again, still trying to quiet his whirling thoughts and focus. "When was the last time you saw her? Where was she?"

"In my building. I never had any neighbors. I used my abilities to convince the man who owned it to let me stay there. I had her in one of the other apartments."

Stone's mind went back to the times he'd visited Deirdre. He'd never thought about the fact that he'd never seen any neighbors going in and out, no matter when he visited, nor any lights in the other apartments. "When did he take her?"

"I checked on her just before I came to your place earlier," she said.

"Then we've got time," Stone said coldly. "Those rituals take hours to set up and perform. Keep talking. I want to hear everything." Part of him was appalled at how callous he sounded—Tabby Wells was in danger, and he should be looking for her, getting her out of there—but he had to know the rest of this story. "You wanted to compel me to perform one of these rituals for you."

She nodded.

He threw himself down on the couch next to her and grabbed her arm again. "Didn't you *listen* to me? Every last one of those rituals requires a human sacrifice. You wanted to force me with your sick little power to kill a human being. An innocent. One of my *students!* Tell me why I shouldn't just turn you to ash right here." His voice pitched louder by the end; he forced it back to normal. "Tell me that, Deirdre."

"Because it wouldn't have killed her," she said, sounding miserable. "I have an alteration to it. It would just…"

He shook her. "Just what?"

"Just…it…would have made her old," she whispered.

He stared at her, momentarily speechless with shock. "Made her…old? You were planning to steal a young woman's life force to assuage your own vanity?" He tightened his grip on her arm again. He didn't care if he was hurting her. He didn't care if he snapped her arm.

She made no sound indicating she was in pain. "It's not just vanity. I'm dying. He…Elias…did something to me. We…my kind…we renew ourselves by taking energy from our…lovers. That's the way it works normally. But…"

Stone closed his eyes briefly. He had to get himself under control or he would kill her where she sat. "So you've not only been manipulating me, you've been stealing power from me as well. Feeding on me."

"No," she said. "That's what I'm trying to tell you. That's the way it normally works, but not for me anymore. Just little at a time. Like black mages can do. It's what keeps me young. It doesn't hurt them." Tears ran down her cheeks. "It doesn't hurt. I've been doing it for…"

"How old are you, Deirdre? If that's even your real name."

"It is now," she said. "We have to change identities sometimes…or else…people get suspicious."

"How old are you?"

She swallowed. "Two hundred and…forty-three."

Stone let go of her arm and slumped back to the couch. His thoughts flew inside his head, so fast he could barely pin them down. "What did he do to you?"

"I don't know," she said, miserable. "I tried to seduce him…it worked for a while, or I thought it did. He caught on to what I was doing."

"And I didn't," Stone said under his breath. How could he have been so blind, so stupid?

"He's very old, and very powerful," she said. "And…"

He looked up. "And?"

"And I didn't fall in love with him," she whispered. "He was just a means to an end. You were…different."

He glared at her. "Don't try it, Deirdre," he snarled. "There's no way you're getting into my head again."

"I'm not trying to," she said. "I'm not doing it. I swear. And…what I said is true. I never expected to fall in love with you, Alastair. That's why it was different. That's why you didn't figure it out, until I started trying to make you do things you were uncomfortable with. Because most of the time, I wasn't doing anything to you, other than making you think I was beautiful."

"Let's get back to Tabby," Stone said. Suddenly, he felt tired, beaten, drained. Every ounce of the exhaustion he'd been feeling ever since Polo Shirt and Leather Jacket's beating had come back and brought friends. "Tell me where he has her."

"I can't," she said.

He reached out to grab her again, but she flinched back. "I don't *know*," she said. "Can't you find her? Can't you do a ritual?"

Before he could answer, the phone rang.

Stone ignored it. "If Richter has her, he'll have her behind wards. Especially if he's planning to do the ritual here, instead of taking her back to Europe."

Deirdre's eyes went wide. "So...you can't..." More tears ran down her cheeks. She buried her face in her hands. "I'm so sorry. This has all gone so wrong..."

The phone rang twice more. Stone heard the murmur of his own voice on the outgoing message, then the beep—and then another familiar voice.

"Al? Are you home? Pick up if you are."

CHAPTER SIXTY-SEVEN

STONE GRABBED THE PHONE from the table. "Jason! Where are you?"

"Al? I don't know what the hell is going on, but—"

"Where *are* you?" he demanded again, more harshly. "Where's Verity? Is she all right?"

"We are gonna talk," Jason said, sounding angry. "You hurt her, Al. You messed up her arm, throwing her into that wall. You're—"

"*Jason.*" Stone hated to cut him off—he deserved every ounce of Jason's wrath—but there was no time. "Is she all right now? Are you nearby?"

"We're on our way back there. And yeah, she healed it up. Listen—you need to stay away from Deirdre. She—"

"I know," Stone said. "I know. I need you to come back here. Both of you. It's urgent. I need your help."

"For what? To find Deirdre?"

"No. She's right here."

"Al—"

"Don't worry," he said, casting a glare in Deirdre's direction. "I know what she was doing now, and she knows I'll kill her if she tries it again. Just get here."

"Yeah. We'll be there as soon as we can. We're in Mountain View right now. We stopped by our motel on the way back. Maybe fifteen minutes? See you then."

Stone almost let him hang up, and then a memory sprang into his mind. "Jason! Wait!"

"What?"

Stone dug in his pocket for his wallet and removed the phone number Kolinsky had given him, for the place that Richter was supposedly staying. "You can find an address from a telephone number, right?"

"Yeah, sure. Reverse lookup. Fran does it all the time. But—"

"Can you do it now?"

"Right now? I'd need a reference book. I don't have one up here. You don't find that kind of thing at the library. Fran's got 'em for the whole state. Maybe more."

"Can you call her? It's life or death. I need to know what address a number is associated with."

"Al—"

"Here's the number." He gave it to him, slowly, and then repeated it. "Get that for me, and then get over here with Verity. I'll explain it all when you get here. Hurry." He hit the button to hang up, flung the phone back on the table, and turned back to Deirdre. "If I see you trying your tricks on Jason—"

"I won't," she said. "I promise, I won't."

"Why didn't you affect Verity with it?"

She blinked. "She's—not a man. It doesn't work on women."

"She's attracted to women."

"I don't know," she said. "I don't know how it works. It's just— part of me. It just *works*."

Stone got up and began pacing again, unable to sit still. "We've got about fifteen minutes until they get here and we have to go. I want answers."

She nodded, and pushed her hair off her face.

How did you find out about me in the first place?" he asked. "What happened with Richter?"

"I…met him at a benefit show," she said. She didn't look at him. "One of those high-society charity events. He was the sort of powerful man I usually…"

"Seduced," Stone said in a monotone.

She nodded. "At first he was charming…we made love, and I…worked my skills on him. I thought I was controlling him, and he played along. But then I came to realize how cruel he was. He wanted to possess me, not love me. He knew what I was…and he was immune to my powers, even though he pretended he wasn't. When I tried to leave, he overpowered me and kept me prisoner."

"And that was when he did something to your abilities?"

She nodded. "I don't know what he did. I didn't find out until later."

"How did you find out about the grimoire? And me?"

"He got the grimoire a few months ago. I don't know where it came from. He told me about it, while he was…we were…" she shuddered. "Told me that it contained magic that would make him immortal. I'd heard of it—rumors, from others like me, years ago. I knew, if it was what I thought it was, there were ways to alter one of the rituals."

"Why didn't he do the ritual right away, once he had it?"

"He couldn't read it himself. He had to find someone to translate it for him. He's a powerful mage, but not a scholar of ancient languages. He had a list of possibilities."

"And he let you see the list?"

"No. He found someone to do the translations—brought him to his home near Prague. When he finished, Elias killed him. He made me watch. I think he wanted me to see what he would do if I crossed him. And then, when he read the translated spells, he was enraged—he'd need something he didn't have as a component for the spell. Something I got the impression was very hard to find. He had to go and search for it. So he left me locked up, and took the translations with him, but left the grimoire."

"How did you get away?"

"His two henchmen got careless. He had an old servant of his bringing me food once a day—he was too old to be affected by my abilities. But these two—they'd seen me from a distance. And they wanted me."

Stone stopped, waited.

"They thought they would sneak in and…have their way with me, and Elias would never know. That I'd be too afraid to tell him, and he wouldn't believe me anyway—or he wouldn't care. But they didn't realize something."

"What's that?"

"I was like them."

"What? What do you mean, like them?"

She gave a faint smile. "There are male versions of what I am, too. But they're different." She shuddered, wringing her hands in her lap. "They can make themselves look beautiful too, to attract women—but while the females of our type get their energy from seduction and lovemaking…the males are more…primitive."

Stone narrowed his eyes and clenched his fists. "Rape."

She nodded. "They would have taken me, both of them—except I'm older than they are, and far stronger in power. Our kind isn't immune to each other's powers, but the older and stronger can always overpower the younger and weaker."

"So you…seduced them?"

"Yes. I was able to compel them to let me out, open Elias's study for me and break down the wards. I found the grimoire, along with his list of possible translators and their locations. Your name was on it."

Stone sat down slowly in the chair across from her. So Richter might have brought the thing to him, and tried to force him to translate it? "How…did you know to come to me?"

Again, the faint, sad smile. "Because of the note next to your name. You were near the top of the list—he had great confidence in your abilities. But he'd crossed you off, with a note: *White mage,* it said. *Strong. Likely impossible to convince.* "

He let his breath out slowly, gripping the arms of the chair. "So you came to me, hoping you could seduce me and convince me to do the translation." Frowning, he said, "But you waited a long time before you even told me about the grimoire. Nearly a month. Why?"

"I had time," she said. "I had to make it look natural—like it was your idea. I was worried that you'd get suspicious if I presented you with the book too soon after I met you. I knew Elias wouldn't be back for a while, and the henchmen would be too ashamed of letting me get away to call him. I knew they'd come after me, but they're not mages, so finding me would take time." She looked at her lap again. "That was my fault too...I'm so sorry..."

Light dawned. "Wait..." Stone said. "The henchmen. They were—"

"The two men who attacked you," she said, nodding without looking at him. "They were trying to get the grimoire so they could take it back before Elias returned."

"That was why they ran, after they attacked me the second time at the parking lot," he said. "You showed up."

She nodded. "They knew if I got too close to them, I could control them again. It wears off after a time...faster, if there's no blood or sexual connection." She looked up then, eyes haunted. "Alastair, I never wanted you to get hurt. By that point, I was already starting to fall in love with you."

He wanted to believe her, even then, and felt disgust at himself for his weakness. Instead, he shook his head. "None of that." He paused, then said, "They're immune to magic. Does that mean you—?"

She nodded. "Yes. But I'm not strong and fast like they are. They're adapted to be predators. I'm just...human, except for my ability. My talents are more subtle."

He paused, letting all that sink in for a long time. Deirdre said nothing while he did. Finally, he looked up. "So, what was your plan once the ritual was finished? Tabby Wells would be an old woman, and what of me? Were you planning to kill me? Somehow incorporate me into the ritual, as another sacrifice?"

"No…" she whispered. "I told you—nobody was meant to die. I was going to…use my power to make you forget that the ritual ever happened."

"And then what?"

She met his gaze. "I was…I wanted to…stay with you. I thought we could be happy together. I know mages live longer than normal humans, so I thought…"

"You thought you'd just continue controlling me."

"I wouldn't need to anymore," she said. "Don't you see? If the ritual was successful…"

"You'd be immortal," Stone said. "Eternally young and beautiful."

"Not immortal," she said softly. "I could still be killed. But I wouldn't age. Not ever. We could have…been together."

Stone scrubbed at his face with his hands. He started to say something, but a loud knock on the door interrupted him. He leapt up and pointed at Deirdre. "You stay put," he ordered, then hurried to the door.

| CHAPTER SIXTY-EIGHT

STONE STOPPED in front of the closed door. "Who's there?" he called. Even though he was sure it had to be Jason and Verity, he wasn't taking any chances at this point.

"It's us, Al. Let us in!"

He flung open the door. For a moment, the three of them stared at each other, all of them looking awkward. "Come in," Stone said at last, standing aside to let them pass. As Verity followed Jason, he touched her shoulder. "Verity...I—"

"It's okay," she said, patting his hand. "I get it. I understand now what was happening. It's all good."

"Like hell it is," Jason said. He'd just caught sight of Deirdre sitting on the couch in the living room. "Al, what's *she* still doing here?"

"No time to explain everything," Stone said. "She knows better than to try anything."

"She's not," Verity said. She glared at Deirdre. "I can tell, too. I know what to look for now. So don't do it."

"Do you have the address?" Stone asked Jason.

Jason looked as if he might object, but he sighed and pulled a piece of paper from his pocket. "What's this about? Whose address is this?"

Stone paused to look at the paper. It listed an address in Woodside, another of the wealthy little towns tucked away in the mountains not far from Palo Alto. "I can't tell you everything right now—there's no time. I'll try to explain later. But I have to go—a student of mine is in grave danger, and it's my fault."

"It's not your fault," Deirdre protested.

"Shut up," Verity said. "You've fucked things up enough already."

Deirdre glared at her, but didn't say anything else.

"One of your students?" Jason crossed the living room and took a stance where he could keep an eye on both Deirdre and Stone.

"She's been taken by a black mage, who's planning to use her as a sacrifice in a ritual. I have to find them before he does."

"Why haven't you gone already?" Verity demanded. "What are you still doing here?"

"It's a complex ritual," Stone said. "I've got a bit of time, and I needed Deirdre to tell me what was going on. I also couldn't go until I had the address. But now I need to get moving. Deirdre—come with me. You started this—you're going to help me end it."

"Wait a damn minute," Jason protested, stepping in front of Stone. "You aren't just leaving us here. We're comin' with you."

"Damn right," Verity said, nodding.

Stone looked like he might protest, but then nodded. "Your help is appreciated," he said. "Fair warning—this is a powerful mage we're dealing with, and black as they come. This will be dangerous."

"Al, you're wasting time. Let's go."

Stone shot him a grateful look. "Come on. We'll take my car."

He headed down the hall toward the kitchen and the door to the garage. As he passed the hall table, he spotted his briefcase sitting there where he'd tossed it when he came in. A corner of a stapled sheaf of papers poked out of it.

Tabby Wells's paper.

He stopped for a moment, guilt hitting him as he remembered her coming into his office to drop off her assignment. What would her father say if he failed and let Richter kill her? What would Matthew Caldwell say? All this time he'd been suspecting Caldwell of being up to no good, when the danger had lain in a completely different direction.

"Dr. Stone?" Verity touched his arm. "Something wrong?"

He spun. "Did you say you could tell when Deirdre was trying something?"

"Uh—yeah." She looked confused by this sudden change of topic. "I can see it in the aura of whoever she's trying to affect. Why?"

He tossed Jason the keys to the BMW. "Go start the car and wait for me." He nodded toward Deirdre. "If she tries anything, knock her out. Not with magic."

Jason nodded. "Yeah," he said, expression grim. "Come on," he told Deirdre.

She followed without comment. Verity brought up the rear, and paused a moment in the doorway. "What are you going to do?" she asked Stone.

"Call in a bit more help," he said.

| CHAPTER SIXTY-NINE

"TELL US ABOUT THIS GUY," Jason said from the shotgun seat ten minutes later. "What should we expect?"

Stone was driving now; they were headed north up highway 280 toward Woodside. By now, most of the commuter traffic had cleared out, so the BMW cruised at a steady seventy in the fast lane. "It's a long story," he said. "He's a black mage who came out here looking for an artifact I'd gotten hold of. Remember when I told you I was spending a lot of time at home because I was working on a project?"

Jason glanced over his shoulder at Deirdre, who sat silently in the back seat under Verity's watchful eye. "Yeah."

"That was the project. It's a book, and I was translating it."

"So he's got it now, and he's planning to use it to sacrifice this student?"

"Yes."

"What for?"

"He thinks doing it will help him become immortal," Stone said.

Jason stared. "No shit? You guys can do that? Do rituals to become immortal?"

Stone shrugged. "No idea if it will work. But I don't plan to let him use Ms. Wells—or anyone else—to find out."

"Who's this help you called?" Verity asked.

"An...associate. Someone who has a vested interest in Ms. Wells."

Jason frowned at him. "Not that guy you were doing magic with before?"

"Stefan? No." In truth, Stone wished he could have consulted with Kolinsky before they left, even if it meant owing him another favor. As a fellow black mage, he might have given Stone some good tips for dealing with Elias Richter. But even if he'd been able to reach Kolinsky quickly, the explanations would have taken too long. "He's a...friend of Ms. Wells's."

He shifted his gaze to the rearview mirror and met Deirdre's. "Tell us what you know," he said. "Anything you can think of. If you really do want to help, don't hold anything back."

"He's very old and powerful," she said. "And cruel. He has no problems killing people to gain more power—or even just because they're in his way."

"What have you seen him do?"

"He didn't let me watch often when he was working magic," she said. "But I heard Lane and Hugo talking about him one day. He...summons things, and makes them work for him."

"Brilliant," Stone muttered. "Just what we needed—extra opposition. Hold on—Lane and Hugo? Those were—?"

She nodded, looking down. "The two who—"

"Got it," Stone said. So Polo Shirt and Leather Jacket had names. "Anything else? He won't have had time to set up anything too elaborate, if he's only been in the area a few days, so we'll have that going for us at least."

Jason peered at a map unfolded in his lap, using a small flashlight. "This address is way the hell up in the boonies. This guy's rich, right?"

"Extremely," Deirdre said.

"Then he's probably rented one of the big mansions up there."

"Which means we'll be in a secluded area," Stone said. "No chance of anyone hearing, for good or ill."

"So what's the plan?" Jason asked. "We'd better have one, if we're going against somebody like that."

"We'll discuss it when we meet up with Mr. Caldwell," Stone said. He glanced at Deirdre in the mirror again. "Deirdre—it would be best if you didn't mention any of the circumstances around Ms. Wells's abduction to Caldwell."

"Why not?" she asked.

"Because if he finds out you were involved, I might not be able to stop him from killing you."

Her eyes widened, but she nodded.

| CHAPTER SEVENTY

THEY REACHED THE RENDEZVOUS POINT, a park-and-ride lot just off highway 280, before Caldwell did. By the time the man's gleaming, dark-colored Mercedes pulled in under the lights fifteen minutes later, Stone and Jason were both out of the BMW and pacing the lot like a couple of caged animals.

Stone hurried over to the Mercedes as Caldwell got out. The black mage wore sturdy pants, boots, and a leather jacket. As Stone reached the car, he leaned in and pulled a bag from the passenger seat and slung it over his shoulder. "Tell me what's going on," Caldwell said, slamming the door. "Where's Tabitha?"

"We'll get there," Stone said as Jason came up alongside him. Behind him, he could hear the BMW's doors opening. "Listen," he said. "We've got to do this properly. The man who has her is bad news. Black as they come—the sort of black that thinks nothing of killing for convenience—and older than both of us put together and then some. We can't just blunder in after him or we'll all get killed."

"Where is she?" Caldwell demanded again. "We're wasting time, Stone."

Verity and Deirdre joined the group.

"We'll go," Stone said, and held up a hand. "We've got a bit of time."

"How do you know that?" Caldwell's gaze scanned the lot as if expecting to see Tabby Wells tied to a telephone pole somewhere nearby. "You mentioned a ritual. What kind of ritual?"

"A very long and complex one," Stone said. "And he hasn't had her for long, so he can't be far with it yet. Just listen to me, Caldwell."

"What do you mean, he hasn't had her for long?" Caldwell stepped toward Stone, and Jason moved over closer. "I told you, she's been missing since Sunday afternoon. That's long enough for any ritual I know."

"I have it on good authority that he hasn't had her that long," Stone said. He didn't flinch back from Caldwell's intensity. "Now, are you going to listen to me so we'll have a chance of getting her out of this alive, or will you waste more time asking irrelevant |questions?"

Caldwell seethed, but moved back to his original spot. Jason did likewise. "Who is this mage?" Caldwell asked. "What do you know about him?"

"Not a lot," Stone said. "His name is Elias Richter. He's from somewhere in Europe—possibly Prague, but that's not important. What's important is that he's gotten hold of an immensely powerful magical grimoire, and the ritual is supposedly designed to make him immortal."

"That's not possible," Caldwell said, shaking his head.

"You may be right," Stone conceded. "You probably are. But does it matter? He means to perform the ritual anyway, and it requires a human sacrifice to complete."

Caldwell went so pale it was visible even under the eerie yellow sodium-vapor lights. "My God."

Stone nodded. "So we need to get there, deal with whatever defenses, wards, and other security he's got set up, and get Ms. Wells out of there before he kills her."

Caldwell took a couple of deep breaths, clearly trying to get himself under control. "What are we expecting? Where does he have her?"

"We've got an address. Probably a remote estate up in the Woodside hills. He's got two henchmen who are immune to magic, as well as being quite strong and fast. I'm told he's also fond of summoning and controlling things. He's had a few days to set up his defenses, and no doubt they'll be deadly."

"One thing I don't get," Jason said. When Stone turned to him, he said, "Why is he doing the ritual here? Now that he's got the grimoire, if he's already got it translated, why not just go home and kidnap some woman there to do it with? Wouldn't it be safer?"

"I can answer that," Deirdre said. "He's impatient. He wants to do the ritual as quickly as possible—he already had the translations, and he must have succeeded in finding whatever component he was looking for, so he'll want to get it over with so he doesn't risk someone stealing the grimoire again."

"He had the translations?" Jason asked. "So why does he need the book at all?"

"Because translations aren't good enough," Stone said. "For magic that powerful, the written rituals actually contain some of the power on their own. That's why there aren't copies of potent old tomes popping up at the magical equivalent of Barnes and Noble. It has to be the originals, or it won't even have a chance of working."

"All right," Caldwell said. "Wards. Summoned beings. Magically-immune minions. Anything else?"

Stone shrugged. "No idea. We'll just have to be on our guard."

Caldwell appeared to take real notice of the others for the first time since he'd arrived. "Who are these people? How are they connected to this?"

"They're friends," Stone said. "Verity here is my apprentice. Jason, her brother, is good in a fight and will likely be one of our best weapons against the henchmen. And Deirdre—she has certain abilities that will prove useful, especially against them."

"Do you know anything about this ritual?" Caldwell asked. "How it's set up? Anything we should know?"

"Yes," Stone said, looking sober. "As I said, it's quite complex, and simply disrupting the circle not only won't end it, but will likely kill Ms. Wells with the backlash. If we're successful in neutralizing Richter, we'll have to dismantle the ritual with care. So no blundering about."

Caldwell bowed his head and took several deep breaths. "And from what it sounds like," he said bleakly, "this man is cruel enough that if it looks like we might have upset his plans, he'll kill Tabitha anyway, just out of spite."

Stone nodded. "We'll get her back, Matthew," he said softly. His expression hardened, and he glanced at Deirdre. "I promise. We'll get her back, safe and sound."

He hoped he could keep that promise.

| CHAPTER SEVENTY-ONE

WOODSIDE, ANOTHER OF THE SERIES of small, tree-filled towns that were home to some of the wealthiest of the Bay Area's residents, wasn't easy to navigate at night, even with a map. Elias Richter had obviously specified both seclusion and security among his requirements when choosing a location for his temporary base. By the time Stone pulled the BMW to a stop on a dirt shoulder a few hundred yards from the address on the paper Jason had given him, nearly twenty more minutes had passed.

"Where is it?" Jason asked, peering out the window. "We already went past where the address should be, but I don't see it."

Verity pointed up ahead, to an ornate, wrought-iron gate. "The sign there has the next house number up. Did we miss it?"

Caldwell, who'd been following them closely since he didn't have his own map, parked behind them, shut off his lights, and got out. He still carried the bag over his shoulder. "Why are you stopping here?" he asked, looking around. "We haven't reached it yet."

Stone glanced at the gate, then back in the direction they'd come. He shifted to magical sight, staring hard at the tree-lined side of the road. For a moment, he saw nothing, but then something shimmered at the edge of his vision. It was as if one section of the trees didn't quite match the rest: as he continued watching, they shifted and glimmered almost as if they were being projected over something else. "Hmm..." he said. "Come on. I've got an hunch—

but if I'm right, it means Richter is even stronger than I thought he was." He started off back down the road.

When he reached the spot where he'd seen the shimmer, he stopped. Up close, now that he knew what he was looking for, the effect was obvious. Richter was good—this kind of illusion must be taking massive amounts of energy to power. Stone suspected it didn't have to remain powered long—just long enough to keep anyone from discovering the house while he conducted the ritual.

Too bad for that. "Here, I think," he said, pointing.

"Where?" Jason looked confused. "I don't see a damn thing, Al."

But Caldwell had shifted too, studying the stretch of trees with the familiar fuzzed-out gaze of magical sight. "My God," he breathed at last. "Illusion?"

Stone nodded. "Damn good one, too. Do you see it, Verity?"

"Kinda," she said, squinting. "Every once in a while I can see something that looks like a wall, or a gate, or something. But it keeps slipping away."

"How is he powering it, though?" Caldwell asked. "Won't he need all his power for the ritual?"

"Apparently he's fond of summoning up things to do his bidding," Stone said. "Perhaps he's assigned that job to one of those." He'd almost revealed that Deirdre had told him that, but caught himself. This was going to be hard enough without having to deal with Caldwell if he found out Deirdre's involvement in Tabby's abduction.

"What are you going to do?" Caldwell asked. "Dismantling an illusion like this will take time we don't have." He craned his neck, peering through the trees as if expecting to spot Richter and Tabitha behind it.

"No need to do that." Stone paced up and down, stopping every few feet to examine something unseen. "Besides, if we take it down, it might alert Richter that we're here. And besides, I don't think it would be a good idea to go in the front door, do you?"

"I see a tall wall," Verity said, still peering hard. "I wonder how long it extends."

"We can go up and over," Stone said. "Let me see if I can get an aerial look first, though."

"What if somebody sees you?" Jason asked.

"They won't."

Caldwell unzipped his shoulder bag. "Stone, I don't know if you ever tried my elixir—"

"I did," Stone said. "In fact, I've brought the last of the bottle with me." He pulled it from his coat pocket.

"What's that?" Verity asked, eyes narrowed.

"Sort of a—magical energy drink," Stone said. "Bit of fairly benign black magic, so if you've a problem with that, don't use it."

"You're using black magic?" Verity's gaze fuzzed out a moment. "Dr. Stone—"

"I've already had this debate with myself, Verity. I don't need to have it with you. Right now, I'm exhausted, and getting Ms. Wells out safely is more important to me than a bit of moral ambiguity."

Verity didn't look convinced. She waved off Caldwell's offer of another brown bottle, and so did Jason and Deirdre.

Caldwell shrugged, poured himself a capful, and swallowed it. After a moment, Stone did the same. Once again, the cotton-packed feeling of fatigue melted away, as did his remaining aches. "That's it," he said to Caldwell, stowing the bottle with its few remaining doses back in his pocket. "Don't give me any more of that stuff. I don't want to get dependent on it." He glanced across the street. So far, no other cars had gone by since they'd stopped. "Right, then," he said. "Let me get a look, and then we'll go in."

Stone closed his eyes, gathered power, and layered two spells: the first was his "disregard me" spell, which was far easier to cast and maintain than true invisibility, and the second was levitation. He didn't add a shield to it—all he wanted to do was get a clear view of the area's size, so he could stay high enough that he wouldn't be seen in the darkness even without the disregarding spell. "Back in five minutes," he said, lifting off.

"Hurry up," Caldwell whispered loudly.

Stone let the levitation spell take him up about a hundred feet before switching direction to head toward the estate. Below, it was hard to see anything, as most of the area was wreathed in trees. A narrow two-lane road snaked from the formidable front gate and through the forest; Stone followed it, and after about a quarter-mile, the trees thinned and the view opened onto a large cleared area with a circular driveway and a wide expanse of lawn.

Beyond that were three buildings: the massive one dominating the scene had to be the main house, consisting of two stories with a pair of large wings stretching out from an even larger central core. The second, off to the right and set back a bit, appeared to be a large detached garage. The final one, behind the main house and nestled in its own small clearing reachable by a paved path, was probably a guest house. A freeform-shaped swimming pool, illuminated by a series of marker lights, took up much of the cleared space directly behind the house.

Stone took a moment to make sure he had a good hold on both spells—it wouldn't do to lose track of the levitation when he was this far up—and shifted to magical sight. He didn't know if anything would be visible; as a black mage, Richter would have a harder time with wards than Stone would, so he might confine them to inside the house where they could most effectively protect the ritual itself.

He didn't see any wards, but he was surprised to see several glowing auras moving around. Some circled the perimeter of the house itself, and several more moved among the trees. It was hard to see the latter, since the trees themselves also had auras that interfered with clear vision, but he counted eight distinct figures. Had Richter hired mundane security guards to patrol the area and keep intruders out? If so, obviously between that and the illusion on the gate he'd put all that time he'd had during the days while he waited for his feelers to come back to good use.

Stone saw no sign of Polo Shirt's and Leather Jacket's (*Lane's and Hugo's*, he reminded himself) distinctive auras anywhere around the area. Were they in the house too? Or had Richter done something to conceal their auras from nosy visitors?

He wouldn't get much more from his aerial survey—for one thing, the strain of holding three spells at once was just beginning to tire him, and he needed to conserve his strength. Even with the focus items he'd charged up, he'd need every bit of it that he could muster. And at any rate, since trees covered the vast majority of the estate and he couldn't see into the house, the tradeoff wasn't worth it. He made a quick mental note of the relative locations and distances of the estate's various features, then turned back and drifted toward the front gate.

As he neared it, he spotted a figure floating toward him. Drawing closer, he could just make out Caldwell's portly form.

Stone swore under his breath. Damn Caldwell and his impatience! He waved the man away, but Caldwell ignored him and continued in his direction.

"Stone!" he called when he got close enough to do it quietly. "Did you find anything? We need to get going!"

"Get back!" Stone called back, also trying to keep his voice down. He cast a glance toward the ground, but nothing seemed to have noticed them yet. "Get back! We'll—"

Down below, something shrieked: a horrific, inhuman sound.

| CHAPTER SEVENTY-TWO

"**B**UGGER!**"** Stone put on some extra speed and closed the distance with Caldwell. He grabbed the man's arm and propelled him back toward the front gate.

"What was that?" Caldwell demanded, looking around.

"No idea. But it knows we're here now, thanks to you. So much for the element of surprise." Stone dropped the disregarding spell and pulled a shield around himself and Caldwell, glancing around to see if anything was gaining on them. So far, nothing was, though down below, some of the trees rustled ominously in the windless night.

The two of them dropped down on the shoulder next to where Jason, Verity, and Deirdre waited. "I told him not to go," Verity said angrily, stalking over.

"Well, we need to get moving now," Stone said with a glare at Caldwell. "They know we're here."

"Oh, gods," Caldwell said, his shoulders sagging. "I'm sorry. I just thought they might have—"

"Just stay with us," Stone ordered. "If you run off on your own, Caldwell, we won't come after you. And you're likely to get Ms. Wells killed. Got it?"

The black mage nodded. "I'm sorry."

"Let's go," Stone said. "Verity, you shield Jason. I'll shield Deirdre. Caldwell, you have your own shield, yes?"

Caldwell nodded. "Of course."

"All right. I know we can't maintain them all the time, but pay attention. I couldn't make out what they've got down there, just that there are a lot of them. I counted at least eight—probably patrolling security guards. Don't know if they're armed. Stay together, but not too close. Verity, Caldwell, keep your magical sight up and stay sharp." He started across the road toward the wall, about fifty feet down from the main gate.

The others followed. "I'll go first," Stone said. "My shield is the strongest, I think, in case they're waiting." Without waiting for a reply, he called his shield back up and levitated upward to the top of the eight-foot wall, which was easier to see now that he knew where it was. He landed silently, ducked low, and looked around to spot the auras of anyone lying in wait, but all he saw were the faint green glows of the trees. He waved for the others to follow and lowered himself to the ground on the other side. After a moment, the rest of them landed next to him.

"How do you want to do this?" Jason asked under his breath as he scanned the area.

"Fast," Stone said. "Let's not give them time to get organized." He turned to Deirdre. "Can you affect any guards we find?"

She nodded. "I'll have to get close to them, but yes."

"Right, then. Let's not kill anyone. I'm sure the guards are just hired locals. Well," he added, his expression hardening, "don't kill the guards. We may have to kill Richter."

"What about Lane and Hugo?" Deirdre asked.

"Who?" Verity asked.

"Richter's henchmen. They're immune to magic. Come on— we don't have time for this. We'll deal with them when we find them. Stay aware. If you see anything moving in the trees, say something."

They continued through the trees, doing their best to stay as quiet as possible. The scant light made it difficult, but the moonlight filtering down through the leaves provided enough illumination for them to avoid tripping over anything. They made it roughly halfway to the house by Stone's reckoning when something rustled up ahead

"Did you hear that?" Jason whispered to Stone.

Stone held up a hand, and the others stopped. "I don't—"

A form darted out of the trees, fast and low. Two more were right behind it. "Dogs!" Verity said.

"Circle," Stone ordered. "Shields up."

"Don't kill 'em," Verity said, moving into position with her back to Stone.

The others took up their spots and the three shields flared around them.

The dogs barked loudly as they spotted their prey, flinging themselves forward only to bounce off the shields, confused. Stone hit one with a stunning spell; it yelped and retreated, watching with fearful eyes as the other two continued scrabbling at Caldwell's and Verity's shields.

"Hold it!" yelled an authoritative female voice from the trees. "Stop right there. Drop your weapons."

"Damn," Stone muttered. "Female guard." He hoped there weren't more of them—if there were, his plan to have Deirdre take control of them and neutralize them harmlessly would be useless.

Three figures stepped out in front of them. All three held guns, and all three were female. *Damn.*

They wore identical black BDUs, combat boots, and light armored vests over long-sleeved black shirts. "I said, drop your weapons," the one in the middle ordered.

"*Three* female guards?" Jason whispered. "What the—?"

"It's Lane and Hugo," Deirdre said. "It's got to be."

"You mean they're controlling them?" Stone asked. He'd been so busy thinking about Deirdre's inability to influence female guards that he hadn't considered the implications of what Richter's henchmen could do to them. He didn't take his eyes off them. The shields shimmered, barely visible in the darkness.

"Probably."

"And you can't do anything about it."

"Quiet!" the middle woman snapped. "I'm gonna warn you one more time: drop 'em and put your hands up, or we shoot."

Stone took a step forward, holding up his hands. "We don't have any weapons," he said. "Don't shoot."

"What is that thing? What's up with the dogs?" one of the others asked, as the two German Shepherds continued trying to get past the nearly invisible protective walls around Stone and the others.

"We can do this the easy way or the hard way," Stone said. "We've no quarrel with you—we're after your boss. Put the guns down."

"Like hell," the middle guard, obviously the leader, said. She swung her pistol barrel around until it was centered on Stone's chest.

Stone sighed. "I'm sorry. We haven't time for this. Verity? Caldwell? Now."

Three stunning spells flew from the three mages, each one taking out one of the guards. The women fell to the soft carpet of leaves and needles without taking a shot. More spells took care of the dogs.

Jason ran over to the fallen guards, checked on them, and collected all three of their guns. "They're fine," he said. He checked the safeties on the guns, stowed one in his waistband, one in the pocket of his jacket, and kept one in his hand.

"The dogs too," Verity said from where she was bent over them. "They'll wake up with headaches, but they're fine." She got up. "Why so many female guards?"

"I'm betting they're all female," Stone said. He dropped his volume so Caldwell couldn't hear him. "Richter's henchmen have an ability similar to Deirdre's."

Jason was still crouched next to the guards. He put the gun in his hand down for a moment, gathered something else from each of them, and then picked up the gun again. "Radios," he said. "We want 'em?"

Stone held out his hand, and Jason tossed him one. He gave the second to Verity and kept the last one.

At the moment, the night was silent. Stone scanned the area for signs of approaching auras, but saw none. "Come on," he said. "Don't know if this lot reported us to the others."

"I can't keep my shield up the whole time," Verity said. "Not if I want to have anything left when I get there."

Stone nodded. "Let's keep them down for now, but be careful. Try not to make too much noise."

They kept moving through the forest. It was easy to stay silent, as their footsteps made nearly no sound on the thick pile of squishy leaves and pine needles covering the ground.

"How far is it?" Jason whispered, coming up next to Stone.

"Not far. Quarter mile or so. We should be seeing it any moment."

He was right: they'd only been walking for a few more minutes when the trees thinned out, revealing a wide expanse of open lawn, a circular driveway, and the dark bulk of the house in the distance. The group stopped at the edge of the tree line. "No cars," Jason said. "Where are they all parking?"

"And where are the rest of the guards?" Caldwell asked. "Stone, you said you counted eight?"

Stone was about to answer when a deafening, inhuman shriek split the air. He got a brief impression of something big dropping with a heavy *thud* down into their midst, and then something hit him and he went flying.

CHAPTER SEVENTY-THREE

STONE GOT HIS SHIELD UP barely a second before he slammed into a tree and crashed to the ground. He scrambled back to his feet, intending to look for his friends, but he couldn't see past the massive form lunging toward him. He flung himself to the side and it plunged past, grasping at the air where only a second before he had been standing.

It stood over seven feet tall, broad and barrel-chested, its too-short legs and too-long arms bulging with muscles, its big hands bristling with long, wicked claws. It shrieked again as it wheeled around; its voice was like the roar of a big cat combined with the harsh scream of a bird of prey.

Around Stone, the others spread out. "What the hell *is* that thing, Al?" Jason yelled. He had one of the pistols out and was tracking the barrel around as he tried to get clear shot on the monstrosity.

"No idea!" Stone pulled himself up again, panting. He didn't, either—he'd never seen anything like this before. Aside from the fact that Richter must have summoned it from somewhere, all he could see was the same thing the others could: it was big, and it was dangerous. "Careful—don't shoot anyone!"

He gathered energy and flung a concussion beam at it as the thing lunged toward him again, and was rewarded by a satisfying *thud* when it made contact. The spirit, or demon, or whatever it was screamed and hit a nearby tree so hard the trunk shuddered.

"Coordinate!" he called. "Verity! Caldwell! Hit it now!" He glanced around to see where the others were, but could only see Deirdre, her eyes wide, shrinking back from the terrifying thing.

It recovered fast, shrieking into the night again, and its gaze fell on Stone. That made sense—he was the one who'd hit it hardest so far. Its tiny legs pumped hard, propelling it forward far faster than should have been possible. Its massive arms reached out, claws bared.

Stone pulled up his shield again, and the thing slammed into it, driving him backward into a tree. But as it did so, it jerked sideways, first to the left and then to the right, its body juddering as if battered by unseen blows. Verity and Caldwell had gotten their attacks off.

He skittered around the tree, keeping the hefty trunk between himself and the creature as it shook off the hits and fixed on him again.

The loud report of a gunshot split the air, and Jason rose into view off to Stone's left. The creature jerked again as the round tore into it, but the resulting hole shimmered and closed up almost immediately. "Fuck!" Jason yelled. "Bullets don't hurt it?"

Stone, still puffing, flung another concussion spell at the spirit, reeling it backward and away from him. They didn't have time for this! Richter obviously knew what he was doing: send something to keep them busy, to waste enough time so he could take the ritual beyond the point of no return before they arrived. "Caldwell! Verity! We need to hit it all at once. Jason—little help?"

He hoped Jason knew what he was referring to—it had been a while since they had teamed up to make use of Jason's "magical battery" ability, but if Stone could tap into it, he could increase his power significantly. That didn't mean he wanted to let Caldwell know about it, though.

"Do it!" Jason called back.

The creature was already recovering from Stone's hit. It hadn't moved quite as fast that time, though. That was encouraging—at least they could slow it down. "Group up!" Stone ordered. He popped out from behind the tree and sent another wave of magical energy at the creature, driving it once more back as it shambled toward them. Then he hurried over to where Jason, Verity, and Caldwell were already converging on a spot about ten yards away. Deirdre hung back, eyes wide and fearful. Stone didn't blame her—nothing in her power would be able to affect this thing.

He reached the others and clamped a hand onto Jason's shoulder. "Right, then," he said quickly. They didn't have much time—the thing was already coming back for more. He glanced to the left and the right, noting the set, grim looks on both Verity's and Caldwell's faces. They couldn't waste the energy on a shield, so if this failed, they'd be in a world of hurt. He hoped he wasn't leading them to their deaths. "Hit it with your best on three. One…two…*three!*"

Gripping Jason's shoulder even more tightly, he let the power course through him, let it sing through his veins and burn off the fatigue and the pain. This wasn't like Harrison's magic—it wasn't as powerful, and didn't suffuse him with the ecstasy/agony sensation that made him feel as if his body were being consumed from within—but nonetheless, the massive infusion of extra magical punch was an incredible rush. He pointed his hands at the creature and released the energy, feeling the heat on either side of him as Verity and Caldwell did the same with their own spells.

What happened next was the magical equivalent of someone being taken apart by machine-gun fire. The creature's shriek of triumph morphed into one of terror, and its body shook and danced as the three separate spells hit it at its center of mass. It lunged forward, taking one last, desperate swipe at the group, before vanishing in a large puff of foul-smelling black smoke.

For a moment, Stone wasn't sure where the other cry of pain had come from—perhaps an echo of the thing's death scream? But then his relief at the creature's demise ebbed away as Jason dropped

to the carpet of leaves, moaning, his arms locked around his chest.
"Jason!"

| CHAPTER SEVENTY-FOUR

STONE DROPPED TO HIS KNEES next to his friend, but Verity was there first. "Come on, Jason, let me see," she pleaded, eyes wide with concern.

Jason didn't answer, but merely continued to moan and writhe. Stone saw dark blood running from beneath his tightly clenched hands.

"Help me!" Verity ordered. She pointed first at Stone, then at Caldwell. "You two! Lay him out so I can see what I'm working with."

Stone didn't argue. In this arena Verity was already more skilled than he was, even at this early stage of her training. With a quick glance over his shoulder to make sure nothing else was approaching, he grabbed hold of Jason's left arm and pried his grip loose. Caldwell did the same on the other side, while Deirdre kept watch.

It wasn't easy—Jason was strong, stronger than either Stone or Caldwell—but with adrenaline's help they managed to pull his arms free.

The wounds weren't pretty: three deep, bloody furrows carved across Jason's chest by the creature's claws. "Can you help him?" Stone asked.

"Yeah," she said, breathless. "They're deep, but it's just muscle. Hold him still and let me focus."

Caldwell looked toward the house. Sweat beaded on his shining forehead, and his eyes were full of fear. "How long will this take? We need to—"

"Shut up, Caldwell," Stone growled. "We'll do what we need to do. Let her work."

Caldwell glared at him, but then nodded, focusing on holding Jason's arm down.

Verity closed her eyes, running her hands over the bloody wounds on her brother's chest, a few inches from touching. Stone watched her as, her jaw set tight and her body tense, she moved her fingers in a circular pattern. He switched to magical sight and saw a warm yellow glow begin to suffuse Jason, seeming to rise up from the earth itself to gather around his chest and swirl beneath her hands.

Concerned as he was about Jason, and about whether the delay would keep them from reaching Elias Richter in time to stop the ritual and save Tabitha Wells, Stone could not remember ever feeling more pride in his apprentice. As he struggled to hold Jason's flailing arm down, his thoughts drifted back to when he had first met her at the Forgotten's camp in San Jose.

She'd been seventeen then, wary and uncertain as a frightened wild creature, frustrated at the strange disorder that had taken hold of her mind from the time she was twelve years old. To see her now, competent and confident, casually giving orders to two men many years her senior—one her own master—and expecting them to be followed because this was the thing she was born to do, filled him with gratitude that he'd been given the charge to guide her magical career.

Hell, to guide her life, at least for these last few years.

He had never wanted a child, never wanted the responsibility required to bring another life into the world and nurture it to adulthood. But if he'd had a daughter, he'd have wanted her to be very much like the young woman Verity was becoming.

Oddly, though, he'd never thought of her in a paternal way, not even when he'd first begun her training. Perhaps it was because he didn't feel it was his place to compete with her own long-dead father. Perhaps it was because her brother Jason, with his protective instincts and strong drive to keep everyone he loved safe from harm, filled the role better than he could.

Or perhaps it was that he was not, in truth, so much older than she was that—

But no. He drove that thought down and back as he always did, almost without any conscious volition. It was simply something one did not think about, and that was that.

Still pressing down on Jason's arm, holding it to the soft earth (it was easier now, as his moans and writhing subsided under his sister's care), Stone glanced back over his shoulder at Deirdre. She stood, bent a little with her palms pressed against her thighs, alternating between scanning the area in front of them and watching the scene on the ground. Her eyes were wide, her expression fearful. She met Stone's gaze and held it for a moment, but said nothing.

Even with her hair in disarray and her clothes dirty and torn from the scratching limbs of the trees, even after all the lies she had told him and the deceptions she had wrought, she was still as beautiful as ever.

He tore his attention from her and focused back on Jason, and didn't care if Deirdre saw the anger and frustration in his eyes.

The healing took several minutes, and by the time Verity rocked back on her heels, her shoulders slumping with effort, both Stone and Caldwell could barely contain their stress at constantly having to be on watch for more threats. Stone looked down at Jason: he lay still now, awake but spent. Verity's healing had closed the furrows on his chest, though the front of his shirt was still soaked in blood.

"That's all I can do," Verity said on a breath of expelled air. She swiped her hand through the beads of sweat on her forehead and gripped Jason's shoulder. "Jason?"

"Yeah…" he answered immediately. He sounded alert but exhausted.

Stone got to his feet and switched to magical sight, but still saw no sign of any other approaching enemies. Though he didn't relax his vigilance, it didn't surprise him that none were forthcoming: Richter hadn't had long to prepare, and between the illusion hiding the entrance to the compound, the female security force with their guns and dogs, and the horrific summoned creature that had taken three mages to destroy, he no doubt thought he'd be sufficiently protected to keep undesirables away from his ritual. That, and he probably didn't know about Caldwell and Verity. Still, they had to hurry.

Stone glanced at his watch: extrapolating from the time Deirdre had told him she'd last seen Tabitha and the grimoire, they were now rapidly approaching the leading edge of how long it would take to construct the ritual. Especially given a mage of Richter's reputed power level.

And they still had to get inside the house and find the ritual.

"Jason? Are you up to this?" he asked. "If not, we'll need to—"

Jason rolled his head back and forth. "Nah, I'm comin'. Just give me a sec." He pulled himself to a sitting position and accepted Stone's hand up, then stood swaying.

"It's the blood loss," Verity said, eyeing him dubiously. "The wounds are healed, but I can't do anything about the blood." She herself looked tired as well. Healing didn't take as much out of her as it used to, but it was still exacting, exhausting work.

Stone glanced between her and her brother. If Jason's blood loss made him too weak to fight, it would be dangerous—both to him and to them—to bring him along. And if Verity wasn't strong enough to use her offensive magic, she too would be a liability. Richter's creature might not have damaged their group in any permanent way, but if the two weren't able to press on, it had neutralized a big chunk of their power just as effectively. Stone didn't want to say it, but—

Before he could speak, Caldwell spoke up. "If I may…"

Stone wheeled on him, ready to snap at him for once again disregarding the situation. "Caldwell, I told you—"

He held up his hands in a conciliatory gesture. "I know. I know. But—" Reaching into his coat pocket, he withdrew a brown bottle. "I know you don't like it, but it can help."

Stone looked first at the bottle, then at his friends. Damned if the man wasn't right. He'd experienced the rejuvenating powers of Caldwell's elixir enough times in the past few weeks to know the effect it would have on Jason and Verity.

"It's black magic," Verity said softly.

"Yes," Stone agreed. "But only indirectly. And it *will* help. We need both of you at your best to do this. But if you'd rather not, I—"

"Give it to me," Jason said. "I'll do it. No way in hell I'm gettin' left behind." He held out his hand to Caldwell.

The black mage poured a capful and gave it to Jason, who downed it without hesitation. Instantly, a shudder passed through his body, his head jerked up, and his eyes went wide. "Holy shit. That stuff's *potent.*"

"You'll pay for it later," Stone said. "The exhaustion's not gone, just…displaced for now. But yes, it works." He turned to his apprentice. "Verity?"

"I don't like it," she said, staring at the bottle in Caldwell's hands as if he were holding a clump of poisonous snakes. She frowned at Caldwell. "You sure it's not addictive?"

"If you don't abuse it," he said. "I promise." His expression became pleading as he glanced once more toward the house. "Please…we need your power. We need to get to them before he—"

She stood a moment, clearly weighing the options and finding them both wanting. "Yeah. Okay," she said at last. "But I still don't like it."

"Thank you," Caldwell said. His expression as he looked toward the house reinforced Stone's belief that he genuinely did care for Tabitha Wells. The man was trying his best not to fall apart, but if they didn't get moving soon, all bets would be off.

"Come on," he said, as Verity downed the little capful of liquid. "And be careful. He might have assumed the welcoming committee would hold us off, but he's still dangerous."

Nothing else attacked them as they picked their way through the forest for the remainder of the distance to the house. Any second, Stone expected more of the enthralled female guards, more cautious now after the loss of their compatriots, to take potshots at them from somewhere in the darkened forest. They couldn't keep their shields up constantly, as it would take too much out of them—especially himself and Verity, who, despite the jolt from the elixir, had still put out some significant magical energy healing her brother's wounds.

"Are they all inside?" Jason whispered, creeping up next to Stone as they reached the treeline.

Beyond the trees, a wide expanse of lawn, about a hundred feet across, stretched out between them and the house. The road ended in a circular driveway ringing a large fountain, and another road snaked off toward what looked like a multi-car garage. All around the house, bright perimeter lights bathed an area comprising about a quarter of the lawn. From here, they could see more lights glowing inside but couldn't make out any detail.

"Let's go!" Caldwell urged. "They've got to be in there somewhere." He started to move out of the trees' cover, but Stone grabbed his arm.

"Wait!"

"*What?*"

Stone glared at him and gripped him by the upper arms. "Pull yourself together, man! I know you're worried about Tabitha—so am I. But if we're going to get her back, we've got to keep our wits. If you can't, you might as well stay here, because otherwise you'll get us all killed before we can get near her. Do you hear me?"

He understood Caldwell's recklessness, now that they were so close: if it were Verity or Jason—or even Deirdre—who'd been held in there, he'd probably have needed the same lecture from someone else. He tightened his grip and then broke it, his gaze never leaving Caldwell's.

The black mage's shoulders slumped. "Yes. I do—and you're right. What's the plan?"

Stone turned his attention back to the house, shifting to magical sight. "Damn."

"What?" Verity asked.

"I was wrong about Richter. He's better than I thought. He's got the place warded."

| CHAPTER SEVENTY-FIVE

"**D**OES THAT MEAN we can't get in?" Jason asked. He leaned forward, peering into the darkness as if expecting to pick out the wards with sufficient non-magical scrutiny.

"Probably not—to ward someplace that large with an impermeable barrier would be—" Stone shook his head. "I'm not even sure I could do it, and I *know* I couldn't do it in that short a time. Even if he's significantly stronger than I am, he's still a black mage. That will work in our favor. As it is, I wouldn't be surprised if he's killed several people just to get the energy to do what he's done."

Behind him, Caldwell shifted uncomfortably, but said nothing.

"So, what then?" Verity asked. "What kind of ward is it? If it can't stop us—"

"Almost certainly an alarm ward." Stone hadn't shifted back to normal vision yet; he squinted at the faint lines, following them down until they disappeared into the ground. "It won't stop us, but it'll announce our presence to Richter as loudly as if we hired a brass band to march in there and do it."

"So what do we do?"

"We dismantle it. Without letting him know we've done it."

"Can you do that?"

"It will take a bit of time, but I think so. Caldwell, how good are you at wards?"

"Not bad," he said. "I can help you."

"Right, then," Stone said. "Let's go 'round the back and see if we can find a spot where anyone prowling around inside won't see us, and we'll get started."

"What do you want Jason and me to do while you're doing that?" Deirdre asked.

Stone had almost forgotten she was there; she'd been so quiet since they'd arrived. "Just...stand guard. Amuse yourselves. Quietly."

Verity glared at her. "And don't fuck with my brother, or I won't need magic to put you in a world of hurt."

They sneaked around along the edge of the tree line until they reached the rear part of the house. "Wait," Jason said, holding up a hand as Stone waved them out.

"What?"

"You're so worried about wards, you're not thinking they might have mundane security."

"I thought that was what the dogs and the guards were for."

"Yeah, but a place like this, I'm guessing they've got cameras. We need to disable 'em or at least get them pointing somewhere we're not. And they might have alarms on the doors and windows."

"Can you tell if there are any? Would they even be using all of that? Do you think they'll be monitoring a security room now, in the middle of a ritual?"

"Who knows? They might have put one of the guards on it, just to be safe. Your disregard spell doesn't work on cameras, does it?"

Stone shook his head.

"Worth checking. No point going through all this trouble to disable the wards if they see us waltzing up to the back door on cameras."

"All right, but make it quick. Verity, go with him. And mind those wards—don't get too close to the house."

The two headed off; Stone watched them as they ducked low and stayed in the shadows while approaching the house. They disappeared around one corner, then quickly darted to the other side and did the same thing. Less than five minutes later, they were back.

"There were cameras," Jason said. "I'm not sure if they were live or just dummies, but we nudged 'em so they point away from the middle part of the back." He pointed at an area with a glass door currently covered by blinds. "If we work there, we shouldn't be in view, at least until somebody figures out the cameras have been moved. I can't tell if they've got an alarm, so we'll just have to take our chances when we go in."

"Best we can do," Stone said. "Come on."

All five of them mirrored Jason and Verity's actions as they approached the house, crouching and darting from shadow to shadow. They pulled to a stop near a window next to the sliding door.

"Verity," Stone said, ducking down below the window line. "I haven't taught you much about wards yet, and I'm assuming Edna hasn't either—?"

"Not really," she said.

"Then your job will be to keep the disregarding spell going on all of us, and keep magical sight up to watch for any approaching threats. The spell won't hide us from anyone determined, but it might give us the edge we need if we have to fight. Can you do that?"

"On it," she said.

"Deirdre—you said you had a gun and knew how to use it. Were you lying about that?"

Her eyes came up, and he didn't miss the hurt in them. "I wasn't lying," she said. She opened her bag, pulled out a small pistol, then slapped a magazine into it.

"Can you shoot someone if they're coming after us?"

"Yes." Her hurt expression shifted to one of resolve. "If it means dealing with Richter and fixing this mess I made, I can do it."

Stone winced, hoping Caldwell hadn't caught her words.

No such luck, though: The black mage turned from where he'd been examining the wards. "What do you mean, this mess *you* made? Did you have something to do with this? Stone, what's she talking about?"

"We don't have time for this now," Stone said. *Gods, don't let this all fall apart now.* "Do you want to get Ms. Wells out, or not? Our window is shrinking rapidly."

But now Caldwell was rising to his feet. "You know more than you're telling about this, don't you?" he asked Stone. His eyes narrowed. "For that matter, how did you know about this Richter? How did you know where Tabitha was being held? I used a ritual to try to find her, but didn't get anything. I was afraid she was dead!" His voice rose, his posture stiffening as he leaned in toward Stone.

Stone stood his ground. "Matthew—yes. There's more to this than I've told you. But we can discuss it later, after we've got Ms. Wells safely back and Richter dealt with. All right?"

"Who is she?" Caldwell hooked an aggressive thumb toward Deirdre. "What does she have to do with this?"

Deirdre stepped forward. "I'm very sorry, Mr. Caldwell. Part of this *is* my fault, and I'm doing my best to try to fix what I did. Please, though—listen to what Alastair's saying. I promise—I'll tell you everything when we're safe. All right?"

Caldwell's glare turned to first a look of confusion, and then to a grudging nod. "Yes…yes, all right. Fine. Getting Tabitha out of there is the first priority."

"Dr. Stone?" Verity spoke up, an odd edge to her voice.

"Not now, Verity," he said softly. He met her eyes for a moment, and nodded once. He knew what had just happened. He didn't like it, but he hadn't been kidding—they didn't have time for dissension in the ranks right now. He shot one quick warning glare at Deirdre, which he hoped adequately communicated his thoughts about any further use of her abilities on their group members.

She merely nodded and looked down.

"All right," he said. "We'll try to wrap this up as quickly as we can. Shouldn't take more than five or ten minutes." He turned away from them and back toward the ward, trusting them to watch his and Caldwell's backs as they worked.

Wards, essentially, were constructs woven of magical threads, and anchored at strategic points around the location to be protected. Some of them were designed for a single purpose: to keep something out, to alert someone to a certain condition such as the approach of a magical being or a mundane, or to injure or kill something that attempted to bypass them. Others, more complex ones, wove multiple types of threads together, such as to detect the presence of a mundane trying to pass through and render him or her unconscious, or to prevent a magical being from passing and alert the ward's caster to its arrival.

The reason white mages had the potential to create far stronger and more complex wards than black mages was that the latter by nature had a hard time with spells designed to be permanent, or even long-term. It wasn't to say they couldn't cast such spells or weave effective wards, but merely that it was far more difficult for them to do it. Most of them did it only when necessary, or, like Stefan Kolinsky, convinced white-mage friends or associates to do the job.

Richter was good—damn good, or he'd never have gotten as far as he had with these. But fortunately for Stone and his friends, warding a house the size of this one, even with a construct snugged tight against the walls, necessitated a certain simplicity of design. The barrier was a strong one and solidly constructed, but it was, as he suspected, single-purpose: it was designed to set off an alarm if anyone attempted to cross it. Probably a silent one, so any interlopers wouldn't even realize what they'd done until it was too late.

"He's underestimated us," Stone murmured to Caldwell as he focused in to examine it. "I doubt he expected us to get this far, but no doubt he thought if we did, we'd be so relieved that we'd just blunder in without checking."

"I almost did," Caldwell said soberly.

"Don't worry about it now—let's get this thing down so we can stage a little surprise of our own, shall we? Let me take a look at this for a moment so I can find its weak spot."

He narrowed his eyes and focused on the latticework of magical threads radiating outward from one of the anchor points. In order to allow them to pass through the ward without alerting Richter, he would need to perform the magical equivalent of defusing a bomb: placing a few new anchor points of his own to form a doorway, and then carefully detaching the threads from those already there and relocating them to these new points. The trick was to do it quickly, under cover of misdirection magic designed to fool the ward into thinking it was still attached to something when it wasn't. It was difficult work, as exacting as surgery, but it was one of the things Stone's master had drilled into him so deeply he doubted he could ever forget the theory.

He just hoped he still had the touch for the practice. He'd built many complex wards in his career (the periodic refreshes he did on Stefan Kolinsky's shop kept his hand in, which is part of why he agreed to do them), but it had been quite some time since he had dismantled one.

He took a deep breath to steady his nerves, and began forming the pattern for the first anchor.

CHAPTER SEVENTY-SIX

JASON SCANNED THE AREA behind the house, his gaze never settling anywhere for more than a second or two. He took in the pool, the barbecue area, the gate leading out into the grounds, both corners of the house, and even up along the roof line. He hated that he couldn't see very far without some kind of vision enhancement; normally he didn't regret his lack of magical ability, but right now a little mystic sight like Stone and Verity were always using would be a big help in spotting approaching threats. His hand tightened on his gun, and he hoped he wouldn't have to use it.

Next to him, Deirdre sighed.

He spared her a quick glance: she looked tense and miserable, holding her own gun aimed out into the night.

"Careful," he said. It came out a little more brusque than he'd planned. Verity had said she could spot it if Deirdre tried to influence him again, but his sister was focused on maintaining the spells Stone had asked her to cast. Would he even notice if Deirdre took another shot at it?

"I'm not going to do it, you know. I promised Alastair."

"Do what?" he asked without looking at her.

"Use my ability on you." Her voice was soft—she clearly didn't want it carrying to where Stone and Caldwell crouched next to the house, conferring in low murmurs.

"Yeah, don't mind me if I don't believe you. You fucked with Al's mind for weeks, and that's not easy to do."

She nodded, still looking at the ground. "I—I didn't know what else to do. I was wrong. I know that now. But I can't change the past. All I can do is try to fix things."

"And then what?" He kept up his scans as he spoke, and didn't attempt to look at her. Could she affect him if there was no eye contact? He didn't know, and he couldn't exactly ask Stone right now. "What happens if we do fix it?"

"I don't know," she whispered. "If we do this—if we get her out—I suppose I'll go away somewhere."

"And start this whole routine up on somebody else."

"No. It wouldn't do me any good."

He glanced at her. "Why not? You could just get yourself some sugar daddy, warp his mind, and have whatever you wanted."

"For a while," she said. "But that's not what I want."

"What *do* you want?"

She clasped and unclasped her hands in front of her, never still, toying with the gun. "I don't know anymore." She paused. "What I want is for none of this ever to have happened. I never wanted to hurt anyone."

"You never wanted to hurt *yourself*." Jason heard the bitterness in his tone, but he didn't care. "It sounds like that's all you give a damn about."

"That used to be true," she admitted. "It's the way of most of our kind. It has to be, or we couldn't do what we do. But it's not true for me anymore."

"How so?" He glanced at her again; she was still staring at the ground, playing with the gun. He was close enough to see that she was nonetheless careful to keep her fingers away from the trigger.

"I love Alastair," she said softly.

Jason's hands tightened on his gun, but he had to look at her then. "Bullshit."

"No." She raised her head and turned her face toward him. "It isn't. I wish it were—it would make things easier. I love him...and even after all this, even though I can't believe it could be possible, I'm sure in some way he still loves me too."

Jason snorted. "Like hell he does. Al doesn't put up with *anybody* fucking with his mind. If you still are—"

"I'm not," she said. "I haven't been since I promised I'd stop. Ask your sister if you don't believe me—she says she can tell. I swear, I never did anything but make him see me as beautiful before…before the night of the grimoire. I didn't have to."

"What do you mean, you didn't have to?" He watched Verity as she paced back and forth between them and where Stone and Caldwell still crouched next to the house, taking apart the wards. She had her back to them, focused on maintaining the spells.

"Look at me," Deirdre said.

"No way. I'm not letting you—"

"I'm telling you, I *won't*. What do I have to gain from it? I want what you want—to deal with Richter and rescue Tabitha. Please, Jason," she said more softly. "Just look at me for a moment."

Reluctantly, with another glance at Verity, he did. "Okay, what am I—"

But he didn't have to finish the question. Already, he saw what she was trying to show him: an attractive face framed by chestnut hair, with eyes dark with worry. It wasn't what he saw, though—it was what he *didn't* see. Her face was pretty, perhaps even more to the right person—but it wasn't the stunning, almost unearthly beautiful that had so captivated him before. "You're—"

"Normal," she finished, and nodded. "I'm pretty, but no prettier than your sister, or any other attractive woman you might meet."

"So—when you're not—" He looked at Verity again. "That's what V saw, isn't it? When she didn't believe me when I told her you looked like a supermodel."

"Yes."

He rubbed at the back of his neck with one hand. "But why does that tell you that Al loves you? You were doing that to him too. He saw the same thing I did—or was it worse than that? Did he see what he wanted to see, and so did I?"

"No. He saw me with my glamour up, same as you. Same as any man, unless I turn it off. And I turned it off hours ago." Her eyes pleaded with him. "Don't you see—I turned it off, but he still sees me the way he always did."

Jason stared at her. "That doesn't mean he loves you. It just means—you've had longer to get your hooks into him. You got a lot closer to him than you did to me."

"None of that matters," she said with a sigh. She looked over her shoulder at Stone and Caldwell. "Nothing matters. Because even if he does still love me, you're right—he won't accept that I used my power on him. As soon as we finish here, it will be over. And I don't blame him at all."

Jason didn't answer—he had no idea what to say.

| CHAPTER SEVENTY-SEVEN

STONE STEPPED BACK from the house, swiped sweat off his forehead with his sleeve, and finally allowed himself to breathe normally. "That's done, then. Let's get inside before someone notices us."

The whole process had taken only a bit more than five minutes, but it felt as if he'd been concentrating for three hours. Bit by painstaking bit, he'd taken apart a small section of the ward and reconfigured it, one strand at a time, to leave an opening large enough for them to pass through without setting it off. Fortunately, Caldwell had proven an able assistant, far more skilled with ward-breaking than any black mage he'd ever met except Stefan Kolinsky. He had stepped in and done as Stone asked with steady competence, making the operation easier than it could have been. Stone was glad he hadn't had to do it alone.

He turned back to his friends, surprised to see Jason and Deirdre in conversation, and quickly tore his gaze away. Deirdre was as lovely as ever, albeit as disheveled as the rest of them. Was she working her skills on Jason? He doubted it, though: Verity, neatly assuming the protective-bear role that Jason usually claimed, would have spotted it instantly with her magical sight and put a stop to it.

"How are we doing this?" Jason asked. "What exactly did you guys just do?"

"We made an opening in the ward," Stone said. "This will be tricky because you and Deirdre can't see the edges, so you'll have to be careful." He indicated the glass doors. "The opening is there. It's about four feet high by three feet wide. You'll have to duck to pass through it, once I open the door. I'll go in first, and help Deirdre. Verity, you next and help Jason. Then Caldwell. Pay attention once we get in, in case there's an alarm on the door. And keep quiet." He turned back to them. "Everyone ready? Last chance to back out."

"Let's *go*," Caldwell urged.

Nobody else said anything. Once again, Stone was struck by Jason's and Verity's loyalty to him—those two would follow him anywhere and stand at his side against anything, as long as they believed in the cause. He just hoped he wouldn't get them killed for it.

It didn't take much effort to open the door: a simple telekinetic tweak to the inside latch did the job. With care he slid the door open, using magical sight to make sure he didn't touch the edges of the ward opening and that the door was open far enough to provide maximum possible room for entry, even for the portly Caldwell and broad-shouldered Jason. He scanned the darkened area inside, but saw no sign of any auras moving around. "Looks clear," he whispered. "I'm going through."

He crouched and stepped through the opening, half-expecting an alarm to go off, or one or more attackers to leap out from behind furniture.

None of that happened, though. He passed through to the other side and found himself in a large, sparsely furnished sitting room. He beckoned Deirdre forward, then held a hand up to indicate the top of the opening. "All right. Duck down and come on through. Carefully."

Deirdre did as instructed, crouching low and following Stone's route through. She moved with her usual grace and didn't come anywhere near the edges.

"All right," Stone told her. "Watch the rest of the room, and if anything comes through, shoot it."

The others likewise made it through without incident: first Verity guiding Jason, who had to turn partly sideways to slip through, and then Caldwell, who was a tight fit.

They crossed the room to where a pair of double doors, wooden and intricately carved with delicately traced trees and flowers, stood closed. "Wards?" Jason asked.

"No." Stone paused to examine them. He detected no magic near them, but the area beyond them was another matter. It wasn't strong from here, but yet it gave the impression of strength, as if something were attenuating it. Odd—a simple wooden door shouldn't be able to block the kind of power he was sensing. A ward on the other side? How had Richter even had time to put all these safeguards into play? He shouldn't even have expected opposition, but even if he did—

"Stand back," Stone ordered. "I'm going to open the door, and I'm concerned about what's behind it. Caldwell, a shield, if you'd be so kind…"

Jason, Verity, and Deirdre all stepped off to the side, and Stone and Caldwell took positions in front of the doors but well back from them. Caldwell gestured, and a glowing shield popped up in front of him and Stone. "Do it."

Stone raised both hands like a conductor and pointed them at the doors. They popped open readily, swinging toward them on oiled hinges.

Beyond them, something moved in the darkness.

Stone stiffened, gathering energy for a spell, but then relaxed. "It's just a mirror," he said. Damn, he was getting jumpy. This wasn't Richter's personal stronghold—it was a rented mansion that normally belonged to some rich Silicon Valley executive. Everything here wasn't—

The mirror shattered with a sound like a musical explosion, and suddenly the air was full of tiny shards. They blew out through the opening at high velocity, hitting Caldwell's shield like a hail of glittering bullets.

"Holy shit!" Jason yelled, grabbing Verity's arm and pulling her down.

There was no more flying glass, though, after the initial volley. All of it had slammed into the magical shield protecting the two mages and fallen with melodic tinkles to the soft carpet.

Stone let his breath out. "Bloody hell! Is he expecting an army?"

Caldwell dropped the shield. "We need to keep moving. They'll know we're here now. We—"

"Look out!" Verity cried.

Stone saw it too, at the same time: the glass shards, which had been scattered harmlessly on the floor, flew up, spinning in mad circles as if in the grip of a tiny, sparkling tornado. Almost too fast to follow, the shards whirled and danced until they formed into a creature of vaguely humanoid shape, taller than Stone, with no legs and long, reaching arms.

It lunged at them.

Taken off guard, neither Stone nor Caldwell got their shields up in time. The shard-thing slammed into them as both instinctively flung their arms up to protect their faces. Tiny bits of sharp glass buried themselves in Stone's coat and Caldwell's leather jacket as the two men reeled backward.

A shield blossomed between them and the creature. "Get back!" Verity shouted.

Stone and Caldwell backpedaled toward the others, both of them unleashing waves of magical force at the thing before it could attack them again. Unlike the dark, muscular guardian outside, this one erupted in another hail of shards as the magic took it apart. This time, the bits of glass littered a much larger section of the carpet: in the moonlight shining in through the door, it looked as if a thin dusting of ice crystals dotted the floor.

Verity swallowed. "That was—" She kept her shield up, angling it so it was between the group and the open doorway.

"That was an ambush," Stone said grimly. "That thing was never meant to stand up to much punishment." Despite his coat, he could feel tiny trickles of blood running down his face, and where the coat had been open, his T-shirt sported small holes where the shards had gotten through. Caldwell was in a similar condition. "Come on. Caldwell's right—they know we're here now, if they didn't before. Keep those shields up, but we don't have time for caution."

"You guys okay?" Verity asked. "You need me to—"

"Later," Stone said. He was already passing through the doors. The feeling of latent, powerful magic was stronger now. Whatever Richter was up to, they were getting close to it.

The hallway stretched out on either side of them, tracing a wide expanse of walls with no doors. Each direction ended at a corner, with hallways continuing around them. Stone paused to examine the intricate mirror frame in front of them for just a moment, shifting to magical sight: it hung blasted and dead, all the glass gone from its wooden backing. He was about to switch back when a faint glow caught his eye, off to the right about ten feet. Holding up a hand to indicate the others should stay put, he crept down the hallway and sharpened his focus.

Yes—there it was. There was magic here, where magic had no sense being. Unless—

"Caldwell," he whispered, beckoning. "Verity."

The two of them came up to meet him, and he pointed at the area where he'd spotted the glow. Both of them peered at it.

"Illusion," Caldwell whispered.

Stone nodded. He'd thought so, but it was good to have confirmation. He pointed left. "Jason. Go look—carefully—around the corner. Tell me if you see a door. Verity, you check the other side."

After a moment, the two came back, both nodding. "Double doors," Jason said.

"Yep," Verity added. "A lot like the ones we just came through."

"What does it mean?" Deirdre asked. "Which way do we go in?"

Stone indicated the blank wall. "Here. They're expecting trouble to come in through the obvious doors, so let's not give them what they want, shall we?" He stepped back. "Caldwell, on three again, we'll hit the spot with concussion spells. Verity, you put up a shield in front of us. Jason, you and Deirdre stay behind us. If they're expecting us, I'm sure they'll have something nasty prepared. Deirdre, if Lane and Hugo are in there, you know what to do."

"I do," she said. "But remember, I'll need to get close to them."

Jason took a deep breath and let it out. He raised his gun. "We'll get you close. Do it, Al."

They took their positions. Verity's shield shimmered into being in front of the blank spot in the wall that hid the illusionary doors. Stone glanced at Caldwell, then focused forward. "Ready? One, two, three."

The two spells arced from their hands and slammed into the wall. For a moment, it looked as if nothing would happen: the wall remained a wall, and the spells glanced harmlessly off it. But then the air in front of the wall shimmered and warped, revealing a pair of doors identical to those they'd just come through—except this set had a large hole blasted through them, and hung askew on their hinges.

"Go!" Stone ordered.

They poured through the hole, Verity's shield moving in front of them.

CHAPTER SEVENTY-EIGHT

THE ROOM WAS HUGE: an enormous hall nearly fifty feet on a side, dark-walled and granite-floored, with a ceiling so high it disappeared into shadow. Stone got a brief impression of the scene before them—furniture pushed off to the side and far end, windows covered with heavy drapes, lighting provided by candles spread out around the room, and an impressive crystal chandelier hanging on a heavy chain from the ceiling.

But his gaze was drawn to the centerpiece of the tableau: a massive circle, at least twenty feet in diameter, painted with precision on the cleared floor. Surrounding it, spaced along the perimeter at irregular intervals, was a series of odd-looking apparatus on stands, like something out of a mad scientist's nightmare. He saw glass globes filled with liquids, tubing and what looked like electrical conduits stretching from one stand to the next, metal arms holding green flames, red flames, blue flames. Some of the tubing snaked across the circle and into its center, where it reached—

"Tabitha!" Caldwell yelled.

An elaborate table had been placed in the center of the circle, and upon it lay the naked body of Tabitha Wells. She wasn't tied—she didn't have to be, as she appeared to be deeply unconscious. Several of the tubes and conduits had been somehow attached to her body, though it was impossible to tell how in the dim light. Seven tall stands were arrayed around the table, each one topped with a crystal of a different color. From each crystal, a beam of light, bright as a laser, spiked out and converged at a point in the center of Tabitha's chest.

At that instant, though, Stone's attention was diverted as several things happened at once.

Shadowy figures rose from behind the furniture's makeshift cover and opened fire on the new arrivals.

Stone gripped Caldwell's arm and yanked him back before he could surge forward toward Tabitha, out of the protection of the shield that Verity was still holding with effort.

Two more figures, who'd been hiding on the wrong side of their cover, obviously expecting trouble to come in through one of the two sets of doors on the sides of the chamber, scrambled around in the direction of the other side.

Jason took aim at one of the figures and fired his own gun. The person—a woman—yelped but flung herself around the barrier to safety.

"Careful!" Stone yelled. "Don't break that circle!"

"Yes!" called a voice from the other side of the circle, mocking and amused. "Don't break the circle. Who knows what terrible things might happen if you do that?"

Stone saw him then, in the shadows on the other side of the room, just outside the perimeter. The man stood behind a lectern on which a book lay open—Stone recognized it instantly as the grimoire he thought he'd destroyed.

Of medium height, with a slim build and silver-gray hair, Elias Richter wore a fine suit and an expression of smug calm. He glanced down at the grimoire as if checking something, then nodded, satisfied. "I wouldn't risk disturbing anything at this point," he said. "Not if you don't want to blow this entire place to pieces."

Stone shifted to magical sight, and immediately spotted the shimmering, translucent barrier enclosing the circle. "He's got it warded," he said under his breath.

"Very securely, too," Richter said as if Stone had spoken aloud. "You might have been successful with the simple protections I put up around the house, but this one will prove more formidable, I promise you." He nodded toward the side of the room nearest where Stone and the others stood.

Stone spared a quick glance in that direction. A pile of old, ragged clothes lay strewn haphazardly around on the floor. *He's killed people to power that barrier.* It shouldn't have surprised him.

"Hey, I've seen that guy!" Jason muttered.

That, however, *was* a surprise. "Where?"

"At the restaurant," Verity said, her voice tight with effort as she continued holding her shield. "We both did. He came through the portal."

"Ah, yes. I do remember seeing you two. I'd put your guns down if I were you," Richter said. He nodded toward the apparatus. "You may be tempted to try to get past my ward, but even if you somehow manage it, this is still a delicate construct. I'm sure you're well aware of that, Dr. Stone, given that I'm certain you've had time to do your translations on the grimoire. If you knock it out of sync, it could be disastrous for the young lady there."

"You're going to kill her anyway!" Caldwell yelled.

"Well—yes. But do you want to kill yourselves too?" He glanced at the grimoire once more, consulted a sheaf of papers that lay next to it, and made an adjustment to one of the nearby stands. "If you were wondering, by the way—I've got a few moments while this reaction completes, so we have a brief time to chat."

"Where are your two lackeys?" Stone asked. He scanned the room again, but aside from Richter, all he saw were the flickering edges of the female guards' auras as they sheltered behind their heavy furniture barriers. "I know they're here—that's why your security force is all women. I thought they'd be front and center for this."

"I'm surprised you're in such a hurry to see them again, Dr. Stone," Richter said. "They've told me about how ineffectual you were against them last time you encountered them." He made a *tsk* sound, shaking his head. "I wish I could have seen it. It must have been humiliating." His gaze traveled past Stone to Deirdre behind him. "And you, my traitorous little thief. I hope you've enjoyed your time with Dr. Stone. I assure you, I've got plans for you once this is over. I guarantee they won't be to your liking."

"Just—let her go!" Deirdre yelled. Her voice shook. "I'll—I'll come back with you if you let her go."

"Deirdre—" Stone began.

"Oh, you'll come back with me in any case," Richter said. He made another minute adjustment to another stand. "There was never any question about that. But it's far too late to stop the ritual now, even if I wanted to."

"You're a monster!" she yelled. She moved up next to Stone, still behind Verity's barrier, which was beginning to waver. "How can you—"

Something dropped down next to her, on her other side, silent and quick as a cat. Stone spun in time to see a tall, muscular figure, dressed all in black. He grabbed hold of Deirdre and flung her backward. Her head hit the wall with a sickening *thud* and she slid to the ground.

"Deirdre!" By the time Stone, or any of them, could react the figure had vaulted away, moving low and fast, wreathed in shadows. He briefly recognized the grinning face of Polo Shirt—Lane—before he was gone, ducking back behind more of the heavy furniture stacked along the walls. A quick glance up confirmed that the room's ceiling, high above them, was latticed with heavy beams wide enough to provide a superhighway for men as strong and agile as Richter's two henchmen. Where was Hugo? Was he still up there somewhere?

"Dr. Stone!" Verity's voice, full of strain, rose. "The shield—"

"Down!" Jason ordered, grabbing Verity's arm once again and pulling her to the floor. He took a wild shot toward where the dark figure had disappeared.

The shield shimmered and dropped.

Two of the female guards popped up and began firing at the group.

Stone and Caldwell hit the ground as well, rolling toward the other side of the room. Two more guards rose and also began shooting.

The one saving grace, apparently, was that while the women were attired as guards, they didn't appear to be as proficient with their guns as real security guards should be. That wasn't surprising: Stone doubted Richter couldn't have found and hired that many female security guards on such short notice. He'd probably hired what guards he could, and supplemented the force with other women under Lane's and Hugo's thrall.

But even so, that many guns firing in such a small space were plenty dangerous even if they didn't always hit what they were aiming at.

Time to get rid of some of them.

"Caldwell—get the near one," he ordered. "I'll get the far one. And don't kill her." Without waiting to see if the black mage complied, he raised his shield, ducked low, and took off toward where the rearmost of the two guards sheltered.

Apparently, neither Richter nor his flunkies had informed them what they were up against—not that it would matter if they were deeply under the control of Lane or Hugo. The woman got two shots off at Stone before he reached her: the first one hit his shield and ricocheted harmlessly away, while the second went wide and took a chunk out of the wall. *Someone isn't getting his security deposit back,* Stone thought as he aimed a concussion beam at the woman. She cried out and fell in a heap, and he snatched up her gun and stuck it in his coat pocket.

He was about to spin around to check whether Caldwell had dealt with his guard when another dark figure landed next to him.

Hugo—still dressed in his biker jacket over black body armor, grinned. "Well, look who it is. Back for more?"

Stone backpedaled, heart pounding, scrabbling in his pocket for the gun. He still had the shield up—it should hold, if he could just—

Hugo lashed out with a savage, steel-toed kick. His foot hit the shield, which flared from invisible to translucent to pink to red in the space of less than a second, and then dropped. His grin widened. "We practiced with the boss," he said. "Seems we *can* take down magic shields if we hit 'em hard enough."

Stone, reeling from the psychic feedback from the shield's destruction, got the gun out, but fumbled it in his hand. He wasn't used to firing guns, and certainly wasn't used to bringing them to bear this fast when his head felt like somebody was tap-dancing on the inside of his skull.

Hugo moved like a snake, faster than any normal human should be able to. His foot flew out again, this time hitting Stone's wrist.

Pain exploded. Stone yelped as the gun flew from his fingers and hit the floor somewhere in the back of the room. He staggered backward again, but this time there was nowhere to go. His back hit a heavy wooden armoire, and he couldn't go back any farther.

Hugo was in his face instantly. The big man grabbed a handful of his shirt and reeled him in. "No fun this time," he said. His hot breath smelled like garlic. "Too bad. Maybe later, after."

Stone forced himself to concentrate. He couldn't hit Hugo directly with magic, but his last two fights had proven that, while the henchman was supernaturally tough, he was nonetheless still vulnerable to physical damage.

He couldn't see anything to hit him with, though—Hugo's bulk was in his face, blocking his view of the various pieces of furniture strewn around. He struggled to move, but Hugo just laughed and pulled back his fist.

And then Stone spotted it. Not past Hugo, but above him. He gathered power and unleashed it in two spells: the first grabbed hold of Hugo's jacket and yanked him backward, away from Stone.

Before the man could regain his feet, the second spell went off, taking a firm telekinetic grip on the chandelier high above, wrenching it free and sending it with all the strength he could muster at Hugo.

But Hugo was faster than Stone expected. At the last second before the enormous hurtling projectile crashed to the ground, trailing its long chain behind it and flinging shimmering crystal droplets in every direction, Hugo threw himself to one side, rolling twice and leaping back to a crouch in one swift and graceful motion. Before Stone could move, he leapt at the mage and took him down hard, his face wreathed in fury.

"Nice try," he said through clenched teeth.

Stone wasn't looking at him, though. Stunned, head pounding, he was nonetheless almost hyper-aware as adrenaline coursed through his body. The chandelier's chain, thick and several feet long, lay trailed out on the floor behind the ruined fixture. Stone focused his will again, snatched it up, and wrapped it around Hugo's neck.

For a moment, Hugo didn't appear to realize just what was happening. Then his eyes widened and his hands flew up to the chain, trying to wrench it free.

But Stone's magical power was every bit a match for Hugo's physical strength. He kept his focus, ignoring everything but the chain, squeezing it tighter and tighter until the henchman's face reddened and his eyes began to bulge.

Hugo, apparently, was not stupid, though. When it became clear his strength wouldn't be sufficient to rip the chain from his neck, he changed tactics, going instead for the source. Face darkening, he lunged toward Stone, hands out, going for the mage's throat.

Stone reacted on instinct—he yanked the chain tighter, and then used it to fling Hugo away from him, using every shred of his power backed up by all of his rage and frustration at his previous encounters with this man.

What he didn't take into account was what was behind Hugo.

He had only a second to react before the henchman hit the barrier, and this time he wasn't fast enough. Hugo flew backward, screaming obscenities as he went. The chain hit the shimmering dome first and he followed immediately after.

At first, Stone thought he'd merely bounce off. He kept hold of the chain in case he had to tighten it back around Hugo's neck again, but—no.

Gods, no...

The shield, as strong as it was, was nonetheless a delicately balanced magical construct. It had to be—to create something that large and that powerful so quickly required a level of magical knowledge and ability beyond even Stone's. He didn't doubt it could have held off physical onslaughts from his friends, and it was probably designed to bleed off any magical energy that came into contact with it, so hitting it with magic would have been useless.

But Hugo was immune to magic.

Whatever he was, he wasn't quite human. Something about his body simply didn't react to magic at all. Stone's shield had stopped him—temporarily—because it was a smaller, cruder version of this big one that Richter had erected.

But when you brought that kind of anti-magical force into contact with a precisely tuned magical construct like Richter's ward...

The chain hit as expected, simply bouncing off.

Hugo did not.

Stone had just enough time to shift to magical sight so he could see exactly what occurred.

Where Hugo's body slammed into the barrier, its shimmering surface lit up brighter and brighter, until it outlined him with otherworldly light so brilliant it almost hurt to look at it. His clothes protected him for a moment, but when they burned off and the rest of his skin hit it, the light's intensity grew even more incandescent.

Hugo screamed, a bellowing, agonized screech that rose up until it echoed from the massive room's rafters. His body jerked and stiffened, very much like what it might have done if it had hit a strong electrical field—and for much the same reason.

Stone wasn't sure whether Hugo was dead before the barrier flashed even brighter and his body simply vaporized, but he did catch a last glimpse of the man's wide, terrified eyes before they exploded from the heat of whatever strange reaction Stone had caused by putting him and the barrier into violent contact.

And then the flash died and Hugo was no more.

One second his body was there, and the next it was gone, vaporized by whatever bizarre reaction had been set into motion by his sudden impact with something he never should have touched.

Stone heard yells and thought they might be Lane, Verity, Caldwell—but he couldn't be sure, and he couldn't tear his gaze away from what was happening in front of him.

The barrier was flickering now, shifting and strobing like an old-style television signal struggling to lock in. The candles guttered madly, as if a powerful wind had blown through the chamber.

Stone stared at it, and had no idea what to do about it. What had he done? If that barrier went down and the feedback upset the even more delicate balance of the ritual inside, he could kill not only Tabitha, but every one of them.

The next seconds were agonizing. Across the flickering barrier, he could still hear the sounds of battle. Caldwell pelted up alongside him and gripped his shoulders, hard. "What did you *do?*" he screamed.

Stone shook him off, but otherwise ignored him. There was nothing to be done now but wait. He couldn't stop it. Whatever happened would happen soon—if the worst occurred, they wouldn't have time to escape. He was certain a ritual this size could take out this entire house and part of the grounds if it went up.

But it didn't go up. Inside the circle, Richter must have discovered a last-minute sense of self-preservation, because he switched his attention from the grimoire to the apparatus in front of him. He had raised his hands and was yelling something in a language Stone didn't know—something authoritative and, though his voice didn't hold quite the mocking confidence it had before, it still came out strong and clear.

The barrier flickered and shifted and winked out.

The stands and globes and tubes inside the circle teetered alarmingly, rattling on the granite floor, and then steadied. The tubes and conduits swayed as if in a gentle breeze, but their ends remained connected to Tabitha's unconscious body on the table in the center. The colorful, laser-point lights remained focused on the center of her chest. She slept on, oblivious to the chaos around her.

"What did you *do?*" Caldwell yelled again. "Tabitha!" He started to move forward, but Stone grabbed his arm and yanked him back.

"No! It's more dangerous now than ever, Caldwell! You know better than this! Damn it, *stop!*"

Something in his voice must have gotten through to the other mage, because he did stop. He stared out with terror and hopelessness at Tabitha's body on the table. "What do we do?"

Stone wasn't listening to him. Something across the circle had commanded his attention now that the barrier was down. He was still viewing the scene with magical sight, so the flaring auras of the combatants on the other side of the room shone bright and colorful against the dark backdrop of the walls. "Verity!"

Verity was down on the floor, flat on her back. She wasn't unconscious, but she looked stunned. Above her, Lane's golden aura, tinged red with rage and malevolent sexual desire, loomed. The two of them seemed to be engaged in some kind of wordless battle of wills.

Stone's own rage rose: the bastard was trying to enthrall her! Where was Jason? There was no way Stone could get over there in time, and the only available weapons from this distance were the heavy pieces of furniture scattered near them. Too much chance of hitting Verity too if he threw an armoire at the man.

"Stone—" Caldwell began.

Stone continued ignoring him, focused on the scene across the circle. Where the hell was Jason? Had Lane already taken him out?

And then, as Lane loomed in closer, towering over Verity with his sneering mad grin, her foot snapped up and planted itself between his legs. "Fuck off, you perv!" she yelled as she rolled sideways away from him.

Lane shrieked—apparently his supernatural speed and strength didn't protect that most delicate area of the male anatomy from a determined combat boot—and pitched forward, revealing Jason standing behind him, clutching something long and thin. He reared back with it and let fly like a batter swatting a fastball, and the sound it made when it hit the side of Lane's head was audible to Stone and Caldwell all the way across the circle.

Lane didn't even have time to scream. He crashed to the ground and lay still. Stone couldn't see him any longer below the line of the various circle apparatus.

"Al?" Jason called, reaching down to give Verity a hand up. "You okay?"

"Enough!"

Stone, Caldwell, Jason, and Verity all spun around.

Richter stood where they'd left him, behind the lectern containing the grimoire. No longer protected by his ward, he nonetheless didn't look concerned. He glanced down at the grimoire and then back up. "We're at an impasse, then, it seems."

"How do you figure?" Stone demanded. "Your lackeys are down. Your ward is down. It's over, Richter. Step away from the grimoire and let Ms. Wells go."

Richter laughed. "You amuse me, Dr. Stone. Certainly your interference has made the process a bit more difficult, but that is all. In fact, in a way you've made things more complicated for yourselves. It might be tempting to try to attack me, but remember—the ritual has begun. It can't be stopped now, not if you don't want to destroy everything in this room, and more. You're out of options, unless you prefer suicide."

Stone glared at him. Why hadn't he put another shield up around himself and the grimoire? Was he concentrating on the ritual much harder than he seemed to be, preventing him from casting other spells? Was he simply counting on the fact that they wouldn't risk disrupting the ritual by attacking him? Or was he bluffing?

"Stone—" Caldwell began, voice tight with worry.

On the table in the middle of the circle, Tabitha began to writhe. It didn't appear that the laser-beam lights from the crystals had been hurting her before, but now her brow furrowed and her features twisted in pain. Liquids that had lain unmoving in the tubing now began to bubble and flow. The glass globes glowed brighter.

"What's happening?" Verity asked. She and Jason had come back around the circle and now stood next to Stone and Caldwell.

"It's the next stage of the ritual," Stone said grimly.

"We've got to stop it!" Caldwell said. He took a step forward, but then stopped himself. He looked like a man contemplating a live bomb, afraid to do something but more afraid to do nothing. He wheeled on Stone. "You started this! Do something!"

For a moment, Stone's mind merely spun helplessly. Every solution he came up with had a flaw, and most of those flaws resulted in all of their deaths. He couldn't risk upsetting the circle, but if he didn't interrupt Richter, the ritual would pass beyond the point where they could safely stop it without going through with the sacrifice.

It may already have done so, but he didn't tell Caldwell that.

And then, suddenly, his mind latched on to an idea. It was a crazy, last-stand idea, and probably wouldn't even work. But given that they had no other choice—

"Caldwell!" He made a sharp beckoning motion toward the black mage.

When he leaned in, Stone said something to him in a harsh whisper.

Caldwell's eyes widened. He backed away from Stone, his face lighting up with rage. "What do you mean, we have to let her die?" he yelled. "Like *hell* we'll do that! I'll kill him! *Tabitha!*"

He threw himself forward and flung a wild bolt of magical energy at Richter.

"No!" Stone yelled. "Caldwell, *no!*"

Richter moved fast—not as fast as his two supernaturally agile henchmen, but a lot faster than a man his age should have been able to. He took a single step backward and raised the hand nearest Caldwell. A small shield flared around it and the bolt sizzled harmlessly away.

And that was Stone's cue. The instant Richter took his focus off the grimoire—the unshielded grimoire—Stone activated the telekinetic spell he'd been holding in reserve. He grabbed the book and snatched it back toward their group.

An instant too late, Richter caught on to the ruse. "*NO!*" he screamed. He shot out a hand and tried to yank the book back, but Stone had caught him off guard just enough to get it to where he wanted it.

As it hung there, suspended in midair outside the area encompassed by the circle, Stone unleashed another spell.

The grimoire burst into flames, erupting into a crackling, multi-hued fireball. The magical fire, hotter and more intense than normal fire, burned it to ashes in the space of a few seconds. For an instant, Stone thought he heard a second, fainter scream join Richter's as its remains fluttered to the granite floor.

Richter staggered backward, almost falling. Stone moved in, pressing the attack while the other mage was weakened. That kind of ritual required a massive amount of concentration and investment on the part of its practitioner, especially when conducting it alone. If that concentration were somehow disrupted, it left the caster in a state of confusion that could last anywhere from a few seconds to several days, depending on the power of the ritual and the strength of the practitioner.

They wouldn't have long, Stone knew, but they still had to be careful not to disturb the ritual.

He hit Richter with a concussion wave intended to throw him backward toward the rear of the room, away from the circle.

Richter swatted it away with his shield, backpedaling again. Another beam hit him—this time from Caldwell—and he took another step backward.

"Your ritual's buggered, Richter!" Stone called. "Give it up!"

Richter's normally calm, mocking face lit up with sudden rage. He didn't say anything, but merely raised both hands in a sharp jerking motion, as if conducting a particularly vigorous movement in a symphony.

All around Stone and the others, the heavy furniture rose and whirled through the air. Some of the pieces flew toward them at high speed from in front of them and behind, while the others rose up above them and then dropped.

"Down!" Stone yelled, grabbing Caldwell and Verity and trying to pull them down as Jason did the same from the other side. He brought up another shield, noticing at the periphery of his vision that two other shields—Caldwell's and Verity's—had likewise gone up.

The pieces of furniture slammed into the barriers and broke. Some of them got past the first layer, but none could penetrate the second. For a few seconds the pieces smashed together with thundering crashes like what it might sound like to be at ground zero in a multi-car pileup.

And then the sound died down as the heavy wooden pieces settled to stops all around them.

Cautiously, Stone dropped the shield and rose. The air was full of swirling dust, but he couldn't see the figure standing near the head of the circle.

"Where's Richter?" Verity demanded, getting up too.

But it appeared Elias Richter had seen the futility of staying any longer and escaped during the chaos.

"Damn!" Stone snapped. "We—"

"The circle!" Jason cried. "Look at it!"

They all spun. The circle had begun to glow an unhealthy shade of green, and the crystals' beams had gone from pure clear colors to muddier, darker hues. Tabitha continued writhing in the center, her entire body paling except for angry red patches where the beams hit her and the conduits were attached.

"Stone!" Caldwell grabbed him by the front of the shirt. "Damn you, *do* something!"

Stone stared in horror, ignoring Caldwell's grip. He remembered the ritual—he had translated it recently, after all.

Something was wrong.

Without Richter's focus to keep it going, it was falling apart. It was sucking Tabitha Well's life force, but instead of doing what was intended and siphoning it into Richter, the conduit was interrupted. The energy, with nowhere to go, was building, like a blockage in a pipe. "Caldwell—" he murmured. "It's too late—there's nothing we can—"

"Can you *stop it?*" he demanded, shaking Stone.

Stone's gaze fell on the sheaf of papers remaining on the lectern—Richter's notes, and his translations. He couldn't complete the ritual successfully with them, but he might be able to power it down safely by draining its energy at a controlled rate. "I think so," he said. "But without a sacrifice, it won't—"

"Then I'll be the sacrifice!"

The voice had come from the area near where they'd entered the room. Stone ripped free of Caldwell's grip. *Deirdre?*

She stood there, swaying, her expression fearful but resolved. "I'll take her place," she said again. "Can I do it, Alastair? Will it work?"

"Deirdre—"

Her eyes blazed. "*Will it work?*"

"I don't *know!*"

"Stone, it's killing her!" Caldwell yelled. "Do something, damn you, or I'm going in there after her!"

Deirdre didn't give Stone time to make a decision. She darted forward, moving with nimble grace as she stepped past the perimeter of the circle.

Stone held his breath, expecting the whole thing to flare when she broke its line, but it didn't. "Deirdre!"

She ignored him. Continuing in without touching any of the painted lines, ducking neatly under the conduits and tubing, she stopped next to the table. "Get ready," she said. "Grab her and get her out."

"No!" Stone took a step forward.

She shook her head. "This is my fault, Alastair. Hurry, before it's too late. I know you can stop it before it kills me."

"Wait!" he protested. "Deirdre, you're immune to magic. How can you—"

"Only to outside effects," she said. "And mine's not as strong as Lane's and Hugo's, anyway. Trust me, Richter's magic worked on me." She gave him a faint smile, meeting his gaze with a ghost of her old vivacious charm. "Come on. I know you can do it, love."

Stone barely felt Caldwell's hand gripping his arm. She was right—Tabitha Wells was innocent. Deirdre was not. As much as it tore at him to do it, he knew she was right, even if it meant that the switch would set off the ritual and take out the room. At least this way had a chance. His only other choice was to do nothing and allow an innocent woman to die.

He clenched his fists, his heart thudding in his chest, and once again pulled free of Caldwell's grasp. He ran over to stand behind the lectern, then spread out the sheaf of handwritten papers.

He recognized the ritual instantly—whoever had done the translation had written it out with a careful, precise hand, and the diagrams were flawless. "All right," he called, and heard the tremble in his voice. "Go on my word. Caldwell, you grab Ms. Wells and get her out—*carefully*. Do *not* disturb the circle."

Caldwell nodded. He was shaking.

"Jason—you and Verity get the hell out of here. Now. Run. If this goes wrong, I won't have your deaths on my conscience."

"If it goes wrong you'll be dead too!" Verity said, her expression set. "We're staying. Do it."

Next to her, Jason nodded.

Damn you all, he thought, but he didn't mean it. Once more their loyalty touched him, firming his resolve. He didn't have time to argue—the energy drain had sped up, and Tabitha grew ever more pale. He had only one chance to get this right.

He turned a couple pages to the correct spot in the ritual, then focused on the circle. When he spoke again, his voice was calm, steady, commanding. "Deirdre. Caldwell. *Now.*"

The two of them moved in concert as if they had trained for this moment for months. Caldwell reached out with his magic and gently plucked Tabitha up, floating her high above the circle and then over toward the group. The laser beams broke, refocusing on the table beneath her. The tubes and conduits thrashed around as if alive, seeking a living being. The circle thrummed with ominous menace.

The moment Tabitha was out of the way, Deirdre rolled onto the table, taking the same position the young woman had been arranged in. The lasers converged on the center of her chest, wavering in their dark, muddy colors for a moment before settling back into their former brightness. The conduits and tubes ceased their thrashing and latched onto her body in the same places they'd done with Tabitha. She gasped and her back arched.

Stone couldn't pay any attention to what was going on at the side of the circle. He didn't know if Tabitha Wells was alive or dead, whether Caldwell, Jason, or Verity were doing anything that might interfere with the ritual, or whether Richter might choose this moment to reappear. None of that mattered now.

All that mattered was that he bring this runaway ritual under control and dismantle its power before it sucked Deirdre dry. As much as he wanted to, this wasn't something he could do quickly or suddenly. Each bit had to be done with care, balancing as much speed as he could risk against a level of precision that made what they'd done with the wards outside look like taking apart a child's building-block castle.

He'd once compared the deconstruction of a powerful ritual to landing a commercial jet: you couldn't simply point the nose downward and head for the ground. Not if you wanted to get the plane down in one piece with the passengers alive and well. You had to take it down in steps, making sure each one had been successfully completed before moving on to the next. He actually had no idea whether you *could* land a jet like that, but it made a good metaphor and you certainly couldn't do it that way with a ritual. Especially not one that had gone as badly awry as this one had.

Worse, he couldn't even restore it to its original purpose. That would have been the easiest—except it wouldn't. To do that, he'd need the grimoire, and this time he was certain he'd destroyed it. Further, even if he *could* do so, he had no desire to—that would require him to take the energy being siphoned from Deirdre's body into himself, combined with the massive amounts of power that had been generated by the ritual itself. Sure, it might make him immortal—but he didn't believe that for a moment. Besides, even if it were true, he had no desire for an immortality brought about by draining the vitality from the woman who, up until a day ago, he thought he'd loved.

The woman he might still love.

He forced himself not to look at her straining, grimacing face as she arched and writhed on the table. All that mattered now was the ritual.

Easy now…

Take control of the energy and bleed it off. Slowly, slowly…

You can do this…

His body burned as some of the power leached into him, even as he tried to block it. He felt as if a current passed into him, through him, and out the other side.

The conduits and tubes swayed again. On the table, Deirdre moaned, but he still didn't look at her.

He thought he heard Verity yell something, but he couldn't pay attention. He blinked sweat out of his eyes and kept his focus.

Carefully, carefully...

He had no idea how long it took. Time ceased to be a concept. All that existed was to reach out with his power, grab the energy coursing out of Deirdre in seven different directions, and slowly bleed it off into the ether, then tie off each conduit in turn so no more could escape.

If he took too little before the next stage of the ritual arrived, he would fail at his task.

If he took too much, it would kill Deirdre.

Slowly, ever so slowly, he began to feel his efforts bear fruit. The thrum of energy began to lessen, and the feeling that someone was pouring a high-voltage current through his body decreased.

The glows around the globes faded. The bubbling half-energy, half-liquid running through the tubing calmed. At the edge of his awareness, he sensed that Deirdre's writhing had slowed.

Had he stopped the ritual?

Was she dead?

Still, he focused. Until he knew for sure it was over, he couldn't get complacent. He raised his hands, shaping the magical forces, gently manipulating them as they continued powering down.

The globes went black. The thrumming ceased, winding down like a powerful engine brought to a successful stop.

The room went quiet, except for the sound of Stone's harsh breathing.

And just like that, it was over.

Stone sank to his knees, exhausted from his effort, gripping the edges of the lectern. All he wanted to do was lie down somewhere and sleep for about two weeks.

"Al!"

It was Jason.

Stone's head snapped up, and he dragged himself back to his feet. What now? Despite all their efforts, had Tabitha Wells's body been too weak to withstand the ritual? "What is it? Is she alive?"

Verity and Caldwell were bent over Tabitha's still form. Caldwell had taken off his leather jacket and draped it over her. Jason stood guard, his gaze scanning the room back and forth, his gun in his hand.

"V's working on her." He looked grim; Stone could see even without looking at their auras that whatever was going on over there, a positive outcome was by no means certain.

And then he glanced toward the center of the circle.

Deirdre.

Something was wrong.

The circle was dead now, dark and inert, no longer dangerous even if he were to knock the whole thing down. He vaulted into the center, shoving aside stands and tubing and cords.

When he reached her, he stared down in shock.

She was alive—that much was obvious. She no longer writhed, but now only moved fretfully back and forth as if in the grip of a nightmare she couldn't awaken from. Her eyes were closed, her brow furrowed, her teeth clamped tightly shut. The bright laserlike beams were gone now, the crystals blasted and spent, the tubes that had been attached to her dropped away like so many dead snakes.

All but one.

That one remained attached to her, fused to her neck as if it had been implanted there. The strange liquid continued to burble sluggishly inside it.

But none of that was what Stone noticed first, what had frozen him there with wide, terrified eyes.

Deirdre was aging as he watched.

Even now, her preternatural beauty remained. But when before she had appeared as a young woman in her middle to late twenties, now her face was crisscrossed with faint wrinkles. Her lustrous chestnut hair was streaked with gray. Her cheeks were sunken, her brow split with lines. She looked to be at least fifty, perhaps even older.

And it was still happening. As she twisted back and forth on the table, her hair lightened as more gray appeared.

In horror, Stone remembered what Deirdre had told him when he asked her if she'd planned to kill Tabitha Wells in the ritual.

It wouldn't have killed her...it would have made her old...

"Verity!" he yelled, spinning to face the group off to the side of the room.

"Not now, Stone!" Caldwell snapped back.

They were all still bent over Tabitha; Verity crouched at her head, her hands still roving over the unconscious woman's body, her face set in concentration.

No help, then. If Tabitha was to survive this—she *had* to survive this—then Verity's healing talents were still needed to help her.

That meant if he wanted to stop this, he'd have to do it on his own. He had no idea how he was going to do it; would her magical immunity prevent him from healing her, even if the ritual had somehow worked?

Deirdre had aged yet more in the time he'd turned away. Whatever was happening, it was happening fast. Her face was more wrinkled now, her skin more sunken. She looked sixty, sixty-five—

Stone had to take a risk. He didn't know what would happen if he removed that last tube, but he surely knew what would happen if he didn't. He took her hand in one of his and wrapped the other around the tube, reaching out with magical senses.

Her familiar aura was still there, but it was weak and close to her body. The outer edges of the brilliant blue had frayed, flickering a darker, more muted hue—similar to what had happened with the beams from the crystals before they'd swapped Deirdre in for Tabitha.

Stone's heart pounded. This was the kind of delicate, organic magic that he'd never been good at. This was Verity's kind of magic. *But Verity's not available, damn you. Stop making excuses and do it!*

It was simple as that. Do it or Deirdre would age until her body simply gave out.

Refocusing his mind, he reached out and gently formed magical energy around the spot where the tube entered Deirdre's neck. Slowly and carefully, he blocked the weird liquid-like energy, a bit at a time, until it began to back up in the tube. Then, with his physical hand, he pinched off the tube and pulled it free.

He expected to see a hole, a sudden gush of blood or energy, but that didn't happen. The end of the tube came away cleanly, leaving nothing more than a faint red mark on the side of Deirdre's neck.

She squeezed his hand and opened her eyes. Haunted with fear, her gaze met his from wrinkled, hollow eyes. She smiled. "Alastair..." she whispered.

She was still aging.

No, no...

Desperate now, he reached out with his magical senses once more. What more could he do? He'd removed the last component of the ritual! That should have stopped it, but yet her body continued to wrinkle and fade.

With no other ideas presenting themselves, he did the only thing he could think of: he took hold of both of her hands, closed his eyes, and poured healing energy into her. It was tentative at first—his technique wasn't as subtle or careful as Verity's—but when he didn't seem to be doing her any harm, he increased the intensity. He was tired, so tired, but that didn't matter. If he could keep her alive by boosting her fading energy with his own, he would do it. It was nothing more than a brute-force effort, using all his power to drive the healing into her, past her barriers. It was working, but it was so slow…

At last, he felt her aura stabilize. He opened his eyes and stared down at her. "Deirdre…" he whispered.

Her hair was completely white now, her face a map of wrinkles, her eyes sunken into hollows. She now looked to be at least eighty-five, maybe older. She smiled at him, her cornflower blue gaze tired but satisfied. She gripped his hands with her thin, spotted ones. "I knew you could do it…" she whispered. "I love you…"

"Deirdre…"

He sank to his knees, letting his head drop to the table next to her. The last thing he remembered feeling passing out was her frail hand gently stroking his hair.

| CHAPTER SEVENTY-NINE

Two days later

"AL?"

Stone looked up from his desk at his Stanford office to see Jason and Verity in the doorway. "Ah. Come in."

The two of them entered and took seats across from him. "Thought we might find you up here," Jason said. "We went by the house, but—"

Stone shrugged. "Wanted to get away. I've got a lot of work to do, and it's quiet up here with almost everyone out for break. Something I can do for you?"

"We just wanted to let you know we're heading back down south," Verity said.

"I thought you might be. Please give my best to Edna."

"Yeah…we will." Verity paused a moment, playing with a loose string on her jacket. "Dr. Stone…are you gonna be okay?"

"Of course I am," he said briskly. "No ill effects from the ritual, other than feeling like I need to sleep until sometime next year. I plan to finish these up and spend the rest of the week catching up with that."

"That's not what I meant."

"Well, that's what *I* meant," he said, in a tone clearly indicating that he didn't want to pursue the subject. He grabbed a stack of papers and put far too much care into squaring them up and situating them just so on the corner of the desk. He didn't look at either of them.

"I've been following some of the police reports," Jason said. "It sounds like they haven't got a clue what happened up there. I guess whatever you and Caldwell did to clean the place up, it worked."

"Yeah, and the security women don't remember anything," Verity added.

"Not surprised," Stone said. "When you're dealing with predators who take power the way they do, it makes sense they adapted so their victims won't remember them after the fact." He sighed. "Too bad Lane got away, though."

They'd discovered that later—it hadn't been a priority before, with everything else going on. But when they went looking for his body, it had been nowhere to be found.

"You think he'll go back with Richter?"

"Probably. I don't know." He glanced up at Verity. "Forgot to mention, though—nice job dealing with him. He tried to take you over, didn't he?"

She nodded, looking troubled. "Yeah. It was pretty awful—I felt him fucking around in my brain, and for a minute I thought he was the sexiest thing I'd ever seen in my life. All I wanted to do was lie back and let him have his way with me." Her face twisted in disgust. "I'm not sure how I threw it off, but...yeah. I'm glad it worked."

"Shame about the people Richter killed," Jason said. "Yeah, they were street people, but that doesn't matter—somebody's gonna care about what happened to them. And now they'll never know." He stood. "Anyway, we should get on the road. Fran's already pissed that I took the extra two days." He extended his hand. "Take care, Al. And answer your damn phone, okay? We need to get together more often."

Stone stood too. He gripped Jason's wrist and nodded. "I promise."

Verity came around the desk, hesitated for a moment, then wrapped her arms around Stone. "You better," she mumbled. "I worry about you, Doc. You need us, and you know it."

He almost said something flippant. Instead, he returned the hug. "I do," he said. "I do need you. And I won't forget it this time." He released her, holding her out at arm's length so he could get a good look at her.

You don't realize sometimes how much someone can change when you interact with them every day. It can be a shock to see them, truly see them, after a long absence and realize that your memory no longer matches reality. It wasn't until that moment that it consciously occurred to Stone that his internalized vision of Verity up until now had been as a bright, eager seventeen-year-old girl, excited to learn magic and to hungry take in whatever knowledge and wisdom he wanted to feed her.

She wasn't that anymore. In truth, she hadn't been for quite some time. It wasn't physical, either—physically, she looked much the same as she had before. It was something in her eyes, a new maturity to go with her ever-present cynical twinkle. He almost felt jealous of Edna Soren, who got to guide this next stage of his apprentice's training. He gave her a faint smile. "Come up to see me now and then. I promise I won't slam the door in your face next time."

She grinned. "How can we turn down an invitation like that?" She turned away, then spun back and hugged him again, hard and fast. Then she quickly rejoined Jason and the two of them left the office.

Stone watched the doorway until long after they were gone, his thoughts far away. After a time, he opened his desk drawer and removed a glossy photograph.

He'd found it in his interoffice mail when he'd come back to campus yesterday, along with a note from Laura, the department admin. "*Thought you'd like this*," the note had said. "*Looks like the only one they caught you in!*"

The photo was from the party at the Rosicrucian Museum. Stone remembered when it was taken, when the roving photographer had happened by and caught him and Deirdre in a candid shot. He gazed at it without really seeing it, but he didn't have to— he'd already studied it until every detail had seared itself into his brain.

It showed him in his tuxedo standing next to Deirdre in her slinky black dress. The two of them were facing mostly toward the camera, looking at something off to their left.

He still recognized Deirdre. The essentials were still there: the chestnut hair; the slim, athletic figure; the blue eyes and sensual lips. She was by all accounts a lovely young woman, but no lovelier than several of the other young women in the background of the photo. No more so than Tabitha Wells, or many of the attractive female students and faculty members Stone worked with every day.

The ones he barely noticed, except in the context of his work.

As always, he experienced a twinge of guilt at the feeling, but it passed more quickly now.

Taking one last look at the photo, he slipped it back into his desk drawer. His gaze fell on the brown bottle there—the elixir Caldwell had given him. Probably only one dose remained now. It would be so easy: he could take it and get these exams graded faster, then go home and get some much-needed, and hopefully dreamless, rest.

He shut the drawer on the photo and the unopened bottle, and returned his attention to his work.

| CHAPTER EIGHTY

E VISITED MATTHEW CALDWELL three days later at the Church of the Rising Dawn in San Jose.

Caldwell hadn't contacted him since the night in Woodside, nor had Tabitha Wells. He knew she was alive, but that was all. Caldwell had hustled her off that night with little conversation, just after he and Stone had completed the magical scrubbing on the mansion that would prevent anyone visiting the scene from connecting any of them with what had happened.

Stone almost didn't go, but he felt he owed it to Caldwell to check up on how things had turned out.

The black mage received him in his office. "I thought you might come," he said. His tone was carefully neutral, polite but without any cues as to his mood or mental state.

Stone took the offered seat. "How are you?"

"I'm well," he said, shrugging. He didn't look directly at Stone. "I'm sorry I didn't contact you sooner. I wanted to thank you for what you did—without you, Tabitha would have died."

Stone waited, hearing the unspoken pause at the end of Caldwell's sentence. When nothing more was forthcoming, he said, "But…"

Caldwell sighed loudly. "But…I also know that if it weren't for you and whatever you were wrapped up in with that woman, none of this would have happened. So you saved Tabitha's life, but you're also the reason she was in danger in the first place."

"Yes," Stone said. He bowed his head. There was nothing he wanted to say—nothing he *could* say—in his defense. True, Deirdre had worked her particular charms on him, drawing him unwittingly into the web of intrigue that had culminated in the scene at the Woodside mansion. None of this had been his fault, not really.

None of that mattered.

"How is Ms. Wells?" he asked, afraid to hear the answer.

"She's fine," Caldwell said, still in the same neutral tone. "I brought her back here and used a couple of my concoctions to stabilize her and help her sleep. She didn't have any lasting physical damage. And she doesn't remember anything about what happened."

Again, Stone heard something unspoken in Caldwell's words. "What aren't you saying, Matthew?"

His gaze came up then, dark and intense, half-angry, half-haunted. "Didn't you hear me? She doesn't *remember,* Stone. She's lost more than a day of her life, and she has no idea what happened to her in it." He sighed again and looked back down at his hands on his desk. "I had to do it—it was either that or have her remember that woman kidnapping her, being held prisoner, the ritual—but—"

"She's left you, hasn't she?" Stone asked softly.

Caldwell nodded. He radiated weariness as the animation drained from his posture. "She told me a couple of days ago that she decided she should focus on her studies—that the Church was taking up too much of her time."

"Where is she now?"

"Home. Back with her father and her sister. She told me she was having nightmares." His fists clenched. "She's thinking about taking the next quarter off. To, as she says, 'get her head together and decide what she wants to do with her life.'"

"I see." Pause. "I'm sorry, Matthew."

"So am I."

"What will you do now?" Not wanting to look directly at Caldwell, he let his gaze travel around the office. Now more than ever, the man looked like some kind of harried, world-weary mid-level administrator amid the file folders and scattered papers.

"I haven't decided yet."

Stone got up, heavily. There wasn't much else he could say, and he didn't think Caldwell wanted to hear any of it anyway.

He wondered if Tabitha Wells would come back to Stanford at all, or if she'd decide to drop out, or transfer somewhere else to get away from the vague, disturbing memories of lights and creepy mad-scientist-meets-H. R. Giger apparatus and the feeling of being drained of her life force. He wondered if her interest in the occult would continue. He wondered how much therapy she'd need to help her get past all of this.

"Be well, Matthew," he said. "I won't contact you again, but if I can help you in any way—"

"I'll keep that in mind."

He didn't say, *haven't you already helped me enough?*

But Stone heard it nonetheless.

CHAPTER EIGHTY-ONE

THE CALL STONE HAD BEEN EXPECTING came on a Friday afternoon, a little over a month later.

He was in his office, glancing through a research book he planned to use for a new paper, when his phone rang. "Yes, this is Stone."

"Dr. Stone? This is Dr. Watkins." The voice was gentle. "I think you might want to come over here in the next couple of hours, if you can."

Stone was silent for a long time, closing his eyes, his hand tightening on the receiver. "Yes...of course. I'll be right there. Thank you, Doctor."

He sat staring at his desk without seeing it for several minutes before getting up to leave.

The facility was in Los Altos Hills, tucked away up a short road passing through scattered copses of trees and emerald-green, meticulously manicured lawns. When Stone pulled the BMW into the tiny parking area, he was reminded, as he always was, of a large, peaceful private home.

He passed the flowerbeds flanking the front doors as he headed inside, and nodded to the gardener working among them. The place was awash with color—red, yellow, orange, blue. Everything about it was clean, bright, and cheerful.

The woman at the desk looked up as he entered, with a kind, sad smile that probably got a lot of practice around here. "Hello, Dr. Stone."

He slid out of his overcoat and draped it over his arm. Under it, he wore a charcoal-gray suit with a bright blue tie. He'd kept it in his office, and changed before he left.

"She's been waiting for you," the woman said. "I don't think I mentioned it before, but she asks about you almost every day. Sometimes right after you leave."

He closed his eyes, briefly. "I'm sorry I wasn't able to make it yesterday. Work's been frightful, with the new quarter starting."

"Oh, I'm sure she understands you can't come every day." She nodded toward the area behind her. "You can go on back. I'll tell them you're coming."

He passed through a set of white-painted double doors and walked down a hallway carpeted in plush, deep red past walls lined with colorful still-lifes and pleasant pastoral scenes. Periodically, a small table off to one side held a bouquet of flowers, a lamp, or a glossy book of nature photographs.

He stopped in front of a door halfway down the hallway, and knocked softly. When there was no answer, he opened it and stepped inside.

The room was of medium size, with a large, sparkling-clean picture window in front of a sitting area containing a loveseat, two chairs, and an oval coffee table. The open curtains let in the day's bright sunlight.

On the other side of the room stood a bed flanked by two nightstands. A multicolored comforter covered it, and a pile of fluffy pillows gathered at the head. A figure in a blue nightgown lay snuggled into the pillows. A young nurse in cheerful blue scrubs had been puttering around the bed, but when Stone arrived he nodded and headed for the door. "I'll get Dr. Watkins," he said, and gripped Stone's shoulder as he went by.

For a moment, she didn't seem to notice Stone, but then her eyes flew open and she smiled. "Hello…" She blinked, and her expression went vague for a moment, and then her smile widened. "Alastair. Hello. I'm so glad you came."

"Hello, Deirdre." He put his coat over the chair and sat down next to the bed, reaching out to take her nearest hand in his. "You're looking lovely today, as always."

And she was, even now. There was no denying the ravages of age: she looked every bit the eighty-five years he'd estimated her to be—every bit the age listed in her official files. Her wispy white hair lay spread out on the pillow, forming a bright halo on the blue pillowcase. Her face was furrowed with deep wrinkles, her lips thin, her nearly translucent skin stretched tight over thin, bony hands. But even with all of that, even with the deep dark hollows around her cornflower-blue eyes, her tired face still lit up with mischief. Her smile still captivated Stone as it had since the night they'd met.

"You're always so handsome," she said, chuckling, patting his hand with her other one. "I don't remember that suit. Is it a new one?"

"I got it just for you," he said. He'd worn it a few other times when he'd visited her over the last month, and each time she'd asked the same question.

"You're sweet." She chuckled again. "All the young men here are sweet. The young ladies, too, of course. But Robbie and Luis always sneak me little things from the kitchen, and Binh brings me flowers. He tells me the flowerbeds outside are so lovely…he says he'll take me out there some time to look at them."

"That would be lovely," he said. Somehow, he kept his voice even. "Perhaps we could go out sometime, just the two of us."

"Oh, I don't know…" she said vaguely. Her hand fluttered away from his. "I'm so tired all the time…Maybe next week."

"Next week, then. It's a date." He swallowed as something clenched inside him, and waited until he was sure his voice was steady. "Sounds like everyone's treating you well."

"Oh, yes. Everyone's lovely here. They make sure I have everything I need."

He remembered when they'd brought her in here, a couple days after the ritual. He'd been concerned about that, especially when he'd confirmed that, just as Jason and Fran Bartek had discovered, she didn't technically exist. There was no record of a Deirdre Lanier anywhere—no Social Security number, no tax identification, no employment record. Her stories about being a fashion designer had all been fabrications, and not only did she not have another apartment in San Francisco, but she'd never even left the Bay Area when she'd told him she'd gone there or to Los Angeles.

These last bits he'd gleaned from questioning her back at his townhouse after they'd gotten her out. He'd offered to let her stay at his place, though he had no idea how he would care for her, but she'd declined. She was lucid enough back then to give him details of bank accounts she had squirreled away in various locations, and between her, Stone, and Jason, they'd figured out the best way to proceed without arousing any suspicion.

Using one of Deirdre's false identities from an earlier period of her life, they'd arranged for her to stay in one of the most exclusive care facilities in the Bay Area. Stone researched it thoroughly, including making two visits—one planned, one unannounced—to make sure it was up to his standards. For her part, Deirdre had done what she could to make the process as painless for them all as possible, though she became increasingly prone to fits of vagueness and her memory quickly became inconsistent.

Stone visited whenever he could get away. At first that had been every day, but as his work became more demanding he'd cut the frequency, with a great deal of guilt, down to two or three times a week. Sometimes he stayed only a few minutes, and others he would sit in the chair next to the bed, silent and contemplative, for an hour or more. The staff members, from the nurses to the food-service workers to the orderlies, were always kind, and never asked too many questions about why a young man his age, not related to the patient, would visit so often.

It had been almost two weeks ago to the day when Dr. Watkins, her attending physician, had taken Stone aside before letting him see her. She'd been complaining of pain, he'd said, so they'd done some tests. They couldn't identify exactly what was wrong—not without a lot more invasive investigation that would have been more cruel than kind at this point—but the end result was that she didn't have much time remaining.

Stone had taken the news with surprising calm—at least on the surface. He'd suspected it was coming. It wasn't just her age—it was the amount of harmful magic her body had absorbed. That kind of unnatural aging, and that level of concentrated dark magic, could not be good for the fragile body of a human—or whatever Deirdre was, he reminded himself. Her immunity hadn't protected her; in fact, it might have made things worse, once the magic managed to get past it.

Whatever it meant, she was dying.

He squeezed her hand gently again. "I don't want to keep you awake, if you're tired. I just wanted you to know I was thinking about you. I'll...I'll sit here with you for as long as you like."

"You're sweet," she said again. She looked up at him, her gaze sharpening beneath her wrinkled brow. "I love you, Alastair. I do."

He leaned in and brushed a gentle kiss across her forehead. Then, after a pause, he bowed his head and kissed her lips. "I love you too, Deirdre. I always will."

"Ah, what could have been..." she murmured, and then her eyes shifted out of focus again and closed. The smile remained, quirking at the corners of her lips as her voice trailed off. "What could have been..."

❖

He remained there among the beeping machines, sitting next to the bed and holding her hand, alternating staring out into nothingness and studying her face as if trying to commit it to the deepest parts of his memory. Not that he had to—he'd already done that many months ago.

The door opened and Dr. Watkins came in. A distinguished-looking black man of about fifty, he had thinning salt-and-pepper hair and the tranquil manner of a Buddhist monk.

"I'm glad you could come," he said as he shook Stone's hand and glanced over the readings on the machines. "Miss Carruthers always speaks so highly of you." Emily Carruthers was the name of the earlier identity they'd used to admit her.

Stone nodded, not wanting to speak.

Watkins made an adjustment to one of the machines, then backed up. "I'll leave you alone," he said. "You can stay as long as you need to."

"Does...does she know?" he asked softly.

"We haven't told her, but I think she suspects. She's informed us she doesn't want any sort of...heroic measures."

Stone thought about the 'heroic measures' that had gotten her into this situation in the first place. He thought of Tabitha Wells, safely home with her family, and squeezed Deirdre's hand a little tighter.

"Please call if you need anything. We're all here for you. Both of you."

"Thank you, Doctor."

Watkins turned to leave, then paused in the doorway. "Dr. Stone, may I ask you a personal question?"

"Of course."

"What are you to Miss Carruthers? Her paperwork lists you as a 'friend,' but I've never seen anyone so devoted to a patient he's not related to—especially not someone your age."

Stone paused, trying to come up with the best way to describe it. *The woman I fell in love with? The woman I almost married? The woman who took over my mind and made me see her as beautiful until I really did? The woman who nearly forced me to betray an innocent student so she could stay eternally young and beautiful?*

She was all of those things. And more.

But in the end, she was just Deirdre, and even after everything, that hadn't changed.

"It's…complicated," he said at last. He shrugged into his coat. "Thank you for everything, Doctor."

She died a little more than an hour later. She didn't awaken as the machines' beeping became more insistent and the numbers began to flash more urgently, but as he watched her eyes moving behind her paper-thin, wrinkled lids, he hoped that perhaps she was having one last pleasant dream.

He took her hand in both of his as a gentle knock sounded on the door. "Goodbye, Deirdre," he whispered.

He didn't speak to Watkins and the nurses as he passed them on his way out, and he didn't look back.

Out in his car, Stone sat in the parking lot for a few minutes, thinking. He hadn't done a lot of that lately—he'd been actively avoiding it, in fact, not wanting to dwell too much on the events of the last few months. But now, at last, he might be able to do it.

He had things to do—his next class was in less than two hours. Next week, he planned to try locating Pete, the old vagrant who'd given him a sweatshirt the night of Lane's and Hugo's first attack, so he could treat the man to a new wardrobe and a good meal. And of course he had Deirdre's arrangements to make.

For now, though, he thought he might give Jason and Verity a call. They'd want to hear the news, of course. Perhaps he'd ask them if they were busy, and drive down for the weekend. It had been too long since he'd really connected with his old friends—and besides, maybe Jason would know a place where the two of them could get good and drunk.

As he pulled out of the parking lot and glanced in the rearview mirror to watch the cheerful building and riot of colorful flowers receding behind him, it suddenly occurred to him that he hadn't had a nightmare in a month.

It was a beginning.

Alastair Stone will return in

FLESH AND STONE

Book 8 of the Alastair Stone Chronicles

Coming soon!

ABOUT THE AUTHOR

R. L. King is an award-winning author and game freelancer for Catalyst Game Labs, publisher of the popular roleplaying game *Shadowrun*. She has contributed fiction and game material to numerous sourcebooks, as well as one full-length adventure, "On the Run," included as part of the 2012 Origins-Award-winning "Runners' Toolkit." Her first novel in the *Shadowrun* universe, *Borrowed Time*, was published in Spring 2015.

When not doing her best to make life difficult for her characters, King is a software technical writer for a large Silicon Valley database company. In her spare time (*hah!*) she enjoys hanging out with her very understanding spouse and her small herd of cats, watching way too much *Doctor Who*, and attending conventions when she can. She is an Active member of the Horror Writers' Association and the Science Fiction and Fantasy Writers of America, and a member of the International Association of Media Tie-In Writers.

You can find her at *rlkingwriting.com* and *magespacepress.com*, on Facebook at https://www.facebook.com/AlastairStoneChronicles, or on Twitter at *@Dragonwriter11*.

To get a copy of the free novella *Shadows and Stone*, available only to mailing list subscribers, sign up at *rlkingwriting.com*.

Did you enjoy *Heart of Stone*? If you did, please consider posting a review on Amazon or Goodreads letting folks know what you thought!

Thank you so much, and I hope to see you back again for *Flesh and Stone,* book #8 of the Alastair Stone Chronicles!

Made in the USA
Monee, IL
19 June 2023

36171660R00249